COPPER AND SALT

BY

ANDREW SHIELDS

A
BLADES
IN THE
DARK
NOVEL

COPPER AND SALT

First Printing: 2020

ISBN: 978-1-7327586-9-8 (paperback)

Cover art by John Harper

https://shieldsuppublishing.wordpress.com/

CHAPTER ONE

The wide-spread misconception that Bluecoats work for the Inspectors is understandable. They are housed together, they both stop criminals, and they are both funded by the city. The most prominent trait they share is that they will brook no disrespect. They will punish the insolent with the law—or they will handle matters otherwise, and hide behind the law.

Still, their difference is foundational and pervasive. The Bluecoats are charged with keeping the peace and protecting the wealthy. The Inspectors are charged with solving crimes and punishing law-breakers. Only a fool would confuse the two mandates.

— From "The Bruised Tide" by Arlen Slane

"We must take the next step," the young man said, "or we begin to lose ground." His hands were clasped behind his back.

"You clearly have strong feelings about this, Inspector Cellar," said Chief Inspector Prichard. "You have an investment to protect. You've been working on the Tick Tock Tea Shop for how long now?"

"Two years."

"At your age," Prichard said, "that seems like a long, long time." He took his time, selecting a cigarette from the box on his desk and leaning in to light it with his desk lamp. He leaned back and exhaled, considering the Inspector.

"In two years, I've documented sixty four deaths," Cellar said, his voice even. "I have documented at least two hundred severe beatings. I've got a whole book of narratives following victims drained to destitution feeding their addictions, and victims degraded into predatory trades by these brutal criminals. They prey on the vulnerable." He paused. "Please, Chief Inspector. If you grant an exception to protect Sparks, I can get the evidence I need to root out one of Silkshore's most pervasive crime networks."

"I like your confidence," the Chief Inspector said.

"Sparks is the street name for Drav Comber, one of the Tick Tock runners," Cellar continued, restraining his sense of urgency. "I almost turned him three months ago, when his mother got sick and he got desperate. I offered medical help for his mother, but he chose to ask the Tock Tock leaders instead. We caught a break when the criminals gave her shoddy care; she died last week. Sparks is ready to cooperate. He can get at least one of the ledgers tracking the financials. Maybe he can get more than one."

"You think the ledgers will be enough to convince the magistrates," the Chief Inspector clarified.

"They are the capstone to a bloody arch I've been pulling together," Cellar replied. "I believe I can connect whatever coded ledgers may hint at to past actions that I've documented. I have over three hundred vouchers connecting experts and witnesses to narratives, and hundreds of factuals that have been established beyond reproach. Connecting those vouchers, factuals, and accusations will build an inescapable trap; for the first time we can strike at the leaders, not just the agents."

"You think you can get Dame Maroden?" the Chief Inspector clarified, raising his eyebrows.

"For a start," Cellar replied, solemn. "I will shutter the whole operation."

"You really believe you can do this," the Chief Inspector mused, more to himself than to Cellar. He cocked his head to the side. "I am occasionally wrong," he admitted, "and while I doubt this is such a time, the stakes are low, so I am willing to gamble. You have the exception prepared?"

"Sir," Cellar said so swiftly the word was percussive. He whipped a folder he held behind his back around to land on the desk. The Chief Inspector flicked it open, eyes skimming the cramped and officious text.

"Let's see what you can do, then," he murmured, taking up his pen and scratching his approval onto the document's final lines. He raised the glass chimney on the lamp and warmed a stick of wax in the flame for a long moment, then he deposited a blob of wax on the paper and stamped it with his seal.

The Chief Inspector lifted the paper, and Cellar took it as quickly as he could without snatching it. Cellar pivoted and slipped out of the office in the same motion, crossing the balcony traverse in a handful of steps, rounding the corner and racing down the bustling hallway to the closet at the end.

"Arm up," he barked, stepping across the cramped office to snatch his massive pistol from its shelf as he swiped his baldric off the wall. "Specials in my shadow!"

"Chief went for it?" a startled man said as he rose.

"Course he did," said the slim woman in the doorway. "Pay up," she grinned at the other special.

"Later," Cellar said through his teeth, headed out as she stepped aside. She was already armed and ready to go. Cellar was down the hall, around to the stairs, his feet fluttering at the steps as he closed in on the watch tower exit. Both specials were right behind him, and the three reached the street together.

The mid-afternoon murk was lit by plasmic lamps, casting harsh glare. Posts flanked the central aisle of broken statues decorating Bookend Square. Floss skirled and drifted in the breeze, pulled and pushed by the breathing of the city, leaving a silken litter to pile up in corners and along alleys. The earthy stink of draft goats mixed with the odor of fried food. The ancient exhalation of wood and stone and iron was a taste at the back of every smell.

The clock tower looming over Bookend Square tolled, marking out each of the nine hours since dawn. Cellar led the specials past the hired rides; they weren't going far. The tolling ceased as they passed the half-way point of the square and turned to follow a cobbled lane that awkwardly skewed around a stone tower before widening out, a space where carriages could pause to let each other pass.

The three slowed their pace, and they glanced around and up. The overbuilt structures flanking the street had been expanded over time. On one side of the street they extended out twice, covering over half the lane. The other side of the street had a rusted fence, its gate lost centuries ago. The shallow courtyard echoed a memory of when the apartment building had been a single mansion with a gracious front sweep. Tucked back at the far end of the courtyard, a massive and ancient dead tree cast a shadow over a stone fountain.

Stairs curved up one side of the fountain, and its centerpiece was a book stand. When the pumps worked, the fountain had been a magnificent podium for conducting music, reading poems, or speaking publically. Long ago, the pool hosted a healthy profusion of radiant algae and moss, so the water shone and underlit the podium. Now only a few patches glowed, rendering the murky water a bit eerie, attracting climbing vines that buried the podium and rambled around the rim of the pool.

"That was ninth bell," one of the specials observed. "That's when you were going to meet. Figure he thought you were late and took off?"

"Come on, Jayan," Cellar said. "We would have seen him."

"Maybe not. He is a sneak," the other special retorted, one hand resting on the butt of her pistol as she scanned the windows overlooking the courtyard. "He's probably watching us right now." She paused. "*Someone* is." A frown creased her forehead.

"Sparks," Cellar called out, trying to project his voice without drawing attention, peering at the shadows. He hesitated a moment, then turned to a special. "Daava, check the street. Don't go far."

She nodded, and slunk out of the courtyard, following the contour of the lane as it pressed its way between slouching buildings.

"Something's wrong," Jayan said. "You tried to get that exception and got delayed until right before the meet." He shook his head. "I don't think Sparks is coming, Inspector."

A croak startled them, and they pivoted to see wings flexing a downdraft over the courtyard as the massive crow landed in the spreading branches above. The black bird cocked its eye at them, croaking again. Lines traced in its beak glinted in the plasmic light. Its pupil was pale, as though it reflected a light invisible to the human eye.

"That's a Deathseeker crow," Jayan said, numb. "It—it's not circling."

Cellar felt his guts drop, a coldness flowing into him, and he stepped over to the fountain under the crow. He looked down.

The boy's corpse gazed up past him, past the arms of the tree, past the Deathseeker crow, lost in the vast senselessness behind the Mirror. A chain connected two rocks, pinning the torso; just enough to hold the body down in three feet of water, for at least a while. Only the thinnest gauzy threads of blood drifted apart in the filthy pool.

Several emotions hit Cellar at once, robbing him of breath. He widened his stance and steeled himself. "Daava," he called out, and he heard her approach. Cellar turned to Jayan. "You keep an eye on this, I'll send the Bluecoats and you can coordinate with the Spirit Wardens when they come." He spared a glance at the Deathseeker crow, who perched regally in the tree.

Then Cellar's eyes narrowed. Past the crow, he saw a lit window in the row of windows, and an unmistakable silhouette. The man on the third floor leaned out and offered a jaunty salute, grinning.

"Spur," Cellar said through his teeth, staring at the man.

Daava glanced up, frowning. "No, Inspector," she said. "This is not the moment. That's a brothel. I'm pretty sure he has all the alibi he needs; why he's there, and witnesses who will swear he didn't step out."

"This is the fourteenth person he's killed that I can document, in the last two years alone," Cellar said. He struggled to let go of the idea of taking action, but he was unable to totally shake the impulse. He slapped his flat, open hand against the side of his pistol, hard enough to suppress the shakes. "He has protected the Tick Tock. Again."

Satisfied that the Inspector had passed up every opportunity to act, Spur languidly withdrew and closed the shutters. Still, Cellar could not tear his eyes from the window.

"We will have another chance," Daava said.

"Sparks won't," Cellar replied softly, something in his chest compacting.

He felt a dislocation, a dizziness; Sparks' mother died, her corpse burned in plasmic flame to assure she did not rise as a ghost. Sparks died, his corpse would be burned in plasmic flame too. Nothing survived that. Their stories were over. A handful of notes in the city's dark symphony, passing in the din, insignificant.

"We should go," Daava said.

"I got this," Jayan agreed, nodding towards the pool. "Don't you worry."

Cellar was transfixed at a crossroads, unable to move without making a decision. He stared at the pool, his heartbeat pounding in his eyes so he could not properly focus. He felt his hands tighten to fists.

The pressure resolved.

Cellar turned to Daava. "Let's go," he said, feeling energy flowing through him, a certain grim peace settling through the turmoil of his blood as his course became clear.

The world seemed a blurred noise as Cellar returned to the Smoke Tower, past the Bluecoat guards and up the stairs, to his office. He let himself in, then pulled handfuls of books from one of the shelves, stacking them up on his desk with the slap of covers against covers.

"What are you doing?" Daava hissed, alarmed. She rapidly closed the door and locked it. "People will know where you stash the good stuff!"

Heedless, Cellar pulled a false back from a section of shelving, and he hauled out several portfolios. Examining them briefly, he put a few back, and tucked two fat files under his arm.

"Put it away," he said, letting himself out of the office. He closed in on the Chief Inspector's office, passed the assistant stationed outside, and let himself in as the assistant realized his bold intent and protested.

"Back so soon?" the Chief Inspector mused.

"Sparks was murdered while I was talking to you," Cellar replied, restraining his emotions. "I ask you to grant an exception to the privacy that the law accords to Brance Hellyers. I want him, his life, his associates." Cellar paused as a tremor touched his voice, and he swallowed hard. "I want them here in the tower."

"Sir?" the Chief Inspector's assistant said, his voice terse as he stood in the doorway behind Cellar.

"I need to speak to Inspector Cellar," Prichard said. "Close the door." The assistant reluctantly withdrew. "Hellyers. That's Spur. The Tick Tock enforcer," the Chief Inspector observed. "I suppose you have vouchers and factuals to back up your request for an exception."

Cellar leaned forward and carefully placed the thick files on the desk. "Dozens of vouchers from those who saw him commit crimes, or those who saw him near crimes, or heard him talk about them," Cellar said. "Factuals to anchor time, place, objects, and ownership. They establish truths to anchor the contemplation." He paused. "Two years of work, and I've got a decade of his crimes documented at some level." Cellar opened the top portfolio and pulled out a prepared exception that lacked only the date and approving seal.

"Some of this is no doubt central to your ambition to take the entire Tick Tock operation apart," the Chief Inspector observed.

"I cannot wait," Cellar replied as calmly as he could. "What happened just now—we must answer it." He paused. "The Tick Tock crew is responsible for a lot of damage," he said through his teeth, "and they have friends in the Bluecoats and in the Inspectors, and the Ministry, and the Fairpole Council, and the Hive." He tightened his fists. "Please tell me that murdering a boy in cold blood is outrageous enough for us to insist on a gesture towards justice."

The Chief Inspector allowed the silence between them to gather some weight. "Inspector Cellar," he said quietly, "Contrary to what you may think, I do like you. I think you have promise. And this? What you propose to do?" He shrugged. "This is a mistake. You take this step and it will not end well. I guarantee it," he said, his tone low and calm. "Let it sit overnight. See how you feel about it in the morning."

"Two months ago," Cellar replied, struggling against the urgency in his voice, "Lenia Arran came to me and showed me injuries in various states of recovery. Her sister resisted Spur, so he beat Lenia in an effort to make her sister cooperate. When Lenia could no longer bear the abuse, physical and mental, she came to me. I promised to get her out. You signed the exception. She was dead by the time I reached her. And her sister? Disappeared." Cellar leaned forward, riffling the top folder. "That's documented here."

"I remember it," Prichard said with a nod.

"You suggested I sleep it off, regain my balance and perspective, keep working the long game."

"It was good advice then," the Chief Inspector said, "and it's good advice now."

"Chief," Cellar breathed, staring at the file, "I can't let this thing get thicker." He opened the file and slid the exception for Sparks on top, then closed it. "If the Inspectors are about building libraries to catalogue the wrongdoing in Doskvol to satisfy curiosity, but not to act as a corrective, then I have made a number of grave errors to bring me to this moment."

"You approach insolence," the Chief Inspector said, a new chill in his tone. "If you prefer the immediate reaction and the short view, I can have you transferred to the Bluecoats."

"This is not the work of an impatient man," Cellar said, planting his hand on top of the files, almost inaudible. "You told me to find my balance, and this is the balance I have found. I can bend this far." He looked the Chief Inspector in the eye. "But no further."

The moment quietly spun between the two men.

"It appears you must fire before you aim," Prichard said, his voice low. "There are some mistakes we must make ourselves. My blood certainly remembers my worst follies, and the warning that came before them. So, I have warned you, and your folly propels you beyond safety." The Chief Inspector shrugged, as though shedding a weight. "Very well. I will not stand behind you." He paused. "Nor will I stand in your way."

Prichard approved the exception.

"You do not have to go with me," Cellar said under his breath, glaring across the street at the looming face of the Tick Tock Tea Shop. "I understand if this is too far for you to follow."

"You don't understand," Daava disagreed, "and if we don't follow you here then we are essentially reassigning ourselves to another Inspector."

"This is a super bad move," Jayan said, trying not to whine. "You know that whatever you hit Spur with, it's not going to stick. Right? I mean, you've *got* to know that."

"This gesture you're about to make," Daava said, "at least admit it's more about trying not to feel guilty than it is about trying to actually accomplish anything." She looked over at the tea shop. "This is petulance. A tantrum."

"They are not as strong as they look," Cellar said through his teeth. "We pull Spur off the street for a week, we suggest he cooperated with us, and we can at least give them some consternation. Beat some bushes. See what flies out. At least try," he gritted out. He rounded on Daava. "Did you sign on to *watch* bad guys, or to *stop* bad guys?"

"Some of each, really," she said, wary.

"You?" he said to Jayan.

"Ladies like the uniform," he replied, deadpan.

"You're really walking in there with an exception in one hand and a gun in the other," Daava said, something like wonder in her voice.

"Yes," Cellar nodded. "I absolutely am."

"I mean, we're *with* you, of course," Jayan shrugged. "This is stupid, with a hefty dash of suicidal, but what the hell, right? We may not have signed on to the Inspectors to seek justice, but we also didn't sign on because it was the safest and smartest thing to do."

"That's certain," Daava agreed. "Specials in your shadow, Inspector."

With a curt nod, Cellar tugged the exception out of his coat and stalked towards the tea shop, the specials at his heels.

Three interlaced revolving doors and two double doors opened the face of the tea shop to the square, and Cellar took the double doors on one side. Once inside, he paused to take in the spacious seating area built around the massive grindstone that connected to the gears above and below. The windmill behind the clock tower allowed the stone to slowly spin, adjusting the view of those seated in chairs attached to its rim. At the back of the room, spiral staircases connected to balcony bars.

The Inspector closed in on the bar. Spur's lanky form lounged against the counter next to a number of glasses, with several runners present to take orders. Behind the bar, Madam Maroden expertly rocked a knife across some small sour fruits, preparing accents for drinks. She was not physically large, but her crimson hair and force of personality drew attention and encouraged respect.

"Hey there," Spur said, "I just saw you over on Greenwater. Taking in the sights." His smile broadened. "Are you here to question me about anything I might have witnessed, or my whereabouts?"

"Yes," Cellar said shortly. "Please come with us."

"And if I don't feel like it?" Spur asked, something chilly in his smile.

"I wouldn't have come without an exception," Cellar replied, "and you're coming with me."

"Am I covered too?" Madam Maroden asked brightly. "Just checking to see how much rope they gave you. How many people you can hang with it." Her smile showed a lot of teeth. "Sounds like just one."

"Is this resistance theoretical, or factual?" Cellar asked Spur directly.

Spur paused for a long moment, looking Cellar over. "Theoretical, I was planning to go with you all along. That's the thing about a tea shop, it puts you in the mood for a little mischief," he explained. "All in good fun. A little game here and there." He rose to his full height. "Do I need an overnight bag?"

"No," Cellar replied. He took a step back and to the side, and Spur sauntered over to him, flanked by specials. The four of them headed for the exit.

"Bring me back something nice!" Madam Maroden called after them, and the runners laughed.

"I see it, but I don't believe it," Spur confessed as they headed out through the double doors, back out to the square. "You are actually taking me to the Smoke Tower. Getting a bit ahead of yourself, aren't you?"

"Not in the least, you'll have an opportunity to see the case against you. It is not trivial," Cellar said.

"No doubt I've generated a lot of heat over the years," Spur conceded. "But I have friends in all sorts of places. I cultivate my friendships near and far, and they make sure to draw down any consequences I might face. I think you'll discover that sooner rather than later." He paused. "How long do you think it will take them to transport that child's body to Charterhall?"

"He's probably there now," Cellar said through his teeth.

"Then he'll be on time to go in the fires tonight," Spur said, something breathy in his tone, a smile twisting his face and subtly shifting his features. "Just like I told him he would."

"That'll do," Jayan said sharply. He pointed a worried look at Cellar's tight shoulders.

"You seem pretty confident," Spur retorted, looking Jayan in the eye.

"Lots of leeway in your job right now," Jayan muttered, "but if you people kill an Inspector carrying an exception, then the law is under direct attack and things get nasty."

"That is a two-way door," Spur chuckled. "The Tick Tock is paid up in protection money through the end of the month. The Bluecoats know better than to interrupt our business. The Inspectors are generally happy with the look-don't-touch understanding. We give you information and you turn a blind eye. This here, what you're doing, it's expensive for your buddies—"

Cellar pivoted, driving a fist into Spur's gut. Startled, the enforcer slid back. The specials struggled to catch Spur so he did not sprawl all the way down to the paving.

"Let's go!" Cellar barked, and the specials dragged Spur up and kept moving towards the Smoke Tower at the far end of the Bookend Square. Spur let out a couple coughs.

A dozen feet later, Spur was limping on his own. By the time they reached the tower, he was walking normally.

"Somehow," Cellar said to Spur, "you've never been through a verification, to establish as factuals your name, history of residences, known acquaintances, and other identifiers. Today is your day."

Spur looked around the busy foyer of the mansion that was converted to a Watch tower, and grinned. "Nah," he said. "I would prefer not to cooperate."

Cellar raised the exception between two fingers, and cocked his head to the side.

"That's a fine thing," Spur agreed, "but it's just an exception to my privacy, yeah?"

"Yes," Cellar said, wary.

"I think I'll cooperate with that guy's exception instead," Spur said, nodding towards a broad-shouldered man crossing the foyer to intercept them, also wearing the coat and insignia of an Inspector.

"Dammit," Jayan muttered under his breath.

"Well well well!" the broad-shouldered Inspector said as he smiled at Cellar. "How are you doing, Digger?"

"Inspector Clelland," Cellar said as politely as he could. "What brings the leading light of the Lantern Tower to the Smoke Tower today?" He forced a smile.

"Got this exception," the other Inspector replied. "Our Chief Inspector urgently needs Hellyers to help him to identify some bodies. It's gotta be him, he's the only one reputed to know all the deceased," Clelland said apologetically.

"When I'm done, he's all yours," Cellar said.

"We may have a complication," Clelland admitted. He looked to Spur.

"Yes, I agree to cooperate with the Lantern Tower, but only if the exception from the Smoke Tower is voided," Spur grinned.

"How about it?" Clelland demanded. "Feeling cooperative, Digger? Or do we escalate this to the Chief Inspectors of the towers? Because I know mine is eager to secure Hellyers' cooperation." He cocked his head to the side. "You sure you've got the backing?"

"No," Cellar ground out. "I—I don't think I do."

"Well then," Clelland said with that awful, too-bright smile. "You transfer custody? And that exception?"

"Right after I see yours," Cellar said. Clelland hesitated only a moment, then handed it over. Cellar spent thirty seconds looking over its details, each moment of time sliding across the situation like icemelt.

"Mr. Hellyers is all yours," Cellar said, toneless.

"Right this way," Clelland said to Spur, and the two of them strolled back out the front doors of the tower.

A number of Bluecoats snickered, gathered in a knot at the end of the long counter. Jayan and Daava did not look at each other or Cellar.

Cellar could not look at his specials or the Bluecoats. He mounted the stairs, closing in on the Chief Inspector's office. This time he did pause to look at the assistant, who returned his look with cool contempt.

"He said you'd be back, and he'll see you," the assistant said.

Cellar stepped into the Chief Inspector's office. Prichard sat at his desk, back straight, fingers interlaced and resting on the uncluttered desktop.

"Third visit in a day," the Chief Inspector observed.

"So it would seem," Cellar replied. He managed to look the Chief Inspector in the eye. "Did you tell anyone about the exception I requested?"

"No." Prichard narrowed his eyes. "Are you suggesting I answer to a tea shop?"

"Of course not, sir," Cellar said with as much sincerity as he could fake. "That's just my frustration talking." He flexed his jaw. "I would like to retrieve the evidence I gave you to justify my exception."

"Request denied," the Chief Inspector said.

Cellar twitched. "Yes sir, I understand." He drew a shaky breath. "Looks like I'm off balance after all."

"Yes," Prichard agreed, "and you've leaned against the railing. Those rails are there for a reason. Railings slow you down before you walk off the edge of a drop that goes all the way down to the short stop. You know who climbs over railings to show off?"

"Idiots," Cellar said softly.

"Now, are you ready to climb back over to our side?" the Chief inspector asked, quiet but firm.

Cellar managed a nod, the movement of his head turning his stomach. "May I go, sir."

Prichard regarded him for a long moment. "Every blow that moves us can drive us down, or it can drive us up," he said. "If you need a few days, take them; you're no good to me like this. Get your head on straight so you can do the work you're assigned, then come back." He looked down to his desk, pulling over a stack of requisition orders. As Cellar let himself out of the office, his bowed shoulders demonstrated his submission.

His eyes did not.

➤ CHAPTER TWO ➤

Here's another example of how ideas kill people. One of the great inflammatory ideologies forty years ago was 'excessive dependency,' provided by Dr. Hope Brahdell. In this view of history, humans were optimized to be independent, with a few chosen dependencies. Civilization built on trading independence for safety and comfort. This trend forced humans to overspecialize and plunge into dependence on their rulers and experts for survival.

Idealists rattled on about how that philosophy should inspire people to pursue greater freedom. The cruelest aristocrats adapted the ideology, suggesting those with 'excessive dependency' who could not provide enough value to secure independence should be exterminated.

During the Smorton Uprising of 618, saboteurs blew up the lightning wall generators around Nightmarket. A tide of ghosts rushed in. At the time, Nightmarket had become the last stop of the desperate, and the district was overcrowded with starving paupers. Thousands died. The slaughter underscored the helplessness of the modern individual bereft of protection.

Was the Smorton Uprising triggered by rebels trying to issue a wake-up call to a slave population? Or was it a purge of the city's neediest parasites by the aristocrats?

— From "Deadly Ideas and their Echoes"
by Dr. Nuss Tyvaria

Rain drizzled across the saturated and warped shingles. Mist hung halos around the plasmic lamps lining the road, filling the eye with light so the shadows became impenetrable. Even in the humid warmth of the morning, the slim man standing under a lean-to by the street shrugged deeper into his overcoat.

He perked up as he heard the approaching echo of a rattling carriage; moments later, a massive draft goat hauled the two-wheeler in view. The goat's shag bounced with something like swagger as he slowed upon approaching the lean-to. As the carriage stopped, the man opened the door and hauled himself up into the cramped interior; the door was not yet closed when the driver snapped her whip, and the carriage clattered along the street.

"You're late," the man in the greatcoat muttered at the big man across from him in the carriage.

"You'll thank me," the other man replied. "There's a wobble in the Lantern revenue. There was an incident, I guess."

"Yeah? What happened?"

The big man cocked his head to the side. "Come on, Spindle, you don't get it both ways. Are you upset I was late, or would you be more upset if I was on time and couldn't answer your question?"

"I'm the boss, so I don't have to choose," Spindle replied, tetchy. "What happened?"

"An Inspector got all excitable about some fallout from internal housekeeping, tried to arrest some muscle from Tick Tock."

"How is that a hiccup?" Spindle asked, forehead creased. "It's good for our muscle to spend some quality time with the Inspectors or Bluecoats now and then."

"I guess Dame Maroden called in a marker and leaned on the Lantern Tower, so we had the guy released. For some reason, she didn't want a verification to get all his factuals recorded. Kind of a big move for low stakes, the Tick Tock was sending a message, but there's going to be some cleanup needed so that doesn't come back to bite us."

"Yeah, Piccolo may have questions about that, and you're the expert now. Answers, Crackstone; you'll have 'em or get 'em."

"Understood, boss," Crackstone said under his breath.

"Anything else that might make Piccolo curious? Anything we need to talk about ahead of time?" Spindle asked, looking out the window.

"Things are running more or less as expected," Crackstone replied. "Anybody else have anything to report?"

Spindle swung his head around to regard Crackstone. "No, just you. Your news breaks my streak," he said. "Means I have something to report. I don't like having something to report."

"Want me to explain to Dame Maroden she screwed up?" Crackstone asked.

Spindle considered that for a moment. "Find out more," he said. "If you think the answer is obvious, then, you know, decide," he shrugged. "If you aren't sure, bring it to me."

"Got it," Crackstone nodded.

The carriage shuddered to a halt outside the noisome back alley of the Sidearm public house. Spindle and Crackstone dismounted, and as the carriage hustled away they strolled down the stinking corridor, past a couple watchful sentries that could be mistaken for vagrants. The two men rounded a pile of crates and headed down the narrow steps behind them, and let themselves in the iron-bound basement entrance.

The thick stench of hagfish glop suffused the air. In the dim luminescence of globes mounted on the wall, they saw a man in waders pushing the offal on the floor over towards an overtaxed corner drain. The man glanced up at them.

"You're expected," he said, and he nodded towards the far door. He continued sweeping the floor around the long waist-high tank that dominated the room.

Spindle was glad to get out of the close quarters, down a flight of stairs, and into the more open chambers somewhere under the Sidearm public house. Globes were mounted on the ceiling over another tank with a table next to it, and block and tackle set up on a pivot. An old man stood by the table, masked and armored in thick leather, viscera smeared on his torso. To the side, a dapper figure sleeved in black leaned against a pillar, toying with a long spike set in a handle. The table's straps held down an injured hagfish. It was a three foot long column of vicious muscle, several beady eyes set in the visible side of its head, its mouth a nightmare of jagged translucent fangs.

"You are late," the man in black said absently, eyes on the torn flesh along the hagfish's flank.

"This won't take long," Spindle said. "Silkshore is gearing up for the Sail Lighting Festival. In general, our operations are pretty smooth right now. Everybody is on track with what we expect them to do."

"In general," Piccolo echoed, eyes wandering the hagfish's amphibious gill assembly, watching it suck at the air.

"Just before I came over I found out about something that the boss has asked about before, so we're keeping an eye on it. Like you said."

"You know," Piccolo muttered, "the boss once told me about the news sandwich. If you have unpleasant news, make a sandwich of it. Lead with good news, stick the bad news in the middle, then have some good news at the end." He looked up at Spindle, his dark eyes almost magnetic. "You trying to feed me a sandwich, Spindle?"

Spindle blinked. "I mean... well... do you want a sandwich?"

Piccolo looked over at the surgeon. "So how does it look. Give me a picture, Grabs. Will Nibbles live to fight again?"

"He took serious damage," the surgeon said, muffled by the mask. "Chutes scored him along the side, but if he was going to get infected I would be seeing the signs by now. I think he'll have some scarring, but as long as his muscles grow in right, he'll fight again. Could take up to six weeks to recover."

"Hm," Piccolo replied, absently testing the point of the spike with his finger, looking at the fighting hagfish as it struggled to breathe. He looked over to Spindle. "If Nibbles dies, I get to put another hagfish in the tournament; I lose my standing, but I can get it back if I can get some key matches lined up. I still have some time to recover. Or, I can trust that Nibbles will have the vicious tenacity of a veteran, and get back in there and bite me out some big chunks of money." He looked back at the hagfish. "If I give Nibbles here another chance and he doesn't come through for me, then I lose my shot at winning the Sidearm's Golden Hook tournament. Next year he'll be too old to fight anyway, so this is where he lives or dies. This is where I figure out who to trust. Who to rely upon."

"Remind me to never get hurt," Spindle said, bland. "Nobody failed you here, Piccolo. Just reporting the news."

"I'm practicing," Piccolo said, almost to himself. "This will be a good anecdote. Somewhere down the line. And this is also where I'm going to figure out whether I trust this guy, who didn't win, or the next guy, who may not even survive."

They were all quiet together for a moment, the silence interrupted by something dripping in the shadows and the labored wheeze of the injured hagfish's breathing.

"Back in the tank, Grabs," Piccolo said. "Nibbles will get another shot." He turned to Spindle as the surgeon unclipped the strap support and lifted the hinged table so the hagfish slid down into the tank with a blast of water. "Tell me what came up. What the boss is looking for."

Spindle turned to Crackstone. "Tell the man," he said.

Crackstone stepped forward, looking especially pale in the underground luminescence. "An Inspector got all enthusiastic and tried to do some verification of factuals on a cutter from the Tick Tock Tea House in Bookend Square. Spur, that's his name, he did some housekeeping and polished off a runner who was looking to go double agent."

"That kind of thing happens all the time," Piccolo said, frowning. "Make it interesting."

"Inspector Cellar traded in a big stack of factuals to get an exception to take Spur in. He's been working on the Tick Tock for a while, he got impatient. So Lantern Tower overruled him, got Spur out, and a bunch of pretty solid material got vanished. Overall a win for us, but it doesn't look good for the Inspectors or the Bluecoats. We're going to have to feed them some wins."

"Yeah, sure," Piccolo said. "We've got some low level people who need some seasoning in Ironhook. We can fix this. And yes, this Inspector... sounds like the kind of thing the boss is interested in." He paused. "Do you know why he stepped out of line?"

Crackstone licked his lips. "I guess the double agent was a kid," he said. "Inspector Cellar was working on him for a while. Thought he was going to get somewhere." He shrugged. "Didn't."

Piccolo looked in the murk of the hagfish tank, and saw the murderous eel-like monster slowly circling, eyes everywhere, furious and wounded. "Good job," he said absently. "Get a file together for the boss."

He jammed the spike into the table by the tank. Today, everybody lived.

HIGH SIX BUSINESS APERTURE, SILKSHORE. 18ᵀᴴ VOLNIVET. TENTH HOUR PAST DAWN.

Piccolo adjusted the cuff on his sleek coat as he stepped into the antechamber. The massive leather couches on one side of the room supported two brooding men with large moustaches and dark suits, briefcases on their laps. The far end of the room had an intimidating desk with a slender man behind it, guarding the double doors beyond. The other side of the room had windows, interspersed with recessed lighting, both covered with stained glass murals. Piccolo strolled past the waiting men to the reception desk.

"Burman," he said with a nod. "Is the boss in?"

"Yes," one of the portly men behind him on the couch said, rising and joining in Piccolo's question. "Is he? We had an appointment for half an hour ago!"

"And we appreciate your patience," Burman said, his sleek features and grace almost mesmerizing even at rest. He refocused on Piccolo. "Go on in, sir," he said with a deferential nod.

Piccolo smirked, rounding the desk and heading through the double doors. "Here to report, boss," he said.

The far end of the shadowed corridor office was lit only by radiant plants, a mass of curated vegetation that grew up the walls to meet overhead. Blossoms tinted the delicate light. A looming desk was anchored on both sides by planters. The light from the glowing shrubbery seemed directionless; there were few shadows at the end of the office. The pale man behind the desk was sleek. His suit was intricately styled and perfectly fitted. He relaxed in his throne-like seat, and smiled.

"Piccolo," he said. "I was thinking we were about due for your report."

"Do we need to wait until after you chat with your other guests?" Piccolo asked as he closed in on the desk. "I hear they've been waiting for half an hour." His smirk widened.

"They're fine," said the man at the desk, waving the concern away. "They're from the Ministry, they have some recommendations for renovating High Six, and frankly their requests are insulting. I'm setting the tone with a little cool-down period." He leaned back. "I'm more interested in what you have for me, I'm going to see Trellis tonight."

Piccolo seated himself in one of the small chairs in front of the desk. "Everybody is scrambling to get ready for the Sail Lighting Festival in Silkshore," he said. "That's a major distraction right now. The biggest thing I have to report is that things are getting serious for the proposed Church of Ecstasy construction on the edge of the Sparkgrounds. If we're going to intervene in that little fracas one way or another we need to declare by the end of the week. Then there's Chief Hamstead; he's ready to give us a hearing if we want to go forward in working out some Ironhook rentals."

The man behind the desk cocked his head. "That's not a stop. It's a pause," he murmured.

Piccolo raised his eyebrows. "I love these briefings, Sanction. I really do." He shifted in his seat. "There is one other thing. You know Trellis told us to keep an eye out for any unusual activity with Bluecoats or Inspectors."

"Right, he didn't say why," Sanction nodded.

"Yeah, I don't care," Piccolo clarified. "But I did hear about an Inspector who blew a pile of factuals trying to take one of the Tick Tock cutters down. We stopped him, but he was apparently right on the edge. Lost his patience, tried to brute force it."

"And you brought me a file."

"I wouldn't send you to Trellis without a briefing," Piccolo said, sliding an envelope across the desk.

"Good man," Sanction said, tucking the envelope away. "Set up a meeting, me and Hamstead. Usual precautions. Then, you work with Trajan. You are our representative with the Fairpole Gondolier Council, we're as invested as they are in making sure the Sail Lighting Festival goes smoothly." He paused. "You're in charge of the shipment coming in on Market Day," he said quietly.

"Yes. I'll use Spindle and his people. No complications," Piccolo promised.

"That's what I want to hear. Now, you've got plenty to do, so I'll let you get to it."

"Want me to send in the bureaucrats on my way out?" Piccolo asked, his smirk returning.

"I'm still busy," Sanction smiled, showing pale teeth but only traces of good humor.

BELDERAN ESTATE, BARROWCLEFT.
18TH VOLNIVET. HOUR OF SONG, 2 HOURS PAST DUSK.

Sanction mounted the stairs, exiting the narrow stairwell into the low-beamed attic space that echoed the shape of the house below. He heard a gritty whine that seemed to grate at the base of his skull, and he crossed the center aisle of the attic to look down one of the peaked corridors that served as a workshop.

An old man hunched over his work bench, illuminated by several lamps and mirrors. The artisan squinted into a loupe as he held a gem, delicately cutting at its surface with a spark-powered grinder. The workshop was well stocked with tools, everything in its place. Radiant materials glowed softly from their lockboxes, and a bookshelf supported lifetimes of research and reference material. The far end had two easy chairs flanking a small round table.

The old man put the gem down, relaxing his face and catching the falling loupe in a single graceful motion. He cocked an eyebrow as he looked over to where Sanction emerged from shadow. "There you are," he observed with something like satisfaction.

"How goes the hobby?" Sanction asked, nodding at the workbench.

"Gratifying," the old man replied, rising and stretching. "May I interest you in some tea?"

"Certainly." Sanction followed the artisan to the table at the end of the workshop. "I trust I am not interrupting."

"You are expected," the old man said, removing the cozy from the pot and pouring two cups of tea. "Catch me up." He settled in a chair, cradling the steaming cup in both hands, narrowly regarding Sanction through the steam.

"Things are running smoothly on our end," Sanction said, "but you wanted an update on Gaddoc Rail Station."

"Indeed."

"The Hive has been making noise. Their investment in Gaddoc Rail Station has paid off. Orris has secured complete control of contraband moving through the station, using a consortium of invested faction representatives to handle internal policing and keep any upstarts from getting a foothold. By consolidating the bribing and chastisement into a single channel, he's realized significant savings for the group, and while they have to share with each other, they're pretty well proofed against other players starting up competition."

"We expected that," Trellis nodded.

"Hive success with Gaddoc Rail Station means all eyes are on North Port," Sanction continued as Trellis contemplated his tea. "That's the next battleground for securing a contraband monopoly. If the Hive wins both, then they're going to be able to undercut all the other black markets combined."

"Lay it out for me," Trellis said. "What happens next."

"The Hive is flush with success, but success also works against them; others are more likely to band together and push back. The Fog Hounds are making a strong move, pulling on their connection with key Bluecoat chiefs. Their captain, Margette Vale, has assigned her second, Bear, to personally oversee efforts there. The big question at this point is whether the Hive is going to back the Vultures, an up and coming band of smugglers trying to develop a network in North Port, or whether they'll form a third contender."

"When we spoke last, I instructed you to do some research so you can explain to me why we want the Fog Hounds to win this one," Trellis said.

"And I did," Sanction said. "It took some digging to find that Captain Vale leveraged the Fog Hound successes into a portfolio that attracted Sagliarre to be their patron and provide a market for the goods." He paused. "Sagliarre is the head of a noble family, one that provides significant backing to the Fairpole Gondolier Council—our closest allies."

"Good, so far as it goes," Trellis smiled.

"Okay, you want more." Sanction tried not to sound peevish. "Sagliarre is also of Iruvian descent, which will go over well with a lot of the contraband smugglers. And we worked to place him in the Ministry in the aftermath of the gondolier reallocation fiasco. He is likely to view the Silkworms in a favorable light."

"I'm just not feeling that satisfying snap of everything fitting into place," Trellis murmured, almost concerned.

"You want to know about Sagliarre's wife, children, history, address? I have a lot of information," Sanction frowned.

"Yes," Trellis said, "of course you do. But do you understand why we want to make this connection?"

"I can see lots of advantages," Sanction replied through his teeth.

"Consider this," Trellis said. "If we consolidate a connection between the gondoliers and a smuggler clearinghouse, like North Port, the Fairpole Council could monopolize Doskvol's black market. No one else has their capacity to move cargo within the city. They can hide it, and adjust protections to counter or manufacture occult tracking and scrying. They can set meets with buyers and sellers undetected." He paused. "I want this ambition to come from them, to grow from their leadership, and to be accomplished on their terms."

Trellis took another long sip of his tea as Sanction felt almost dizzy, his mind rapidly processing the possibilities. A fleet of small boats in constant motion, run by crews with basic adept traditions to cope with ghosts and curses. Endless nooks and crannies, makeshift boathouses and drydocks, family homes, all intermingled. The trust that grows between close-knit family-based businesses, a culture of visitors in a strange land bound together for mutual advantage. Their smuggling had focused within city boundaries previously, in Silkshore mostly, its maze of canals their home. But seeing them as a resource for a much grander smuggling operation... Sanction shook his head.

"Why not make a bid for Gaddoc Rail station, if this is the ambition?" he asked.

"The gondoliers won't pull together. Not without having a strong outside competitor to resist, to defeat. They have too many feuds and rivalries. The Hive has proven they are serious. Considering how the Hive once controlled the Fairpole Gondolier Council, as well as other elements in Silkshore, there's bad blood there. We've got a boogyman to invoke," he said with a smile that was almost hidden behind his teacup.

"And if the Fog Hounds don't lead the way to victory in North Port?" Sanction asked, cocking an eyebrow.

"Then we make a move on the docks," Trellis said, "and the military. We have contingencies. Each conflict fuels and outlines the next."

"Yes," Sanction agreed, thoughtful. Quiet followed.

"I have time," Trellis clarified.

"Excuse me?"

"For the next item. The one you're trying to decide whether or not you'll mention." Trellis shifted in his seat. "I have time."

"You said you want to hear about any Inspectors or Bluecoats acting out of character," Sanction said, almost reluctant. "I heard of one. Inspector Cellar, based out of Silkshore. Gambled big for low stakes and got shut down anyway, took a pretty catastrophic hit to his carefully curated effort to bring down the Tick Tock operation. I guess he was upset because he was trying to turn a child to be a double agent, and the operation sent a cutter to kill the kid. Cellar tried to arrest the cutter and got outmaneuvered; messy point-blank interference, we'll have to settle down the locals by giving the Inspectors and Bluecoats some arrests to prove they're properly invested in fighting the bad guys."

Trellis let a small private smile grow on his face. "You don't have to understand. Just leave the file." He rose to his feet, putting the cup aside. "Now, if you don't mind, I would appreciate it if you'd run an errand for me. I commissioned a flask of flecked plasmic essence from the Mistress of Tides, in exchange for this." He picked up a small box, then opened it, tilting it so the light reflected and refracted from a handful of exquisitely cut gemstones. "Please give this to her, and get the essence, and bring it straight to me. I don't want to lose it, and I trust you completely."

"Of course I'll help," Sanction said, "but why me and not Piccolo?"

"Why indeed?" Trellis asked, challenging, eyebrows up.

Sanction scowled. "Alright, it's not too difficult to guess. We haven't seen much of her lately. And should something come up, you want to be sure she's alright, and ready to step in on our behalf." He paused. "And you think I'm a better judge of that sort of nuance than our handy young lurk."

"Very good," Trellis smiled. "I don't mean to discourage you from asking questions. There's tremendous value in checking your impressions against what other people say, or what they think, even if you understand them better than they understand themselves. Still. You want to get into my head, to see things the way I do, so someday you can outmaneuver any challenge we face. You won't build those muscles if you don't exercise them yourself."

"I've got a start," Sanction said, perhaps less confident than he had been at the beginning of the conversation. "For example, I know before I leave, you're going to give me a small personal gift for the Mistress of Tides herself. You want to show regard, not treat her as a vendor. I bet you've got something with occult significance worth more than this whole box, and you were waiting for me to ask for it."

Trellis said nothing in return. He simply smiled, and tossed Sanction a small box.

"Your brilliance warms an old man's bones," he said.

MAURO OVERVIEW, ZEPHYR STREET, MASTER MARKET, SILKSHORE. 18ᵀᴴ VOLNIVET. HOUR OF FLAME, 5 HOURS PAST DUSK.

Sanction was built lean and sleek, but he felt almost logy compared to the slim acolyte he followed up the last curve of stairs to the main gallery of the temple. Her sea-colored robe had no sash or tie, and her woven sandals made no sound on the stone.

"She will meet you here," the acolyte said. She offered a deep bow, then turned and left Sanction alone high above the colorful patchwork of the Ease. Sanction leaned against an ancient stone column, taking in the ripple of life, light, and color drifting up from the earth. Land was invisible below, indistinguishable from the canals, boats, docks, rafts, and rooftops. Thousands of lights of all kinds glowed, through paper shades and silken drapes, reflected on wood, metal, stone, and water. The torn and blasted sky had long ago surrendered its stars to the Void Sea, and the torment of the clouds was invisible against a blackness not yet interrupted by moonrise; the moon was late tonight, but it was sure to rise before the Hour of Pearls.

Sanction half-turned. "It's no wonder you don't visit," he murmured. "This view is difficult to leave."

"What you see and what I see are very different," the voice behind him replied, cool as marble. Sanction turned to see the Mistress of Tides, draped in her embroidered vest and robes, her face veiled and indistinct in shadow. "What did you come here to see?"

"Trellis sent me," Sanction replied, offering the box full of gems. "Something about flecked plasmic essence."

She considered Sanction as her acolyte stepped in from somewhere out of sight nearby and took the box with a deep bow. The Mistress of Tides pulled the flask from a pocket in her robes and handed it to Sanction. It was bitterly cold, even through the glyph-stitched iron of its container. He slid it into his messenger bag.

"Do you have questions about it?" the Mistress of Tides asked.

"Oh, no, I'm happier not knowing," Sanction replied. "That is between you and Trellis."

"Yet he did not come," she observed.

"He's working an angle on something," Sanction said, "and you know how he gets. He does send his regards," Sanction added, freeing the smaller box from an inner pocket and holding it out for the Mistress of Tides. She took the box and opened it. She looked inside, and gasped.

Sanction saw a gem the size of the last segment of a pinkie finger, polished to a peculiar sheen with a color he could not describe.

"If he cut this himself," the Mistress of Tides mused, "his talents have grown considerably."

"Looks like it has radiance," Sanction murmured. Then he shrugged. "Of course it does," he sighed.

The Mistress of Tides tucked the gem away, and stepped over to share the view with Sanction. "I have not sent an update to Trellis for a while," she confessed. "I mean to send an acolyte, I have several I can trust, but..."

Sanction nodded, not taking his eyes off the cascading puzzle of the city below. "Any news you have, he appreciates," he said.

"The Foundation is making a move against the Church of Ecstasy putting a church into the edge of the Sparkgrounds," she murmured. "Something in that area is part of a larger pattern in the geography of the city; the Foundation would not interfere otherwise. And I suspect the Church of Ecstasy knows it, and is deliberately making a move to surface resistance."

"Good to know," Sanction nodded.

"You are familiar with the Lost, out of Coalridge," she continued. "They are planning an assassination at the Sail Lighting Festival. I hear they are working with the Weeping Lady poverty berths as part of the plan. I don't know more about that."

"I will tell Piccolo, he's running security on that."

The Mistress of Tides turned to face him. "We are in a shadow," she said so only he could hear. "Change looms over us. We will be over-taken by it."

He looked for eyes somewhere behind her veils. "Change always comes," he replied in the same hushed tone. "When it arrives this time, will we rise, or will we sink?"

She paused. "This time," she breathed, "it is not that easy."

Sanction nodded to her, and sensed his audience was over. He turned, heading back down the stairs.

Alone, the Mistress of Tides contemplated Silkshore as the future silently approached.

CHAPTER THREE

*He didn't grow up on the streets, he grew up in the back
workrooms of Ink Lane shops. He devoured the sensational and
lurid accounts of criminals and their philosophies, worshiping
powerful figures who could rise above and beyond the law. He
was one of those well-fed and plump-faced kids who would
talk in awe about The Life and Crimes, if you know what I
mean. He ached to be cool, to grow into the image.*

*Sometime around puberty he got the biography of Lye, the
Iruvian assassin—I think it was called Lye and Truth. For a
whole month he reverently recounted this story from the book
to everyone he met. In the story, an inspector was grilling Lye
about a murder weapon. Lye was in the middle of a music
lesson, and he insisted that he didn't care about the weapon;
anything could kill if you become a weapon. The inspector
scoffed at him, so Lye jammed his piccolo through the law-
man's eye socket.*

*Bored with the brat's lust for shock value, one of his uncles
said he could be a murder weapon—he could be a piccolo. It
stuck because the kid adopted it, all "hell yeah I'm a piccolo
murder weapon." This was an early example of his stubborn
refusal to let people shame or praise him; that's the core of his
character, and the reason I let him into my crew. If he lives, I
think he could really make something of himself.*

*— Saint Suran, factuals attested to Inspector Flywin,
Bridge Tower, winter 846*

"Here you are again," grinned the elderly man in the threadbare Blue-coat uniform. He gestured around the dim, smoky chamber. "I was just thinking the place needed another target dummy."

"That's hilarious, Taff," Inspector Cellar said with half a grin. "I've got a night's work for you. Factuals surrounding the murder on Westerline Canal and Greentree, from all the witnesses," he said as he put a modest folio of papers on the desk. "Here are factuals surrounding incidents of theft from the rising pickpocket threat in the Market of Steps. And the factuals surrounding the disappearance of Dame Lacha's stablemaster." A third folio topped the stack.

Taff chuckled. "The murder was Eben the Lesser, he crossed Niles Talbosh and got knifed for it. The pickpockets are that new gang, the Damselflies, but we won't catch them because they answer to the Fairpole Gondolier Council, unofficially, and they're paid up through the end of the month," he said with a wink. "As for Dame Lacha's stablemaster, I think everybody knows he was poisoned for his indiscretions." Taff tossed the folios of factuals in the filing bin against the back wall. "Sounds like you're still on the Chief Inspector's bad side."

"Think so?" Cellar asked mildly, leaning against the counter. "After months of well-earned autonomy in my investigations, I've been assigned to assist Bluecoat efforts by interviewing witnesses and establishing factuals to support some eventual contemplation." He paused. "Mainly contemplations the Bluecoats know will never go forward."

"Seems a waste of paper and ink," Taff agreed sympathetically.

"It's a waste of *me*," Cellar growled. "At least my specials are reassigned to evaluating potential problems with the Sail Lighting Festival—something useful."

"Only one in a hundred clues makes a difference," Taff admonished, wagging his finger.

"But the clues that do? They are worth the ninety nine that don't," Cellar replied. He shook his head, squinting around the archival dungeon. "Taff, how do you know all this? I feel like there's a whisper network all around me, just out of earshot."

"It's only fair," Taff said. "I've heard Inspectors complain that when you look over some broken furniture and a blood spatter you can see the whole story, and you can get all sorts of conclusions out of an interview like you hear things nobody else can."

"Charmer," Cellar said with a wry glance at the old man. "Really though. You didn't leave the building all night, and you know more about the cases I documented than I do."

"That's easy enough to explain," Taffer said. "If someone tells you a secret, does that mean you're going to tell them a secret later? Something they're not supposed to know?"

"Of course not," Cellar frowned.

"There you go," Taff sighed. "You get standards instead of gossip." His grin showed off a number of gaps between brown teeth.

"So you think I should give up my standards."

"What? No!" Taff replied, almost baffled. "We each have a foundation, our strength, and we work from that. Switch foundations and your whole life gets unsteady. Me? My foundation was gossip," he said. "Yours? Conviction. You are sure you can serve the law and unravel deceit." Taff gestured vaguely behind Cellar. "That's why you Inspectors get shadows. Extend your reach. Use people who think differently."

"You sure are a smart old man," Cellar said.

"Absolutely right," Taff agreed with a sage nod. "Far as you know." He grinned.

"And there's too much I don't know," Cellar said, his smile fading. "Do you know who tipped off the Lantern Tower that I was going after Spur?"

"No way," Taff said. "We don't give children guns to play with." He paused. "Maybe when you're older," he said, eyes twinkling with good humor to counterbalance his patronizing tone as he put his hand on Cellar's forearm.

"Blood and bone, Taff," Cellar said, teeth locked and tone mild. "That's not funny. Not to me."

Taff looked him in the eye for a long moment, taking his measure. "Cellar, my boy," he said quietly, "you screwed up. You lost the hand, and since you kept upping the ante, that's going to sting." He slid his hand across the counter, spreading a deck of pasteboard cards facedown.

"You always keep a deck of cards up your sleeve?" Cellar asked, cocking an eyebrow.

"Pockets, sleeves, lapels, palm of my hand," Taff agreed. "Now pay attention, I'm saving your life right now. You can get tetchy with me, I'm old and indulgent; you take that tone with the Chief Inspector again and you're likely to disappear into the Ministry's filing pool, which may be worse than drowning. Now, you know these cards," he continued, tilting one end of the row of cards up so they all flipped over.

"Standard Dimmerdeck," Cellar agreed, looking at the celestial suites; the Sun, the Moon, the Stars, the Void.

"Just one deck," Taff nodded. "It's standard, everybody's got one. But you could find yourself playing Hunt the Leviathan, Corpseriddle, Jumping Three, Settle, or Fishflank," he observed. "So many ways to define a win, to frame the competition. These games look at random chance, people reading, and managing your risks. You get some cards and some people willing to play by your rules, and you can unpack the challenges forever."

"How have you not retired to become a card shark?" Cellar asked, deadpan.

"This isn't just for games, Cellar. You can do divinations. Read the past, the future, your own secrets, the secrets in other people. Even the plainest truths filling up your blind spots." He tilted the cards back and forth along the line, then swept them together with a wince. "I used to be able to make these things *dance*," he said, flexing his swollen knuckles. "Now I can barely shuffle."

Cellar took the cards and twisted the deck into a pair of stacks, blending them with a crisp rattle and snapping the deck against the counter.

"This city," Taff said, watching the deck of cards. "It's like a deck of cards. You can play all kinds of games. There's rules set up by the City Council, another set of rules for basic human decency, your family will give you a set, the Bluecoats got one, Inspectors got one, Crows got one, Church of Ecstasy, the Skovs, the Whispers... Everybody at the table, everybody using the same cards." He looked Cellar in the eye. "It's a rare few who focus so hard they only play by one set of rules at a time."

"Sounds like a mess," Cellar said quietly.

"It absolutely is, in case you haven't noticed," Taff replied, a shadow of a smile under his stained stubble. "Cellar, there's nothing special about the law," he murmured, leaning in close. "Written-down laws are no stronger than orders to keep the peace. There's blood rules, son," he added as his red-rimmed eyes bored into Cellar. "Rules of revenge and love and sacrifice. Life and death. You know that better than most, and that's where you got pinched." He poked Cellar in the chest, hard. "Between the games."

Cellar studied the old man. "So... what's your game?"

Taff chuckled. "I wanted to get old. I wanted to get enough coin to retire in style and get laid constantly until I dropped dead." He paused, thoughtful.

"How did that work out?" Cellar asked with a grin.

"That's the trouble with getting old," Taff replied. "You find out the hard way that you wanted the wrong things all along. The trick is to stay flush without drawing attention or committing to anything 'no matter what.' I was lucky. My desires were pretty selfish. That's what drives all this, you know. The desires you choose and the desires that choose you."

"You're awfully philosophical today," Cellar observed.

"I guess I don't want to waste all this," Taff replied. "We're hours past dawn and night is still in my bones. The world is colder than it used to be." He sucked a tooth, looking down at the counter. "Only a few hands left."

"Come on, Taff," Cellar said, resisting the mood. "You were old when I was born. You think old age will catch up to you now?"

"I would never have guessed it, with the swagger of youth," Taff replied, still not meeting Cellar's eyes. "Age. Of all things." He blinked. "Every cough. Every slip. Every cut. Everything got dangerous."

Cellar tried not to see the hollowness in Taff's cheeks and throat, the vagueness in his hands. "So if you had to boil it down," he said quietly. "How you'd want to be remembered. The most important things you've learned."

Taff's eyes were bright again as he looked Cellar in the eye. "Boil it down? No, I've never done that, never will. Let it stay all messy. You figure it out yourself." He managed a smile. "Make your own mistakes, boy!"

Cellar smiled at him, hiding his relief as best he could as the moment passed. "Take care of yourself, old man. I'll be back tomorrow morning with more useless paperwork."

Taff waved him off, and Cellar hesitated only a moment before mounting the stairs, leaving the dungeon archive and returning to the main floor. He spotted Jayan approaching, urgency in his step.

"What is it?" Cellar asked.

Jayan did not slow down, but steered Cellar to the side door, across the street, under the shade of a balcony. Out of earshot.

"Okay boss," Jayan said. "I heard that the Bluecoats got paid off to look the other way for a shipment coming in to the Tick Tock on Market Day. Something important." He paused. "Do we let it go?" he asked, studying his Inspector.

Cellar looked him in the eye. "No, we absolutely do not," he replied through his teeth. "Tell me everything."

CHIMEWATER CLOSE, SILKSHORE.
20TH VOLNIVET. HOUR OF SILVER, 3 HOURS PAST DUSK.

Finally, the door opened and closed. The lean man looked up from his book, his mild gaze taking in the trim figure in a greatcoat. The newcomer shed his outerwear and hung it in the entryway closet.

"Looks like the rain started up again," said the man with the book.

"That will happen," Sanction said, his tone sharp as he stepped into the living room. "I don't suppose you left the house at all today."

"Just a little shopping, then the museum," the lean man replied, looking Sanction in the eye. "Did you have a good day at work?"

"Sure, why not," Sanction muttered. "Good as it can be. Can't really talk about it." He frowned. "Rutherford, what's that I smell?"

"Eelish stacked plate," Rutherford replied with a characteristic smile that always carried something like sadness behind it. "It's on the table if you'd like some."

Sanction squinted for a moment. "Oh, right, tonight was that, you know," he said with a vague gesture. "Something about the museum."

Rutherford rose to his feet. "I've served three months at the Ease Cultural Museum part time, now I'm curating the Bluecoat exhibits and archives." He shrugged. "A little celebration."

"How did it go?" Sanction asked, hiding behind a smile.

"Predictably dull," Rutherford replied.

"Well, that's museums," Sanction said. "Did you sort out that confusion with the cleaners for my tailcoats? I'll be needing one before the end of the week."

"Dealt with it yesterday, your coats are in the closet," Rutherford said. "How about your errands, for your uncle?"

Sanction paused, then turned to watch Rutherford, a glint in his eye. "Probably best we do not discuss Lord Belderan," he said quietly.

"Or work. Or the museum." Rutherford squared his shoulders. "How about the weather?"

"Oh, is that what we're doing now?" Sanction retorted, brow furrowed. "I'm sorry I can't dazzle you with conversation the second I cross the threshold. It's been a hell of a day, I finally get home, and the last thing I need to deal with—especially here in my own house— is an ambush." He pivoted and crossed to the kitchen, almost stamping his feet.

Rutherford watched his shadow retreat, then sat back down and opened his book. His eyes wandered the page, unseeing, until a few minutes later when Sanction mounted the stairs to the bedroom.

Only then did Rutherford allow himself a deep breath.

MAURO OVERVIEW, ZEPHYR STREET, MASTER MARKET, SILKSHORE. 20TH VOLNIVET. HOUR OF FLAME, 5 HOURS PAST DUSK.

The acolyte padded up to where the Mistress of Tides sat at the table, the heavy book open before her. "I have come at the appointed hour," he said reverently. The neighborhood bells that tolled the hour were still resonant.

"Thank you, Neap," the Mistress of Tides replied, her face concealed behind a veil. She closed the book, and regarded her acolyte. "What is going on tonight?"

"The Fairpole Gondolier Council wants to give you a new gondola as a symbol of their regard for you. They would like to present it in the next couple of days." He paused. "They have some requests for you as well, I am certain of it."

"Set it up," she said quietly. "What else."

"Spirit Warden activity has intensified around the Sparkgrounds," Neap said. "And, possibly related, Levyra has requested an audience."

"The medium Levyra?" the Mistress of Tides clarified. She paused. "She has never contacted me before."

"Not directly," Neap agreed, "but we have had contact on routine matters. We shop in similar circles, have overlapping dealings with some nobles. Also, she has some fame, and I believe maybe a year or so ago she informed me that if you wanted an audience she would grant one."

"She is an adept, not a Whisper, yes?" the Mistress of Tides said.

"Correct," Neap nodded. "Her gift focuses around internal control; she lets ghosts ride her so they can exchange some last words with the family, that sort of thing. She's skilled at blocking off the ghost's access to her if things go wrong, ejecting the spirit. More to the point, she has a somewhat friendly relationship with the Spirit Wardens; she hands over ghosts after they have their last say, and the Wardens destroy them."

"She may have heard something," the Mistress of Tides murmured. "Tell her I will grant her an audience."

"That brings us to a pair of supplicants," Neap said. "They want to join your cabal."

"Names," the Mistress of Tides said absently.

"Nevi and Yelsir," Neap replied.

"Weren't they with Crestwine?" the Mistress of Tides asked. "I think he worked the west side of the Ease."

"Yes, Crestwine was their Whisper. He has been missing for a week, and they are confident he is dead," Neap said. "I asked around and the word is he was doing divination and spectral interrogation to discover obscure facts about Silkshore landmarks. As a consequence, it is generally believed he fell afoul of the Foundation, and they arranged for his death."

"He was no slouch," the Mistress of Tides said. "He had two spirits bound to his staff, and one to a tooth in his head; even if taken by surprise, he would put up a real fight."

"The Foundation doesn't fight," Neap cautioned. "Chances are he was drugged or poisoned, then put into a stone box, then buried in a street or the foundation of a building. Informed speculation favors Paving, an operative of the Foundation who specializes in burying targets alive in rune-scribed boxes so even when they die the Deathseeker crows cannot find them." He shivered slightly.

"What do we know about Paving?" the Mistress of Tides asked.

Neap blinked. "Nothing, except by his reputation and method of disposing of foes," he said. "I will ask around."

She rose from her seat. "Very well. Let us have a look at these supplicants."

Once she was seated on her throne in the main audience gallery, two acolytes on each side, the far door opened to allow two women in thin robes to enter the presence of the Mistress of Tides. They approached reverently, their heads freshly shorn, and lowered themselves to their knees before her.

"You come beneath my gaze, wishing to be seen," the Mistress of Tides murmured in Hadrathi, the syllables slithering out.

"Breathe our air. See our flesh. We offer you both," replied the supplicants in unison, practiced.

"Let us speak plain," the Mistress of Tides said, switching to the clipped tones of Akorosian. "You wish to join us and receive my instruction."

"Yes," they both said fervently, not even exchanging a glance.

"There will be a period of observation. Tests. You may not survive. Walk away now and there are no hard feelings," the Mistress of Tides said quietly.

"My Lady," Nevi said abruptly. "Some things are worth dying for. I would serve you, unto death."

"And beyond?" the Mistress of Tides asked.

"And beyond," Nevi agreed.

"Why me?" the Mistress of Tides murmured, almost to herself.

Nevi hesitated only a moment. "My uncle is Alzaro Feylide, also an adept, he owned a gondola that was in the family four generations. When the Ministry foreclosed on his gondola he was in despair, but before he could act foolishly, his gondola was restored to him—to us." She paused. "Since that day I have sought to find a way to repay you."

The Mistress of Tides let that stand for a moment, then turned to the other supplicant.

"I am Yelsir," the dark woman said quickly. "I long ago chose a path of murder, and I would not have my talents wasted in service of thugs. Nor can I escape my past, even should I wish to do so." She paused, studying the inscrutable veil. "Let me kill for you," she said. "My former master said you would ascend in blood. I want to be part of your ascent."

The Mistress of Tides considered them in the deep quiet of the gallery, far above the noisy street below.

"Neap," she said, "I will allow them to have a chance to become my acolytes. See what they know. Make a place for them, for now," she said. Cocking her head to the side, she turned her attention back to the women kneeling before her.

"Looking within and without, we shall see," she said in Hadrathi.

"See and be seen," they replied, completing the ancient saying. Rising, they bowed deeply, then left the chamber following Neap.

"See and be seen," the Mistress of Tides echoed, lost in thought.

CHIME ERA BOOKSTORE, FOGCREST, SILKSHORE. 21ST VOLNIVET. FOURTH HOUR PAST DAWN.

Rutherford relaxed at the table, his wineglass half full, finely milled sporebread in a basket before him. The small round table before him was enough for one, maybe two patrons. There were only a handful of tables in the corner; the rest of the ground floor was taken up with shelves and racks of books, and the occasional seat. A counter by the frosted glass at the bookstore's front hosted the attentive clerk who watched the patrons and managed their purchases. Outside, thunder muttered and lisped as a steady rain rinsed the city.

A trim elder with pixie-like features and silvered hair approached the table, arms wide. "Rutherford," she said warmly.

Rutherford rose and gently hugged her, then resumed his seat. She sat across from him and gestured at a server, who ducked a nod and headed to the back to get her usual order.

"Thank you for meeting me for brunch today," Rutherford said. "It's good to see you, Nebs. I don't know how you manage to look more fantastic every time I see you." He smiled, an almost wistful expression that stayed with those who saw it.

"Flatterer," Nebs observed. "Don't slow it down, we'll need a steady stream today. Tell me about my eyes," she demanded with a puckish grin.

"They are the deepest green, a forest lost in their hue," Rutherford replied, "and they've watched Kreeger his whole life." He paused significantly.

"Trouble with the husband," Nebs sighed. "I am sorry to hear it. I like you better than him, even though he's my nephew." She shrugged at the feeling. "You've got balance, Rutherford. Kreeger... his whole life he's been off kilter. You were the only one who could ever change that pattern in him."

"I love him, in my bones," Rutherford murmured. "But he's forcing me away. He knows just how to do it. First he withdrew, then... he wants it to be easy for me to leave."

Nebs regarded Rutherford with a steady look as her roast coffee and crispy wafers arrived. The server retreated as Rutherford met her eyes and took a slow sip of his coffee.

Rutherford did not tell her about the mismatched rouge he got out of Sanction's collar. He did not tell her about the scratches on Sanction that his husband did not even try to explain. He did not tell her how Sanction had been working late, irritable, dismissive. He did not tell Nebs about the partitioning of finances so Rutherford could not see all the expenses, or the overnight strategy sessions Sanction lied about with the carelessness of someone who considered a falsehood to be a kindness.

"You know who?" Nebs said quietly.

"His assistant at work," Rutherford said. "There's an artist, too, and someone at the Ministry offices." He shook his head, tightening his jaw. "I have not told anyone," he said, his voice stiff.

"Oh, Rutherford," Nebs said, her eyes glinting. "I am so sorry." She paused. "What are you going to do?" Her eyes narrowed. "If you need help, I will provide it," she said, some steel under her tone.

"I have to leave him," Rutherford ground out, every word a struggle. "But—I don't think I can survive letting him go."

"You can," Nebs said firmly. "You absolutely can, Rutherford."

"There is no hope for salvaging what we have now," Rutherford said, his chest locked up. "I'm going to have to burn it all down."

"It sounds like you already have a plan," Nebs said.

"I was a Bluecoat for years before I met Kreeger," Rutherford replied. "That's how you defend yourself, when there is ambiguity, when there is that hopeless feeling. You make a plan, and you take action, even if it's just symbolic." He tightened his jaw. "This plan, these actions, will be far more than symbolic." He met her eyes once more. "Thank you for seeing me, Nebs. I haven't had anyone to talk to about this, and I need to hear it out loud, at least some of it, to muster the courage for the next steps."

"I have never known a man with less need of additional courage than you, Rutherford," Nebs said directly. "Before this goes any further, you know there's someone you must consult before you do anything rash."

"He is second on my list," Rutherford said, a wintery smile tugging at the corners of his face. "He will see things my way. But... I needed to talk to you first." He paused. "I got your blessing before I consented to courtship with Kreeger. I want your blessing now that it's time to... redefine that relationship."

Nebs put her hand on Rutherford's forearm. "Do what you must," she said, her whisper almost a hiss.

BELDERAN ESTATE, BARROWCLEFT. 21ST VOLNIVET. TWELFTH HOUR PAST DAWN.

"Thank you for agreeing to see me, Lord Belderan," Rutherford said to Trellis as the escorting servant withdrew from the study, closing the double doors.

"Nonsense, Rutherford," Trellis said with a warm smile, rising from his desk and extending his arms, pulling Rutherford into an affectionate embrace. Then Trellis held him at arm's length, studying his eyes and face with a discomfiting and penetrating scrutiny. "What can I do for you," he mused.

"I value your friendship," Rutherford said quietly, "and I love your nephew Kreeger."

"But," Trellis said, cocking his head to the side as he released Rutherford, heading back around the desk to his seat. "Kreeger is restless." Trellis lowered himself into the chair slowly. "And deliberately careless." He leaned back, looking to Rutherford as he steepled his fingers. "And you come to me."

"I must act," Rutherford said quietly. "You know I must."

"If ever you were worthy of my nephew, of course you must do something," Trellis replied. "How long have you known?"

Rutherford seated himself across the desk from Trellis. "Known?" he murmured. "Suspected, three months. Believed, about one. Confirmed, a few days."

"And now?" Trellis balled one hand into a fist and clasped it with the other.

Rutherford let the moment simmer before he spoke. "I cannot be invisible. I cannot be dismissed. To Kreeger, I have become a piece of outdated furniture cluttering up his new floorplan." Rutherford swallowed hard. "I am going to recapture his attention."

Trellis waited.

"I must burn down what we have now," Rutherford said quietly, "because he has fouled it beyond repair."

"Do you plan to kill him?" Trellis asked.

"No," Rutherford said sharply. "That's not the kind of love I have for him. I want—I need him to be happy. But that doesn't happen, not like this; not unless I turn his world upside down." Rutherford rose to his feet. "I really didn't come to talk to Lord Belderan," he said. "I talked to family when I visited Nelytha Bel for lunch. I made the long trip out to Barrowcleft because I need to talk to *Trellis.*"

"How very unlike you," Trellis replied, unreadable.

"Desperate times," Rutherford replied. "I do not trust you to know when you're out of your depth, or to restrain your need to meddle. I do not trust you to tell the truth, or to recognize your transgressions when you are manipulating everyone around you." He paused. "I absolutely trust you to look out for those you care for, and to develop elaborate plots, and to keep secrets." He leaned forward, almost whispering. "So I am entrusting you with my secrets. I am telling you my plan, if you'll hear it. Of the two of us, I trust you more than me to make the most of what I'm about to undertake."

Trellis watched him and said nothing.

"My heart is broken," Rutherford said quietly, "and that's not something to waste."

A bleak smile suffused Trellis's features. "You're going back to the Bluecoats," he murmured.

"I'm going back to the Bluecoats," Rutherford nodded. "For a start."

Trellis snuggled back in his chair like a cat settling on a cushion, and Rutherford explained his plan.

CHAPTER FOUR

Harden your heart! You survive as your heart flexes, again and again, striving towards impenetrable density. Our bodies reflect our world; we have bone for the world's rock, blood for the world's seas, and meat for the world's earth. Our distinctives, the brain and sense-takers, are the living things of the world. Then there is the heart. It is the physical symbol of life, the Moon and her Dimmer Sisters, and purpose.

Oceans move through us! We drive those oceans with our hearts, as the Void Sea is driven by the moon and her shadows. When the moon fills with light she is strong, and when she empties she is weak. As blood flows through us, we reflect her influence.

If we do not harden our purpose with blood, then we cannot push that ocean to its life-bearing purpose. We must reach a pinnacle of flexed determination and flowing blood to create new life, to sustain our strength, and to exert our will. Your heart beats out a drumbeat of necessity—yet your weaknesses force you again and again to soften, to show mercy, to falter. If your eyes make tears, consider that a call to harden your heart, following its rhythmic exhortation to never remain in weakness.

— From "The Dust Day Sermon Series" by Sister Alamarias

Sanction's strides were long and rapid, carrying him through the last stretch of his return home. His head was lowered, lost in thought, but the shifting of the crowds drew his attention back to the present. People were jogging in the same direction he was, and an excited murmur spread from the corner shop and the small crowd gathering in the street. Only then did he breathe in the bitter stink of burning, and glance up to see the flickering orange light reflected from windows and adding a dull glow to buildings up ahead. He heard the thin, high-pitched whistle the Brigade used to call their volunteers.

Breaking into a run, he rounded the corner and stopped short, confronted by a pillar of flame roaring up into the night at the end of the street—his street.

His home was gushing flame.

Questions and reactions raced to the forefront of his mind, colliding and tangling as his eyes widened and his pupils shrank in the face of the inferno writhing out of his living space. Sanction shoved all that aside with an act of will. He shook his head, then scowled at the crowd, dashing over to a Bluecoat who was hollering at the forming crowd to stay back.

"Hey!" he yelled, moving into the Bluecoat's immediate reach. "Any crows? Are there any crows!"

The Bluecoat glanced over his shoulder at the grim Brigadier who was organizing the fire-fighting effort. "Cort?" he shouted.

The Brigadier spared them a glance. "No crows! Not yet!"

The Bluecoat returned his attention to Sanction. "This your place?" he demanded. When Sanction nodded, the Bluecoat pointed to a lean-to in a nearby alleyway. "Wait there!"

"Like hell," Sanction muttered, fading back into the crowd and pivoting to trot down the stairs to the canal level. He followed the walkway along the canal, and flagged down a gondolier who was distracted by the roaring flames that sent reflections glittering up from the water's surface.

"What heading?" the gondolier asked absently. Then he blinked. "Sir!" he said. "Anywhere you like."

"Sallyport Quay," Sanction said, grim.

"Yes, sir," the gondolier nodded. He leaned into a thrust with the pole, against the floor of the canal under the water, propelling the gondola into a smooth glide. Hesitant, the gondolier cleared his throat. "Is—isn't that your house, sir?"

"It was," Sanction replied.

Sanction gazed into the billowing smoke and sheets of fire as the gondola passed, then turned away from the fire. Once he turned away, he did not look back. The rest of the short trip passed in silence.

The gondola nosed around a poultry delivery boat covered with clucking crates, sliding by a barge to tilt adjacent to a houseboat. "This is as close to the quay as I can get you," the gondolier said apologetically.

Sanction stepped off the gondola, crossed the houseboat deck, and jumped over to the steps leading up to the quay walkway. He followed the walkway to the corner and climbed a staircase up to the street level. Leaning against the wall of a boat house, he glanced around as he drew a thin blade from a concealed forearm sheath. Moments later he had made short work of the boat house's primitive door latch, tucking the blade away and letting himself into the dim interior.

Below, a long and sleek gondola was moored at the dock, isolated from the canal by a massive door. Several glowing lanterns hung on the twenty foot craft, and several more illuminated a camp-like area adjacent to the water where four big men sat at a flimsy table playing cards.

"It's me," Sanction said, brusque as he descended the stairs towards the big men, forestalling their reaction towards weapons. Still startled, they sat back in their chairs as he passed them, crossing to the deck of the luxury gondola.

"I hope I'm not interrupting anything," Sanction said loudly as he stood by the cabin on the middle third of the craft, crossing his arms over his chest. A moment later the door opened and Piccolo stepped out, fully dressed and scowling.

"This is kind of a private party," Piccolo said. "What went sideways, that you gotta come here yourself?" He sniffed. "You smell like a fire," he said, brows contracting further.

"My house is burning down right now," Sanction said. "We need to check the cellar." He raised his eyebrows, watching Piccolo process the news in a flash; shock about the fire, various questions about possessions and Rutherford, memory that the Silkworms hid a substantial treasury in the walled-off cellar corridors under the house.

"Skelranna," Piccolo said, "get this thing underway." He bounded off the gondola and strode over to the capstan controlling the boathouse door, slotting the pole through its center and leaning in to shove it around in a circle to crank the door open. Meanwhile a lithe woman with dark eyes came out of the cabin and pushed past Sanction, firing off a string of Iruvian commands that spurred the four sturdy crew into action casting off the lines and readying the poles.

By the time Piccolo joined Sanction where he stood with his arms crossed at the prow of the ship, it was already sliding forward out of the boat house.

"So, you okay?" Piccolo asked. "Any injuries? Any word on Rutherford?"

"No crows spotted at the scene," Sanction scowled, not looking at Piccolo. "My body is fine, but I've got a powerful urge to strike back. The size of that blaze, it had to grow fast. Too fast to be an accident."

"One thing at a time," Piccolo said with a sage nod.

Sanction's scowl intensified. "You know how you reacted every time someone in your life has ever said that to you," he muttered.

"Those were *my* problems," Piccolo explained, "and that made them way more urgent than *your* problems."

"How are you still alive?" Sanction wondered aloud, not looking over at him.

"Too useful to die," Piccolo shrugged. "Your house burns down, first man you go to?" He cocked his head to the side. "Me. Of course."

"Do you have what we need?" Sanction asked. "Sledge. Chisel. Poles. You know."

"I do know, and of course I do," Piccolo replied. "I wanted to get myself some shallow racing boat, but I ended up with this thing so I'd always have my stuff when I needed it. And, I was kidding myself, thinking I could have some privacy if I relocated constantly. I thought maybe if I kept moving, even my closest associates—like you—would *occasionally* not know how to reach me." He wasted a meaningful look on Sanction.

The gondola's superior size claimed the right of way on the canal, and soon the craft nudged up to the quay. Above, Sanction's burning house overhung the canal.

"If my boat catches fire, you're paying for it," Piccolo said as he hefted the tools. He led the way off the gondola as the crew quickly tied off the bow and stern, standing by for a quick cast-off. Piccolo and Sanction closed in on a weathered door. Sanction unlocked it with an iron key, opening the way to a chamber under the house. The air inside was close and warm, smelling of smoke, but there was no fire down here. They crossed to the hidden door, opening a section of wall, and they entered the brick-lined vault.

Piccolo's eyebrows raised. "Is that yours?" he asked, pointing at the blue and silver scarf that was draped over the lockboxes that filled the center of the room.

"Dammit," Sanction ground out. "Damn it." He glanced around. "Rutherford wasn't even supposed to know this was down here."

"Wait, what now?" Piccolo demanded, eyebrows raising even further.

"Let's get this done," Sanction replied, hefting the sledge and approaching the far wall, taking a big swing that knocked several bricks through the wall. Piccolo hefted one of the lockboxes, carrying it out by the gondola. By the time he returned Sanction had revealed the safe behind the wall, opened it, and removed several large folios of papers and boxes of valuables. Two of the crew returned with Piccolo, and together they made short work of ferrying the contents of the hidden vault to the gondola. Minutes later, the canal-level door was locked again and the gondola nosed back out to the central current.

"Business first, then the rest of the business." Piccolo crossed his arms over his chest as he faced Sanction, quoting the ancient adage.

"Yes, that scarf," Sanction said distantly. He leaned his back against the prow. "That scarf belongs to Wester Scora. He is an artist. I once had him paint my portrait."

Piccolo blinked. "Okay, so there's a message you got that I didn't," he said.

Sanction gritted his teeth. "Earlier this evening I was with Wester. He noticed his scarf was missing, but we didn't think anything of it."

"Oh," Piccolo said. "You were *with* Wester. Like, cheating on Rutherford."

"Yes," Sanction said. "Cheating on Rutherford. Now, it is possible that Rutherford doesn't know, and isn't behind this; it could be someone from Wester's background acting out. We should not jump to conclusions." He rubbed his eyes. "I'm going to put Spindle on this, to find Rutherford and figure it out one way or another."

Piccolo suppressed a number of witty comments that came to mind, and leaned back to sit on one of the big lock boxes they had retrieved from the hidden cellar. "So... if Rutherford knew about the vault, maybe he knew about the upcoming Market Day deal."

"I don't think we can assume he didn't," Sanction sighed. "I didn't tell him, but apparently he can figure some things out anyway. We will have to change our plans."

"Trellis won't be happy," Piccolo said.

"You let me handle Trellis," Sanction growled, pushing hard against the creeping unease rising around him. "And Rutherford," he added, his scowl intensifying.

Piccolo had nothing to say to that.

SMOKE TOWER, BOOKEND SQUARE, FOGCREST, SILKSHORE.
23ᴿᴰ VOLNIVET. FIRST HOUR PAST DAWN.
SAIL LIGHTING FESTIVAL, DAY ONE

Rutherford strode into the squad room. His Bluecoat uniform was the only one that was crisp and stainless, and also the only one with the white armbands of an inactive member. The officers looked over at him with various expressions of reservation, surprise, and hostility. He passed them, nodding at the front desk, and followed the corridor back further into the tower. Striding down an aisle between heavy desks, he reached the door at the end and rapped on it hard.

"Enter," said the woman inside. He opened the door and stepped into the compact but organized space, standing in front of the desk.

"Captain Smiles," he said, serious. "I request reinstatement in the Bluecoats."

"Yeah, I guess you do," she muttered, looking over his spotless uniform. "What, you get all inspired with your work at the museum? Curating Bluecoat history?" She sucked on a tooth, recasting her face into a mask of disdain.

He looked her in the eye. "Yeah, let's go with that," he said.

"Can't say I care for your entitled tone," she replied, her voice flat.

"I don't need you to like me," he replied. "I'm ready to resume the service. Had a great vacation, but I'm rested and ready."

"I'll give you that," she shrugged. "You're the only Bluecoat I ever saw leave the service who could still fit into the uniform a couple years later. And it's good you don't need people to approve of you, that's one of the biggest weak points a rookie has to get past. Still." She narrowed her eyes. "I never liked you, and you know that. Why come to me? You've got two other captains I know of who would flip to have you back."

He tilted his head. "I've got reasons. The main action item here is the request itself."

"No good," she said. "You tell me your reasons or I won't give you a hearing, and you'll have to go to some other tower to work this out."

Rutherford only hesitated a moment. "I do not want to resume where I left off," he said. "I'm here to start over. Maybe go some other directions. I want Canal Watch duty. I want service reviews from someone who is not inclined to favor me; I will earn your reviews in spite of your bias against me."

"People don't volunteer for service with me," the captain said. "The pay is terrible. No paths to advancement. I might as well be the penal captain of the Bluecoats, people get sent to me for their mistakes."

"Leaving was not a mistake," Rutherford said, "but I got another view of the city, and there are some things going on unchecked that need to stop. You're right, you don't have friends. That is, you don't have *lots* of friends, but you're still a captain because you've got the *right* friends. You are the most expensive to influence. The least likely to bend. Even when some connected people push. You're given an unpopular assignment here because you won't cooperate." He paused. "I need to work for someone uncooperative."

"Ah," she said, leaning back. "This is about the Silkworms. Your husband, wasn't he some crooked Ministry official who got a cushy desk job at the High Six to launder his criminal earnings?"

"Yes," Rutherford nodded. "I'm done with him." He looked the captain in the eye.

"Right," she said slowly. "Ready to make a difference in the city, huh. Or maybe just squeeze some pain points." She cocked her head to the side. "Or are you a really stupidly obvious plant?"

"You want some wins?" Rutherford said. "I want to get some feelings out of my system before my inside knowledge ages out."

"Say you're honest right now, for purposes of discussion," the captain said. "What do we do to make a difference?"

"We bring in a fixer named Spindle, and wrap up his people," Rutherford replied. "Then we wash some laundry." He cracked his knuckles, echoing a habit abandoned for years; the unpleasant pop of cartilage was thick with memory.

The captain shrugged. "Okay," she said, "you're provisional, pending the outcome of this course of action." She opened a drawer in her desk and rummaged for a moment before pulling out two red arm bands to go over the white armbands. "Show me what you can do," she said.

Rutherford took the red bands, turned, and left the office. "Time to get to work," he growled to himself, and for the first time in a long time a smile creased his face unbidden.

He took the tight spiral staircase next to the former great hall that had been repurposed as a squad room. One level down, he followed a hallway out to the cramped boat house, two of its four berths occupied with Bluecoat watercraft.

"Okay," a Bluecoat said, stepping out from behind a stack of crates repurposed to serve as wall and desk, "you're going to have to change before you touch anything. I have never seen squad gear with that texture," he added, squinting at Rutherford's greatcoat.

"They've changed the fabric since mine was new," Rutherford replied. He looked over the mop-topped officer in the stained wrap, standing in his way. "You're Clamp, right?"

"Yes," the officer replied, almost comically wary. "And I can explain."

"Your name?" Rutherford asked, momentarily off stride.

"No, whatever little wrinkle sends you looking in my direction," Clamp replied.

"I want your help," Rutherford said. "I'm looking for a seasoned partner, and I want to get you on board before my provisional status is sorted out," he added as he tugged the red stripes up the sleeves, over the white armbands of inactive status.

"This is weird and I might just have to shoot you," Clamp said. "I don't like anybody looking in my direction." His brows contracted and his moustache bristled. He shifted his stained coat, revealing the butts of four non-standard pistols and several blade handles strapped around his torso. "I've left Bluecoat partners in the canal, and I'll do it again," he growled.

"You had to do it," Rutherford said, "because they were going to shut you up; they needed you to agree to be silent, or they needed to make sure you wouldn't be able to talk anymore." He paused. "I'm going to inconvenience some people. They won't like it, and they won't take it standing still. I need backup brave enough to step on some well-protected toes."

"Yeah?" Clamp retorted. "What, the Red Sashes? River Stallions? Or are you tough enough to take on the Fairpole Council? The Iruvian Embassy?" Somehow his bushy moustache accented his grin more than hiding it.

"Silkworms, Clamp," Rutherford said with a straight face. "I'm going to pinch the Worms until they squeak."

"Who *are* you?" Clamp demanded. "We can get a head start on your last will and testament, get next of kin sorted out, save on the paperwork we gotta fill out after you can't help do it anymore."

"Yeah, we'll get around to that," Rutherford said. "Meantime, who do you know? Who would you trust to play catch with a hornet nest?"

"You've got me all wrong," Clamp said, shaking his head. "I'm on Canal Watch because I lost a bet, and I am not looking to make waves. I'm not some crusader." He looked Rutherford over. "Provisional, even. Look at that frock. I wouldn't follow you down the street, much less into danger." He spat to the side.

"Okay," Rutherford shrugged. "Forget I asked. I do want you to come with me, though. I am going to secure Spindle, wrap up his gang. Bring them in, ask them some uncomfortable questions."

Clamp squinted at him. "There are a dozen Bluecoats kicking around the tower, and you're coming at me hard." He gestured around. "Go bother somebody else."

Rutherford looked him in the eye. "It's got to be you," he said. "You have the very best moustache in the tower."

Clamp thought that over for a long moment.

"I'm in," he shrugged.

MAURO OVERVIEW, ZEPHYR STREET, MASTER MARKET, SILKSHORE. 23RD VOLNIVET. THIRD HOUR PAST DAWN. SAIL LIGHTING FESTIVAL, DAY ONE

The iron door clanked as the key shot the latch back, and it creaked open. Two acolytes stood aside, and a veiled woman in a deep cloak passed them, entering the stone chamber. The door whined on its hinges, then banged shut.

The Mistress of Tides sat at one side of the table in the rectangular chamber, and there was one single chair across the table from her. The guest released the catch on her veil and lowered it, revealing her narrow features. The Mistress of Tides' veil remained firmly in place.

"Welcome, Mistress Levyra," the Mistress of Tides said in Hadrathi. "Let tomorrow bear its share of troubles."

"For today, we stand tall," Levyra answered, completing the ancient verse. "As you apparently expected, I have come here today because I must stand tall, and currently I am bowed beneath the weight of a secret." She gingerly lowered herself into the chair, then clasped her gloved hands before her. "Thank you for agreeing to an audience."

"I am intrigued," the Mistress of Tides said, her tone cool. "Per your instructions, this is a place where we will not be overhead. Not by my people, nor yours, nor anyone else."

"I have chosen to trust you," Levyra said. "That decision was not easy to reach." She paused. "I have a... working relationship with the Spirit Wardens. As an adept, I have certain gifts, but one of my greatest talents... I am a medium. I have a way with ghosts. And," she said reluctantly, "I offer that gift as a service to some; a ghost may inhabit me, and allow others to interact with it."

"Yes, I have heard," the Mistress of Tides murmured.

"This service is permitted in large part because the Spirit Wardens expect to discorporate the ghost afterwards," Levyra said. "However, that is not the extent of what they require of me." She swallowed hard, eyes pointed at the table rather than the expressionless veil across from her.

The Mistress of Tides said nothing, allowing the silence to gather weight.

"I know there is no love lost between you and the Spirit Wardens," Levyra continued. "In the past, after each session where they required rigorous service, they swore me to secrecy with terrible oaths. Binding oaths," she clarified, glaring at the tabletop. "You see, they sometimes have accidents when they are interrogating prisoners. Sometimes prisoners die before they are finished. They have techniques for interrogating ghosts, a whole portfolio, more extensive than anyone realizes. And, one of those tools... is me." Levyra looked up at the Mistress of Tides' veil. "They bind a ghost to me and connect it to my physical sensations, so they can pour a fresh kind of pain into the spirit." Levyra paused. "Does that shock you?"

"I wish it did," the Mistress of Tides said quietly.

"This time," Levyra said, pushing on, "there was a homeless seer they found somewhere in the depths of the Ease, his name was Maragaya. His gift of prophecy unhinged him, so he could speak only in symbols and riddles. The Spirit Wardens had some experts with them, scholars and cultists of Forgotten Gods. They drew forth his spirit from a bottle and bound it to me, and then they began the cruelest of torments. For days. I have just now healed enough to seek you out."

"Why *did* you seek me out?" the Mistress of Tides asked, expressionless.

"Maragaya invoked symbols I do not know, they were either obscure or distorted by his madness. The Spirit Wardens were following a previous line of questioning begun before his death. Apparently he knew something about the Dark Tooth. All he would say was that the Dark Tooth would complete the Fourfold Circle, and that it had already begun. They were determined to extract the identity of the Dark Tooth, but he genuinely did not know more. All he could add was that their only salvation lay in Venisana. The last thing he screamed was 'look to the worms' over and over." She paused. "The Spirit Wardens almost pushed too far this time," she said, the hoarseness at the back of her voice filtering through. "I nearly expired at their hands. They were... desperate. Terrified."

"You said they swear you to secrecy," the Mistress of Tides said.

"Every time, without fail. There's a ceremony," Levyra nodded. "I tried to position myself to comply, when they finished and withdrew the ghost from me. I asked them to proceed, but they just stared at me, then turned away. It's not that they forgot, or that they assumed I would keep their secrets," she said, a haunted look in her eyes. "They deliberately left me free to speak if I chose. I do not understand why." She closed her eyes, touching at them with her gloved hands. "After a good long sleep, thinking over what the madman babbled, I realized he might have been talking about the Silkworms when he said 'look to the worms.' And the Silkworms have a powerful Whisper." Levyra dropped her hands to her lap and cocked her head to the side. "I thought you might know more."

"Are you looking for my help to solve the riddle?" the Mistress of Tides asked.

"No, no," Levyra replied quickly. "I don't want to know the answer. I just... did not want to bear the secret alone. I want out of this." Something in her torso twinged, and she was arrested by pain for a breathless moment.

"Do... you need medical assistance?" the Mistress of Tides asked, almost reluctant.

"No, thank you," Levyra replied, her smirk pained. "The Spirit Wardens give me excellent care when they are done. A leech is assigned to address... side effects. They want me returned to peak condition quickly. Sooner or later, they need me again."

The moment hung between them.

"If you want to be free of that arrangement," the Mistress of Tides said, her voice low, "I can offer you a new arrangement."

"Thank you, that's kind, but no," Levyra replied, her expression hardening. "I've heard stories about what your outfit is capable of as well. There are no heroes. We just... we make our choices, from a terrible menu, and we eat the dish that results."

"You may reconsider," the Mistress of Tides said. "If you do, I will open the door to you."

"Thank you," Levyra said, something distant in her tone. "In the meantime, now you know about Maragaya. The Dark Tooth. The Fourfold Circle. Venisana." She winced slightly "The Spirit Wardens. So, for what it's worth, I hope that does you some good." She rose, taking her time to lever herself out of the chair. "I had best move on."

Levyra slowly left the room, doing her best to leave the riddle behind. The Mistress of Tides eventually returned to her quarters, carrying a new weight.

CHAPTER FIVE

The Sail Lighting Festival is the single biggest economic event in Silkshore's fiscal year. Back in 762 the Sail Fire leveled a third of the Ease; there were always fires, but it was a dry year and cheap, thin sailcloth flooded the market. That year, when enthusiastic sail arsonists ran fires up flagpoles so every breeze carried sparks, the Ease burned for two weeks. Minister Salmek earned an unpopular reputation by cracking down on illegal sail burning and mandating that the celebrations would refocus on using light on sails symbolically.

Most people in the Ease grumbled, but those who took this as an artistic and cultural challenge made art with billowing silk, luminescent paints, directed light sources, and public displays. Numerous Ministry-sponsored art competitions drove innovation, and crowds of the curious returned now that they were no longer in danger of burning to death. Now, the Sail Lighting Festival is a cultural touchstone and a must-see attraction for visitors to Doskvol.

— From "Innovations in Governance" by Dr. Uras Kyne

"We should be right behind them," Rutherford said through his teeth. He glanced over at Clamp, who was perspiring heavily and struggling to keep up. "End of the street," he said. "Across from the Ministry roughage cart."

"I see it," Clamp said tightly. The once-white statue of the Weeping Lady stood on a chipped column, high enough to be visible down the length of Greenwater Street as it followed the crooked canal.

Rutherford lengthened his stride, combining the strength of his frame with its leanness as he moved through the crowd, significantly taller than most of the people bustling around the busy street. The Bluecoats moved through knots of people gathered around hollering vendors, rounding the back of a crowd watching a sword-swallowing busker, closing in on the shadows at the far end of the lane.

They passed a brothel where several fancy lads and ladies stood on the balcony with dishes of luminescent soap, breathing through bubble wands and sending cascades of thinly glowing orbs spilling over the crowd. Excitable festival-goers leaped around swinging hats and scarves, laughing, trying to burst the bubbles and cover each other with glowing flecks. The turn-around at the end of the street attracted a number of amateur musicians who were scraping out an ancient Iruvian dancing drone with viols of various sizes and shapes while passers-by paused to clap or dance.

Rutherford abruptly stepped to the side, blocking the mouth of a narrow alleyway as he stared through the crowd. Clamp sagged against a building beside him.

"There, just where his brother said he'd be," Rutherford said. "That's Spindle. Stay sharp, the rest of his gang is likely to be nearby, he's here on business."

"Think his people have got word to him that we're looking for him?" Clamp asked, trying to be nonchalant as he struggled to catch his breath. "I mean, probably not, unless they've got messenger bats; we made—good time," he said, picking his words.

"No assumptions," Rutherford said, taking his eyes from his target long enough to check his pistol.

"You know, we, ah... no backup," Clamp said with a bit of a shrug. "No exception. No mandate. What are we doing here?"

"We're taking them in," Rutherford said, steel in his tone. "Spindle made it easy for us; I can see he's armed, and the privacy rule is relaxed during festival so we can act expediently in the public interest."

Clamp squinted at him. "Why do I get the feeling you actually know most of the Mandates and Provisions?" he growled.

Rutherford's smile was bleak. "I may be provisional now, but I was a captain, Clamp. Mandate the First is the ground upon which the Blue-coats are founded, everybody knows that one. Protect life and safety. Let's go wrap up that rook." He practically dove into the crowd, moving fast, Clamp at his heels.

The milling people around the impromptu concert provided a screen of cover that let Rutherford get close to Spindle before the rook realized his danger. Spindle stood around the corner from the entry to the Weeping Lady poverty berth, checking his pistol; his glance flicked up as movement drew his attention, and his eyes widened as he saw a Bluecoat looming over him.

"What—" he started as Rutherford slapped his pistol, knocking it from his grasp as Clamp leveled a gun at him. Reflexively, Spindle relaxed into a smile.

"Officers, there must be some confusion," he said. Then he blinked. "Rutherford?" he hissed.

"Consider yourself bound," Rutherford growled. "I have some questions for you."

"Hey, fun time later, man!" Spindle choked out. "This is important!"

"Not a costume," Rutherford said as he pulled flexible mechanical irons from a belt pouch, gripping Spindle's shoulder and pivoting him to face the wall, snapping manacles on one wrist—

"Hey!" was his only warning, as Clamp oriented on the big man who had been standing by the roughage cart, now closing in on Rutherford with his massive arms spread wide.

Rutherford smoothly ducked and stepped wide, spinning out of the way. His attacker stumbled forward, unable to quickly change direction. Making the most of the distraction, Spindle reached into his coat and came out with a stiletto that drove right at Rutherford's chest. Rutherford took the spike in his forearm and stepped into the rook's momentum, rebounding him back against the wall and catching him with a savage punch that slammed his head back against the stone.

"Do it!" Clamp yelled, pointing his gun unerringly at the big attacker as he regained his balance. "Come on!" The big man hesitated, then reluctantly straightened and opened his hands, surrendering.

"Now I've got every reason I need to take you two in," Rutherford said, stepping away from where Spindle swooned, sliding down the wall. He frowned at the stiletto, and gripped the handle, setting his nerve for a moment before tugging it out of his arm. Blood gleamed on an inch of the blade.

"Put 'em on," Clamp growled at the big man he held at gunpoint, tossing him the manacles. Frowning, the big man slowly cuffed himself. Only then did Rutherford squat before where Spindle sat splayed against the wall, cuffing his wrists too.

"Time to march to the canal steps, far end of the street," Clamp said without enthusiasm, watching the big man, his gunbarrel unwavering.

Spindle blinked against the wavering of his consciousness, struggling. "You—you can't think—we're going with you," he slurred.

Rutherford hauled him to his feet and snapped a connector chain between Spindle's manacles and the big man's manacles. "Here we go," he said through his teeth, and he gripped Spindle's upper arm and guided him around the crowd's thinner fringe.

They made it halfway down the street before three Bluecoats moved to intercept them, frowning at Spindle's bloody face and unsteady walk, and at Rutherford's provisionary bands. "What's this then, fellows?" demanded the pike in charge.

"They posed a threat to a festival crowd," Rutherford replied. "Then they attacked Bluecoats."

The big Bluecoat leaned in, brow furrowed. "Of course they did, nucoat," he growled. "These guys are paid up through the end of the month. What the hell are you doing, bothering them?"

Spindle managed a hazy grin and lifted his wrists towards the Bluecoat, who reached of his keys. "I'm letting these guys go," the pike said, sharp. "It's festival. Loosen up. We don't want to feed them." He looked Spindle in the eye as he dangled the key ring from his finger. "Are you real sorry?" he demanded, patronizing.

"Real sorry," Spindle agreed.

"Yeah, no good," Clamp said as he stepped forward, uncomfortably close to the Bluecoat pike. "This is Lantern Tower coverage, right? Well I'm Canal Watch, I'm taking these guys back to base. Nucoat here is just muscle helping me out," he said, looking the pike in the eye. "You don't want to cross Canal Watch, do you?"

The pike stepped back, frowning. "Okay, Canal Watch," he said. "What's the charge?"

"Stabbing, assault, and me not liking their faces," Clamp frowned, chin jutting as he squared off with the much bigger Bluecoat.

"Oh, it's like that," the pike said, his voice flat, eyebrows raised.

"You want to make this a thing during festival?" Clamp pressed. "You want to explain why you had to pick this battle to see through, when your captain asks, once the festival nonsense dies down and there's time to get really pissed off about it?" He cocked his head to the side. "Or do you want to just shrug and blame the Canal Watch?"

"They *are* all bastards," the pike said, his frown tightening. He crossed his arms over his chest. "I guess we'll just blame the Canal Watch."

Clamp nodded, gripping Spindle's arm, dragging him forward as the smile evaporated from the prisoner's face.

"Wait—"Spindle said. "Hey!"

Rutherford was behind the big man, prodding him too. The Bluecoats looked away as the prisoners finished their trip to the canal steps, staggering down them and awkwardly stepping into the wide-hipped patrol skiff.

Rutherford leaned down, cuffing the linking chain between both prisoners to the ring at the bottom of the boat, then he sat back, regarding his prisoners with a strange little smile.

"Okay, fun is fun," Spindle said to Rutherford in a low voice. "What the hell are you playing at? Last I heard, Spindle told me to figure out what was up with you; where you are, whether you're even still alive, what the hell happened to the house." He paused. "You know your house burned down, right?" he squinted.

"So I hear," Rutherford replied, unreadable.

"I don't know what's going on," Spindle said clearly, his voice still low, "but you have *got* to let us get back to that berth. Belltongue, that's an assassin with the Lost, out of Coalridge. He's in that berth, and he's going to try to assassinate Master Drassle, the owner and operator of the Coreside Mill." He raised his eyebrows, leaning forward. "During the festival," he prompted. "We have to stop it."

"You are in no position to strategize our next moves," Rutherford said.

"What are you doing," Spindle hissed, unnerved. "This is about keeping the peace *and,* you know, business; we all win here, and nobody wins if Drassle gets shot. You don't understand. Belltongue, he's a *sniper.* If we don't catch him here, today, he could strike from anywhere tomorrow!"

"Sounds bad," Clamp agreed, looking sideways at Rutherford's impassive face.

Spindle studied Rutherford for a long moment, then slouched. "Okay, you want to play games? Great. Put me in the gaol in Smoke Tower and we'll see if we can mop up this mess before it soaks in." He shook his head. "You got a squabble with Sanction, you work that out with Sanction, but this is *business,*" he insisted, pained.

"There's a drunk tank in the boathouse," Rutherford replied, "and you're going to spend a couple days out of circulation. Sorry to spoil the festival for you."

"That, uh... that could cause us some trouble," Clamp winced.

"Right," Rutherford replied, and he cracked his knuckles. "So, what *is* our next move?" Clamp demanded. "Warn Drassle?"

"No," Rutherford said, sweeping the canal traffic with his gaze.

"Okay, check out the assassin?"

"No," Rutherford said.

"You gonna let me in on the plan?" Clamp said, exasperated.

"In due time," Rutherford said, examining his prisoners as they glared back. "In due time."

"Your husband is gonna be *pissed,*" Spindle muttered, shaking his head.

Rutherford laughed.

"So yeah, thanks for your cooperation," Piccolo said to the Whisper of the Fairpole Council, a tall man in golden robes. "Trellis has done a really ridiculous amount of skullduggery to get this shipment in, and if anything goes wrong, he's gonna be grouchy." Piccolo paused. "I mean, I think he's fond of me, like you'd be fond of a pet, but if we screw this one up? I might have to leave town," he explained. "And I like it here."

"Understood," intoned the Whisper. "The Fairpole Council will take great care in concealing and protecting this shipment until the Silkworms call for it."

Piccolo looked him in the eye for a long moment. Outside the narrow, triangular office, canal traffic bustled through an intersection two stories below. The customs station was decorated with the bright colors and subtle sigils of the gondoliers, normalizing the tall man's garish robes somewhat. Crowd noise was muted in the chamber above the Fairpole Gondolier Council's most public leadership nexus.

"I mean, as long as we're clear," Piccolo clarified. "Normally I know you'd be talking to Sanction about this sort of thing, but I'm running the handoff." He turned, alert to the battering of feet rushing up the stairs. He casually put his hand near weapons.

The door banged open, and a breathless woman tumbled in. "Piccolo—Spindle—Crackstone—Bluecoats—custody, didn't—didn't get Bell-tongue," she managed.

"What?" Piccolo demanded, on his feet. "They missed?"

"Couple Bluecoats wrapped 'em up," she gasped.

"You're busy," the Whisper said, somewhat patronizing. "Another time."

"Yes, and thank you again," Piccolo said as he frowned. He turned back to the messenger as the robed man strolled down the stairs. "Okay, that's pretty bad timing."

"Thought—you'd wanna—know," she said.

"Oh, you're right, we can't waste any time. What did they find out? Where did this happen?"

Fortunately the messenger was in fine physical condition, so her breath was returning to her. "Checked around, tracked him to Greenwater street, name Belltongue, figured he was a sniper, they were going to take him down," she reported. "At the last minute, Bluecoats came out of nowhere."

"You check our contacts and find out where they were locked up, and get them out. Use Ortaz and Flay, they can work that out. I'm headed to Greenwater Street. Damn!" he swore vehemently. "This is really not good."

They headed down the stairs, and as the messenger broke off to flag a gondola, Piccolo crossed the crowded café area by the office and closed in on a corner booth.

"Tine," he said to a burly man whose face was scarred into a permanent half-grin. "I need the Gaffhooks for a while. Let's go." He turned and started walking as the burly man struggled to his feet and let out a couple liquid whistles. Half a dozen toughs gravitated into their trail as Piccolo and Tines headed out of the Central Landing.

"What's up," Tine muttered, keeping pace with Piccolo.

"We're going after a sniper," Piccolo growled.

WEEPING LADY POVERTY BERTHS, GREENWATER STREET, THE EASE, SILKSHORE.
23RD VOLNIVET. SEVENTH HOUR PAST DAWN.
SAIL LIGHTING FESTIVAL, DAY ONE

Piccolo stalked in, Tine and three of the Gaffhooks at his heels. The narrow central corridor was empty, the pale plaster overhead a stark contrast to the shoulder-level and lower walls that were various shades of brown, stained by human bodies. The straw on the floor was freshly changed, and the space was oddly quiet.

A woman in a worn brown robe stepped out of one of the side corridors. "May I help you?" she asked, reserved.

"Figured I'd come while all the beggars were out begging," Piccolo said with what he meant to be a charming smile. "Just need a minute of your time, and some insight. I'm looking for someone. You know how it is, long-lost family, I'm extending a helping hand. Right?" he said, raising his eyebrows.

"Sure," she agreed, noncommittal, drawing her own conclusions.

"I'm looking for someone who has a big load, like a case or a bundle or something. Real protective of it. Probably keeps to himself, or herself."

"You don't know if you are looking for a man or a woman?" the attendant clarified.

"It's a long, really sad story we don't have time for," Piccolo lied casually. "Anyway, has anyone like that been in here?"

"We have many people here who must carry what's left of their possessions," the attendant replied coolly.

Piccolo paused, and looked her in the eye. "Well this person would stand out. Kind of shadowed, you know? Dangerous."

The attendant examined him for a long moment, making up her mind. "We do have someone like that, been here for few days."

"Yes, good," Piccolo said with a tight grin. "Where's the berth?"

"Eighteen, there," the attendant said with a gesture.

Piccolo turned from her, leaving the central chamber and crossing the arcade flanking it. He pushed aside the curtain next to the deep alcove with "18" on the wall by it in flaking paint. The alcove only had room for a cot and a rickety wooden chest that could serve as a seat. Piccolo dropped to his hands and knees and peered under the cot.

"Yes," he said to himself quietly. He reached under the cot, then stood. "Okay, so we have a pile of rocks under the bed, and one of these." He held up a gleaming bullet for a large-bore sniper rifle. "This is Belltongue. He may not know we found him, so Tine, pick one of your guys—somebody you don't like much."

"Yeah, Devin," Tine said with his expressionless scar grin. One of his men swore softly.

"Devin, you're up," Piccolo said. "You're going to stay here and keep an eye out for Belltongue, and if he shows up you send word, and follow him. We cannot lose sight of this sniper, you get me? He'll be back for his rocks," Piccolo said with a dismissive gesture.

"But—beggars, man. This place is crawling with—at least *lice*," Devin frowned, trying not to whine.

Piccolo paused, and looked him in the eye.

"No problem," Devin mumbled, looking away. "I can shave all my hair off, sure."

"Then it's settled," Piccolo said as he headed for the door. Tine and the others (except Devin) followed.

"What now?" Tine asked.

"Things got complicated," Piccolo said. "We have to stop this sniper, there's no choice. We need to find him and stop him."

"But you wanted us to provide security for the shipment tomorrow," Tine said in a low voice as they left the berth.

"Now you have to do this," Piccolo said, "and I've got to track this bastard down if I can, and—we'll just have to trust that all my schemes to cover the shipment work out," he finished, jaw tight.

"Yeah, sounds like a plan," Tine said to Piccolo's back as the lurk strode away, mind already awhirl in next steps.

CANAL WATCH BOAT HOUSE, SMOKE TOWER, BOOKEND SQUARE, FOGCREST, SILKSHORE.
23ʳᵈ VOLNIVET. HOUR OF SONG, 2 HOURS PAST DUSK.
SAIL LIGHTING FESTIVAL, DAY ONE

"I trust you're uncomfortable," Rutherford said as he strolled into the drunk tank chamber. It was somewhat makeshift, a metal grating with a sally port roughly built-in to divide a somewhat spacious room in half.

"I do like the privacy," Spindle admitted. Crackstone, brooding in the corner, said nothing. "What do you think happens now?" Spindle asked.

"Tell me what's going on. What the Silkworms are up to. How they're using you these days," Rutherford replied.

"Hey, I get to be cooperative," Spindle shrugged. "You know most of what I know already. Something big is coming in on Market Day; normally I'd die before I told you that, but since you disappeared, Sanction and Piccolo were going to reshuffle all the arrangements anyway. So, no real danger, right? And there's the matter of that sniper, one of the Lost. I already told you about that too," he said. "So now that I've been so forthcoming—"

"I have some follow-up questions," Rutherford said. "What's the shipment? The one on Market Day?"

"Something for Trellis," Spindle said. "He didn't tell anybody, I don't think Sanction knew. Whatever it was, he wanted it bad; blew a fortune on tracking it down somewhere in Iruvia, he's been researching it and investing in it for half a year. He's spent more coin on it than I've ever touched," Spindle said, eyebrows raised. "So whatever it is, I don't think you're going to be the guy to keep him from getting it."

"And the sniper? How did you find out about that?" Rutherford pressed.

"Mistress of Tides," Spindle said. "You'll have to ask her your follow up questions." There was something defiant in his eyes. "You know, if this is a game, you're good," he said, his tone more muted.

"It's not a game, except in the sense that everything is," Rutherford replied, the echo of a sad smile somewhere in his features. "What Kreeger and I had in the past, that's over. I have some new priorities."

"Are you sure you're not overreacting?" Spindle asked quietly.

"Pretty sure," Rutherford replied. "I'll be back. Don't go anywhere." He left the cage room, and Clamp was waiting for him in the hall outside.

"There you are," Clamp said.

"Shouldn't you be off duty by now?" Rutherford asked, eyebrows raised.

"Yes, but when we put the tank off-limits to the Canal Watch during festival, we burn through some of that sweet, sweet favor bank. So, it's time to let me in on what we're up to. Since you dragged me into it."

"That seems fair," Rutherford agreed. "Tomorrow's a big day. We know where lightning is probably going to strike," he said, and the explanation followed.

NINE VEILS BRIDGE FOOTING, FOGCREST, SILKSHORE. 24TH VOLNIVET. FIRST HOUR PAST DAWN. SAIL LIGHTING FESTIVAL, DAY TWO. MARKET DAY

"Ugh, thought you'd never get here," Daava growled as she blearily looked over at Cellar. She leaned away from the building that had sheltered her from the drizzle of rain, watching Cellar approach. "No blue wagon," she reported as he handed her a fresh biscuit and a cup of something hot.

"It's festival," Cellar said. "Takes longer to get everywhere. I forget every year," he sighed. He looked at the rear dock of the Tick Tock Tea House, built out from the structure and descending down to the canal out of general public sight. From several blocks away by the footing of a bridge, they had a decent view. "What's our readiness?"

"It's pretty flimsy," Daava replied, and she took a sip from the cup. "We've got a pike and a squad of Bluecoats who have agreed to be on call, they are stationed at the Bookend Tournament of Lights officially. Just like I'm officially troubleshooting for the festival," she added pointedly. "Couldn't your hot tip have waited a week or two until all this blows over?"

"Smugglers have a heyday with festivals," Cellar muttered. "Too much traffic, overwhelms the normal channels. Easier to slip things through. Anyway, our intelligence suggests that the shipment isn't due until noon, and it will most definitely be concealed in a blue wagon, so... probably fine. See anything suspicious?"

"It's festival, of *course* there's suspicious things, everywhere," Daava replied with a vague gesture. "There was activity on the street all night. Some of those buskers showed up during the Hour of Coal and..." she shook her head, gesturing towards where the three musicians with steel drums put out chords and atonal thrumming. "All night." She gazed at the long streamers hanging from the bridge, decorated with luminescent sigils. Across the bridge, a man in a robe dropped something in a cauldron as a crowd looked on, and with a snap hiss the cauldron emitted a searing glow.

"False dawn," Cellar breathed. "Man, I forgot about that." A small smile warmed his features. "Day two of the festival."

Scattered applause rose from the crowd as the brilliant yellowish light lit up buildings from below, revealing them as though they were the faces of loved ones only dimly remembered.

"Do you... I mean, if you want, you can go over. Have some Dawning Pie, sing the old songs," Daava said hesitantly.

"That was a long time ago," Cellar replied, still not able to take his eyes off the outpouring of light that was just beginning to falter. "Time never retraces its steps."

"Shows what you know," Daava said with a faint smile. "Less than you think."

"That's an Iruvian saying, right?" Cellar said, turning to her.

"Maybe, but it's true everywhere," she said. "I am going to check in and get some sleep, if that's alright. Long night."

"Yes, do that," Cellar nodded, settling himself on the stone. It was still warm from her body. He studied the back of the tea house. "Get some rest."

Daava left, and the vigil continued.

CENTRAL LANDING, THE EASE, SILKSHORE.
24TH VOLNIVET. THIRD HOUR PAST DAWN.
SAIL LIGHTING FESTIVAL, DAY TWO. MARKET DAY

The slim man entered the upstairs meeting room, seeming much more imposing because of the ceremonial robes and garb weighing him down. The two women who entered with him began unbuckling and unlacing the bulky costume as soon as he stopped walking. Across the room, Piccolo rose to his feet.

"Trajan," he said with a nod. "I take it the False Dawn went well."

"Of course," Trajan replied. "Everything smooth, just like we promised the people." He paused. "You look like hell," he said.

Piccolo waved that away. "We have a problem," he said. "I'm having to shuffle my gang assignments to cover, the Bluecoats picked up Spindle and Crackstone, bad timing. We've lost sight of the assassin that's supposed to be planning to take a shot at Master Drassle at the noon ceremony. You know, the big contest."

"Yes, the False Dawn Competitive Showing," Trajan said slowly. "That—that cannot happen, Piccolo. The competitive showing is very important to us."

"Right, of course, I know," Piccolo agreed. "This sniper, he didn't come back to his berth last night, so I've been leaning on people, looking for him." He rubbed at his eyes. "Damn this festival," he muttered.

"The Silkworms require a high price for their protection," Trajan pressed, worry creeping into the edges of his expression. "Rates for 'we'll try' are much lower than 'you're covered.' Are you making excuses?" he demanded.

"No, your promises are safe, and ours are solid," Piccolo retorted. "Just giving you an update. Don't get tetchy with me."

"I don't need to remind you," Trajan said, "Master Drassle has not been to Silkshore in almost a decade. He didn't think it was safe enough, and wouldn't do business with us because he thought of us as a mess of passion crimes and sloppy operation. The last couple years, we've managed to persuade him to trust us, to have confidence that we can deliver. If there is so much as a thrown shoe," he said, alarm rising.

"Nobody is throwing shoes!" Piccolo said sharply. "I said I'd take care of it, and I will." He looked out the window as the women flanking Trajan pulled off the heavy shoulder yoke, hanging it from the dressing mannequin. "I've got three hours before the big speech." He flashed a rakish grin. "We're fine." Then he passed Trajan, headed down the stairs.

The crease of worry now marring Trajan's forehead did not smooth over.

NINE VEILS BRIDGE FOOTING, FOGCREST, SILKSHORE. 24TH VOLNIVET. FIFTH HOUR PAST DAWN. SAIL LIGHTING FESTIVAL, DAY TWO. MARKET DAY

"Blue wagon!" Cellar blurted, on his feet in a moment. Below, in the canal, a caravan wagon was lashed in place on a barge that was navigating the crowded canal, potentially closing in on the rear dock of the tea house. Adrenaline coursed through Cellar as he raced up the stairs to the makeshift Bluecoat station at the edge of the exhibition, waving at the pike in charge. "Now!" he mouthed, and the pike grimly nodded, whistling up his Bluecoats and falling in behind Cellar as the Inspector ran down the Bookend Square towards the front of the tea house.

Cellar led the Bluecoats through the square's goat stable that flanked the tea shop, out the back and down the crumbling stone stairs that connected to the walkway. He crouched, struggling to catch his breath, the Bluecoats right behind him. The barge was tying up to the dock, and several rough men and women were standing by as the barge crew untied the blue wagon, muscling it into position and heaving it towards the ramp so the tea shop workers could maneuver it onto the dock. Dame Maroden's red hair was unmistakable as she emerged from a back door, shaking the barge captain's hand and giving him a satchel.

"Now!" Cellar hissed, and he ran forward. "Halt!" he shouted. "Stand-by for inspection!"

The tea shop workers spun, startled, as the Inspector led the Blue-coats over a makeshift bridge from one dock to the next. The wood rattled under their heavy boots. Dame Marodan signaled her people to stand down, so they did not bolt or try to resist as the Inspector and the Bluecoats cut them off, standing between those on the dock and the relative safety and anonymity of the tea shop rising with the elevated embankment behind them.

"Nothing to hide, Inspector," Dame Maroden said with a wide, gleaming smile. "I am *so* glad you came by."

Then Cellar felt that coldness, as though he had fallen into the canal. He felt that sick moment of realizing a crash was imminent, but lacking the brakes or maneuverability to avoid it.

"Well, here I am," he said through his teeth. "So let's see what's in that wagon."

━━┑ CHAPTER SIX ┝━━

My predecessor at the Ministry saw Kreeger's rising star, back when he was a bureaucrat, and dug into his background. Turns out Kreeger's influential family took pains to conceal its many interconnections. You can follow those bloodlines to several nameless luminaries in the Hive, a few holy figures in dark cults of Nameless Gods, and a tradition of criminals. Assassins and fixers. Architects of society and trade on both sides of the law. Uncovering those links shines lights on subtle and old secrets. Their owners have a variety of ways to restore darkness.

Still, Kreeger rattled him, so he couldn't let it go. Therefore, someone arranged an accident for him. At the memorial gathering, I resolved to keep an eye on this young man and his various potentials. Of course that didn't work out, but when he resolved to leave, I let him go.

As for the name Sanction, he got that from a Whisper, the Mistress of Tides. She somehow knew this fresh-faced kid's blood inclined him to a life of dark influence. Granting permission, threatening penalties. I don't think he knows his own connections. He is protected, to a point, but shadows in his bloodline would dispose of him if his trouble drew enough of the right kind of attention. Or, if he threatened to bring them to light. Sometimes I wonder if the Mistress of Tides agreed to work with him just to get a step closer to the secrets in his extended family.

— Marcus Barrsly, Director of Distribution — Silkshore.
Clearance Interview notes, Suran 18, 848

Cellar walked deliberately at the workers flanking the wagon, and they reluctantly stepped out of his way as the Bluecoats surrounded the narrow caravan. Everyone was on edge, eyeing each other, assessing risks and choosing targets should the situation collapse into violence; hemmed in between the stone embankment and the sullen canal, there was little cover, and there were only a couple risky escape routes. Bluecoat activity always attracted attention, and several passing boats slowed so a scattered crowd of witnesses could watch the showdown from the water.

Opening the back door of the caravan, Cellar saw long, narrow crates slotted into the space inside. "Pull it out," he said with a gesture, stepping back. Two Bluecoats reluctantly came forward, dragging at a heavy crate, lowering it to the dock. They looked at Cellar, thoroughly unwilling to take initiative. Frowning, he glanced into the caravan and pulled out a prybar secured by the back door. He dropped to one knee, examining the crate.

"I lodge an official request not to open my belongings," Dame Maroden said with a sultry and provocative smirk. "You mean ole Inspector." No one could quite laugh; the tension became unbearable.

"Noted," Cellar said through his teeth, and he jammed the prybar into the crate joint, heaving down on the makeshift lever so the lid lifted with a screech of stressed nails.

A jumbled thrash of motion—something inside the crate was startled, and a dark shape thrust out of the gap, narrowly missing Cellar. He swore, scrabbling back, and the narrow crate bucked as its contents flexed hard against the breached lid, opening it further.

"No!" yelled a Bluecoat, lunging towards the crate—not fast enough. The lid twisted back as a dark mass writhed inside, and a number of skull-sized hard shapes banged on the sides of the crate as the glistening bulk of flesh twisted free of confinement, flopping out onto the dock.

"Stripers!" the pike yelled, opening fire with his pistol and shattering one of the shells, spraying viscous ichor as the bullet pulped something wet. Like the starting pistol at a race, the report inspired a gush of motion as snails the length of a forearm squirmed, tumbling out of the crate or sliding towards the edge of the dock. The dock workers retreated as the Bluecoats opened fire at the snails without hesitation, blowing several apart and slapping fans of slime all over the dock and bystanders.

One of the snails twitched, shooting out a tongue-like appendage that punched into the side of a Bluecoat's knee, twisting as the barbs delivered their venom into the screaming man. A docker had recovered his wits enough to whack the snail with an oar. He knocked its shell sideways. The snail's belly broke its seal with the wood of the dock with a sucking pop.

Another docker joined him in battering at the snail with oars, and as the shell snapped, the wriggling snail dragged its sharp foundation along as it reached the edge of the dock and plopped down into the water. Its "tongue" ripped off and recoiled towards the Bluecoat's knee, plunging the rest of the venom into the breach. The Bluecoat convulsed, several others grabbing him and lowering him to the dock as his eyes rolled back in his head.

Some dockers and Bluecoats headed for cover, while others desperately tried to head off the snails before they could slide off the dock into the water; the snails vented mucus sacs so they could slide on a pool of snot, their version of a sprint, and several made it to water while the rest were savaged with whatever weapons were close at hand.

"Canal snails!" Cellar shouted. "Those — illegal! Those are illegal!"

"Not if you have a permit to serve them as a delicacy," Dame Maroden said, producing an official document from a pouch in her sleeve. "What's illegal is allowing them to reach the canal, where they can multiply and threaten the public safety." She cocked her head to the side. "You did that."

"The crates, you have to mark them!" Cellar retorted.

"Failing to mark the crates is a civic misbehavior," Dame Maroden agreed, "and the fine is fifty eels." She offered him a pouch of pre-counted coin, her smile predatory. "I apologize for the oversight. But releasing them into the canal—well, that's a minimum sentence of a month in prison and five hundred eels, unless you get specific dispensation from the Chief Inspector. Isn't that right?" she said sweetly, focusing on the Bluecoat pike.

"She's right," he said, and Cellar noticed the Bluecoat had already stepped back away from him. "We better go back to the tower. You know. Report the breach." He abruptly stopped talking, but his face was red and he radiated embarrassment and stress.

Cellar locked eyes with Dame Maroden. "You really put a lot of thought into this," he said through his teeth.

She snapped her fan open and cooled herself with a coquettish wrist action, unfazed. "Good thing one of us did," she taunted, her roughened voice almost seductive. She threw her head back and laughed.

Cellar turned away from her and followed the Bluecoats back up to the street.

PULSERIDGE SQUARE, THE EASE, SILKSHORE. 24TH VOLNIVET. FIFTH HOUR PAST DAWN. SAIL LIGHTING FESTIVAL, DAY TWO. MARKET DAY

There was barely room in the chamber for Rutherford and Clamp, and in the confined space the muffled sound washing up from the crowd below was like the grumble of the ocean.

"Six zip lines?" Rutherford asked Clamp, not looking at the other Bluecoat as he deliberately wound a tough strip of fabric around his wrist, palm, and knuckles.

"Took almost seven hours, but yeah, we got them all in place," Clamp replied. "We didn't have time to test them. Your plan is crazy."

"I know it," Rutherford nodded. "But you've got the shout line set up like I asked?

"I do," Clamp said. "Bluecoats are busy, it's festival, but I hired about fifty urchins. Begging is sure money during festival, so I had to pay them triple rate to lure them away to be the shout line. This is going to cost you."

"I've got money to burn," Rutherford observed, tugging at the wrapping on one hand.

"I'll take some," Clamp said.

"You get something better than money," Rutherford replied, twisting his wrist around to settle the protective wrapping on his other hand. "The pikes? They have squads ready to respond to the shout line?"

"That's expensive too," Clamp said.

"And everybody has a flare."

"Everybody," Clamp agreed.

Rutherford looked him in the eye. "I'm going up."

"According to the plaque on the side of the building," Clamp said, "We're at about 290 feet high or something like that. And there are another 15 rungs up that ladder to the base of the lookout tower."

Rutherford smirked. "I knew you'd look up to me eventually."

"This goes a hair off plumb, I'll be looking down at you," Clamp retorted. "Way down."

"Don't you worry about me," Rutherford said. "I was a Nightmarket roofer for about six months. Compared to that, this is a patrol."

Clamp blinked at him, then shrugged. "Bye," he said.

Rutherford's grin was full of sharp teeth. He climbed the ladder, up towards the last trapdoor between interior atmosphere and rarified space.

PULSERIDGE SQUARE, THE EASE, SILKSHORE. 24TH VOLNIVET. SIXTH HOUR PAST DAWN—NOON. SAIL LIGHTING FESTIVAL, DAY TWO. MARKET DAY

Piccolo's breath burned in his chest as he battered open the door at the top of the staircase and stepped to the rooftop railing. He looked down six stories, then alongside the roof. The steep pitch rising from the catwalk at the roof's edge had a small crowd of onlookers for the festival below; they relaxed in roof hammocks slung between chimneys to provide a space to sit against the tiles. Others had portable platforms with supports folded out, lashed to cornices or gables. Enough people gathered on the rooftops that his entrance did not draw much attention.

He leaned his forearms on the railing, and for a long moment he dropped his forehead to his arms and felt the swarming needles of stressed pain flowing through his overtaxed muscles.

Then he was up, moving fast, trotting along the walkway by the railing and moving around spectators who were already filling up spots in the front row. He reached the spiked fence at the end that isolated the penthouse balcony, and even though his limbs felt like wet cement, he kicked up off the raked roof and grabbed the bars, swinging himself over just clear of the spikes.

He landed unsteadily on the patio, and the glass doors opened as Tine joined him from inside the house. "How goes it?" Tine asked, face contracted in a frown.

"I've checked six of the eight best shooting positions," Piccolo replied, struggling to catch his breath.

"It's—" Tine started, then the belltower at the far end of the ridgeline tolled, the first of six strokes.

Noon. No more time.

Scattered cheers and applause drifted up from the crowd. A dozen enclosed stalls on platforms were spaced throughout the square below, and each one had a radiant animal specially bred and developed for the competition. The patrons that could afford tickets to the ground floor access were a refined bunch, so their display of enthusiasm was somewhat muted.

Second peal. Trajan was smiling on the main stage, flanked by other gondoliers, as well as a few special guests. Piccolo could not make out detail at this distance, the people looked like smudges of color, but his heartrate forced a faster pace as he frantically stared around at the impossible volume of detail that his brain could not process in time.

Somewhere, a sniper was setting up or taking aim. Third peal.

Relying on instinct, Piccolo darted his gaze around the whole environment, taking in everything he could. Something registered as out of place, and he refocused on an adjacent building. What? What didn't fit? Fourth peal.

Exterior staircase. Bluecoat just now heading to the roof—alone. With a long rifle. Fifth peal.

Piccolo let out a ragged noise, and threw a hand signal at Tine as the bell's tolling continued—cover my exit. No time to talk. The lurk hurled himself at the spiked fence on the other side of the patio, jumping up to plant both feet on a table and leap. He hit the spikes and rolled over, leaving some of his shirt on the fence. Sixth peal.

He hit the roofwalk running, shoving spectators out of the way, pain and exhaustion forgotten as his body dug deep to match the fear that sluiced through him.

Too far away.

Trajan's voice was a dim echo lost in the stone box of the square below. Welcoming Master Drassle, founder of today's feast, sponsor of the competitive showing. Piccolo's senses reverberated with a driving analysis of possible routes, what speed might cost him, what threats might stop him. Those roof tiles were too loose, the ledge below didn't have a good enough jumping off point to get to the adjacent building the sniper was climbing. Only one way to go.

Piccolo's heart nearly burst as he sprinted diagonally up the steeply pitched roof, reaching the ridgeline just in time to launch out into space. He sailed across the space between buildings, losing a story in the fall, crashing into a decorative circular window and landing inside, resolving a bashing roll as glass rained around him. He bled freely as he popped up out of the roll and kicked the door to the interior atrium open, sprinting to pick up speed before jumping up to kick off the railing, snatching the exposed rafter and twisting as his arms ignored their agony and guided his body's momentum upward to slam into a catwalk; he rolled up onto it, scrambling up a short flight of stairs towards the door that opened to the rooftop garden party. He blasted right past the door guard and plowed into a waiter, sending the unfortunate sprawling as he barely kept his feet well enough to bound up onto a bench, a table, over the fence and onto the rooftop.

There: two stories down, a quarter of the square's width away, on the roof of a covered balcony. The Bluecoat impostor was already laying down, checking the gun.

Still too far away.

Piccolo drove everything he had into the sprint, and he flew along the rooftop. He focused on the sniper, and the rest of the world went gray; a flare went off somewhere to the side, but he spared no thought or energy for it. For a cold instant the sniper looked towards the noise of his approach and their eyes met. Then the sniper refocused on the rifle as Piccolo felt his lungs spasm.

Piccolo no longer needed lungs. He knew Master Drassle had stepped up to the podium because he saw the sniper flick the scope open, lining up, breathing out. Piccolo's nerveless fingers tore his pistol out of its holster and blasted at the sniper, knocking a chunk of tile off less than an arm's length from where the sniper concentrated; the sniper didn't even flinch.

Momentum drove the lurk towards the edge of the roof, and he sprang out into space two strides earlier than was wise, counting on his trajectory to carry him to the sniper. Piccolo was midair when the sniper's rifle recoiled, blaring out a plume of smoke—

The edge of the balcony crumpled as Piccolo smashed into it, and his betrayed footing spun away over the four story drop as he rebounded. The sniper rolled over out of easy reach, rising with practiced ease as Piccolo dragged at his last reserves of strength and cunning to roll onto the roof, blood streaking in his wake.

The rifle barrel swung around towards him, and Piccolo exploded up at the sniper, knocking the gun aside and bashing into the sniper's chest; he didn't know what was off the other side of the balcony, but he was past caring as dread suffused him.

The Silkworms didn't stop the sniper.

Piccolo was driven by emotions as failure solidified in his mind; he would tear this damned sniper apart with his bare hands. The two killers staggered back, and the other side of the balcony roof gave, dumping them a story and a half onto the pitched roof of another balcony. They tore through that and crashed down on the balcony; the sniper twisted hard, muscling the rifle to the side and flinging Piccolo off him. He gave up the rifle, springing up to his feet with a knife in hand.

Leaving himself wide open, Piccolo drove at the sniper with a knife of his own; the sniper parried the attack and struggled to get out of the murderous lurk's way as the backstroke whipped uncomfortably close to his face. The battle sprawled into an open dining room as exclaiming servants pulled back, and the sniper sprang up on the dining room table.

Piccolo threw his knife sidearm, catching the sniper in the elbow and distracting him as the lurk yanked another knife from its harness and lashed out at the sniper's knee; the staggered man didn't fully avoid either hit, and now Piccolo stood on the table and squared off with him. Was he still unable to breathe since he was on the roof? It didn't matter.

Maybe Piccolo could not live with his failure.

The sniper caught a vicious stab in his forearm and managed a cut in reply, then Piccolo's forehead smacked into his face; he felt the sniper's nose give as black spots swarmed his vision and his balance skewed. The lurk jammed the knife into his torso hard, sending him staggering back off the end of the table to trip on a chair back and smack down in a clatter of furniture.

Piccolo heard a bang from the balcony, but he did not turn to investigate. He leaped at his fallen foe, a knife in each hand—

Gunfire exploded from the balcony. The shot caught Piccolo right in the torso, sharply adjusting his leap. He hurled into the wall and dropped, landing on all fours as the knives clattered out of his grip.

The sniper dragged himself to his feet using the back of a chair for support, gauging his distance to the door out of the dining room. The attacker on the balcony flung a chain; the handful of metal hit with enough force to knock the sniper off balance. The click of the pistol's hammer to firing position managed to get through to both the sniper and Piccolo.

Rutherford stood in the doorway connecting the balcony and the dining room, a gun in each hand, covering the sniper and the lurk. For a moment, no one moved.

"I used a shout line," Rutherford said, his voice flinty. "There's a Bluecoat squad at the end of the row one floor up, and word will reach them in seconds so they know where I am. Where you are. You don't get out of this."

Piccolo's mind was out of synch, starving for blood, awash in pain from broken ribs; his armor saved his life, but his lungs were hard knots that could not fuel him to fight back.

"Did I get the bastard? Drassle?" the sniper demanded, hoarse as he pressed his hand around the knife wound, the hilt jutting out of his torso.

"You sure did," Rutherford replied, bleak. "Now you'll die for it."

"We all die for something," the sniper growled.

As Bluecoat boots pounded in the hallway outside, Piccolo could no longer force himself to stay conscious.

Sanction stood impassive, waiting in the stone alleyway, a modest locked case held at his side. An arm's reach away, the Fairpole Council Whisper waited with him, cloth-of-gold veil in place and occult wrap intricately decorated with glyphs and sigils.

"Where is Piccolo," the Whisper asked, breaking the silence. "He was my contact for this."

"He is personally overseeing the security for Master Drassle," Sanction replied. "We need to get this over with quickly, I'm due back." He frowned at his pocket watch, snapped it shut, and tucked it in a pocket.

A slow wagon creaked down the street, pulled by a single weary draft goat. The wagon turned from the quiet byway into the still-quieter alley where Sanction and the Whisper waited. It was a battered old Ministry of Preservation carriage, painted blue and repurposed to haul supplies for the Department of Roughage. The figure on the buckboard was dressed in a heavy coat in spite of the warm day, and the flickering lamps hanging from the corners of the carriage did little to chase the shadows away.

The wagon stopped, and the driver rapped a five pattern knock on the roof. Both side doors opened, and large half-naked men stepped out, loosely holding hatchets. They scanned the rooflines and projected menace, ignoring the two men waiting for them.

Four more people exited the carriage. Two more big bodyguards headed to one mouth of the alley, watching the street and covering the escape route. The other two advanced towards Sanction and the Whisper. Both were turbaned and cowled, faces covered, shapeless shadows straying from the corners and basements where they belonged.

"You Trellis?" one asked, her light voice accented. "I here, on time. You got the price?"

"I'm Sanction," he said, "and I represent Trellis. Do you have the package he requires?"

"Yes, no problems, easy," she said. "Me and Trellis work it out, high trust, no problems, easy. I swear package ready for pickup, so you give me payment for taking big risk coming here, and I give you package. Everything fine. Nobody nervous."

"I want to see your face," Sanction said. "Trellis told me the sign. How I would know you are not an impostor."

"Sure yes, easy," the smuggler replied. She ducked out of the turban and dropped the scarf from her face, revealing delicate bird-like features, olive complexion, tousled white hair. Her eyes were milky blue, with no irises or pupils, and they glowed faintly.

"Welcome to Doskvol," Sanction said with a sardonic smile. "We don't often get luminaries like you, Cacophony Sideways."

"You so lucky," she said. "Now you show me price."

Sanction approached, and hefted the case. He snapped a hidden catch, and the side opened to reveal a pale stone the size of a thumb, set in a platinum medallion. Sanction did not suppress his smile as he heard the Whisper gasp.

"Is—is that the Star Cascade?" the Whisper demanded.

"Better be," Cacophony Sideways retorted. "May I?" Sanction nodded, and she picked up the medallion and squinted at it through a loupe. A few tense seconds passed, and she swore passionately in Iruvian. Relaxing her face, she dropped the loupe to her hand, and looked Sanction in the eye. "Is good, we good," she shrugged. She pocketed the medallion.

"So where is Trellis's package?" Sanction asked, forcing himself to remain calm.

Cacophony Sideways paused, looking him over. "So he no tell you what it is, hah? No clue. No hint. Just trust Cacophony Sideways."

"That's the size of it," Sanction agreed. "I'm surprised too. He's not the trusting sort."

She let out a bark of a laugh, and shook her head. "No, not so much," she said. "Okay, here is package. Here is Trellis prize." She gestured, and the other cowled figure stepped forward. Cacophony Sideways pulled her hood and mask down, revealing a girl, maybe twelve years old, with an unsettling serene gaze. "This Cromlech. Say hello, girl."

The girl did not say hello. She fixed Sanction with a level gaze.

"Okay," Sanction said, burying every tell of surprise he could. "Thank you. We'll take it from here."

Cacophony Sideways nodded, then turned her back on Sanction and retreated into the carriage, followed by her four bodyguards. Sanction, Cromlech, and the Whisper stepped out of the way and let the goat drag the creaking carriage past, through to the other end of the alley, to leave a different way than they came.

"This is madness," the Whisper muttered to Sanction. "The Star Cascade—that occult gemstone was stolen from the Tomb Tower in Charterhall eight months ago. That was the Silkworms? For *this?*" he said with a gesture at the girl.

"You don't need to understand," Sanction replied without looking at him. "You had an arrangement with Trellis—the Fairpole Council would take his package and conceal it so no one would get to it except Trellis." He slowly turned to look at the Whisper. "The Council's honor is at stake. You will take this girl, you will hide her and keep her safe."

The Whisper nodded. "That was the bargain," he agreed. He turned to the girl. "Come with me. I will keep you safe."

She looked him in the eye, almost sad.

The Whisper snapped his fingers twice, and half a dozen armed gondoliers emerged from various shadows. They joined the Whisper as he escorted Cromlech through the back door of the shuttered stone building, leaving Sanction alone in the alleyway with his questions.

"I think it's time I had a talk with Trellis," Sanction murmured to himself, his mind racing. Then he turned away from the inscrutable back door, and vanished into the city's shadows.

TATTLER'S TOWER, IRONHOOK PRISON, DUNSLOUGH.
24TH VOLNIVET. SEVENTH HOUR PAST DAWN.
SAIL LIGHTING FESTIVAL, DAY TWO. MARKET DAY

The gibbet chain squeaked slightly as the cage shifted. Inside, Piccolo was bandaged and tied into an inmate coat, sleeves without wristholes wrapped around his torso and buckled with the other restraints in the back. His bare feet dangled out of the cage. Windowless stone walls hemmed in the narrow cell. One high-up vent let in outside air, and there was a metal door connecting to the hallway. A key rattled in the lock, and the massive door groaned open to admit Rutherford.

"Here we are," Rutherford mused, crossing his arms over his chest, looking Piccolo over. "I'm told your injuries are superficial. Cuts, a cracked rib or two."

"Provisionary? You're a nucoat?" Piccolo said. "What are you doing, Rutherford?"

"Starting over," Rutherford said. "I'm offering you the same opportunity."

"You think I'll flip on the Silkworms?" Piccolo clarified, eyebrows up. "Are you serious?"

"You'll come around when the deal is right," Rutherford said. "It's too soon, I know that."

"I'd rather swing," Piccolo said through his teeth.

"That's not an option," Rutherford replied. "There are a number of ways this could end, but you have my word I'll keep you from the hangman's noose. You are far too valuable, in too many ways."

"Why didn't you stop the shooter?" Piccolo demanded. "And don't tell me you couldn't have."

"We'll never know whether I could have or not," Rutherford said. "But you're right; I didn't try." He paused. "I don't pose much of a threat to Silkworms operations. As long as they are closely allied with the Fairpole Council, that is." A faint smile shifted his features. "It's about options. Without you, they lose some choices. Without the Fairpole Council's backing, they lose more choices. Step by step, they will be boxed in." He considered Piccolo. "You of all people know how fine the line is—how short a distance between projecting a powerful image and losing all confidence."

"How do you want this to end?" Piccolo asked, hostile.

Rutherford considered the question, then shifted his weight. "We'll talk again later," he said. Turning, he let himself out of the cell, and the heavy lock slammed in place behind him.

Piccolo did his best to push the day's events from his mind. Time to start contemplating escape.

◄── CHAPTER SEVEN ──►

Entering Silkshore can feel like exploring another world. You've got Ankhayat Park, the largest open area in the city. You've got the Spark Grounds, with acrobats and spark fliers performing death-defying stunts or airing exotic kites, lightning playing across the various tumbling feats as the fliers pull energy from the lighting wall. You switch out the regular street traffic for canal traffic. Even the food is unique, as various cultures blend and fuse their styles into a distinct cuisine.

This sense of dislocation is worse for civil servants and law enforcement than it is for visitors. Due to a special agreement with Imperial agents centuries ago, Silkshore has some archaic laws unique to the area. They draw from Iruvian tradition to make a hybrid code not faithful to Akoros or Iruvia. Reporting structures, mandates, statutes, uniforms, penalties; there are idiosyncrasies that defy centralization and stubbornly anchor modern practice in archaic rules even if no one remembers why.

If you get assigned to Silkshore, remember that ambiguity serves somebody (and if you can't tell who, watch for who defends unique practices.) Remember that the intent of the rules never ever reflects all of their consequences. Most importantly, remember that the sharpest operators on every side of the law can compare and contrast how the rules work in different areas so they customize their tactics to maximize strengths and minimize vulnerabilities.

— Captain Selina Davian, "Bluecoat Best Practices Supplemental Handbook" Third Edition

VITAL CATHEDRAL, PULSERIDGE SQUARE, THE EASE, SILKSHORE.
24ᵀᴴ VOLNIVET. SEVENTH HOUR PAST DAWN.
SAIL LIGHTING FESTIVAL, DAY TWO. MARKET DAY

"There you are," Trajan said through his grimace, almost trembling with the strain of keeping his voice even as he strolled into the echoing chamber of worship. A haze of incense imitated a wisp of cloud cover overhead. Only a handful of people were in the tall space, clustered towards the front, conversing in low tones well out of earshot of where Sanction waited towards the back. There were no benches in the wide corridor facing the altar and podium; during services, the crowds stood shoulder to shoulder while the wealthy occupied the upper tiers.

Sanction could not repress the urge to scan the balconies and catwalks as Trajan approached. He could keep his breathing calm and his face expressionless. "We will fix this," he said quietly. "We will work out incentives. Redirect blame. You—"

"Stop." Trajan's tone was cold, and he took a few long seconds to inhale and exhale, unwilling to look at Sanction. "You don't know what your carelessness has cost us," he said through his teeth. "We had one potential partner in Coalridge, and we barely convinced him to take a chance working with us. Now?"

"A setback—"

"Stop," Trajan repeated, more forcefully. "You don't get to talk yet. Not at all. You have nothing to say," he growled. His eyes locked on a glittering mosaic above, unpacking a circulatory system radiating from a heart, trailing along the upper balcony frontispiece. "Honor weights words with meaning; without honor words are—they are *noise*," he spat. "You are *noise*." Slowly, he turned to look Sanction in the eye. Trajan's new vulnerability touched off a fountain of fear that flowed directly into anger. "The Fairpole Council will only hear an apology and offer of compensation from Trellis himself. Until this—this *breach* is repaired, you are *inaudible* to us." He snapped his mouth shut, pivoted, and stalked out the cathedral's main door, where several worried gondoliers met him.

Sanction watched him go. "That could have gone better," he muttered, if only to distract himself from a sense of relief that the conversation hadn't turned violent. He followed the wall around to the side door.

In the square, the bustle and disruption was still churning. Aristocrats and their privately contracted guards argued with Bluecoats, demanding access to their displays and the supplies needed for the displays. The Bluecoats and Inspectors continued the arduous process of interviewing those near the assassination and managing the scene. Bluecoats were releasing people as quickly as they could while still trying to be thorough, but some scuffles had broken out, and resourceful spectators had already slipped away through side doors and oblique exits. The unhappy crowd still present was invested in the False Dawn Competitive Showing exhibits, and those were harder to transport subtly.

Sanction skirted the crowd, closing in on a Bluecoat pike. "Harlass, what happened here?" he asked quietly as he approached.

The pike turned to fix him with a grim stare. "Some nucoat with the Canal Watch spread a lot of money around, set up zip lines and yell lines, like he expected trouble. They caught the assassin and your man Piccolo," he muttered.

"Where the hell were you while this was going on?" Sanction demanded. "What do I even pay you for?"

"Protection," the pike replied, his tone sharp. "We were here to make sure nothing went wrong. I was assigned patrol by the stage. We got hit with a sniper; he only got one shot, but it was a good one." He winced. "Gondoliers are pretty pissed, huh."

"Yeah, let me know where Piccolo and the shooter end up," Sanction replied. "You know how to reach me." He turned and headed towards one of the gates out of the square, striding past the Bluecoats guarding the portal without sparing them a glance. They did not move to stop him.

CANAL WATCH BOAT HOUSE, SMOKE TOWER, BOOKEND SQUARE, FOGCREST, SILKSHORE.
24ᵀᴴ VOLNIVET. NINTH HOUR PAST DAWN.
SAIL LIGHTING FESTIVAL, DAY TWO. MARKET DAY

"That was a hell of a mess, eh?" Rutherford said conspiratorially as he entered the stone chamber. He pulled the heavy door shut behind himself, and turned to regard the prisoner who sat chained to a chair, his wounds bandaged, dressed in a simple tunic. "I guess you're called Belltongue."

"I am now," the sniper replied.

Rutherford settled in a chair in the corner of the room. "So I guess you're Lost."

"I know where I'm going," Belltongue replied.

"You're with *the* Lost, then." Rutherford paused. "Or is that a catch phrase? I asked around about *the* Lost, when I heard about you. I guess you people attack business owners, foremen. Looking out for the oppressed worker. Am I close?"

Belltongue looked him over for a moment. "I'm not sure where you are, how close."

"I guess you try to counter evil influences to atone for unforgivable sins you've committed," Rutherford mused. "That's what the Lost do." He cocked his head to the side. "I know how it is, trying to take action, trying to deal with feelings that are too big to carry."

"Is that why you didn't stop me?" Belltongue asked, eyes intense.

"You think I could have?" Rutherford countered, eyebrows raised.

"Urchin scouts, zip lines, flares," Belltongue said. "Kind of a waste, if you didn't spot me until after I fired. You knew I was coming somehow." He shifted position. "I'm trying to figure out what you wanted then. What you want now."

"Maybe I'm just trying to get a sense of how it works out for you. Trying to find your way back, to make peace with yourself."

"If it's all the same to you, I'm done with this conversation," Belltongue muttered. "I'm going to hang for the killing. Doesn't matter anyway. Drassle is finished."

"Maybe I'm *not* done with this conversation," Rutherford said. For a long moment, both men were quiet. Rutherford narrowed his eyes. "Drassle got hit in the chest. They rushed him off the stage. He's got the kind of money that can pay for survival."

Belltongue leaned forward. "Tell me." His stare was intense. "Tell me he died."

Rutherford raised his eyebrows. "We all want to know things," he replied.

Belltongue set his jaw. "Some sins are too heavy to carry," he said under his breath. "We center each one in a stone. I had eight under my cot. Looks like I'll die with seven unpaid. It's not about the weight, or the sin; in the end, it's about the trajectory and momentum. I've turned it around, with this killing. I've made a difference and I know what I'd do with more life if I got it. That's all the fortification I've got holding back the past."

"And that's enough?" Rutherford murmured.

"Enough for what?" Belltongue retorted. "Enough for peace of mind? No. But it's enough to carry on. To try again." His eyes burned with conviction. "It is my honor to die for taking righteous action, because that's an easier fate than living under the weight of shame. The stones—they are ballast, to hold steady when the wind tears at the sails to go another way. There is no repayment. Only inspiration, and strength to take the harder course."

Rutherford studied him for a few seconds, then nodded. "Drassle's lung collapsed, and while they were trying to re-inflate it he seized up. Took him a messy few minutes to die proper. But the bell tolled for him and he got his own Deathseeker crow."

"Thank you," Belltongue said, serious.

"You have about a week until your trial," Rutherford said. "Maybe another week before they kill you."

Belltongue looked him in the eye. "They've done worse," he murmured.

Rutherford let that sink in for a moment, then he rose to his feet and crossed to the door, rapping it twice. The view slot snapped open, then the door bolt shifted aside and the door swung wide to let him out.

"You don't have to do it," Belltongue said abruptly.

Rutherford paused, and turned to face him. "Do what?" he asked.

"Whatever it is," Belltongue replied, his eyes penetrating.

A faint smile drifted across Rutherford's features, a thin veil over a much deeper feeling.

He closed the door.

"Why are you here?" Sanction demanded as he strode down the hallway towards the study. "We could have used you today! Master Drassle was shot and killed by the Lost assassin."

"That's not ideal," Trellis mused, his attention not dislodged from the book he studied through the half-moon reading glasses perched on his nose. Light pooled from the glass-chimneyed lamp on the desk, unwavering as it lay upon the pale pages.

"Not ideal?" Sanction echoed, confronting Trellis across the massive desktop. "Trajan won't even listen to me. He demands an apology from you, as well as some suggestion for how we make it up to them. Our failure. We guaranteed Master Drassle's safety, and he's *dead*. Also, Piccolo was captured. He tried to stop the assassin and wasn't quite in time."

"Regrettable," Trellis agreed absently.

Sanction stared at him for a moment. "If this meshes with your master plan somehow, I think it's time you let me in on it," he growled.

Trellis raised his eyes from the book, but there was still distance in them as he regarded Sanction. "I'm more concerned about the delivery of my package."

"That went fine," Sanction replied, restraining the energy that wanted to pour through the words. "The timing was not great, as it lined up with arguably the most important commitment we've made in months with our closest allies, and pulled me out of position in a critical moment, and now we're in breach of trust and there is a long and ugly series of consequences ready to build on that turn of events."

"We'll work it out," Trellis soothed. "Don't get exercised over this."

"Don't—I *had* to get exercised, I came all the way out to *Barrowcleft* to find you! I thought you delegated all the planning for today because you were going to work behind the scenes, not—not sit it out altogether. Reading," Sanction said with a tight gesture at the desk.

"I can see how you would think that," Trellis observed, cocking his head to the side. "It's not so unusual for you to draw the wrong conclusions."

"I need you to take this seriously," Sanction breathed, leaning forward, planning his knuckles on the desk as he stared into Trellis's eyes. "We can talk later about why this package you paid a fortune to acquire is a *girl*. Right now we need to solve this problem with the Fairpole Council."

"Do we?" Trellis replied, mild.

Sanction blinked. "Yes!" he protested. "We do! Our protection agreements, our premium tithes and operating expenses, our livelihood is grounded in our reputation—which is going to be worthless if we don't patch this up fast!" He was vaguely aware that his tone escalated towards shouting.

"Oh, I wonder if Trajan is angry enough to try and have us killed. What do you think?" Trellis asked.

"What—I think it's possible," Sanction replied, his voice brittle. "Were our situations reversed I would consider it. We made assurances. This assassin was supposed to get wrapped up yesterday! But we didn't stop him."

"Do you know where the assassin is now? Or Piccolo?" Trellis asked as his eyes strayed back towards the book.

"Do *I*?" Sanction echoed. "You generally have your ear to the ground, your contacts give you answers before we've formulated the questions! You have a role here! I don't expect you to run the rooftops with Piccolo, but this? The damage control, the contingency plans, the next steps, this is *you!*" Sanction yelled.

"And I'll get to it later," Trellis shrugged. "I'm working on something else right now."

"Something else?" Sanction almost squeaked. "If we don't deal with this fast, we won't have 'later' because our enemies are emboldened right now, they could make a move. We are on the edge."

"Well, fix it," Trellis said in a querulous voice. "You're so smart, you've got the plan, you figure it out."

Sanction stood up straight, staring. "You have *never* refused to pitch in before," he said, almost hushed. "What the hell is this."

Trellis rolled his eyes. "This is *maintenance*, boy. I work the big picture, you run the day-to-day. Yes, it's a shame this one got away from you; we knew it wasn't going to be easy all the time. Our fortunes ebb and flow. Figure it out. I'm busy." He returned his attention to the book.

"No," Sanction said, frost in his voice. "This is too important, you don't blow me off now. I don't know what game you're playing, but I need you in *this* one."

Trellis paused, then slowly closed the book. He leaned back in his chair, stripping his reading glasses off, looking down his nose at Sanction. "You rely on me," he observed. "You're hurt. That I wouldn't rise to this particular challenge. Fix it for you."

"This is not about feelings," Sanction snapped. "This is *business*. And personal safety." He gestured tightly. "And our *future*."

"Yes," Trellis suddenly agreed. "We don't want our feelings to interfere with business." He looked Sanction in the eye. "Do we."

For a long moment, Sanction was speechless. "This is about *Rutherford?*" he protested.

Trellis tossed his glasses on the desk. "I try and I try," he said. "I point the way, and you stare at my finger. Tell me this, do you know who arrested Piccolo? Which Bluecoat?"

"No, I—it didn't seem important," Sanction replied, puzzled.

"It is," Trellis replied, curt. He let the silence stand for a moment, then he picked up his glasses and slid them back on, returning his attention to the book.

When he looked up later, Sanction was long gone.

THE EASE CULTURAL MUSEUM, THE EASE, SILKSHORE.
24TH VOLNIVET. ELEVENTH HOUR PAST DAWN.
SAIL LIGHTING FESTIVAL, DAY TWO. MARKET DAY

Rutherford strolled through the archway with his hands clasped behind his back, soaking in the scent of chilly stone and glass polish. The old man tucked by the entry blinked rheumy eyes at him and grinned, showcasing a few teeth.

"Rutherford!" he said. "Good news—say, that's quite a uniform," he said as his face shifted rapidly from boredom to enthusiasm to puzzlement.

"Hello, Cap," Rutherford replied, something kind in his tone. "I'm going to have to resign my post as curator for this exhibit. As you see, provisional again." He gestured at the armband.

"Sure, and you fit into your old Bluecoat uniform. That doesn't happen," Cap mused, leaning back. "You're a hell of a specimen, Rutherford. So, what does your man think of this relapse?" he asked with a long-fingered gesture at the uniform, keeping it light.

"I'm sure he'll let me know," Rutherford said quietly, looking to the side, seeing his ghostly reflection in the polished case displaying the evolution of Silkshore Bluecoat uniforms over the centuries. "Did we get the rush we expected from the festival?"

"Oh, we did indeed," Cap said, squinting down at the ledger on his narrow desk. "We've had twenty two visitors to the exhibit in two days!"

"By my blood," Rutherford said with half a smile. "Could you keep up with it all?"

"I managed," Cap said diffidently. "It's not like Drowner's Row downstairs, they've been wall to wall with the festival action. They've kept the grill going sixteen hours a day. Just like in real life, the criminals will keep the Bluecoats funded and operational."

"That's how it goes," Rutherford chuckled. "Our gallery is on the third floor at the back of the building. There is no path of least resistance to reach it."

"Yet reach it you did," Cap observed. "Did it get to you? Too much time around the Virtues?"

Rutherford's smile faded as he looked at the Virtues carved in the wall. Duty. Purpose. Protection. "You know how it is, Cap. Once you acquire a taste, the thirst never really goes away. For justice, right?" he said with a gentle, almost painful humor, not looking over at the old man.

"I know my affair with duty outlasted three wives, a husband, two children, and half my joints," Cap sighed. "It may be one-sided, you accept early on that duty will never love you back. Still." He shook his head. "I think we have too much in common with the criminals."

"Oh?" Rutherford retorted, raising his eyebrows.

"You let them out of Ironhook, the ones that have had decades in there. Some of them are in half their life or more. Some go in as kids." His smile was crooked. "They get out, and they miss the structure. The consistency. The rules. It's not hard to find your way back."

"I've certainly helped a few find their way home," Rutherford agreed.

"It's so easy to forget," Cap continued, looking down at the desk, "that the guards spend all their time in the prison too."

"Cap," Rutherford protested gently, "you're in a hell of a mood today."

"Festival crowds have me on edge," Cap replied, sardonic. He gestured at the three people wandering along the wall of displays at the far end of the room. "And I just got some devastating news. My curator is leaving his new duty to get back together with his former duty. It's always messy, with the ex." He paused. "How is Kreeger taking it, really."

"Oh, Cap, you know I wouldn't go back to the Bluecoats while I was with Kreeger," Rutherford replied. He turned to examine the badges mounted in a wall display, his eyes lingering on the first Canal Watch sigil. "We haven't spoken in a while. Not face to face."

Cap let the moment simmer, then he sighed. "I'd offer to round up some of the boys and scold him for you, but I know you can handle yourself," he said. "Frankly, I wouldn't want to get in the middle of whatever you've already got planned."

"You think I'm vindictive?"

"I think you never fit in with the Bluecoats because you like things to be fair," Cap replied. He pointed at the virtues. "Duty. Purpose. Protection. But that's not enough for you. You said it yourself. You give a damn about justice. Makes you dangerous as hell. Chasing justice is disruptive. Bluecoats, *true* Bluecoats, like it quiet."

"Is this an excerpt from your recruitment speeches, back when you worked the academy?" Rutherford teased, something serious behind his eyes.

"It's an excerpt from the talk I had to give the battered unfortunates I patched up as they weathered the turbulence of the academy," Cap said, examining his fingernails. "The ones considering whether or not to drop out. Deciding how much pain it was worth, how much fire and iron they had for challenging their reality." He paused. "You never talked about your time in the academy."

"And I don't plan to," Rutherford agreed. "But I know what you mean. I've have a finger that never healed right and some pretty exciting scars I got learning my lessons." He crossed his arms. "Some of those lessons never sank in. I took my low marks and carried on."

Cap smiled in spite of himself. "That's what made your reputation. As long as you got those big square shoulders, and allowed your superiors to steer you in useful directions, and kept that full head of hair, you were the hero the Bluecoats occasionally need to show off. Could have used you for those recruitment drives. All brash and noble and stern."

"The uniform helps," Rutherford said, droll.

"Well if you're trying to show your man what he's missing, then, you know, that's the outfit," Cap grinned. "Is that what you came here for? Show off the outfit?"

"There's this," Rutherford said, pulling an envelope from his coat and putting it on the desk. "Resigning the curatorial post. I was really looking forward to it, too," he said wistfully. "My circumstances shifted, and I don't have time for a hobby right now."

"Your timing is awful," Cap sighed. "Lord Straden's daughter deeded us his Bluecoat memorabilia collection, and now I'm going to have to sort it with Jen and Talbot."

"They are keen for the work," Rutherford said. "You'll be fine."

"I'll miss you, that's all," Cap said. "You know the Mandates and Provisions front to back. You can sort the regalia by time period and district. They are more interested in bloodstains and back story."

"Bloodstains and back story, eh," Rutherford mused. "That does describe a fair portion of the job." He shook his head. "I'm going to be busy for a while, Cap. I think often of our talks. I don't want you to feel neglected."

"Just abandoned," Cap shrugged. "Still, you could have posted the letter, and I'm glad you stopped by instead." Craning his neck, he looked over at a pair of old women whispering to each other and pointing at the wall of firearms. "I don't even mind tearing myself away from my duties during festival to catch up."

"I had better let you get back to it," Rutherford said. "I'll be by from time to time, as my circumstances allow. I must be on my way."

"Eyes up," Cap said.

"Eyes up," Rutherford agreed. He looked around once more, then left the Bluecoat exhibit, following the hallway, its polished floor reflecting his purposeful gait as he strode to the broad stairwell in the center of the museum and headed down.

Once he reached the main floor, he skirted the throng filling the foyer. Festival goers were queued up to pay admission, or gathering to watch buskers performing thematic acts to advertise for exhibits inside. A light rain sifted over the scene, but the crowd's enthusiasm was undimmed. The coffee shop by the museum was packed, an unusual circumstance; Rutherford paused, then crossed the lane to sit on a bench instead of waiting in line. Quiet and watchful, he was aware of the dampening effect his uniform had on passersby, and he knew he would have the bench to himself as long as he wanted it.

Rutherford did not have to wait long.

Sanction approached. Rutherford noticed Sanction deliberately relaxing his hands, releasing fists. A small, barbed smile lodged on his face.

"Well well well," Sanction said, his voice tight as he closed in on the bench. "You are a hard man to find."

"Am I?" Rutherford replied, almost lazy. "I told your Chime Bookstore snitch I would be here around the eleventh hour."

"You consider a lapse in your secrecy a summons?" Sanction retorted, eyebrows up.

"Here you are," Rutherford shrugged. "Have a seat if you like. Or don't. Please yourself."

Sanction stared at him for a moment. "I thought you were done with that nonsense," he said with a curt gesture at the Bluecoat uniform. "Provisional. Couldn't get them to reinstate you?"

"They will," Rutherford replied evenly. "I'm pursuing what I want for a change. I consider myself free to do so. I suppose I should thank you for that freedom, whether I wanted it or not."

"I never told you what to do," Sanction snapped. "This—acting out is bad for everyone, including you, whether you can see it or not. If you want to go, then go. You've got money, you can live anywhere in the city. Travel if you want to. Go dig for broken pottery in Iruvia, whatever."

"I like digging here," Rutherford replied, cool. "I'm not leaving Silkshore."

"If you think you're going to put me in Ironhook—"

"That's not my plan," Rutherford interrupted.

"What *is* your plan?" Sanction demanded.

A slow smile shaped Rutherford's features. "For one," he said quietly, "it's been too long since you asked me that." He rose to his feet, enjoying the sensation of being taller than Sanction. "You did me wrong, husband," he said quietly.

"Then you burned down our house!" Sanction retorted. "You're reliving the past now, is that it?"

"You feel so safe, taking that tone with me," Rutherford replied, looking Sanction in the eye. "Maybe we'll try this again later." He turned to go.

"This has to stop," Sanction said. "You've made your point. It's time to let Piccolo go and end this interference before you force me to stop it *for* you."

Rutherford let that sink in for a moment as Sanction stared at his back.

"That's the difference between us," Rutherford replied, his voice as even as he could make it. "You hurt me and then threaten me. I've threatened you. Now I'm going to hurt you."

He walked away.

Sanction did not follow.

ATTIC, CRAMDEN'S PUBLIC HOUSE, SILKSHORE. 24TH VOLNIVET. HOUR OF SONG, 2 HOURS PAST DUSK. SAIL LIGHTING FESTIVAL, DAY TWO. MARKET DAY

Thunder growled, a gentle sound, all the more erratic in contrast to the steady patter of rain on the attic roof. The dim room was lit only by luminescent paint, a giant stylized bloom on the far wall. Sanction lay in the bed, arms crossed over his chest, staring at the indifferent workmanship of the rafters bracing the narrow room's roof.

"I didn't expect you," the slim man next to him murmured, "but I'm glad you dropped by." He grinned, his teeth pale in the luminous shadow, his mop of tousled hair unrestrained.

"Rough day," Sanction replied, almost to himself.

"Do you have the night off?" his lover inquired, arching an eyebrow.

"Not for the foreseeable future," Sanction sighed. He rolled off the bed and rose, pulling on a silken house robe and pouring himself a glass of wine. "Things went wrong today. People may try to kill me. I've been expensive to a number of operations who may be doing the math to determine if wiping out my people is more profitable than continuing to pay us."

"Maybe I'm *not* glad you dropped by," his lover teased.

"Well," Sanction reflected, "I know I'm faster than you, so this seemed a reasonable stop. If they come for me, slow them down, will you?" He smiled, suddenly and painfully aware of how much easier it was to smile here than it had been at home.

"I have practiced a *number* of dangerous poses," the young man said, "and I'm pretty sure I could project some aura of menace for at least a few seconds."

"Now, Card, listen to me; on a more serious note, you may want to relocate for a little while. Stay out of sight. Bluecoats may come for you." Sanction sipped his wine.

"I thought you had an understanding with the Bluecoats," Card said, rising and reaching for a house robe. "What changed?"

"An arsonist burned my house down," Sanction said, his voice distant as he looked out the round window at the end of the loft. The whole street seemed to glow, hundreds of luminous lanterns shaded and placed to drive out shadow. A massive mast stood at the end of the street, sporting a sail that local artists had all painted on. Street buskers set up on either side of the street played enthusiastically; Sanction felt their overlap in the space between them. He savored another mouthful of wine.

"That—that's terrible," Card replied. "Was anyone hurt?"

"Yes," Sanction said, eyebrows drifting up. "The arsonist left a clue in my saferoom. It was your scarf." Sanction turned, looking Card in the eye. "Rutherford torched our life and left me. He knows about you." Sanction cocked his head to the side. "And he's rejoined the Bluecoats."

"That hits me in my joints," Card said faintly.

Sanction nodded. "You'll want to get out of range. Rutherford may go for collateral damage." Sanction touched Card's face. "I don't want your pain. But he might." Troubled, he turned away. "I suspect he might want my pain too. And I care about you." The lie came easy.

Card lowered himself to sit on one of the crates pulled up to the makeshift table. He sensed the tilt of his world. He felt his life sliding, rearranging.

"What about—about your portrait?" he asked, gesturing towards the partly finished painting that was on the flattering side of representational.

Sanction looked over at the portrait, and was silent for a long moment. "It is unfinished," he said quietly. He looked Card in the eye. "That's not always worse than how something ends."

Card nodded to himself, biting his lip.

Sanction gathered his things, dressed, kissed Card gently on top of his head, and left.

HIGH SIX BUSINESS APERTURE, SILKSHORE.
24ᵀᴴ VOLNIVET. HOUR OF SILVER, 3 HOURS PAST DUSK.
SAIL LIGHTING FESTIVAL, DAY TWO. MARKET DAY

The key rattled in the second lock, and the bolt shot out of the way. Sanction leaned into the heavy door, and hesitated as he saw a lit lamp in the closed and locked antechamber to his office. The lamp tightened the eye, deepening shadow; he did not see anyone else, but he knew he was not alone.

Instinct kicked in, and he stepped into the room and to the side, moving his silhouette out of the doorway. He drew his pistol and dropped to one knee, concentrating on adjusting his vision. Seconds passed, he felt his blood quicken as he dropped his mouth open and breathed as quietly as he could.

"No need for drama," murmured the woman who waited for him in the shadows. "I wanted to be sure you were alone. We need to chat." She stepped into the light around the reception desk at the end of the long foyer.

"Mother Grine," Sanction said, rising and pulling the door closed. He tugged a glass orb from his jacket and shook it, waking the algae within to a dim glow. He approached the desk. "So good to see you. What news from the Church?"

"No news from the Church," she replied, seating herself somewhat regally in the assistant's chair that flanked the desk. "This is a little backchannel communication. Just between us. Clarifying expectations."

Sanction poured two glasses of wine from the sideboard cabinet, and brought one to his guest. "Go on."

"We are working through the bureaucratic process of approvals to build a new edifice at the edge of the Sparkgrounds. Resistance has aligned against our efforts. Given the Silkworms history with the Church, and your influence in Silkshore, I wanted to be sure you understood that we are counting on your support." She looked him in the eye.

"You have it," he nodded, agreeable enough. "Why not arrange something a trifle less informal?" He sat in one of the spindly chairs in front of the big desk.

"Your home address is somewhat in question," she replied, "and by now everyone knows about Master Drassle, owner of the Coreside Mill. His assassination. That the Silkworms were *supposed* to prevent," she added, raising her eyebrows.

"A setback," Sanction said quietly.

"We all have them," Mother Grine said reflectively. "Anyway, it seemed best to intercept you somewhere quiet. I don't know for certain where you're sleeping right now," she lied, "and I figured you'd need to do some planning; where better than the relative security of your office?"

"This meeting doesn't make my office feel safer," Sanction pointed out, twirling the wine in his glass, half teasing. "Still, thank you for checking in. Our alliance remains important to the Silkworms."

"Swift blood," she nodded to him.

"Strong bones," he echoed. She was already on her way past him, and moments later she vanished into the shadowed hall.

"At least we're still friends with the Church," Sanction murmured. He finished off the wine in his glass.

CHAPTER EIGHT

Panma Say was an exquisite spark flyer, one of the best in the Copper Era that finally closed out around 830 when the towers on the barrier were re-sheathed in the wake of Propeller of Gant's unfortunate death. Panma was a big shot at the Nine and Nine tavern, as it was at the edge of the grounds. Sometimes, when it was late and the bustle quieted, his big flashy stories would run out and he would wax philosophical.

He once told me why people came to see the spark flyers. "I become everything that people in Doskvol cannot be," he said. "I am alone in space, with overwhelming energy all around. My only thought is the moment itself. I am beautiful in the light, untethered, swift, individual. When I fly, the only thing I have in common with them is easy access to a quick, if painful, death."

— Sagacious William,
"Confessional Mugs: A Bartender's Secondhand Stories"

The Mistress of Tides heard the grunts and sloshes and the ruthless tapping of the stick, and a smile tugged at her face somewhere behind the veils. She noiselessly approached, invisible in the shadows of the stone corridor, unobserved as she watched her adept train her new acolytes.

The high-ceilinged room had a channel of water through it, and Neap sat on a ledge opposite the channel. Nevi and Yelsir struggled, each one gripping the end of a mass of cloth that was half submerged in the channel.

"Tide," Neap barked, calling out maneuvers and rapping the floor in a rhythm echoing the dominant beats of a heart. The acolytes grunted, lifting the heavy wet cloth, raising their arms above their heads without releasing the shapeless burden. The acolytes pivoted under their arms and lowered them, then hauled the wet cloth up again, a slow and strenuous twirl along the wet paving by the channel. They dragged the cloth along the side of the channel, but the bulk of it remained underwater as they worked with the fabric they held.

"Riptide," Neap barked, and the bone-weary acolytes reversed direction, pivoting the other way, the muscles in their arms, legs, and core burning with the strain.

The Mistress of Tides moved out of the corridor entry, approaching Neap as he called out "Surf!" and the acolytes gratefully lowered their arms, then dragged at the cloth, trying to run alongside the channel as quickly as they could, water sloshing as the fabric dragged in their wake. Their knuckles were beyond white as they fixed their grip on the material, unrelenting.

Neap noticed the Mistress of Tides, and his stick stilled. The acolytes looked up, surprised.

"Continue," the Mistress of Tides murmured, and Neap nodded.

"Upon rocks," he called out, resuming the cane's driving pattern. The acolytes widened their stances, facing the channel, and raised the wad of cloth as high as they could, then relaxed it down, then hefted it again, the clacks of the stick driving them.

"I'm looking for Ebb," the Mistress of Tides said to Neap.

"I haven't seen him," Neap said, almost apologetic. "Surf!" The acolytes staggered, but adjusted to jog by the channel, dragging the fabric. "What is he up to?"

"Workers are building a scaffold along the canal side of the Overview. I sent him to get me an explanation," she said.

"Low tide!" Neap called out, the stick rhythm steady. "Crisp! Crisper!" The acolytes were exhausted, their movements sluggish as they crouched, letting the fabric slap down on the water's surface and pick up fresh weight. They straightened, hauling it up, then crouched again, the stick pacing them. Neap looked sideways to the Mistress of Tides. "They may do better when fresh," he murmured.

"Of course," she agreed. "We all do." She watched them struggle.

Yelsir cried out, and the fabric slid out of her grip as she toppled over clutching at her back. Neap looked warily at the Mistress of Tides.

"Keep it going," she said, gesturing at him, and he continued the stick beats as the Mistress of Tides approached Yelsir. Unsure what to do, Nevi looked on, the agony of her grip and the fire in her muscles forgotten.

"Acolyte," the Mistress of Tides said to Yelsir. "Do you accept failure and death?"

"Mistress," Yelsir gritted out through clenched teeth, face red, veins visible in her forehead. "I—I will accept—whatever comes—next—" She gasped at her pain. "I must."

The Mistress of Tides regarded Nevi. "The choice is also yours," she said quietly. Nevi blinked, then winced as she dropped down with her burden, and again hauled it up, chained once more to the endless pattern Neap rapped out.

The Mistress of Tides turned her attention back to Yelsir, who puffed out her cheeks and struggled to breathe, pain overflowing her. "Your limits advocate for themselves," the Mistress of Tides said. "Sometimes we must bow to them. Sometimes not. This is one way we learn the difference; by crossing into spaces where our limits have more power than we do." She turned to Neap.

"Care for her, and let her choose her duties for a week," the Mistress of Tides murmured. Then she left, and as she did, the beat of the stick stopped.

Slack was waiting for her in the corridor, his expression somber. "I have news," he said under his breath. The Mistress of Tides nodded, and he continued. "Trellis will not be able to make the meet with Chief Hamstead, of Ironhook. They were to have supper together tonight at the Hour of Song. Trellis sent a request that you attend in his place."

The veils hid the Mistress of Tides' expression, but her displeasure radiated clearly. She paused for a long, long moment. Considering her limits.

"I will do it," she said through her teeth. "You will come with me." She paused. "This is not like him," she mused.

"He rarely changes his plans unless another hidden plan motivates him," Slack agreed.

"If I didn't know better," the Mistress of Tides said thoughtfully, "I would think this almost looks like sharing power."

They followed the corridor towards the rest of the day's plans.

SMOKE TOWER, BOOKEND SQUARE, FOGCREST, SILKSHORE. 24ᵀᴴ VOLNIVET. FIFTH HOUR PAST DAWN. SAIL LIGHTING FESTIVAL, DAY TWO.

The Chief Inspector's office bustled. One Bluecoat approached with papers, out of breath. Another took papers from the Chief Inspector, who stood by the sideboard, scrawling approval on an exception. Two more Bluecoats and his assistant were also in the office, which no longer felt spacious. Cellar stood by the door, uncomfortable.

"Cellar, get in here," the Chief Inspector said. "I hear you opened a crate of stripers, and some of them made it into the canal."

"Yes sir," Cellar replied, helpless in the face of the cold fact.

"You acted rashly," the Chief Inspector barked, still not looking at him. "You should have checked. But you didn't. The law is clear. During *festival*, I don't have time for this." He glanced over at Cellar, who stood with his eyes fixed on the floor, furiously blushing. "Duty respite, until I restore you. I will communicate through your specials, when they are freed up—after festival," he clarified. "Out." He turned to one of the Bluecoats. "Take this to the Sparkgrounds, Captain Falden will be looking for it." He did not need to glance over to confirm that Cellar was no longer in the office.

As Cellar descended the staircase, he felt out of synch, moving in slow motion. Everyone seemed to have six or more things to do, rushing from one to the next, gaining new tasks as fast as the current list was checked off. Off to one side, a brawl with a thoroughly drunk Skov. At the counter, a bleeding man yelling his story, complete with wild gestures. To one side, a corral of grim victims of pickpockets, lodging their factuals. Cellar blinked with surprise as he saw Jayan pressing through the action to reach him.

"I've been checking, and there are three or four places we're needed," Jayan said, suppressing the need to gasp. "I've been catching up on the news."

"Not the *right* news," Cellar retorted, unable to contain a bitter tone. "I've got a duty respite. You're on your own."

"What?" Jayan yelled. "During *festival?*"

"Yeah, I opened a crate of stripers," Cellar said through his teeth. "Goddamn tea shop."

"Ouch," Jayan winced. "So... huh."

"Hey, Cellar, tough break," called one of the Bluecoats behind the massive front desk. "Come here!" She waved him over. He noticed her black eye and skinned knuckles as he approached.

"What is it, Leen?"

"Got some news, figure you give a damn," she said, her voice pitched to project through the noise. "I heard Taff had some seizures last night. Not looking good. You've got time, maybe you want to swing by. See how he's doing." There was something sympathetic in her tone, blunting his immediate irritation that she already knew about his duty respite.

"I'll check it out," he said with a quick nod, and he turned, pushing through the crowd towards the exit.

He knew Jayan wouldn't follow. Couldn't. Festival, after all.

A very busy time.

Cellar disappeared through the doors.

The Mistress of Tides set her teacup down on the table as Ebb escorted a portly woman into the gallery.

"Ministry Director of Structures Nalaya," he announced. He bowed, retreating.

"Please, sit," the Mistress of Tides said with a gesture. "Refreshment?"

"Certainly, certainly, that would be fine, whatever's handy, don't go out of your way," the Director beamed as she settled at the table, brushing a stray lock of gray hair back from her round face. She considered the Mistress of Tides. "I understand you wanted an update on the project outside."

"The scaffolding," the Mistress of Tides agreed. "I did not expect to inconvenience a Director with my humble inquiry."

"Well, I was in the neighborhood reviewing the plans with the architects when your man showed up, and I've been meaning to meet you for the last year or so anyway; you are a pillar of the community, a respected figure in Master Market. I'm pleased to have the opportunity," she beamed. "First things first; I apologize that this construction was a surprise. We sent notice of work to everyone on the canal, I am dismayed that somehow you were not aware of our plans. The Ministry is working on the west side of the Zatha Route Six canal embankments," Director Nalaya said. "Any questions come up, you can always check in with the roster of improvements." She glanced up at Ebb, who arrived with a nibble plate and teacup. "Thanks, love."

"I appreciate the Ministry's transparency," the Mistress of Tides replied.

"We'll do our best not to hinder you any more than is completely necessary," the Director smiled. She watched Ebb leave, and sipped at her tea. "And now that it's just you and me, that's not the only reason I'm here." She put her cup down, regarding the Mistress of Tides frankly. "We all have more than one role to play. Like you, here. Teacher, wise woman, scholar. Whisper."

The Mistress of Tides said nothing.

"And that's just how it goes in Doskvol," Director Nalaya shrugged. "Take me, for instance. I also hold the role of Master of Stone for the Silkshore Foundation. They have concerns," she confided, "but I didn't want to speculate. I wanted to talk with you directly." She sipped her tea again. "This is really good," she observed.

"Concerns."

"About the Silkworms, specifically. And we're not having this conversation. I'm just having a little off the books recon with you," she winked. "About the Sparkgrounds. The Church is looking to put in a cathedral." She shook her head. "The Foundation does not approve."

The Mistress of Tides waited, and Director Nalaya chose a couple morsels from the nibble plate with her two-tined fork.

"So," Director Nalaya continued, "my people survey the land and draw up plans before they take action. That's just a natural impulse for us. Consider this a survey." She looked at the veil, unable to make eye contact. "We are determining where the Silkworms are in all this. You've got friends in the Church. But you could also be well positioned to advocate for the Foundation, should you want friends among them too."

Director Nalaya had ample opportunity to savor the nibbles; strips of fish in delicate sauces, pickled curls of eel, braised caps. The Mistress of Tides said nothing.

"I come to you because you're the one that complicated this," Director Nalaya said, eyes on the plate as she savored the appetizers. "You took on new acolytes. Previously, they served the Foundation's enemy." Director Nalaya shook her head reflectively. "Makes some people nervous. Seems like a signal."

"It isn't," the Mistress of Tides replied. "Daggers do not remember the blood they shed. I am wiping them clean. They serve only me."

Director Nalaya leaned back in her chair, considering the Whisper.

"As to alignment," the Mistress of Tides said slowly, "I do not want the Silkworms to be the Foundation's enemy. I truly do not." She paused. "We may not align, precisely. But I do not want us to clash. There is no need for that."

"Good," Director Nalaya said, and she smiled again. "That's good. No one wants more enemies." She rose. "Thank you for the hospitality," she said. "If you have any further questions, send that adorable little chap around and we'll work it out." Her smile widened, past the point of plausibility. "Glad we've reached an understanding."

"As am I," the Mistress of Tides said, standing. "Thank you for the update."

"I live to serve," Director Nalaya replied, and she turned. "Well. Enjoy the festival."

"Enjoy the festival."

The Director did not need any further assistance finding her way out. The Mistress of Tides was aware that Spring was in the doorway behind her, waiting for orders.

"Find out more," she murmured. He nodded, and withdrew.

PARMI LODGING, BOOKEND SQUARE, FOGCREST, SILKSHORE. 24ᵀᴴ VOLNIVET. SEVENTH HOUR PAST DAWN. SAIL LIGHTING FESTIVAL, DAY TWO. MARKET DAY

Cellar was lost in thought as he trudged through the festival crowds towards Taff's apartment building. He returned his attention to his surroundings as the flaring tones of an argument pierced the din of the crowd.

"—harpy, back your tits off or I'll pop 'em!" yelled the hunched woman with wild hair.

"You keep after what's mine and I'll fix both your teeth for you!" the iron faced woman retorted. "Sevel, clear the way. It's time we had a look." The tall man at her side looked intensely uncomfortable.

"I don't need my girls with me to put *you* in your place," the hag snarled. "Taff promised me things, now I'm here to collect—"

"Nothing!" the other woman snapped. "You get *nothing*, even over his dead body!"

Dead?

"Ladies, ladies," said a hulking man as he carefully navigated down the stairs towards the scene. "I'm Lowell, the landlord here. Before this gets out of hand—"

Both women spoke over him and each other, gesturing for emphasis.

Cellar strode forward. "Calm this down," he said, jacketed up in his Inspector voice, officious. "Inspector Cellar, I'm here for Taff, where is he?" Cellar leaned into the intimidating symbol of his uniform, a bulwark of impassive authority, free of emotion.

"Well," Lowell said with a bit of a sneer, "he was late before you were. The old man kicked off in the deep night, corpse is long gone, now it's time to figure out redistribution. I'm owed—"

"Not till I'm done you don't!" yelled the younger woman. "You and Hen can take a look when I've got what—"

"You got the clap to remember him by!" Hen shrieked, startling a blush from the other woman. "And that's all you get!"

Sevel stepped forward and gave Hen a shove, and the old woman swallowed the rest of her bilious comment, rebounding with a notched knife that sent Sevel back behind his mother in a hurry.

"Occupancy debt," Lowell insisted, ignoring the others to speak directly to Cellar. "He had his chance to divvy up his goods and he missed it, the law is on my side." He spared a glance to Hen, and his eyes reflected long experience with cruelty to the weak. She took an involuntary step back, the knife in her hand forgotten.

"The law is on *my* side," Cellar replied, cold. "He may have had some clues I need for an investigation. I'm going in first, and when I'm done, you're in," he nodded to Lowell. He looked at the others, who stared at him, bristling. "Then the leftovers," he said.

He walked past them, down the filth-choked stairs, opening the door to Taff's basement apartment as the arguments behind him struggled to regain some enthusiasm.

Cellar stepped over the dusty strip of nails jutting up from the floorboards, just inside the door, a common enough deterrent in Bluecoat homes. Slow down the intruder, make some noise. Many Bluecoats had no reason to expect company.

The apartment's dimensions matched the narrow cross-section of the block's foundation. Its interior was choked with the accumulated flotsam of an unexamined life, lived out beyond its walls. Taff often caved to the temptation to keep castoff junk found here and there that was good for something, eventually, surely. The thick smell of a dying old man saturated the air. The table and wall both had a harrowmaze, but the mice in them had died a long time ago. The Iruvian bayonets in the wall mount had dulled. Speckles of rust on the foreign blades had grown to patches, freezing them in the brackets. One sagging chair had a fabric cover, an attempt at style. The cover was stained by gradual buildup of oil from his head and hands, the fabric on the chair arms worn to a limp shine. Something scuttled in the back counter of the kitchen.

The only clear spot in the kitchen was at the table, where a half finished solo game of chance was laid out with crooked and stained cards. The game had no point but to distract the mind from an unpleasant stretch of time.

Now it had no purpose at all.

A sudden dizziness swept Cellar. Without a doubt, there were treasures of all kind squirreled away in this mass, but the thick corruption and neglect, the sheer density of material, repelled him.

"Let it stay messy," he said through his teeth.

Abrupt, he pivoted and pushed through the door, up the stairs, past the argument and calls for his attention, into the city that could drown out anything.

Cellar tried to outrun the looming sensation he was too late.

SMOKER'S CORNER, FOUNDRYSIDE ROW, FOGCREST, SILKSHORE.
24TH VOLNIVET. NINTH HOUR PAST DAWN.
SAIL LIGHTING FESTIVAL, DAY TWO.

Like water rushing through a net over its course, the sound flowing out of the massive wall of residences was fragmented and tumbling, intermixed and senseless. Cellar followed the structure's face, the mottled sky a strip between the buildings that formed canyon walls. He was drawn along the pedestrian-only pavement between two towering blocks that were connected here and there by makeshift catwalks and laundry lines.

At the end, supports formed an uneasy foundation for extensions overbuilt from the end of the row, hanging over a smithy and multi-story foundry. Cellar mounted the stairs, through the smoke, rising into the cloud one turn at a time. Near the top, he saw a young man crouched by the door to an apartment on the end, a few worn tools at his side as he flexed, pulling a patch tight on one of the balusters.

Hey, Hale, Cellar said with his hands, the sign language flowing from him instinctively. *All good?*

"Screw that," Hale said loudly, face red.

"Ah," Cellar said with half a grin. *Festival a no-go?*

"Ask Gran, you care so much," Hale said, sullen. "Or help me get these chores done."

Cellar chuckled and tousled the young man's hair as he passed him, headed through the open door into the slightly foggy interior of the apartment. The ceaseless clangor of machinery and hammers from the foundry and smithy punctuated all other sounds. The hiss of frying fish released a savory smell. Three people bustled in a one person kitchen. The apartment's high ceiling allowed two levels, and the narrow gallery with windows looked out over a sooty cloud, allowing a filtered view of the Ease.

Two babies were strapped into chairs at the table, both wailing as loud as they could. Cellar stepped in to give his grandmother a kiss on the cheek, and she absently swatted at him with a spoon.

The hell you doing here? she signed. *Festival! Serious! Mid-day!*

You got lucky, Cellar signed back with a grin he didn't wholly feel.

Uncle's chowder; be useful, she signed back, and she dipped into the big pot on the back of the stove, filling a bowl and handing it to Cellar with a wink. *Staying for lunch? Frying fish for us.*

Cellar plucked a runcible spoon out of the jar of cutlery on the counter, pretending to miss the question. He took the chowder to the gallery where his uncle sat in the overstuffed chair, resting his elbow on his upright prosthetic leg next to his throne.

Hey kid! Uncle Feld signed, eyes lighting up, his ruined face creasing upward. *Kim's back soon. Going to the Sparkground. Thought you couldn't come.*

Can't, Cellar signed with a shrug, his smile fading. *Just stopping by,* he signed, realizing it was true even as he signed it. He patted his uncle on the shoulder, then stepped past him, headed for the bunks in the back.

"Hey, cuz is here!" yelled a boy standing at the railing of the low loft. "What's up with you showing up here?" he demanded with a grin.

"Oh, I gotta tell you?" Cellar shot back. He ducked through a curtain into what had once been a pantry, where his narrow cot was made up

113

on two chests, with two shelves above it, and just enough room for the wash basin and seat bucket.

"I don't know what I was thinking," he murmured to himself, struggling, knowing there was no rest here. He pulled a worn box from the top shelf, snapping it open and pulling out bullets, pocketing them as the curtain lifted to the side.

Hey sis, he signed.

Yeah, midday, she signed back, a concerned look in her eyes. She studied him.

Saya, relax, he waved at her concerns. *Just picking up something I forgot, I was in the area. Festival*, he shrugged.

Her eyes darted to the side as a fistfight broke out a little deeper in the apartment. "Damn you Tris!" someone hollered. "I'm seeing Kim tonight! Quit messing with my stuff!" Thudding footsteps transmitted through the floorboards, yells vibrating in the thin wall Saya touched.

We all got duties, he signed, half a grin on his face.

Later, she signed back, unconvinced. She stepped away. "Knock id off!" she yelled, the accurate edges numbed off the words she could yell but could not hear. "Bowf ov you!" Sharp yelps followed, and the swish and crack of a switch.

Cellar shook his head once more, climbing out of his uniform and pulling on more innocuous clothes, one of the four outfits he owned. He set a cloth cap on his head as the curtain twitched aside again.

Cause if there's a problem you tell me, Saya insistently signed, worry shadowing her elfin features.

I'll be out late. Going undercover. I love you, he gestured, and he kissed her on the forehead as he maneuvered past her. He didn't look back as he headed for the door.

He wasn't ready to tell her about duty respite. Which was unpaid. During festival, the peak moneymaking season in Silkshore. The season where the family annually caught up with increasingly insistent debts.

Maneuvering out the front door past Hale felt like the last easy escape he would have for a while. He tried unsuccessfully to push dark thoughts from his mind as he descended through the spark-traced cloud from the foundry that drifted up through the slick, blackened steps.

The tavern was full of friends and questions, as was his home. Everywhere he would go was a place he was known, fraught with conversations he did not want to have.

"Blood and bone," he muttered under his breath as the sense of isolation bit deeper.

The sensation pushed him to the landing half a block down, then he was on a festively decorated gondola, drifting on the interlocking net of ripples from the busy boat traffic, floating away from the stone quay.

"What heading?" the gondolier smiled at him.

"I want to get lost," Cellar replied without looking at him.

The gondolier nodded, pushed off, and found Cellar's destination.

SAROOL'S HOUSE CUISINE, UNITY PARK, BRIGHTSTONE. 24TH VOLNIVET. HOUR OF SONG, 2 HOURS PAST DUSK. SAIL LIGHTING FESTIVAL, DAY TWO. MARKET DAY

The Mistress of Tides ruthlessly suppressed the unease that twitched through her body and her thoughts. She waited, composed. Her evening wear was highlighted by the glow of radiant plants. She was seated in a back nook of the mezzanine on the second floor. Several paces away, a glass column held three small sharks with glowing cartilage skeletons and glittering teeth, drifting aimlessly in the confines of the tank in endless spirals, dead eyes backlit and mouths working on reflex.

Slack approached the table. "The staff have not seen Chief Hamstead," he said quietly.

"He is half an hour late," the Mistress of Tides mused, thinking through the possibilities.

Slack hesitated only a moment, then seated himself on the servant bench outside the alcove. He arched an eyebrow as he spotted Ebb walking towards the table, looking like he hastily upgraded his wardrobe to be allowed to enter the luxury restaurant.

"I have news," Ebb said, doing his best not to blurt it out, the strain of his exertions written across his beet-red face. "Master Drassel was shot and killed at the noon speech, the False Dawn Competitive Showing. And the Bluecoats caught Piccolo as well as the assassin." He allowed himself a shaky exhale and inhale, his heart and lungs still pumping from a recent sprint.

"That was *eight hours ago*," the Mistress of Tides hissed. "I'm *just now* finding out?"

"Festival," Ebb replied with a helpless shrug.

A long moment of silence covered rapid thinking. "Chief Hamstead apparently heard," Slack said unnecessarily.

"This isn't good," Ebb agreed. "If Piccolo—"

Slack silenced him with a gesture. They all turned to see a Bluecoat approaching, somewhat out of place in his dress uniform.

"The Chief sends his apologies," the smug Bluecoat said, his hat under the crook of his arm. "He has been unavoidably detained. Please forgive a little Ironhook humor," he added conspiratorially, a profoundly unflattering smirk smeared across his features. "Got a message I can take back to him?" His eyes held challenge.

Slack glanced at the Mistress of Tides, and nodded almost imperceptibly. "Please thank him for his consideration, and for the message," he said calmly. "We look forward to rescheduling."

"Sure," the Bluecoat replied with half a shrug. He smiled at them, aiming for politeness. "Another time." He nodded, then turned and headed out.

"Ebb," the Mistress of Tides said, her voice low. "Find out the rest of it." He bowed from the waist, then turned and headed out of the restaurant. "Slack," she added, "you stay with me." She hated the slight tremble at the back of her voice, and the sense of exposure that rippled through her. "We need to get back to Silkshore. Now."

They left.

AFTDECK OF THE DOOMSDAY, ANKHAYAT PARK, SILKSHORE. 24ᵀᴴ VOLNIVET. HOUR OF FLAME, 5 HOURS PAST DUSK. SAIL LIGHTING FESTIVAL, DAY TWO. MARKET DAY

Cellar sat with his elbows on his knees, gazing across the river at nothing. His bench was mounted on the afterdeck of the Doomsday, a Leviathan hunter shorn into three parts, with the prow and the stern built into the park as observation decks half a mile apart. Behind him, he heard the festivities at full tilt, the park's many amusements all on display during the festival. He felt so invisible his features blurred in his own mind's eye, warping and sliding away and leaving him face-less.

Or maybe it was the fungal brew. He looked down at six empty bottles, and the one in his hand still half-full of the sudsy swill.

Far below, small boats unfurled underwater luminous sheets, creating the illusion of a reflection of glowing sails on craft with empty masts. A knot of judges commented on the various entries in low voices, fifteen feet away in a reserved corral by the rail with a perfect view. Cellar ripped the loudest belch he could manage, but he was thoroughly ignored. Festival, after all.

The belch did attract the attention of a beer vendor, who closed in on him with a cheery smile. "Top you off, sir?"

"Yep," Cellar slurred. He squinted at the vendor; a different one every time, it seemed. "You can see me, right?"

"Yes sir. Two eels." The vendor smiled, somehow polite even in the middle of the public celebration.

Cellar fumbled the coins at him and pressed the cool bottle against his sweating forehead. "I'll get to you," he whispered to the bottle.

He knew the lookout was anchored firmly to the shore, but he could feel the world turning, tilting, out of alignment. Something was wrong, deeply wrong. Something was coming.

Or maybe it was the beer.

The next time the vendor checked in on customers, Cellar was sound asleep on the bench, curled around his unopened bottle.

CHAPTER NINE

Nothing stuck. He had more enemies than most, and there were generally half a dozen nicknames circulating; String-bean, Cod, Fuse, Slick, Pliers. There just wasn't anything that was sufficiently apt to get a critical mass of usage. You may call him Ram, but if no one else does, it's more an inaccuracy than a nickname.

He was dignified, but grounded. Rutherford didn't need to bend for your approval. He never secretly preened when he heard you talk about him. He overwhelmed that human im-pulse to escape your given identity, to put your own mark on it, to be known by your exploits rather than traits and titles assigned to you as an infant.

I think it was his instinct for letting others keep their dignity that ultimately protected him from a nickname of his own. You inquired why I recommended an academy graduate for a promotion before he even served, and here is my reason: Ruth-erford is the caliber of leader that could elevate the Bluecoats. Make them better. Whether they like it or not.

— Academy Warden and Mandates and Provisions Instructor Uria Donnel, private correspondence to Captain Welsmith. 841 (eight years ago)

The Mistress of Tides felt her breath swell in, then flow out. She withdrew towards fullness and pressed towards emptiness. The battering clangs on one of the overview's street entrances were far away, but the echoes reached to where she drifted as a quiet observer of her own thoughts and rhythms. The intrusion was not unexpected.

Two minutes later Spring entered the long chamber, Sanction at his heels. "Mistress, Sanction requests an audience," he said softly.

Unhurried, she let the last of her breath drain. Then she reached for her headdress and twisted it on, adjusting her veil with the ease of long practice. She listened to Sanction fidget, the scuff of the sole of his boot, the friction of cloth.

"I am not sure which surprises me more," she said. "That you are so early, or that you are so late."

"Hilarious," he said through his teeth.

"Not really," she retorted, rising and turning to face him. "The background is shifting, Sanction. Can you feel it?"

"Can I *feel it?*" he snapped, almost a shout. "I don't have to *feel it*, we—" he stopped abruptly as she raised her hand to interrupt.

"Please, keep your voice down. Ebb is all worn out from chasing news that you should have brought me." She gestured to an alcove where her acolyte slept propped up against the wall. Sanction did not glance over, instead fixing his eyes on the Mistress of Tides.

"I'm short-handed," Sanction said, his tone urgent but much quieter. "This morning I'm picking up Spindle and Crackstone, they were in a Canal Watch cell. Piccolo is in Ironhook. Trellis has gone limp on me. I'm trying to drag this crew to safety, but I need you to pull some weight," he scowled.

"That is *enough*," she said, her voice no louder, but with an edge seldom heard.

"Please excuse my frustration," he said with a curt and only partly sarcastic bow. "Right now we are all doing things we don't want to do, for the sake of the Silkworms and our future. For example, I had a charming conversation with Mother Grine. She was testing the

Silkworms position on this merry little clash the Foundation and the Church have about the cathedral proposed for the edge of the Spark-grounds. I assured her we did not plan to cross them."

"I had a similar conversation with a representative of the Silkshore Foundation," the Mistress of Tides said. "She offered us friendship in exchange for our advocacy on their behalf, as it is known we have church ties."

"What was your reply?" Sanction asked, wary.

"I told her we don't want a fight," the Mistress of Tides replied, "but I did not give her the level of specificity she was after."

Sanction's jaw flexed. "We have *got* to stay out of this one," he said. "We are far too vulnerable right now." He gestured to the side, towards where Ebb slept. "So what did you discover in your inquiry?"

"I had Ebb checking on the Ironhook context, once I got the news of Master Drassle's assassination," she replied. "Spring was assigned to find out more of the Foundation inquiry context. Neap is checking on Paving, a feared Foundation assassin. My forces are already spread thin."

"Well you can relax on the Ironhook inquiry," Sanction said. "Trellis met with Chief Hamstead last night. I'm going out to Barrowcleft later to find out how that went."

The Mistress of Tides cocked her head to the side. "Trellis declined to attend, and sent me in his place. Chief Hamstead eventually sent a Bluecoat to let me know he wasn't coming. Hamstead got the news about Master Drassle long before I did." She paused. "Do you think Trellis knew before he asked me to go?"

"No idea. I do not understand what is going through his head right now," Sanction seethed. "If ever there was a time we needed him at the top of his game, this is it. I know he's old, but—"

"Mind your tongue," the Mistress of Tides interrupted again. "I understand you are frustrated, we all are. You may wish to show more care in how you talk about those who support you."

"Right now I need some signals that this support you mention is not just theoretical," Sanction replied. "We need some damage control, and for that it is all hands on deck. Piccolo is in Ironhook, and this is not an ideal time for us to find out we moved too slowly and we do not have a presence there, or the kind of influence we need to keep him safe. Look, just to cover the basics, I need you to assign your acolytes to some of our key operations. Send some of your disciples out to pick up some of the observation and communication work. I don't trust contract work at this point, we don't know who might deliberately mislead us or grant access to our enemies."

"That is not my role, nor theirs," the Mistress of Tides replied quietly.

"Time and treasure are thin," Sanction said, "and if you choose to withhold full support, support beyond capacity, *right now*, we may not have a crew to back you up later on. If one of us goes down, we are all in more danger. Think it over." He pivoted, and strode out of the chamber without a backwards glance.

SMOKE TOWER, BOOKEND SQUARE, FOGCREST, SILKSHORE. 25TH VOLVINET. FIRST HOUR PAST DAWN. SAIL LIGHTING FESTIVAL, DAY THREE.

Rutherford's stool was pulled up by a clear spot on the cluttered sideboard. He leaned on his elbow, staring down at the cheap pulpy paper that bore his scrawl. He re-read the only line that wasn't scratched out: *In the event of my death*

Frowning, he drew a line through it with the pen. For a long moment, he considered the half of the paper that was still blank. Then he rolled his eyes, balled up the paper, and held it over the low glass chimney of the lamp; in moments, fire trickled up one side of the paper, and quickly spread as he turned the wad over so the whole thing merrily flickered. He tossed it in the metal can by his knee.

"This is your fault!" Clamp yelled from the far end of the office corridor as he stormed around the corner, almost unrecognizable in his basically clean uniform. His hair was slicked back, and his moustache had been ambushed by a comb but it seemed to have put up a good fight. "I'm supposed to go see the goreflushed *captain*. And bring *you*. Get over here." He pivoted, and stalked out of the office as Rutherford rose, holstering his weapon and tucking his notebook and pen into their custom belt pouches.

Rutherford paced himself so he didn't quite catch up to Clamp until they were passing by the upstairs desks in the tactical strategy chamber outside the captain's office, but he was at Clamp's elbow as the Bluecoat paused outside the door.

"Come in," barked a crisp voice inside, and Clamp's face clenched in a scowl before smoothing towards indifference. He opened the door and entered, standing stiffly beside the captain's desk as Rutherford followed.

"Close the door," Captain Smiles said reflectively, glancing over a report. As Rutherford complied, her eyes flicked up to Clamp. "Well here we are, good morning," she said.

"Good morning, Captain," Clamp replied as tonelessly as possible, at attention.

"I'm releasing Spindle and Crackstone," Captain Smiles said, eyeing Rutherford. "They have friends, and the justification for bringing them in was at best flimsy. There was no justification whatsoever for holding them as long as we did, or for separating them out into our questioning berths. That's not what the Canal Watch holding pens are for, especially during festival." She cocked her head to the side. "Had the front desk known we had those two down in Canal Watch they would have been released immediately."

"Yes, captain," Rutherford agreed, looking her in the eye.

Quiet settled as Rutherford passed on the opportunity to say more.

"Two days ago," Captain Smiles continued, "you stood right where you're standing now and asked for provisional status. I granted it," she said with a nod to the red armbands on his uniform. "Since then, you've pulled in Spindle and Crackstone, then Belltongue and Piccolo. Remarkable initiative," she said, ticking items off on her fingers, "oblique methods, and improper use of holding cells." She leaned back. "I've gotten complaints from a number of prominent citizens, they have insisted you should be reprimanded for procedural missteps. Silkshore's Minister of Bluecoats has staff rushing you through the commendation process for bagging Belltongue. And members of the Fairpole Gondolier Council? Not a word," she said.

Rutherford let the silence stand for a moment. "I can justify each and every procedure," he said.

"I don't doubt that," Captain Smiles replied, "but that's not the point." She arched her eyebrows. "Is it."

"The point," Rutherford said, "is that you are deciding whether or not I am the kind of Bluecoat you want in Silkshore right now."

"So, Clamp," Captain Smiles said, not taking her eyes from Rutherford. "What do you think? You're a senior officer. You know the work. Evaluate the nucoat."

Clamp's features twitched, and he cleared his throat. "Ah, Rutherford here," he said, staring at the opposite wall, his formal stance stiffening further. "He is determined to make a lot of people angry and cost a lot of people money. While he's doing the job."

"There you have it," Captain Smiles said with a shrug, and the tone shifted. "Give me those armbands, nucoat."

Rutherford began working an armband off, waiting.

"You aren't provisional anymore," Captain Smiles clarified, "because you're reinstated. And I'm giving you a squad."

Clamp could not suppress a twitch. "Captain, he's a pike?" he asked before he could choke the question back.

"No, he's not promoted, but he's assigned a squad all the same," Captain Smiles replied as the first band hit her desk and Rutherford started working on the other one.

"Orders?" Rutherford asked, a glint in his eye.

"Get me a win," she responded, challenging him.

"Yes captain," he said with a crisp nod, tossing the other armband on the desk.

"Dismissed," she replied, a somewhat feral smile crossing her features.

Rutherford turned and headed out of the office, Clamp at his heels. As soon as they were ten paces and a closed door away, Clamp shoved at Rutherford's shoulder.

"You silly son of a bitch," he snarled, "you dragged me right up next to the fire and I'm all dried out now so you owe me a bonesnapped drink!"

"Yes," Rutherford agreed with a grin. "Many drinks. But not now. The day is young, and we've got a squad to pull together. We've got to move fast, outpace news of my reinstatement." He was flushed with a fever heat.

"Now?" Clamp clarified, eyes wide. "That's it, you get here in the morning in your freshly ironed costume, toddle in to a chat with the captain, get reinstated *and* functionally promoted, then grab your squad and go save the day in time for the afternoon papers?!"

Rutherford gripped his shoulders. "*Nothing* gets past you!" he replied, something ferocious in his stance. "Now, speed is key. Keep up." He turned, striding towards the stairs, Clamp at his heels.

"Nobody says I have to be on your squad!" Clamp protested.

Still. He followed.

Rutherford clattered through the metal grating into the Cave, the low barrel ceiling of the vault under the tower. It was jammed full of desk stations, trunks, equipment shelves and racks, and sweaty Bluecoats. Confident, Rutherford walked right down the middle, aiming for a knot of half-dressed Bluecoats ingesting various drugs as they steeled themselves for the day and examined their gear.

"There you are, Welker," Rutherford said with a smile as he approached.

A hulking Bluecoat shifted to cock an eyebrow at him. "Well if it isn't the nucoat. Lose your bands?" he mocked, enjoying the sniggering from his squadmates as they looked on.

"That's right, I'm no longer provisional," Rutherford agreed.

"And you're looking to join the Sweetwater Regulars?" Welker clarified. "Son, that's not how this works. *We* pick *you*."

"Oh, I'm not looking to join the Sweetwater Regulars," Rutherford said. "Captain Smiles assigned me a squad, and she wasn't choosy about who I picked. So. You're with me, gear up," he said past Welker. "We've got business, and we leave in ten."

"Spread the sweet cheeks, this is *not* happening," Welker swore as his expression darkened. "Your meat is a little too fresh for this kind of joke. It's Festival, and there's no time for pranks."

"Saw it with my own eyes," Clamp said, shaking his head. "Captain Smiles reinstated him *and* promoted his ass. Functionally," he clarified.

"*The hell she did*," Welker snarled, and he shoved past Rutherford, storming towards the stairs. Rutherford leaned with the shove and straightened after it, squared off with the squad.

"Suit up, full arms," Rutherford said calmly. "We're going heavy."

"But, no, wait," one of the Bluecoats said. "We are assigned to the Exchange today, and practices state we don't go heavy during Festival." He gestured at the racks of armor and rifles.

"You have an assignment and you adhere to practices," Rutherford agreed. "Unless what."

A broad shouldered woman stepped forward, considering Rutherford. "Unless your pike says otherwise," she said. "You a pike?"

"Functionally," Rutherford replied. "So suit up. We leave in nine." He turned to Clamp. "Get us a wagon."

"A wagon," Clamp echoed. "During Festival."

Rutherford looked back to the squad. "Nine minutes, west gate, heavy gear. Any halfcoat doesn't make it on time is off the squad ongoing, get me? Move." He pivoted and continued through the Cave towards the back entrance, Clamp at his side.

"A wagon!" Clamp demanded.

"We are racing news," Rutherford repeated. "Only a few people alive could predict in two days I'd go from provisional to getting a squad and leeway to work, we need surprise."

"How about you?" Clamp shot back, dodging a sweaty knot of Bluecoats who entered the Cave, weary from a Festival night. "Were you surprised?"

"Get the wagon," Rutherford replied, and he headed up the stairs as Clamp stared after him. Making a decision.

Clamp got the wagon.

SMOKE TOWER, BOOKEND SQUARE, FOGCREST, SILKSHORE. 25TH VOLVINET. FIRST HOUR PAST DAWN. SAIL LIGHTING FESTIVAL, DAY THREE.

Spindle and Crackstone left the shadow of the tower, approaching where Sanction waited in the coach. They climbed up inside, and the door snapped shut behind them.

"That took a long time," Spindle said through his teeth.

"There was some confusion around where you were held, and in fact *whether* you were being held. While we were sorting that out, we had troubles of our own," Sanction replied.

"I heard about Drassle," Spindle nodded.

"You heard more in a cell than some of my associates managed while at liberty," Sanction replied shortly. "We must talk about next steps. Before you got pinched, what did you find out about Rutherford."

"He's a canny bastard," Spindle said. "I mean, you already knew that, but he saw this coming and we didn't. He could take steps while there weren't eyes on him. Did Piccolo really get nabbed?"

"Yes," Sanction said. He rapped on the ceiling in the cab with his cane head, and the carriage jolted into motion, one of the goats letting out a throaty yell as the driver's reins twitched. "Rutherford is playing games. Burned our house down, let Drassle die, *then* caught the assassin while Piccolo was fighting him."

"Where are we headed, boss?" Spindle asked, expressionless and reserved.

Sanction leaned back and looked out the window. "Barness. Call in a few favors. Do some damage control."

Spindle and Crackstone stared at Sanction. "But... boss," Spindle said. "Barness? I mean, he's Hive, and everyone knows it; I thought we were keeping our distance."

"These are desperate times and I'm short on resources," Sanction replied, eyes flickering around the landscape that shifted as the carriage rolled. "I don't like it either. Now is the time to work some angles and deploy some resources in the Fairpole Gondolier Council that I've been saving for a special occasion." He looked Spindle in the eye. "Barness has some influence with the gondoliers." He left the rest unsaid.

"They didn't give us our weapons back. Just a knife each," Crackstone said, frowning.

"I didn't bring you weapons because we're going to a meet and they'll check you over anyway," Sanction replied. "If you need weapons in the moment, take them from Barness's guards."

Crackstone nodded, satisfied, then they all held on as the carriage heeled around a tight corner, headed towards the riverside.

A few minutes later, they climbed out of the carriage, and it rattled off. Sanction led the way, closing in on a low wall with a metal gate. "I'm here to see Barness," he said to the guard. "Sanction, with the Silkworms."

"Wait here," the guard on the other side of the gate said. He withdrew as another guard stepped up in his place.

Looking through the grating, they saw an unassuming building squatting on the paved riverbank, "Quality Drydock" lettered across its flank in ancient, peeling paint. Past the wall gate, two guards leaned by the front door, dressed to blend.

Sanction didn't wait long. The guard immediately returned, hauling the gate open, and Sanction headed through. The guards by the door patted the three visitors down for weapons, letting them keep their knives, and one guard escorted them inside the musty building and up the stairs to the office.

Barness sat behind his desk, comfortably reclined with his feet up, enjoying a pipe of something that burned with a thick and bittersweet tang. His cleanshaven jaw gave his features a narrow look, and his mane of hair was elaborately braided.

"Welcome, Sanction," he said without rising. "Considering we keep our communications low profile, showing up here with two agents is a bold move."

"This is not a time for being careful," Sanction replied. "What are we going to do with the gondoliers?"

"Straight to business, I like that about you," Barness nodded. "Did you bring Trellis? That's who they want to deal with directly, you've not made the best impression with them over the last couple years." He took a deep pull on his pipe. "They don't feel you made the most of the benefit of the doubt that they extended to you because of your connections."

"I did everything I promised to them, and more," Sanction replied, "until Drassle."

"Not all of them would agree," Barness observed. "Some feel you adjust your promises after the fact, so they fit the outcomes better than the expectations."

"Like getting permits for a drydock then using the building for a warehouse?" Sanction replied with the suggestion of a wry smile.

Barness did not return his smile. "The Ministry is a stickler for rules, and the gondoliers are too. If you want—" He paused, then rose and crossed the office to look out the window.

Four Bluecoats at the gate, in armor, with rifles. Shoving past the guards. Raised voices. A gun, then two plumes of fire and a dead guard, melee in the courtyard.

"Let's move the conversation," Barness said shortly as he snatched up his jacket and a chest small enough to tuck under his arm. He stepped into the back alcove and tugged a hidden switch, snapping open a secret door. Sanction and his people followed closely as Barness headed down the narrow steps and out the back door.

"Hey!" yelled a Bluecoat from the mouth of the alleyway by the drydock. "Hold fast for questions!" She ran towards them.

"Off we go," Barness muttered, and he broke into a run towards the quay and the gondola moored there. Sanction was on his heels as they approached the boat. Gunfire crackled and popped on the other side of the drydock.

"Surprise," said a hard voice, and Barness stopped short as he was confronted by a Bluecoat on the gondola already, leveling a rifle at his chest. Glancing to the sides, they saw a Bluecoat blocking each direction. One of them was Rutherford.

"We are witnesses," Rutherford said. "You were told to hold fast for questions, and you ran. That's enough by itself to establish some factuals and grant exception to your freedom."

"Are you seriously having me *followed*?" Sanction demanded through his teeth.

"Happy accident, us meeting like this. I'm here for him." Rutherford smiled at Barness. "And his warehouse."

"Right, you're Rutherford," Barness said as comprehension dawned. He shot a sidelong glance at Sanction. "Fantastic."

"Now what?" Sanction said, defiance in the set of his shoulders.

"Bluecoats have discretion with whether or not to grant exception to freedom to those who run from them," Sanction explained. "Barness, we keep. You two," he said to Spindle and Crackstone, "my apologies for detaining you earlier, consider this some restitution. Off you go."

"Nice," Sanction said through his teeth. "And me?"

"On your way," Rutherford said, with an almost lazy grin.

More Bluecoats were approaching, and it was clearly the wrong moment to continue the conversation. Sanction turned and walked away. Spindle and Crackstone followed while Barness shook his head.

"You utter bastard," he muttered. "I'll have your job for this. Your life."

"My loved ones?" Rutherford said, sardonic.

"*Everyone* knows better than to take a closer look here," Barness said calmly. "When your superiors realize what you've done, how you've put them at risk, they won't be pleased."

"I know," Rutherford confided in him, his grin almost boyish. "This is *so naughty*. Still. It's not you I'm after."

"Well there's no one else here," Barness said with a touch of acid behind his tone.

"There is though," Rutherford replied, looking Barness in the eye.

Barness worked through some very swift calculations, then nodded. "Behind the central drawer," he said under his breath.

"Clamp, take the box, then follow me," Rutherford said. He turned, striding towards the secret exit Barness had used. Clamp only hesitated for a moment, then he gestured towards Barness, who grimaced and handed over the box. Clamp tucked it under his arm and jogged after Rutherford. The remaining Bluecoat kept his rifle trained on Barness, glancing back and forth between Rutherford's retreating back and the detained suspect.

Barness squared off with him, arching an eyebrow. Inviting him to make a decision.

The Bluecoat swore under his breath and ran after Rutherford. Barness watched him go, then stepped down into the gondola and cast off.

Rutherford was up the stairs in a handful of heartbeats, in the office. As Clamp clattered up the stairs, Rutherford dropped to all fours and climbed under the desk, squinting up in the dimness. He banged on a knee switch, then rose to his feet, pulling the drawer all the way out, reaching behind it. He pocketed the leather-bound diary as Clamp entered the room with a Bluecoat on his heels, and the door to the hall banged open as another Bluecoat found the office while he was clearing the building. He was shocked to see Rutherford and Clamp, but he quickly regained his composure.

"We're all good, Welker. Report," Rutherford said calmly.

"Thugs at the gate put up a show, but no casualties on our side," the massive Bluecoat said. "Says 'drydock' outside but it's used as a warehouse, pretty sure there will be customs questions."

"Carry on," Rutherford nodded. "Search the place. Draw up charges. Any prisoners?"

"The guards. Anyone to add?"

"The rest got away," Rutherford replied. "Secret exit," he gestured towards where Clamp stood. "Carry on, I'll search all this. You, help him," he said, pointing to the Bluecoat by Clamp. Rutherford turned to the shelves behind the desk. Welker and the other Bluecoat returned to the search.

Clamp approached him. "You play like a pro but I can't see the game," he said quietly.

"Coded ledgers," Rutherford said with a satisfied smile, drawing a leather-bound book from a shelf and slapping it down on the desk. He flicked it open, revealing scrawl.

A breathless Bluecoat rattled up the stairs from the drydock. "Sir!" he yelled. "We found cash! Guns! None of the crates here have customs seals!"

"Good job!" Rutherford barked. "Four of you stay here and pack it up, the other two go with Clamp and take the prisoners to the tower. Let's get this place processed." He cracked his knuckles. "See who shows up to claim all of it." He grinned at Clamp.

"What just happened here?" Clamp muttered. "Is this the captain's win you promised?"

"The start of it, yes," Rutherford replied, squaring off with him. "I know you don't understand some of this, and I know you can see the backlash coming. But it feels good. Doesn't it." He didn't have to explain.

"Yeah," Clamp replied. "Now we'll see if it's worth it."

Rutherford chuckled, a low and unpleasant sound. Then he started piling up books.

FOUNDRYSIDE ROW, SMOKER'S CORNER, FOGCREST, SILKSHORE. 25TH VOLVINET. SECOND HOUR PAST DAWN. SAIL LIGHTING FESTIVAL, DAY THREE.

Cellar limped towards the end of the long, long row. He felt his blood batter its way into his skull, and fall out the bottom afterwards. His sinuses were full of what felt like the residue of beer continuing to ferment in him. His surroundings wavered with every step, but refused to resolve into a more pleasant picture. Almost home.

After an eternity of stairs, he leaned on the door to his home, fumbling with the knob so the door opened before his shoulder's weight. He stopped short.

Daava sat at the table, with a number of family members joining her, and more standing around behind. They had quieted as they heard his approach. All eyes were on him. Daava forced a smile.

"There you are," she said as casually as she could. "We need to have a chat!" As if it was a joke.

Cellar didn't have to look to feel the worry radiating from Saya and several other family members. He rolled his eyes.

"Spend all night undercover and here we are back to work," he complained. "Arright, let's go," he added with a sweeping gesture as though he was holding the door for Daava.

"Thank you so much for your hospitality," Daava said to the family as she rose, and she bowed deeply. "I'll keep him out of trouble!" she yelled, and several focused family members grinned and offered various thumbs-up and other signs of encouragement. She headed out the door, and Cellar pulled it shut, following her down the stairs, trying his best to leave his family's worried looks and awkward questions as far behind as possible.

"So that was great," Daava said, focusing on the stairs as she led the way down. "They didn't know, and I didn't tell them. But they saw I wasn't in your shadow."

"Yeah," Cellar growled. "Great. Look, it was a long night. What is this." He stopped, three stories down from his home.

Daava turned, halfway down the next flight. "Where were you last night. Really. Honestly." She was watchful, tense.

"I was at the park. Getting drunk. Watching the idiots." He shrugged. "Disappearing. You heard I'm off duty, right? Anyway, whatever. Who is asking?"

"Pull yourself together," Daava hissed. "The hammer is whistling down. You just got duty respite for crossing the Tick Tock, and you disappeared without a word. Same night, *Spur turns up murdered.*"

"What?" Cellar gasped, the shock concussing him all the way out of drunkenness and deeper into his hang over. He clutched at the railing.

"That's just the start of it," Daava said through her teeth. "Chief Inspector Prichard is already on the site. He demanded your presence. We gotta go. We gotta go *now.*"

Cellar lowered himself to sit on the top step of Daava's flight, his face ashen, his eyes wide, his mind racing. "We need—we need to find someone—confirm where I was," he said, "nail down some factuals."

She winced at his smell. "Do *you* remember?" she asked.

"Mostly," he waved towards her question. "I mean... oh, this isn't great."

"It really isn't," she agreed, an unusual distance in her eyes.

Cellar squinted at the look as he realized what it was.

"You believe me, right," he demanded.

"I do," she said, reserved. "I choose to. We gotta establish your innocence."

He blinked three times, then rose to his feet.

"Let's go."

━━┐ CHAPTER TEN ┌━━

The Exchange is so named because its waters pass the banks of the Ease, Fogcrest, and Eastbank, allowing transition from one to the other. Day and night, the Exchange bustles with river traffic that continually restores the vitality of Silkshore. Running water is a universal symbol for renewal, drawing inspiration from the blood ceaselessly flowing through each of us and the life that represents. Some mystics call the Exchange the Heart of Silkshore. Certain powerful Iruvian families only solemnize marriage on a platform towed to the center of the Exchange, as the ceremony represents a commitment to stability resting on ceaseless change.

— From "Venues for Ritual: Location and Legacy in Doskvol"
by Gerard Feenworthy

The cab jolted, and Cellar involuntarily swore as his head banged off the wall.

"Seriously though," Daava said, just loud enough to be heard over the clatter of the metal-shod wheels on cobblestone, "are you holding together?" Only a hint of worry escaped her cool expression.

"That's the purpose of the heavy drinking," Cellar growled, wincing as he rubbed his forehead. "I don't really care to know the answer to that question myself."

"Right," she nodded. "So, your family. They aren't all deaf," she clarified.

"Course not," he shrugged, and he squinted out the window as his grip shifted to massaging the back of his neck. "But the family work is factories, foundries, smithies. Enough of us were deaf that basically everybody learns the signs young, and it's an easy way to talk in a noisy place or with someone who cannot hear you. Becomes second nature. The bigger challenge is when people lose their vision too, and you have to sign by touch into the palm of the hand. I can never remember anything past the basics," he sighed. "Bedpan? Where hurt? Hungry?" He tried to chuckle.

"They seem really sweet, really open," she said. "I know you didn't expect—you know, respite—so for the basics, food, or—if..." Daava bit her lip, unsure how to go on.

"Blood and bone, Daava," Cellar gritted out, staring out the window.

"If you asked me," she said clearly, brows contracted, "I would—I know you are important to them and I don't want them to lose anything. Basic needs, in the short term, if you *asked me* I might—" She frowned, clenching her jaw. "So you know."

"Now *that's* out of the way," he said, "why the hell is Prichard on the site? Why is he asking for *me*?"

"I hear the murder was—spectacular," she replied, withdrawing. "Causing quite a stir. Lots of Bluecoats on the scene for some reason. I didn't ask around, I figured you'd want to get into this as fast as possible. Sir." She drew out her pipe, tucking in a pre-packed ball, managing a hand-held sparker. The rattle of the carriage crossing another bridge didn't faze her as she lit up.

Cellar gazed sightlessly out the window as they passed a choir on a tavern balcony singing over the dining area, a street hastily converted to a patio for the festival. The soaring harmony shifted in and out of dissonance as they clattered by.

"Don't even know what that means," Cellar muttered to himself, fighting hard to push back the murk he had deliberately wound around the machinery of his keen investigative mind. A nightmarish tinge settled in the bleary corners of the world. The details in his vision were not nearly sharp enough yet. The carriage slowed once more, approaching another canal bridge and a cordon of Bluecoats.

"Go round," one barked, already angry before they arrived. "Closed off, go round!'

"This is where we get out," Daava said around the pipe stem clenched in her teeth, jabbing at the door handle and stepping out of the carriage with long-legged ease. Cellar struggled out after her as she flashed credentials at the Bluecoats.

"Special, Inspector Cellar reporting, executive request," she said crisply, pipe in one hand and credentials in the other. The Bluecoat nodded and stepped aside, and Cellar trudged after Daava as she headed up the bridge.

"Snap the big and little bones," he breathed as he reached the top of the short bridge's arch. His eyes widened as he looked over the swarm of Bluecoats and commandeered support that seethed across the Exchange dockside.

"Missive said he'd be at the Salvage," Daava said, not looking over her shoulder as she headed down into the chaos. Cellar set his jaw and followed, trying not to feel like he was in her shadow.

They approached the looming profile of the public house jutting out on the foundation of multiple piers, overbuilt into the most famous establishment on the Fogcrest shore of the Exchange. A crowd impatiently shifted in a corral to one side as six Bluecoats noted factuals before releasing them, and a lantern-lit tent sheltered exhausted Bluecoat runners in service to the leadership inside. Three Bluecoat towers planted standards outside the Salvage Site, headquarters colors. Adrenaline peaked in Cellar at the sight, submerging his hangover.

Daava and Cellar leaned through the foot traffic, entering the cavernous common room of the public house, orienting on the standard propped up by the bar with the Smoke Tower colors and the Chief Inspector bars.

"Tolja so," drawled a Bluecoat stationed by the door as they entered, tossing the comment over his shoulder at a disgruntled comrade. "Digger showed! You owe me a dozen eels."

"Dumbass," the other Bluecoat muttered as Cellar ignored him, closing in on the back corner.

Cellar swallowed hard as he recognized the Chief of the City Navy, face red, yelling at the Minister of Bluecoats for Silkshore.

"*Our* barge, *our* site, it may be parked in *your* waters but the Naval Code is clear!" the Chief of the City Navy shouted.

"You want to invoke Code, Chief Vale?" the Minister of Bluecoats replied, one eyebrow arched, her hawkish face unmoved. "I have the discretion to deny any towing across the Exchange for any other agency pending review, should I deem it necessary. This goes smoother if we all cooperate, this jurisdictional flexing is not a good look for you," she observed. "If you had not sent your troops aboard to disrupt the area, then there would be more clues for my Inspectors—"

"Your Inspectors," the Chief of the City Navy scoffed. "Minister Tralin, all due respect, they take hours to draw scribbles of blood drops, and we need decisive action!"

Cellar flinched as an iron grip snatched his elbow, steering him to the side. He found himself face to face with Chief Inspector Prichard, who stared him in the eye.

"Did you do this?" the captain hissed, the smell of a rough morning on his breath. His features were drawn, and energy surged under the cold severity of his face.

"I swear I didn't," Cellar protested, quiet but intense.

"You better be able to prove it," Prichard snapped. "Factuals. Credible ones. Where were you."

"Drunk and out of pocket, people-watching at the park," Cellar said clearly, struggling not to wince at the news.

Prichard stared at him for an impossibly long moment. "Witnesses?" he demanded.

"I was dressed to blend, an idiot among idiots," Cellar replied.

The Chief Inspector sucked a tooth, releasing Cellar's arm as he leaned back. "Find someone. You need factuals. This isn't jail time; if this is pinned on you—" He glanced back over his shoulder as a harried messenger pushed past, then returned his attention to Cellar. "Daava, stay in this fool's shadow. Even though he's on duty respite. When the facts come to light," he growled under his breath, staring into Cellar's eye, "everyone will look at you. Get out of the way. Stay home. Establish factuals for every point from here to when you're called. Multiple witnesses, not just family and friends." He leaned in close. "Don't provoke anyone. Don't even breathe sideways. Do you understand."

Cellar managed a curt nod, and the Chief Inspector suppressed the rest of his thoughts and feelings, turning away. "We'll be quick," he said, cutting into the argument between the minister and the chief. "Twenty minutes and out, and we'll have leads."

"How can you be sure?" demanded Chief Vale.

"My people are the best," the Prichard replied, correctly assuming that Cellar had already moved on from behind him.

Cellar resisted the impulse to gulp at the air as they slipped out of the Salvage into the differently-textured thick air outside.

"Yeah, we're going back to your place *right now*," Daava said through her teeth, glancing around, fear barely visible at the edges of her neutral expression. She tapped out the spent bowl of her pipe.

"The hell we are," Cellar replied, eyes closed as he sought his balance. "I'm going to take a look at the murder site."

"Oh?" she retorted, arching an eyebrow. "We're past protecting your dignity, Cellar; this is your life, the lives of everyone around you. If this murder sticks to you—"

"I know that!" he said, eyes snapping open and locking with hers. "I am absolutely aware of that, and there's a reason I'm an Inspector and not a Bluecoat." His eyes had the gleam once again, the scent, the hunt. "I must investigate, this is self-defense." He squared off with her. "Or you trust the other Inspectors to solve this and clear me. I go down, that's not good for my Specials. We solve it, together, and pin the noise where it belongs."

"Go, special in your shadow," she said with a tight gesture, looking away.

Cellar was on his way through the bustle, Daava close behind, and a few minutes of navigating the crowd brought them to the knot of Bluecoats and tangle of rafts that could go out to service the barge anchored in the middle of the Exchange. His heart sank further as he saw the insignias on the outfits and felt the tension radiating from the Bluecoats; all three districts of the Exchange shores, multiple Towers from each district, the Stevedores, military officers, Ministry functionaries, a Fairpole Gondolier Council speaker organizing festival activities...

"Your plan?" Daava demanded.

"Hang back. A moment will present itself," Cellar scowled, and he stepped out of the throughway, between two piles of boxes. Crossing his arms and ignoring his own smell, he leaned back against the wall, his face set. Daava kicked over a box and seated herself, watching the way they came, her thoughts loud but unshared.

Minutes passed, sifting away, and Cellar shrugged against the sense that his hourglass was emptying. Then he frowned at a broad-shouldered figure approaching. "Damn," he swore softly. He took a deep breath, steeled himself, and stepped back into the roadway, closing in, Daava at his heels.

"Inspector Clelland," Cellar said, "I need a word."

Clelland turned, looking over at him, and raised his eyebrows. "Dress code, Digger," he said with what was meant to sound like camaraderie.

"Undercover," Cellar shrugged. "Look, I need to get out to the barge." He looked Clelland in the eye.

Clelland nodded. "In my shadow, Digger, let's go," he said crisply. Turning, he approached the various factions bristling by the rafts.

"Look, fellas, I got four seals," he said to the crowd, holding up his investigative exception. "Took me an hour to get it. That's all the bosses we could get in one place as we're coordinating this nightmare. Just need a raft, I'm headed out with my Specials. Anybody want to make this difficult, step on up," he said, an easy comfort with physical and bureaucratic violence oozing from his relaxed stance and his confident tone.

His reputation preceded him. No one stood in his way as he followed the edge of the pier and dropped down on a raft. "You're rowing," he said with a toothy grin, nodding to Cellar, who gripped the sculling oar and set his stance as Daava cast off the mooring line and jumped down on the raft. They bumped clear of the other rafts, headed out towards the massive military resupply barge anchored in the middle of the Exchange.

"So you heard it's Spur," Clelland verified, not looking back at the others.

"I heard," Cellar replied.

"I heard you were on duty respite, something about stripers and the Tick Tock," Clelland continued, examining the barge. "What, about ten days ago you tried to bring Spur in? Establish factuals or something?"

"You were there," Cellar replied, trying to keep his tone even.

"I sure was," Clelland agreed. "Crazy move, trying to brute force it. Drag Spur in. He's connected, you knew that. It's like you're getting more and more frustrated."

"Yeah, it looks that way," Cellar agreed. "Just ask." He focused his energy on shoving the oar back and forth, aiming the raft's traversal of the sluggish current.

"Tell me about your alibi," Clelland said quietly, thoughtful.

"I drank my way to Ankhayat Park and passed out. I don't have an alibi," Cellar said through his teeth.

"Heh, you didn't do this," Clelland said with half a grin. "You're an idiot, but you know better than to skimp on factuals. If you were going to kill somebody you'd have four ways to prove it wasn't you." He looked back over his shoulder, something like pity in his eyes. "Even if you did have a total mental breakdown. You know you aren't above the law, that's not the kind of drunk you are when you get a taste of that sweet, sweet authority." His smile was almost real. "You're just convenient."

Caught between an exasperating variety of feelings in the moment, Cellar had no reply.

Clelland returned his attention to the barge. "Still. This is embarrassing for lots of people, and they need to solve it fast. You're close at hand and defenseless. I don't like your odds."

"I don't either," Cellar grunted, hauling at the oar.

As the raft drifted into the shadow of the barge, a Bluecoat staggered to the edge of the barge and explosively vomited over the side, the puke splatting down in the river.

"Great," Daava muttered, neatly looping the mooring line over the footing on the barge and tugging it into place. Clelland was first to swarm up the short ladder, Cellar and Daava right behind him.

"Steady," Clelland said, his voice crisp as he clapped the shaken Bluecoat on the shoulder, helping him straighten. He took in the Bluecoat's ashen features, tinged green, and the tremble in his limbs. "What's the situation?"

"S-securing the scene," the Bluecoat replied, feebly wiping at his mouth. "I saw it. The—the victim," he managed.

"Over this way?" Clelland gestured, ruthless direction clear under his sympathetic tone.

"Yes sir," the Bluecoat nodded, and he coughed slightly, turning back towards the water. The Inspectors crossed the narrow apron onto the central deck, climbing another ladder to the watch deck of the resupply barge. A number of Bluecoats were finishing a canvas wall stretched on a framework around the center of the watch deck, around the tower. They deferentially stepped aside, letting the Inspectors pass.

"Finally, we have Inspectors," said a tall woman in a smock, tinged green by the algae lamps in the canvas enclosure. She tucked her notebook under one arm, cocking her head to the side and regarding them. "Inspector Clelland, Inspector Cellar. So pleased to see you." Her smile was hollow. The last years of middle age had slipped away from her, but she had the authority of a matriarch ingrained in her wrinkle-mapped features.

"Doctor Vanwhyle," Clelland replied with a smart bow. "I feel better already." He glanced around, noting that there was only one stone-faced Bluecoat in the enclosure with them, as required by procedure, to prevent adding or subtracting evidence from the scene. "I am relieved you're here, what have you done so far?"

"Marked out the area, examined what I could without touching anything, noted my initial observations," Vanwhyle said. She paused, and looked over at the Bluecoat. "Thank you," she said clearly, dismissing him.

Something in his face relaxed, and he stepped out of the enclosure with almost comical speed. Vanwhyle waited a moment longer, then returned her attention to the Inspectors, her features grim "This is ugly," she said under her breath. "I sent out an identification of the victim, Spur, he was with the Tick Tock. I'm familiar with his work. I could identify him based on a number of tattoos."

"He's unrecognizable? Something happen to his face?" Clelland asked.

Vanwhyle weighed the question for a moment. "Let's just have a look together," she said, her voice tight.

"Come on," Clelland protested. "You've presided over more death scenes than the god of vultures. This one is special?"

She turned away, walking around the base of the tower, not answering. Rattled, Clelland followed, with Daava and Cellar in his shadow.

The smell grew stronger as they approached; the almost-sweet stink of the death slipping in after the last breaths, the full-bodied exhalation of all life from a corpse. The copper tang of blood flavored the air, as well as the last convulsive excretion of a body sinking into death's relaxation.

Cellar frowned at the cable wrapped around the base of the viewing deck tower, and he saw the victim was tied to the pole. As the Inspectors rounded the scene at a distance of a few paces, he suddenly stopped, feeling his own stomach buck in sympathetic rejection of the horrific sight before him.

"No, no no no," Clelland frowned, eyes wide. "That's—that's not right."

"I know what you mean," Doctor Vanwhyle said, crossing her arms to hug her notebook to her chest.

Spur's corpse was tied to the pole. Loops of cable supported his weight, securing his forearms to the pole and holding his body weight up by his elbows. Hair hung around the gory ruin of his head, a slick shine of muscle and bone where his face should be. His face was cut off his head with surgical precision and care, a clean line along his jaw and forehead—and his face had been tacked on to his chest, stretched and nailed in place over a welter of blood. Chest hair sprouted through ragged eye-holes and spilled out of his lipless mouth slit, his features flatly distorted.

"This is—the Skullface Killer did work like this," Clelland said, taking a step back. "But those killings—they were done about what, six years ago? Eight?"

"The last one was ten years ago," Doctor Vanwhyle replied. "They pulled me in to work the last four. It's not something you forget."

"Does this match?" Clelland demanded, rounding on her. "The details, does it—are we looking at the Skullface Killer? Maybe a fan stepping up instead, or a distraction from some other motive?"

"If so, it's a good copy, very precise," Doctor Vanwhyle said, eyes fixed on the corpse. "There is one detail that only four people would know to look for, and one of them would be the killer. I wanted to wait for another Inspector before I verified, but I am going to do it here rather than waiting until I get the body back to my lab."

Cellar and Daava exchanged a shocked look as the implications tumbled past them, but they said nothing.

Doctor Vanwhyle's features twitched as she tugged a set of pliers from her belt and handed her notebook to Daava. Then she approached the corpse, and began working the nails out of the chest, her other hand pressing against the face to hold it in place. The sounds were nauseating; subtle squishing, slithering exits, and clinks of the discarded nails dropping into a metal pan.

"Body is still cooling," Doctor Vanwhyle said through her teeth. "Whoever killed Spur did it around dawn. During festival. In full view of river traffic, on a patrolled barge. And got away. Same cuts to the vocal cords and stab by the diaphragm as the Skullface Killer used. After that attack, maybe Spur could moan; tied in place, he couldn't make any other noise. Ball of muslin with numbing drugs stuffed in the mouth, bite marks on the tongue, as in previous cases; poor bastard couldn't feel the damage he was doing by working his jaw, but the numbing trickle into his throat and sinuses robbed him of power to cry out."

She tossed her pliers aside, straightening, her hands pressed against the face on Spur's chest. "Ready?" she said grimly. As though it mattered.

She peeled the face off the chest. Horror deepened the furrows in the foreheads of the onlookers as they stared at the complex glyph carved into a shaved area the size of the palm of a hand, right in the center of the chest, covered by the face skin.

"What." Clelland's voice was flat.

"Cartilaginous," Doctor Vanwhyle swore softly. "This confirms it. I guess the Skullface Killer took a decade off but..." she trailed off, the skin of the face hanging from where she pinched its corners. "Here we go again."

Daava tucked Doctor Vanwhyle's notebook under one arm and pulled out her own pad, steadying her hand as she squinted at the glyph and back at her paper, sketching a copy.

"You realize now there are seven people who have seen this glyph," Doctor Vanwhyle said quietly. "Do what you need to do to solve this. But be careful to keep this detail quiet." She aimed a sideways look at them. "Understand?"

"Absolutely," Clelland replied as Daava and Cellar nodded mutely.

The blood had become tacky in the last couple hours, and when Doctor Vanwhyle pressed the skin back over the chest it slid on with an oozing squelch. "Give me a couple nails," she said. Cellar was at her elbow, but Clelland pushed him away.

"Don't you touch *anything*," he said sharply. "You're the most likely killer, you fool. If any ritual, any close examination, anything points to you that will be enough." He bent down, picking up a couple nails, handing them to the doctor. She lightly tacked the skin back in place, using existing holes.

"What can we do," Clelland asked, "to get this thing packed up, on its way. Clear the area. We need to get moving." The tremble in his voice was almost inaudible.

Doctor Vanwhyle turned to regard Cellar, and there was a new hardness in her eyes. "This one is suspected?" she demanded.

"He's the likely pick," Clelland agreed, "but I only let him come with me out here because I didn't think he did it. Silly bastard doesn't have an alibi. But this—you would have been, what, ten years old when the killings stopped? Eleven?"

"Some would say it couldn't be you," Doctor Vanwhyle agreed, eyes narrowing.

"Hell of a cover if you somehow did find out who did it, what that glyph was about," Clelland agreed, studying Cellar. "It's a clumsy look not to have an alibi. Too clumsy for this kind of detail work."

"Hey," Cellar said sharply, face flushed with emotion. "*I did not do this.*"

"That's the trouble," Doctor Vanwhyle said quietly. "Whoever did this is both completely insane and very detail-oriented, with nerves of steel and... I mean, so public. Just like the others." She shook her head. "I'm not sure we can assume anything about what kind of thoughts drive this sort of work."

"Yeah, I guess Cellar here isn't the only idiot on the barge," Clelland said. Several emotions drove an energy into his step as he closed with Cellar and got a fistful of his shirt, leaning close. "Don't make me sorry I trusted you here."

"We're gonna solve this," Cellar retorted, fumbling towards confidence. But he felt the echo of the great minds that had bent all their energies and resources towards trying to catch the Skullface Killer a decade ago. Tried and failed. And he felt his world collapsing in on him. "I—I need to look around, see if there are any footprints, discarded tools or trash, scuffs—"

"No," Clelland said. "No, you've seen enough, and I've taken a bigger chance than I realized. You are going back to the dock now." He looked at Daava. "You're going with him."

"In his shadow," she agreed, shaken.

Clelland turned his back on Cellar, facing Doctor Vanwhyle, an unusual apologetic cast to his demeanor. "What do you need from me," he said.

She deliberately looked at Cellar, who nodded curtly and turned, stepping through the canvas barricade, passing the Bluecoat, scrambling down the ladder, heading for the raft. Daava was in his shadow.

"Too tough to row upstream back to the dock where we started," he said through his teeth. He jumped down to the raft. "We'll have to aim for landfall downstream."

"Yeah," Daava agreed. "I think that's best." She unmoored the raft, and the current started them off with a gentle, insistent tug. Ignoring the burn in his muscles, Cellar set his stance and sculled towards the dim shoreline.

"Blood and bone," Cellar said, a distant look in his eye. "This barge. It's City Navy. The Exchange is the Canal Watch. Each shore has multiple towers, that's at least two each for Fogcrest, the Ease, and Eastbank. The Stevedores are involved; if so much as one crate needs to be moved from one place to another, they will want in. The Fairpole Gondolier Council. The Inspectors." His mouth was dry. "No one is going to get clear control on this, but everybody is going to know about it."

"Spur humiliated you publically. Proved you couldn't touch him. Tick Tock got you put on respite, for a start, and all those consequences haven't landed yet," Daava said, her back to the shore as she looked him in the eye. "Bad timing."

"For me," Cellar retorted, "but great for somebody else." He shook his head. "We have *got* to make sure I can establish factuals for every movement from here on out. Maybe get some more Specials involved, protect your reputation."

"Thoughtful of you," Daava said, her tone neutral, her eyes expressionless.

"I need you to believe I didn't do it," he said through his teeth.

"No, you need me to be trustworthy when I'm establishing your factuals," she replied. "If our people think I'd lie for you, then my word is worthless."

"Of course you're right," Cellar agreed, the admission costing him something. He felt the distance between them as more expansive than two paces. Daava looked down at her notebook, eyes tracing the strange glyph.

"At least we have a place to start," she murmured.

"I will need to check with some mystics, somebody with a deep background with occult lore, Forgotten Gods, that sort of thing," Cellar agreed. "Somebody outside Silkshore, for sure." He frowned. "Who do we know?"

"That's a good question," Daava replied. "And how well do we know them?" She cocked her head to the side. "I suppose you have an idea of just the person."

"I do not, actually," Cellar replied, stung and trying to suppress the feeling. "We'll check with Jayan, he's got some weird friends." He looked out over the water. "Friends of friends. Meanwhile, what do you know about the Skullface Killer?"

"I'm younger than you," she retorted.

"You're my special because you're damn sharp," Cellar sighed. "Anything?"

"Well," she said, "there were ten killings over the span of about a week, all in Silkshore, in 839. All of them in public places, with this kind of surgical mutilation; Skullface Killer because he cut the faces off the skull. There was a lot of noise about how the victims were still alive until shock killed them at the very end, the killer knows surgery and drugs. And cruelty." She swallowed at the bile climbing her throat. "It's different in black and white, on paper," she observed.

"We need to know everything we can find out about that last killing spree. And if there were ten a decade ago, maybe there will be a pattern that emerges this time. We can get ahead of this. Catch the killer in the act."

"We'd be heroes," she said, looking back at the squat silhouette of the barge.

"I don't even know what that means," he replied, the oar getting heavier as he pushed and pulled. "I just need to get free of this. Feels like a net. Closing in."

The misty shoreline didn't seem to be getting any closer.

CHAPTER ELEVEN

The Mortal Reflex, or "yawning," is the primeval attunement. As life energy drains through weariness or proximity to unconsciousness, the body signals a need to recalibrate the senses. You stretch and flex the jaw and surrounding flesh, ingest a mass of air, and imitate the tight rigor of death stealing through muscle. The yawn rebalances the normalized perspective. Adepts and Whispers can refocus their awareness on a whim. However, even newborns can shift the range of their perceptions with a yawn, so if an apparition or shadow in the Ghost Field is near they are more likely to detect it. Yawning provides adjustment to pressure shifts in the Ghost Field as well as shifts in air pressure.

— From "Physiological Signals"
by Dr. Talis Eubarrian Keenwither

The butler graciously opened the door and stepped aside so Sanction could enter the echoing tiled space of the bath chamber. Trellis relaxed in the massive tub on the dais, obscured to the chest by soapy water, surrounded by candles. The slow scraping harmonies of a string quartet wavered from the cylinder player in the corner.

"You look comfortable," Sanction observed, clasping his hands behind his back.

"I've been working hard, thought I would treat myself," Trellis replied with a wry smile. He shifted position, leaning his head back and closing his eyes. "Nothing like a good soak."

Sanction examined a number of possible responses, but found himself speechless.

Trellis opened one eye, then heaved a sigh and sat up straight. "Of course you're right. On to business. Set up a meet with Bear, it's time to give him some leverage against the Hive."

"Bear?" Sanction retorted. "You're still looking at North Port?"

"Of course," Trellis agreed, "that's our next move. Orris is not ready to make the pitch to Vale to recruit the Fog Hounds, and he's not positioned to antagonize Sagliarre directly at this point, so as he moves against Bear that's our opportunity to counter. As long as Bear is holding Orris's attention, we've got more space to maneuver behind the scenes in getting our strategy in place." He cocked his head to the side. "We already talked about this."

"We have talked about *many things*," Sanction agreed carefully, "including Master Drassel's assassination, the Fairpole Council's fury with us to the point where they won't even talk to me and instead they want a meet with you, Piccolo's imprisonment, this mess between the Foundation and the Church; while our own affairs are in disarray, this is—timing may need some consideration, yes?" Sanction said as diplomatically as he could.

"Timing is key to all of this," Trellis sighed, leaning back. "I believe Orris is about to decide that Bear can be safely ignored, and I think he may be right. So we need to refocus him on Bear, and that means he's got to lose something to our man. I think it is time to cash in Barness."

He reached a sudsy arm out of the tub, catching up the wineglass from the conveniently placed table and taking a sip.

Sanction gave himself a few seconds to regulate his tone. "Do you think I can be safely ignored?"

"No, that wouldn't be wise, you've got a petty little mean streak and a penchant for tantrums," Trellis replied, something lazy in his tone. He savored another sip from the wineglass.

"I'm demanding you pay attention to the Silkworms and our trifling troubles before we go on meddling with others," Sanction said through his teeth. "Are you prepared to ignore my demand?"

"Oh, yes, your demands," Trellis agreed. "I'll ignore them. But not you." He looked Sanction in the eye, still relaxed. "You are out of your depth. Unequal to the task. Now you are drawing attention to your failure. And, I think, at some level you want pity. Acknowledgement of your difficulty. Possibly even praise for your leadership, not sure about that," he murmured, considering Sanction with a clinical dispassion.

"I'm not—you listen to me," Sanction growled. "I am drawing your attention to some very real dangers that surround you that have nothing to do with me, and I'm asking you to please defend yourself. The Fairpole Council. The Foundation. The Church. The Bluecoats. The Hive. As we look vulnerable, everybody else we've stepped on or threatened in the last few years, everyone who wants some of what we have, is thinking it over. Maybe the Silkworms are at a vulnerable point and it's time to make a move."

"All right, all right," Trellis soothed. "It's a very scary time, I understand. I'll meet with the Fairpole Council and patch things up. Better?"

Sanction stared at him for a long moment. "They've got your special package for safekeeping, you know," he said. "Do you still care about that?"

"Very much," Trellis said mildly.

"Then get this sorted out with them, please," Sanction said over the tightness in his chest.

"I will. And you'll follow up with Bear, give him Barness," Trellis insisted.

"I would if I could, but the Bluecoats hit Barness this morning," Sanction replied. "I barely got away. Barness is going to disappear for a while."

"Hm," Trellis frowned. "Seems bold, considering the leverage he's got, the Bluecoats on the Hive payroll."

"It... was Rutherford."

"Oh." Trellis looked down his nose at Sanction. "Well. *You* cost us that one. I suppose we'll have to give Bear what he needs to take Dalia."

"What?" Sanction blurted. "Dalia? No, that's too far, that's too much." The last of his restraint was fraying.

"So, I have told you what needs to happen, and you are telling me no," Trellis clarified.

"To be fair, I'm distracted from our conversation by the persistent question of whether or not you've completely lost your mind!" Sanction retorted.

"What if I have?" Trellis said. "How does that change the situation? I do not expect you to understand why I give you orders, but you eventually fall in line because you like where you are in my big picture."

"I may not always understand, but I'm not your lackey, and I never was," Sanction shot back. "I want you to get out of that tub and make some moves to counter what's coming at us, I do *not* want to watch the Silkworms get blown apart because we were idiots! Dammit, Trellis, this is no time for suicide!"

The vaguest smile touched at Trellis's features. He shook his head. "My boy, suicide is just a matter of choosing your timing. All of us will die, after all." He opened his mouth, then closed it, something distant in his eyes. "Today is turning out to be a very strange day," he confessed. "And you, you are doing your best to ruin the relaxation I'm trying to extract from this bath."

"I want a little more tension in you," Sanction replied, loud. "Please stop relaxing."

"Oh, all right," Trellis said with a tinge of petulance. "I'll meet with the Fairpole Council today. But you had best meet with Bear, *before dusk*, and you give him what he needs to take Dalia out. Agreed?"

"Fine." Sanction pivoted and stalked out of the bath chamber.

Trellis slid lower in the tub, suds to his chin, and let his focus drift.

Ignoring the butler, Sanction strode through the mansion, shoving through the front door and rejoining Spindle and Crackstone by the coach in the circle drive. He let out a shout and slammed the wall of the carriage with his forearm. Stunned, the others said nothing. They warily watched Sanction as he struggled to master his frustration.

"The old man just ordered me to give Dalia to the Fog Hounds," Sanction said through his teeth, staring at the wall of the carriage, not yet ready to enter it.

Spindle's eyebrows shot up. "Dalia? Like, Dalia with the Hive, the 'bought heavily into the High Six so she can see all the books and track what we're up to' Dalia?"

"Yes."

"But," Spindle continued, "doesn't that mean if she's threatened she triggers an audit with Ministry allies and they get everything they need to take the High Six and pretty much destroy the Silkworms?"

"YES."

Spindle blinked, and struggled towards a follow up question. A few seconds passed before he found one. "So... you're going to do it?"

Sanction pulled himself up into the coach. "Go. High Six offices." Crackstone jumped up on the buckboard and Spindle climbed into the coach as Sanction slumped back in the seat, resting his chin on his fist, staring sightlessly out the window. The goats bawled under the crack of the whip, and lurched into motion.

**MAURO OVERVIEW, ZEPHYR STREET, MASTER MARKET, SILKSHORE.
25TH VOLVINET. THIRD HOUR PAST DAWN.
SAIL LIGHTING FESTIVAL, DAY THREE.**

The door drifted open, and the Mistress of Tides looked into the study chamber as Yelsir glanced over. The acolyte lay face-down on a thin mat, trying to read a book, immersed in pain. She struggled to adjust to a more respectful position, but the Mistress of Tides raised a hand to interrupt.

"All is well," the Mistress of Tides murmured. "I have come to address your pain."

"Thank you," Yelsir managed to say, eyes averted, voice soft, hoping gratitude was not a mistake.

The Mistress of Tides approached, and gracefully lowered herself to kneel by the acolyte. Splaying the fingers on one hand, she passed a gesture over the Yelsir's back. She felt the agony of muscles out of alignment pulling anchoring bones and lubricating cartilage into each other's way. The nerves carrying the mind into and out of the rest of the body nested in the misaligned spine.

"The question," said the Mistress of Tides, "is whether you suffer because of damage done, or whether the damage is ongoing unresolved." She paused, feeling the vertebra that was slightly crooked against its neighbors. Placing both cool hands down on Yelsir's lower back, she bounced her shoulders slightly, driving down the weight of her torso, and the spine clicked back into alignment. Yelsir let out a dull groan.

"This injury is a gift," the Mistress of Tides said, rocking back to sit with her legs tucked beneath her. "You now understand in your flesh and bones the importance of moving energy through your whole being. The stances, postures, and movements we use to channel energy must use our bodies as the conduit, and we must hone our sinew to focus the load." She paused. "The path to power and the path to healing must ever echo one another. Otherwise gaining power is drinking embers."

"Yes, Mistress," Yelsir managed, face-down on the mat.

The Mistress of Tides tilted her head, and turned to see Neap waiting in the doorway. She paused, then gently pressed her palm on Yelsir's back. Rising, she joined Neap.

"The Fairpole Council Whisper," Neap said without preamble. "He sent a runner with an invitation for you to come to the Gifting Line this afternoon, he wants you to receive that new gondola as part of the ceremonial gifting event. Apparently the whole event has been moved away from the Exchange, deeper into the Ease. Eighth Hour, regalia." He was expressionless, watching. He did not need to raise the various questions of what a gift from an angered ally could mean. Or what might follow if the gift was refused.

"We accept, send the message," the Mistress of Tides said. "I'll take a retinue of three, but not you. Not this time." She heaved a deep sigh. "We need to back up the Silkworms, the festival overload and current circumstances require it. Take two initiates and handle collections to-day. Be seen doing it. Send Ebb to Central Landing to catch up with the Fairpole Gondoliers, and to inform them I'll be present this afternoon."

"Spring will guard your person?" Neap pressed.

"Spring is checking into the Foundation," the Mistress of Tides re-plied, "and that's certainly a way to guard my person. I'll be fine."

"I've been working with the new acolytes," Neap said. "Yelsir is likely the finest fighter in your service, including me. Since she's injured, I recommend you take Nevi, she's a close second."

"Praise? From you, that's a rare treasure," the Mistress of Tides mused.

Neap quietly agreed.

"Alright, I accept your judgment on this," the Mistress of Tides said. "I will take Nevi with me, *and* Yelsir. Bind her up, salve the pain, and prepare her for service."

"Looking within and without, we shall see," Neap murmured in Hadrathi.

"See and be seen."

HIGH SIX BUSINESS APERTURE, SILKSHORE.
25TH VOLVINET. FOURTH HOUR PAST DAWN.
SAIL LIGHTING FESTIVAL, DAY THREE.

Sanction rounded the tight corner in the confined space, and trig-gered the lever opening the secret door. Soundless, the door drifted open, not even disturbing the curtain of delicately glowing fronds hanging down before it. Sanction ducked through the curtain of plants as the door shut behind him. He paused for a moment, then walked around to the front of his desk, looking at the magnificent and ex-pensive glory of blooms covering the back wall and growing from the planters flanking the desk. He felt a twitch of terror, grief, resentment, and panic pushing out of his core in different directions, and he sud-denly needed a breath, the air nearly driven from him by the emotional reaction.

"Built to last," he murmured to himself, touching the desk, feeling the pressures all around pulling his roots out of this place.

Dalia.

He scowled at the thought, resuming his place at the desk and settling into the high-backed throne. May as well enjoy a moment here before he threw the whole thing away.

The main office door clicked, then opened, and Sanction's assistant Berman slipped in before closing it. He rounded on Sanction, schooling his features towards blandness.

"Sir," he said. "I am *so pleased* to see you. I spotted Spindle downstairs and thought to look for you here. Once we get through some of the most pressing matters, you can give me some guidance on how to re-schedule the appointments you've missed the last few days. And how you want me to handle those who cancelled."

"Sounds like quite a mess," Sanction said.

"I don't have to tell you how full your calendar is, sir," Berman agreed. "Did you speak to the Ministry representatives about the shipment we offered them for this afternoon's banquet at the Administrative Plaza? The foreman has a disagreement with their agent about which blooms you were discussing, and there are some—"

"Doesn't matter," Sanction said, raising his hand to cut his assistant's explanation short. "Give them whatever they want. And for the rest, too. Work with the foreman, make decisions, I don't give a damn," he said, feeling the unsteady tilt of his life, the importance sliding off of some things altogether in the face of fresh demands.

Berman smoothly recovered his balance. "We've been planning some of these things for months, sir," he said. "I know you were keeping some of your long-term strategies under wraps, and aiming to shatter the financial records of previous festival weeks." He did not turn his statements to questions.

"I certainly was," Sanction agreed.

"Do you want me to send a runner up to the Ease Commissioning Nexus to inform them you will not be attending the association meeting that started on the fourth hour?" Berman asked.

"I think they'll figure it out," Sanction reflected.

Berman nodded to himself. "I see," he said, mentally jettisoning the rest of the slate of questions. "If I may be so bold... I heard about Rutherford." He took a step closer, drawn by his sympathy. "What do you need?"

The slightest smile curled in Sanction's face. "What do I need," he echoed. Then his eyes narrowed as an idea resonated in him; the way he felt about the High Six, reduced to an inconvenience in the face of the threat to the Silkworms. The way he felt about Berman, reduced to a pastime as he struggled to outmaneuver Rutherford's attacks. And the complete disinterest from Trellis, apparently apathetic about the future of the Silkworms.

What unseen threat could be so massive that it trivialized Trellis's investment in the Silkworms?

"I need answers," Sanction said to himself. Berman's perfect features flexed with puzzlement, and he hesitated; that was not the answer he had expected.

Sanction rose to his feet. "You're fired," he said, calm. "Take your things and go. Best if I don't explain."

Berman's eyes widened, and he was speechless for a moment. "Sir?" he almost squeaked. He twitched, anger flowing into the wound he felt. "What are you doing?!"

"Firing you," Sanction replied quietly. "There will be severance pay, and a bonus. If you leave now," he added with a shrug that twisted the knife.

"This—is a very—*brave*—thing for you to do," Berman gritted out.

"Threaten me, and the severance pay goes to a different expense," Sanction said, looking Berman in the eye so there could be no confusion.

Berman restrained an ugly chuckle as he rolled his eyes, then pivoted and stormed out, slamming the door to the office hard.

"No point burning *some* of it down," Sanction murmured, then he shifted his tongue to try and dislodge the awful taste of that encounter. Turning his back on the front door, he attuned to one of his rings, and touched it to the plate of the hidden safe. Opening it, he took the contents, then snapped it shut. Taking one last look around the office, he tried to fix it in his mind.

Then he left.

The Mistress of Tides felt the slow trickle of sweat down towards the small of her back, and the slickness of her face behind the veil. Her ceremonial garb was stitched with pearls and glittering thread in an eye-twisting pattern of greens and blues. Her three acolytes were motionless, enduring the stifling heat, kneeling on the plinths at the base of the bridge alongside the pungent canal.

The water's surface was dotted with small floating lanterns, and an arrhythmic reel was scraped out by a string ensemble on the balcony of an adjacent bridge. Buskers worked the crowds lining the bridge as the Fairpole Gondolier Council's small flotilla of gondolas for this parade drifted down the canal distributing gifts. Some of the gondoliers threw handfuls of candy into the crowd, along with small trinkets. Various stops had been assigned to those receiving more substantial gifts, such as the landing where the Mistress of Tides waited with her acolytes.

The broken sky lit the back of the mid-afternoon clouds with a dull red so they glowed between the dim patches visible behind them. Flies buzzed and whirled around the crowd, stirring the thick light, intoxicated by the welter of smells and food.

Parents tugged at their children, hissing at them not to stare. Some people only stole glances at the Mistress of Tides and her mysterious acolytes, others couldn't look away. The Mistress of Tides could almost feel the confusion of emotion from those who registered her presence and saw her retinue. Admiration, awe, disgust, revulsion, longing, fear, pride. All was as it should be.

The Mistress of Tides had time to isolate her anxiety, the alarming hiss of passing seconds evaporating painfully against her sense of urgency. One by one, she raised the crisis points in her mind and studied them over, reviewing what her acolytes had reported from their investigations. Nothing trembled at that deep level, nothing shortened her breath and provoked the dizziness that almost nauseated her. Not the Foundation, not the Church, not the Fairpole Council, not the Bluecoats...

It was the Spirit Wardens. Maragaya. The medium Levyra. The Dark Tooth.

Venisana.

Breath hissed into the Mistress of Tides as she suddenly found herself in need of it. Revisiting that moment. That name. As soon as the encounter with the Fairpole Council was over, whatever it turned out to be, she would focus on the Dark Tooth. That was the conflict that mattered.

Time eased its grip on her somewhat, and she was able to refocus on her patience and awareness as the parade finally floated near to where they waited.

As the flotilla drifted closer, the Mistress of Tides saw the gondola near the front that must be intended as a gift for her. Twenty five feet, trim waist, shallow draft, but the Hadrathi glyphs and prayers layered in with lacquer and layers of wood radiated protections that she could feel from forty feet away. The ornate sculpting of the trim and the brilliant green and gold paint drew the eye and satisfied it with echoes of form and brilliant flourishes of complimentary color and shape. In spite of herself, the Mistress of Tides felt a smile warm her face.

"To the Mistress of Tides!" boomed the Whisper of the Fairpole Council. He was tall, lanky, and impressive in ceremonial garb, standing at the prow of the gift gondola. A retractable folding gangplank on rails slid into place on the gondola's waist, and extended to the plinth. The crowd surrounding them cheered as the Mistress of Tides glided forward and down the ramp without hesitation, her acolytes following.

"Looking within and without, we shall see," the Mistress of Tides intoned in Hadrathi.

"See and be seen," echoed the Whisper with a courtly flourish. "Welcome aboard the Sight. We have labored on this gift for you for no reward but your pleasure."

"You have my pleasure and my thanks for this gracious offering," the Mistress of Tides said, as expected by the forms of the festival. They clasped hands and bowed to one another, and the gift was accepted. The cheers of the crowd continued, but the Mistress of Tides noticed that the Whisper only had a single acolyte sculling the gondolier. No one else was in easy earshot. The Whisper turned, leading the way to the narrow tented privacy corridor down the center of the gondola. The Mistress of Tides' acolytes waited outside, two on the prow and one joining the sculler at the gondola's stern.

"I confess to some surprise," the Mistress of Tides said in the relative privacy of the gondola's center, reclining on a cushioned lounge seat opposite the Whisper. "Considering the tensions."

"Tensions, yes," the Whisper replied. "That's adjacent to why I wanted a word with you." He paused. "The future of the Silkworms seems increasingly uncertain."

The Mistress of Tides waited for the rest.

The Whisper nodded to himself. "You were trained by the gondoliers, named by the gondoliers, you are immersed in our traditions. We mourned when you left our ranks to join with a criminal crew, though we appreciated your ongoing studies and your investment in tradition." He studied her veil, inscrutable behind his mask. "I am offering you a place as my right hand, serving the Fairpole Council, in line for a number of advancement opportunities. Resources. Prestige."

"And in exchange," she prompted.

"Nothing strenuous or unusual," the Whisper replied. "Just work towards the Fairpole Council's best interests and do nothing to harm them."

"And side with them," the Mistress of Tides continued, "should they clash with the Silkworms."

"That is but one tributary of the river of our cooperation," soothed the Whisper. "You are well respected by members of the Fairpole Council, even those you've countered in the past."

"Yourself included," the Mistress of Tides observed.

"Myself included," the Whisper agreed. "I have experienced frustration in our interactions, that is true. I still do not truly understand why you would choose the life you've chosen when you could be so much more with the Fairpole Council."

"I am fortunate that I do not need to explain it to you," the Mistress of Tides said. "Still. I appreciate your offer, and I will consider the possibilities."

"That is all we can ask for at this point," the Whisper said. "Though I had hoped you would be more... receptive."

"I face a number of complications right now," the Mistress of Tides said. "I must choose my course carefully. There was a time I would have dismissed your offer, but I have come to see the generosity and opportunity behind it." She paused. "Thank you for this magnificent gift," she said with a gesture along the gondola's flank. "I will always value the people who shaped me, and I will never forget my debts."

"Gifts given in the Gifting Line do not obligate their recipients, that's an established tradition," the Whisper said with an audible smile.

"I understand," the Mistress of Tides nodded. "Your traditions are mine as well."

"That affirmation is a gift I hoped to receive," the Whisper replied, and he rocked forward to a crouch, rising through the side curtain of the tent. He called his acolyte in Hadrathi, and the two of them stepped over to another gondola that approached at his signal. By the time he left the Mistress of Tides' gondola, Nevi had joined her in the tent.

"Orders, Mistress?"

The Mistress of Tides was reflective, sensing the flow of the water beneath the prow, the noise of the crowd, the dim light dappling the outside of the tent from various directions, and the slither of instinct through her veins.

"Steer out to the Dosk, upstream to the center. Let's visit the Tangle."

Nevi rose and stepped up out of the tent, headed astern with orders for navigation.

The Mistress of Tides absently touched at the railing under the tent fabric, feeling her body heat's tumble into the protective script of the hull.

"Choosing a course," she murmured. "Mindful of shallows."

CENTRAL LANDING. THE EASE. SILKSHORE.
25ᵀᴴ VOLVINET. EIGTH HOUR PAST DAWN.
SAIL LIGHTING FESTIVAL, DAY THREE.

"Cheer up," Trellis said, his tone warm as he clapped Ebb on the shoulder. The morose acolyte jumped, almost spilling his brew, wild-eyed with surprise at Trellis's sudden appearance on the bustling veranda overlooking the river traffic.

"Trellis! Sir! I understood you were otherwise disposed," he said as he pulled himself together.

"It's not about you," Trellis confided in him, his small crooked smile letting the acolyte in on a private joke. "The gondoliers are experts in the various arts of clique crafting and outsider shunning. They can instinctively send you a thousand signals you don't belong without doing any single thing to provoke anger. Or they can be less subtle," he added, gesturing at the purpling bruise under Ebb's eye.

"Oh, the shiner; yes, that was an 'accident' with buckets on a yoke," Ebb said. "They thought it was *hilarious*," he added as he looked over to where several tough pilots and stevedores were drinking and watching outsiders.

"That's why I'm here," Trellis explained, sliding onto the seat next to the acolyte. "Sort things out with the Fairpole Council. I'm supposed to kiss some ass and smooth things over." He threw a long-suffering glance at the acolyte. "I don't know if I can cool them off. Seems un-likely."

"We rely on your cunning and insight," Ebb said diplomatically.

"I like you," Trellis smiled. "Tell you what. I'll pick up the news, you go on back to the Mistress of Tides and tell her I'm here having this conversation I'm supposed to have. Yes?"

"Yes sir," Ebb agreed, and he rose to his feet and bowed. "I will do as you ask."

"Off you go," Trellis said, his eyes already roving the crowd, the con-versation over. Ebb did not need to be told twice; relief lent him speed as he headed out of the crowded landing.

Trellis slipped through the crowd, ending up outside the trade office. A surprised gondolier boss spotted him, and crossed his arms.

"Well well well, there is the elusive presence himself," the boss frowned. "You didn't make an appointment."

"Trajan will be here soon, his mistress has already arrived and he planned to skip the Gifting Line," Trellis replied. "When he gets here, you let him know I'm available. We'll see if he sends me away or makes time for a chat." Trellis flagged down a server and ordered a drink with gestures common in the noisy taverns.

The boss's frown deepened. "Maybe he's already here."

"Then stop wasting everyone's time and let him know I'm available," Trellis said. "Or stand there and scowl, that seems more your speed." His smile was aggressive.

The door to the inner office opened, and a grim gondolier stepped out. "Trajan will see you now."

"Well let's make sure it's okay with Canaran here," Trellis retorted. "He may not be done flexing and growling. Look at those scary muscles." Trellis cocked his head to the side, arching an eyebrow, giving the gondolier boss every single opportunity to rise to the bait. "No? All done?" He turned to the other gondolier. "Let's go see Trajan then."

They crossed the inner office, into the back room. Trajan was hanging the last of his ceremonial garb on the dressing dummy, now wearing a simple tunic and breeches. He did not turn as his servant ushered Trellis in and closed the door, leaving the two of them alone.

"I have decided to end our friendship and its benefits," Trajan said coldly. "Change my mind."

"No. Are we done?"

"It would seem so," Trajan growled, his scowl intensifying.

Trellis opened the door and turned to go.

"Wait," Trajan said, pivoting to glare at Trellis. "What the hell are you thinking?"

"About what?" Trellis asked, eyebrows raised.

"The Silkworms rose to power with the assistance of the Fairpole Council," Trajan said. "Your people operate in our territory. Without our support you're nowhere. If you cannot respect our relationship, our *friendship*—if you place no value on our word and our mutual benefits, then we will not tolerate your disrespect."

"I understand that," Trellis agreed. "Believe me, I know that feeling." He tossed the door shut with a bang, and turned to face Trajan. "The Silkworms rose to power by cutting Hive agents out of the Fairpole Council, curing the disease that was sickening its most attuned mystics, and cracking the Ministry open so the boat people could finally have a seat at the table in the government that exploits them. You want to make a point of the Silkworm debt without a nod to what that debt purchased. That's not friendship. You are upset because you relied on the Silkworms and they didn't come through. Sometimes that happens, and there is a difference between friends and contractors." He stared at Trajan. "Isn't there."

"This is the tone you take?" Trajan demanded, blood rising. "With *me*?"

"Because if we're just contractors then we take our services elsewhere and we find some *clients* who can use our services. Clients who might target the Fairpole Council and Silkshore. I don't even need the Hive," Trellis said, his voice low as he took a step towards Trajan that seemed to shrink the whole room. "I go to the Church, the Foundation, the Ministry, or half a dozen others. You lose spirit wells. Mystics. Boats. Territory. Lose them to my *clients*," Trellis said, "who understand setbacks are a cost of doing business. With *clients*, there's no apology. That's for *friends*. So end our 'friendship.' Maybe you kill us. Get me, for certain," Trellis said, his ruthless voice low and pitched to crack stone.

Trajan was white to the lips with fury. "Your friendship was pretty goddamn expensive," he snarled, "and you made promises. Now, when I give you a chance to make up for your failure, failure I was *promised* would not happen, you try to shake me down?" He trembled, rage coursing through him. "You speak to me this way and think I will not have you killed in this room? That I won't do it *myself*?"

"I subdued your people once," Trellis said quietly. "Maybe next time I *destroy* them. Remember. The Gannethel family. The Syvatch family. The Dinmakai family." He raised his eyebrows. "Where are their voices in the Council song? How have you filled their silences?" He cocked his head to the side. "Trajan, hm. You belong to the Bennen family. Sweet Linala. Chubby little Lokso. Your uncle Van. The Greensilk Street operation for nine generations."

Trajan convulsively snatched at the dressing dummy, yanking a curved knife from its sheath, eyes wide with murder.

"*Take one step,*" Trellis said, "and I will bring down the Grotto." His gaze was steady, boring into Trajan. "End your people," he whispered.

Trajan was frozen in place, rage and horror wrestling in him and leaving wreckage in his heart and mind.

Trellis stepped nose to nose, in easy stabbing range, not releasing Trajan's eye. "You wanted to be clear, and you are," Trellis murmured, barely audible. "This friendship is over. Your mistake was to think that you *ever* had the upper hand." Trellis let five seconds build an insupportable weight between the two men.

"Threaten me," he mused, and his eyes filled with disgust. He took a step back, and shook his head. Then he turned and walked away.

CHAPTER TWELVE

The Silkworms! Hardly a mascot that strikes fear into the hearts of their foes. Don't let their name put you at ease! You won't see their leaders in the Investigator cautions, but a shadowy new crew pulls the strings for the behind-the-scenes puppet show of corruption infecting Silkshore. These subtle newcomers took their name from a gondolier threat.

In the summer of 847, their leader was the Trellis of Barrow-cleft. According to eyewitness accounts, the Trellis approached the retired-but-still-legendary assassin, Khyro, where he held court at the game tables of the Ease. The Trellis explained his crew was going to take over, becoming benevolent masters when the Fairpole Council was under their sway. Furious, Khyro reminded him that the gondoliers were the dragons of the canals—Trellis and his lackeys were just worms!

A year later, Khyro is still at his game table—but those "worms" influence crime for a third of Silkshore. Today as you shop the Ease for silk sheets or a breezy blouse, you help those businesses pay their protection money—to the insidious Silk-worms, weaving a fabric of influence to cover up crime!

— From "Catalog of Crime! Summer Edition, 848"
published by Eel Press Entertainment

Daava struggled to shorten her stride, slowing down for Cellar. He was almost staggering by the time they walked in front of the foundry next to his family's building. Jayan leaned against the wall at the base of the stairs, waiting for them.

"I thought you'd never get here," Jayan said.

"Aren't you lucky we did," Daava sighed. "We need to establish factuals for Cellar, make sure we've got credible eyes on him every moment from here out. He's half-swallowed by hagfish."

"I heard you are a suspect for that murder at the Exchange," Jayan winced. "Rough break." He paused.

"I didn't do it," Cellar said, louder than he meant to.

"I know!" Jayan protested, too quickly. "Of course you didn't. Don't be stupid. Nobody thinks that."

"Anyway," Daava frowned at him, "I'm going to go do some research on an old case." She exchanged a meaningful glance with Cellar, then looked back at Jayan. "You keep him here, keep witnesses around, and take it easy for once." She tried on a smile. "Right?"

"Absolutely," Jayan nodded.

"Right," Daava echoed. "Okay, be good." Turning, she took off down the street with a long stride, headed for a carriage.

"Yeah, we're not going to do any of that, are we," Jayan mused, almost to himself.

"Of course not," Cellar scoffed. "We've got a case to crack." He hesitated. "You know it was Spur."

"Yes," Jayan confirmed. "I thought if we moved fast we might get a look through Spur's room in the Tick Tock's sublevels before the Bluecoats think to check it out. Fortunately Sparks told us about that secret passage to get down to the wine cellar from the common room. The one Spur used to come and go undetected." He looked over at Cellar. "We can sift his crap. There might be a clue."

"I like the way you think," Cellar grinned. "Let's go. Hail a carriage, I'm not up for the walk."

"About that," Jayan said, handing him a metal canteen. "Granny Crockwizer's hangover remedy."

"No way, not after last time," Cellar said as he recoiled.

"But you weren't tired for hours, right?" Jayan shot back, eyebrows raised.

Cellar hesitated a moment more, then took the canteen.

TICK TOCK TEA SHOP, BOOKEND SQUARE, FOGCREST, SILKSHORE. 25TH VOLVINET. FIFTH HOUR PAST DAWN. SAIL LIGHTING FESTIVAL, DAY THREE.

"Your beard is unsticking," Jayan said, adjusting the fake beard on Cellar's face.

"Yours is unsettling," Cellar retorted. "Please don't ever grow a beard."

"Hah!" Jayan scoffed. "You are just jealous because your baby face won't. Now, I think we're set." They were wearing cheap hooded half-cloaks and fake beards, altering their appearance enough to not be immediately recognized. They headed for the tea shop, mingling with the festival crowd.

The double doors were propped open in the warmth of mid-day, and the panels had been removed so the revolving doors were doorways with a central pole. The tea shop bustled with customers and revelry, a shaded and inexpensive place for lunch. Cellar led the way into the throng, Jayan in his shadow.

The back of the tea shop was a collection of dim booths and nooks, and Cellar closed in on a recessed space between two of them. Even though there were patrons in the booths on both sides, there was enough of a crowd for him to get close unremarked. He leaned into the gap, and squinted up to see the unobtrusive button worked into the overhead panel. He pressed it, and leaned on the wall, pivoting through to a stuffy dark space that stank of vinegary wine. Frowning, he pulled a glass globe from his half-cloak and shook it so it glowed. He stepped down the staircase so Jayan could follow him into the narrow space. The crowd noise was muffled, though they could clearly hear the conversation in the booths on either side of the secret passage. Jayan pulled the panel doorway closed, sealing them away.

They headed down the stairs, around the corner, and over the boobytrap cable that Spark had warned them about. They emerged from the shadows between two tuns of wine in the cellar under the tea shop. Jayan gestured to the left, and they followed the corridor to the gated and barred reckoning office.

"You know," Jayan said philosophically as he handed lock picks and a prybar to Cellar, "this is objectively a bad idea."

"I need somewhere to start, a way into this, and I'm not keen on any of my options," Cellar growled as he fiddled with the picks in the lock. It was dark, but this had to be done by touch anyway, so he focused and felt through the picks as though they were his fingers. The lock was simple, popped open with a few expert jiggles.

"It's open," Cellar said, rising to his feet, looking to Jayan. Jayan looked at Cellar.

"Probably trapped," he observed.

"Maybe; have a look," Cellar replied with an expansive gesture. "This jaunt was your idea."

Scowling, Jayan approached the door and listened at it, then gingerly pushed. The door drifted open without a squeak, its hinges well-oiled and balanced.

Jayan leaned in, looking around, his expression troubled. "Huh. I would not have figured Spur to be quite so... tidy."

The bed was smooth and carefully made up. The desk had a tray with a stationary kit. A footlocker was next to the desk, with a washbasin and pitcher. No pictures on the walls, hardly anything in the former office. They stepped in for a closer look.

"The only thing under the bed is a bedpan, and it's empty. Shiny, even," Jayan observed from the ground. Cellar gazed at the wall. He focused on four pegs, and the scratches behind them.

"He hung his weapons here," Cellar said. He opened the footlocker. "Just clothes and an ammo pouch." He frowned as he closed the chest. "I'm missing something."

"Spur was such a seedy bastard, I kind of expected a pile of dirty dishes and playing cards," Jayan said. "Not... this. Looks like a monk lived here."

"Yes it does," Cellar agreed. Then he stretched out his arms, took a step sideways, and stretched out his arms again. He turned to the doorway and left the room.

"Okay," Jayan said agreeably, following in time to see Cellar repeat the motions outside.

"Just as I thought," Cellar said. "I bet that back wall is false; there's almost four feet difference between the inside and the outer wall!"

"Ah, I hope it's not gross," Jayan groused. "I really don't want to find a trophy room. Even if it's full of clues."

Cellar ignored him, dropping to all fours and closely examining the wall and the corners, all the seams, everything. He drew his pistol and twirled it, rapping on a peg with the butt. The peg clicked in deeper, and half of the wall rose up on a pivot. Cellar pushed it, opening the way to the secret room beyond.

The chamber was bigger than five feet by ten feet; almost four times bigger. There was an exercise circle in the middle of the floor with strange glyphs around the border, a big desk with built-in scroll cases and a bookshelf, and a far more robust weapons rack next to a shallow wardrobe.

Caution tingled in Cellar as he approached the desk, eyes darting from shadow to shadow. Jayan followed. Cellar felt the hair on the back of his neck rise. Almost unwilling, he stood by the wardrobe, looking it over.

Jayan squinted at the book spines. "These look like some kind of... I don't think it's Hadrathi," he said, and he scratched his head.

Cellar opened the wardrobe. He came face to face with a mask. On the shelf underneath, he saw pressed ceremonial garb. A peculiar spicy smell flowed out of the cabinet. His skin crawled.

"No. Way." Jayan breathed next to him.

"That's a Spirit Warden mask," Cellar said, brittle.

"Why—why would Spirit Wardens—why would they work with a scumbag like Spur?" Jayan said, forehead creased with puzzlement.

"Spirit Wardens are anonymous," Cellar murmured. "Some of them are monks. But maybe—maybe some have other identities." A glyph-scribed tonfa. A sash with amulets worked into it. Custom-fitted boots. Weighted gloves.

This was not a costume.

"Wait, you think *Spur* was a *Spirit Warden*?!" Jayan gasped, staring at Cellar.

EMPRESS OF GULLS' WORKSHOP SLOOP WRECK, TANGLETOWN, CROW'S FOOT.
25TH VOLVINET. NINTH HOUR PAST DAWN.
SAIL LIGHTING FESTIVAL, DAY THREE.

"Welcome, it is so good to see you," the Empress of Gulls crooned in Akorosian. She was perched on her throne, a magnificent structure made of interwoven driftwood and bone that formed a tree-like shape rooted in the floor and supporting the ceiling in the crooked audience hall in the shipwreck. Scantily clad men flanked the Mistress of Tides. She deferentially bowed to the Empress of Gulls. Though both Whispers were veiled, they could see each other clearly enough.

"Once again I am beyond my own studies and expertise, and I come here," the Mistress of Tides murmured in Hadrathi.

"You are welcome now as you have always been," the Empress of Gulls replied, relaxing back on the throne. "I am not surprised to see you."

The Mistress of Tides hesitated, then waited, cocking her head to the side.

"Why, you wonder," the Empress of Gulls confirmed. "Because the end of the world is upon us. I can feel it." She gestured at her well-oiled servants, who bowed and withdrew, leaving the two Whispers alone in the warded and enchanted room. "This is my space, and I prefer you begin the conversation," the Empress of Gulls said sweetly.

The Mistress of Tides thought that over for a moment, then sighed. "I am troubled," she said. "The medium, Levyra, came to me. She said the Spirit Wardens tie ghosts to her then extract information from them. Normally the Wardens bind her with oaths of secrecy. This time they did not, and she was disturbed by the conversation she enabled. Burdened by the weight of the mystery."

"So she came to you," the Empress of Gulls nodded.

"Yes. The Wardens tortured a mad beggar. Apparently he had the gift of prophecy. His name was Maragaya, and he could only speak in symbol and riddle. The Wardens involved experts on the Forgotten Gods, and were keen to decipher his message."

"The curse of vision," the Empress of Gulls mused. "Seeing with sufficient clarity robs us of the capacity to communicate what we have seen. You have the message, yes?"

"He said the Dark Tooth had already begun, and would complete the Fourfold Circle. That the only salvation was with Venisana. Apparently he screamed 'look to the worms' over and over until the end." The Mistress of Tides paused, then crossed her arms. "What does that mean to you?"

"Hm," the Empress of Gulls murmured. "Look to the worms. That brought Levyra to the Silkworms. With a problem discomfiting the Spirit Wardens. Quite the riddle."

"Do any of those names mean something to you?" the Mistress of Tides pressed.

"Some, certainly, but I am more curious to hear what about this caught your attention," the Empress of Gulls replied. "I sense you are holding back, that you want to test my knowledge before sharing your own. Something about this makes you *very* uncomfortable."

"Yes," the Mistress of Tides said, reluctant. "There is a secret I have kept, known to no one but myself. A secret that Maragaya could not have known, it is impossible. So, yes, I fear this may be... cosmic." She shifted. "Demonic. Profound. Can you help me? *Will* you help me?"

"I will, if you will then share this secret with me," the Empress of Gulls replied, eyes bright behind the veil.

"I will share my secret," the Mistress of Tides said slowly. "Yes."

"Very well," the Empress of Gulls said, a note of triumph in her tone. "Your Whisper training grows out of the fluid forms and patterns the Iruvians developed, striking a balance of life and death on the canals, allowing the gondoliers to protect the people of Silkshore from the vengeful dead before the Spirit Wardens were founded. Those patterns and forms are a potent enough lore, they are very pretty," the Empress of Gulls said. "They adapt the older forms, the precursors, the rituals learned from demons that serve as the underpinning of all ritual casting lore. Your prophet, your Maragaya, he is babbling about the old stuff. Limmer magic. Leviathan exhalation. Human sacrifice."

"The Dark Tooth?" the Mistress of Tides ventured, unsure.

"The Fourfold Circle. The old rituals had this for their foundation; to channel or contain energy, you had to complete four interlocking circles. Physical, ethereal, chronological, relational. That is how you set the scope, built the container, shaped the effects. Your acts and objects bounded the ambition of the conjuring. Maragaya was telling you that a demonic agent is working a ritual, and the ritual has begun."

For a long moment, neither Whisper spoke. The room was lit by glowing chips of stone in braziers. The protective writings on the walls reflected the light with their own dim shine. The off-kilter floor from the angled wreck of the sloop that housed them felt almost level as the rest of the world seemed out of balance.

"Human sacrifice," the Mistress of Tides echoed. "Well, some demonic agent with a ritual in progress... That doesn't point towards a lot of follow-up leads, does it."

"You've got the Spirit Wardens," the Empress of Gulls said, ticking items off one finger at a time, "and the worms, and Maragaya, and Venisana, and the Dark Tooth. Each of those could bear some further investigation. How they fit together. Where they intersect. What they might mean that they do not *seem* to mean without more context. Why do the Spirit Wardens care about this prophecy? For example. It is not like them to get flustered," she said, something flinty in her tone.

"Help me solve this." The Mistress of Tides was centered, direct.

The Empress of Gulls was quiet. Then she nodded. "I will help you understand the threat," she said.

"Thank you," the Mistress of Tides said. "Now, you were not surprised to see me. Why not?"

"Surely you've felt it; the shift behind the Mirror," the Empress of Gulls said. "Something big is coming. Energy is building, or drawing near somehow. Pressure," she mouthed, the hiss alive in her mouth.

"I have felt it," the Mistress of Tides agreed. "Something coming, some future event compressing the time around it."

The Empress of Gulls nodded. "Indeed. Now a deal is a deal. Tell me your secret."

The Mistress of Tides glanced around. "You know I arrived in Doskvol as a refugee. A storm capsized my family's craft and I was the only one who made it to the shore alive." Deep breath. "I was a child. No one knew me in my homeland, I arrived very much alone."

"Yes."

"I was nameless, but gifted," the Mistress of Tides continued. "Gondolier adepts took me in. I surpassed their teachings and became what I am now. All my life, I have kept a secret that arrived in this city with me."

The silence was full of struggle, as though the Mistress of Tides lifted something half-buried.

"My name is Venisana."

After a moment, the Empress of Gulls rasped out a chuckle.

"Of course it is," she grinned, sardonic behind her veil. "To be fair, I knew of you before we met. While we're being so truthsome."

"How is that possible?" the Mistress of Tides frowned.

"I knew you only as a cypher. That there would be a Whisper who would emerge, at the end of the world, an anchor in the storm of the cataclysm. Like an unfinished ritual, the prophecy set up all things and held energy, but did not complete to trigger the effect. The outcome, unknown. But I knew it was you the moment I saw you. Never you mind how." She paused. "It is likely the Dark Tooth will also recognize that you have a role. I have cherished you," she said in her dry, thin voice, "as though the world depended on you. I believe it does. So, you must be strong."

"I need more light," the Mistress of Tides said through her teeth, "to see the machinery that is apparently intertwined with my fate and shaping my path. How do we find out what we need to know."

"I suspect a divergent path," the Empress of Gulls replied. "The ritual lore of the Leviathans was unevenly printed on the minds of those they altered. As some adepts refined the Whisper tradition to face the dead, other adepts expressed their gifts through the Foundation to collect energy and shape effects with elements of the Fourfold Circle." She paused. "I read of you in a prophecy from the Foundation's archives. They have hundreds, and all are of course vague, but that one... it mentioned me as well. I am one of two Heralds. My role is to set you upon your path, and all your life I have attempted to do that. The Dark Tooth has a Herald as well."

She shook her head. "Perhaps you can locate the prophecy, if you've got a contact in the Foundation. My access was closed off abruptly years ago. The Foundation archives list this prophecy as the Bellweather Locus, recorded in 512, distilled insights and patterns from the dying rants of four members of the Corsalia clan. They were all limmers. The vision boomed through their blood so loud it killed the prophets."

"Seems likely this Maragaya fellow was of the Corsalia bloodline," the Mistress of Tides said grimly, mind racing. "The vision may echo here as the event itself approaches."

"That seems likely. Maybe the Leviathan behind the vision is the one behind the ritual, maybe a rival Leviathan is interfering with some plan beyond the scope of the human imagination. There is no way to know at this point." The Empress of Gulls paused. "These rituals... the old ones, Leviathan magic. They are transformational in nature. They change the caster, the target, the surroundings. They often align with the demon-driven stars themselves, and the shifting of the constellations. I will start by looking at the star charts. Perhaps you should look into the Foundation."

"Yes," the Mistress of Tides agreed. "Perhaps I should."

SMOKE TOWER, BOOKEND SQUARE, FOGCREST, SILKSHORE. 25TH VOLVINET. NINTH HOUR PAST DAWN. SAIL LIGHTING FESTIVAL, DAY THREE.

"I hear you've cracked it," Captain Smiles said as she entered the evidence vault. The noise from the tower entry chamber echoed and rebounded down to the corridor outside, which also connected to the Cave and the raucous shouts there. In the sweaty dimness, several Bluecoats were hunched over coded ledgers, scribbling on pads of paper with charcoal sticks wrapped in tape.

Rutherford rose to his feet and faced the captain. "Yes, Captain Smiles, we were able to break down the cypher used to track payments the Hive made to various individuals and groups in Silkshore. Some of this information may lead to contemplations, but we will surely be able to round out some factuals and vouchers to support accusations. If nothing else, there's a mountain of leverage here." His satisfaction was grim.

"You can't tell from here, but it's mid-afternoon, nucoat," the captain said as she cocked an eye at Rutherford. "We don't pay extra for long hours, you know."

"Right now there are a lot of people hearing that we've got these ledgers," Rutherford said. "They are likely scrambling to cover their tracks and hide their valuables. I want to move faster than they move."

"Oh, I get that impression," Captain Smiles agreed. "You helped our code people crack the cypher, and I commend that effort," she said with a gesture at the other Bluecoats at the table. "Finishing this out is above your station, officer. I'm reassigning it, captain level prerogative." Her eyes narrowed. "Do you have a problem with that?"

"No, captain, I do not," Rutherford said. He tossed his pencil on the table, and looked her in the eye. "You count this a win?" he asked quietly.

"It's early yet," the Captain said. "I will let you know."

"Fair enough," Rutherford said easily. "These ledgers transfer a lot of the Hive's leverage and influence away from them, squarely to you. I think you will know how to be responsible with that." He smiled, the peculiar strain of sadness behind every expression especially haunting. "We've been naughty."

"Indeed, and now you're headed home," Captain Smiles said. "You have done enough for one day. A big day with the analysts, and no fatalaties. You looking for assignment to the Inspectors?"

"No," Rutherford said. "I'm not interested in the Inspectors. I'm a Bluecoat."

"I guess you are," Captain Smiles said. "Now you are going to go home. Get some rest. You need to support the festival, not just your passion projects."

"Yes, captain," Rutherford responded crisply. "Thank you, captain."

"Just one more thing before you go," Captain Smiles said. "You've deciphered some names, some amounts?"

"Yes, the process is started," Rutherford said.

"Find any Bluecoats? Any Inspectors?" Captain Smiles asked directly.

"No, Captain. None so far," Rutherford replied.

"Hm. Dismissed." Captain Smiles considered Rutherford as he gathered up his coat and baldric. As he passed her, headed out, she pivoted. "Oh, and Rutherford."

"Captain."

"Don't go upstairs. Don't go lay down somewhere in the tower. Leave. Out. Somewhere else. Don't come back before dawn." She turned her back on him, picking up a page of notes, and the analysts watched Rutherford go.

As Rutherford strode through the tower, he glanced down at his outfit. Aside from a few charcoal smudges, his uniform was just as crisp as it had been when he arrived for work. He felt the trickle of sweat inside the heavy fabric, but the uniform did not easily show blood or sweat, instead projecting a square-shouldered and clean-lined aesthetic.

He ducked out the front. Down the stairs, across the square, towards the adjacent canal. He walked along the congested channel, then hopped onto a gondola. From one to another, and then to the opposite bank, running up the stairs three at a time.

Rutherford flagged down a carriage, but instead of entering it he jumped up on the footman's step on the back; the driver shrugged, drove a ways, and didn't even notice when Rutherford dropped off as the carriage turned a corner. Rutherford stood in the shadows of the alleyway, watching the street, and smiled to himself as he saw the out-of-breath pursuer run to the intersection, glancing around wildly, trying to figure out which way he had gone. The pursuer was one of the Bluecoats, out of uniform. Once again, Clamp and his allies were trying to follow Rutherford to find out where he was staying.

Not today.

Rutherford followed the alley, crossing the street on the other side, entering a restaurant and heading through to the kitchen and out the back, up a ladder, across a gantry, and around a pigeon loft. He seated himself on a conveniently placed chair and waited for about ten minutes. Then he opened the box he had left on the roof previously, and changed into street clothes, folding his uniform into a backpack and shrugging it over his shoulder before taking the stairs down through the apartments below and exiting the bakery on the ground level.

Rutherford spent an hour executing switchbacks, watching his back trail, and making confusing jumps between carriages and gondolas. Satisfied any observers had been foiled, he finally closed in on a line of barges moored against the wall of the canal long-term berths, a block or two from the River Dosk. He strolled up the gangplank, feeling weariness suffuse him as the pressure ebbed and he approached rest. Inside, cooking eel and greens simmered in oil, and the smell woke up Rutherford's stomach.

"There you are," the sprightly woman said with a smile as he opened the door and stepped down into the barge interior. "I thought you'd never get back."

"Here I am," Rutherford agreed, answering her smile. "Celia, I hope some of that is for me," he said with a nod at the stove.

"Oh yes, you mentioned you like the speckled twin eels, and they had a fresh batch at the market," Celia said. "Do please help yourself." She stumped over to the table, maneuvering easily on her peg leg without a crutch in the confines of her home on the barge.

"You may have just saved my life," Rutherford said as he tilted the pan, loading his plate. He slid the rest onto her plate, and took both over to the table as she expertly snapped the cork out of a dusty bottle. "How was your day?"

"Mine is only half over," she replied, settling at the table and taking up her two-tined fork. "Got the salvage permits for next season worked out, that's the one office that isn't swamped during festival. Went to Ankhayat Park for the buskers, saw a juggler who used globes with fish in them. Damndest thing," she mused. "You?"

"Chased bad guys. Caught some, let some go," he shrugged.

"Good thing you're not a fisherman," Celia sniffed, teasing him.

"I'm after the big ones," Rutherford said with an echoing grin. He chewed the eel, studying the ranks of railings on the building faces across the canal, looking for signs and signals that might be aimed at him.

"Do you think you can sleep now?" Celia asked, as innocent and carefree as she could pretend to be.

"I think I have to," Rutherford admitted. "I'm knackered." He sipped at his wineglass.

"It does me good to see you eat first, I was beginning to wonder if you planned to survive on street vendor food," she said. "I don't recommend trying that; I had a friend, Daveel, and he had this time efficiency plan to only eat from stalls and carts to and from his workplace. It didn't end well," she said conspiratorially.

"Well, I don't want to be a cautionary tale like Daveel," Rutherford said, and with a couple big bites he finished his supper, leaning back as he chewed.

"That's impressive," Celia admitted, eyeing his plate. "Did you taste it?"

"Oh yes," Rutherford said. "And now I need a chaser, the sweet nectar of unconsciousness. This will help." He finished his wineglass in one pull.

"Part of your efficiency plan?" Celia inquired sweetly.

"Thank you for supper, the brightest company I've had all day, and a place to sleep," Rutherford replied as he rose to his feet. He turned, and crossed the narrow barge interior to the bed with a curtain around half of it. Kicking off his shoes, he stepped in and pulled the curtain around the rest of the bed, and it was immediately quiet.

Hours passed as Celia finished her leisurely meal, washed up, tidied the barge, chatted with a neighbor, ran an errand for some more groceries, and resumed reading her book.

She was startled by the shift and creak of a man stepping on the gangplank and strolling up on the barge, tapping on the door. Hauling herself out of her seat, she cautiously looked out.

"Who is it?" she called to the visitor.

"Laraman, I've got a message for Rutherford," the big man replied as he peered in through a porthole by the door.

"Nobody by that name here," Celia yelled, hefting a pistol from its shelf under a cabinet and cocking the hammer.

"I'll wait at the end of the block," the man replied, and he followed the gangplank off the barge to the canal walk.

Frowning at his receding shadow, Celia reluctantly turned to look over at the bed. Rutherford stepped through the curtain, pistol in hand.

"I told him—" Celia said, but Rutherford raised his hand.

"Thank you, Celia. I'll handle this." He shrugged on a coat, stowed the pistol out of sight, then ducked out of the barge.

He did not make it all the way to the corner before the shadows of an alcove shifted, and a man lit his pipe. Rutherford squared off with him.

"You must be Laraman," Rutherford said.

"Yes. The Hive wants a word with you."

Rutherford grinned and cracked his knuckles. "I thought they might. Let's go."

━━ Chapter Thirteen ━━

Knowledge is about using the hammer of information and the chisel of nuance to carve shapes into the faceless block of ignorance, revealing the shapes of truth within.

As a swordsman, you scoff at those who think all fighting is basically the same brutish process. You see the gulf between the technique of a master and an adept in the Falling Star style. You can explain how the rhythm of the Falling Star style differs from Rising Moon technique; who could confuse cloak-fighting and sash baffles with dual wielding and daggerplay? Those distinctions that have absorbed your life are still confined in the broader field of Iruvian bladework!

If you think these differences are important and you are annoyed at someone who figures it's all knife fighting, then I want you to hold on to that feeling. You told your ladyfriend that you didn't put much confidence in "all that mystical nonsense" and in so doing you revealed yourself to be an insentient dolt lacking basic curiosity or education. You lumped into a single block of ignorance the occult worship of the Forgotten Gods, the reverence of the Church of Ecstasy, the ritual forms of the adepts, and the disciplines of the Whispers. In one casual dismissal, you said you can't be bothered to care about the difference between the Foundation and the Spirit Wardens, much less the limmers and the mediums. You said this to an adept who could have spent a day telling you about which tradition contextualizes her studies—and where her expertise is located within that tradition.

You thought you were judging the world, but she heard you reveal your ignorance. How would you would feel if she said her familiarity with spirit bottles mattered, but your "stabby hobby" was a waste of time? In short, yes, I think you should apologize; but all things considered, I think you should look for a girl with lower standards.

> — *From personal correspondence between*
> *Master Sarzayle and a former student*

Two mugs clattered down on the stained table, suds oozing down the sides, and the server was on to the next errand without a backwards glance. Cellar and Jayan exchanged a wary glance, and Cellar grimaced as he swept up his mug and drained it down, ignoring the sediment and bitter sinus-searing flavor.

"You know it's bad," Jayan growled, staring down at his mug, "when *this* is my idea for getting an awful taste out of my mouth." He sniffed at his reservations, then took a long pull from his mug.

Cellar leaned back into the shadows of the stall in the hasty and temporary tavern built into the half-demolished stable leaning against a restaurant's outer wall. The building was packed with festival-goers even though it didn't serve food. The shattered red sun strained at the dim sky, shedding what light it could, and the crowd near the waterfront was making the most of the revelry. A roar of laughter emerged from the crowd watching the puppet theater set up on the street outside.

"Well?" Jayan said, squinting at Cellar. "What are you thinking?"

"Spirit Wardens do not accept members who were born in Doskvol, or have family here; I think those are the rules, anyway," Cellar murmured. "I don't know where Spur was from. That outfit, the uniform—it wasn't neglected, it had been oiled and maintained within the week, I'd swear to it. Who else could it belong to?" he breathed, eyes wide as he stared at nothing, his mind racing.

"More to the point, *why?*" Jayan asked. "If I was a Spirit Warden, I don't think pretending to be a petty criminal would be much of a thrill."

"If Spirit Wardens can have double lives, then that means they've got an invisible spy network they don't have to pay for information. One they can trust," Cellar said through his teeth. "Think about all the conversations Spur could overhear. The access he could get." He shook his head, then took Jayan's beer and drained it off too. "Events they could influence. People they could kill."

"So who can we trust? If Spirit Wardens may have undercover personas?" Jayan mused.

"I am certain they'd kill to protect this secret, and the secrets connected to it," Cellar mumbled as he stared into the glistening pit of the empty mug. "I'm sure they have." His face contracted in a scowl. "That's why they resisted so hard, when I tried to establish some factuals. They don't want details in the record, they wanted Spur to be..." he shrugged. "Untraceable."

Both men sat thinking so hard the tumble of their half-formed ideas was almost audible.

"Okay," Cellar muttered, watching the bar as patrons came and went. "Okay. I sent Daava to find out more about the Skullface Killer's activity a decade ago. The last rash of victims." He shook his head. "There will be more deaths, that seems certain. We don't know enough. We are behind."

"Do you think any of the previous victims were Spirit Wardens?" Jayan asked, breathless with the force of the possibility.

Cellar watched him unblinking for a long moment. "The symbol. On the chest. Maybe... maybe deserters? Traitors?" His eyes widened. "The Skullface Killer may well be a Spirit Warden."

"Or a *rogue* Spirit Warden," Jayan whispered.

Cellar abruptly rose, stepping out of the stall booth. "Too far, this is all too far," he said. "We need more—more facts. Spinning conjecture, we'll just start—we need to know more."

"Daava went to check the archives," Jayan said. "I need to make sure you're with somebody who can establish your factuals, before I go looking for her."

"Send a runner," Cellar said. "You stick with me. Tell her to meet us here," he said as he looked over the crowd.

"Why don't you come with me to the runner's station," Jayan said, his voice flat.

Cellar looked over at him for a long moment, then nodded.

"Let's go."

THE GIBBITY JIG PUBLIC HOUSE, FOGCREST, SILKSHORE.
25TH VOLVINET. TENTH HOUR PAST DAWN.
SAIL LIGHTING FESTIVAL, DAY THREE.

"What do they drink, over there at that back table?" Sanction asked the harried young server.

"What, the Fog Hounds?" the server said. "They like the Exhalation Rum; tarry stuff. I don't recommend it, that's an acquired taste," he grimaced.

"Three bottles to their table," Sanction said. He slapped a handful of coin on the table and slid it towards the server.

"You want them to know their benefactor?" the server asked.

"Oh yes," Sanction replied, leaning back. He was watching the table several minutes later when a server brought the bottles to the Fog Hounds' table, and pointed towards him. The big man seated in the back scowled, and had a quick conversation with the frowzy ginger woman at his side. She rose, nodding towards Sanction; the third man at the table got up, managed his very fancy hat, adjusted his baldric, and minced over towards Sanction. The ginger sidled around the edge of the room, approaching at a slower pace and a more oblique angle.

"Salutations and felicitations," the dandy said with a bow and a flourish of the hat, a feat in the crowded room. "I understand you wish to offer us a generous gesture."

"The first of many," Sanction replied. His eyes flicked over the dandy, taking in his layered pancake makeup, balding wig, and threadbare clothes. Every part of the dandy's kit was on the edge of wearing through from frequent use—including his thin sword.

"Gestures tend to have several meanings," the dandy continued. "Generosity generally offers something small to ask for something bigger." He arched an eyebrow.

"I want to talk to you without a gun in my face," Sanction replied mildly, "so I sent a gift to invite you over here. I've got a job for your people."

"Iruvians?" the dandy sniffed.

"Fog Hounds," Sanction corrected, loud. He cocked his head to the side. "For being invested in etiquette, you certainly have taken your time introducing yourself."

"Me? I am Zalrin, at your service," he said with another bow as he bent a leg. "I refrained from announcing myself, as then etiquette requires me to ask for your own name if you have not offered it yet—which you have not," he pointed out.

"You know I won't tell you who I am," Sanction said. "I want to hire your crew for a job that doesn't get connected back to me. That can't be unusual."

"Indeed not," Zalrin replied airily. "Have you sufficient coin to retain our services?"

Sanction slowly rose from the table, looking Zalrin in the eye. He said nothing. He allowed Zalrin to look him over. Where Zalrin was foppish, Sanction's quietly expensive clothes were tailored and refined. Where Zalrin's sword drew the eye, Sanction did not display any weapons. Where Zalrin projected his personality, Sanction inhabited his. The dandy let out a nervous titter, then shrugged the feeling away.

"Follow me then, let's consult with our second-in-command," he said with a fluttering wave.

Sanction followed the dandy to the Fog Hound table, aware that the ginger woman fell in behind him. He stood across from the big man draped in fur, who scowled at him through a majestic bristle of facial hair and scarring.

"What the hell do you want," the big man grunted.

"I'm going to hand you some tools," Sanction replied, "so you can smash the Hive in Silkshore."

"Oh, smash the Hive," the big man echoed, skeptical.

"I can see why you'd doubt it," Sanction said. "After all, the Hive just consolidated the Gaddoc Rail Station. Wrapped up all the smuggling through that portal. They're making a move on North Port, and they're going to control that portal too if you don't move fast."

"Aren't you just the king of the Ink Rakes," the hairy man sneered. "Reporter?"

"Better," Sanction replied, narrowing his eyes. "Your name is Ethan Bear. You, Corly Zalrin. Goldie Tellermach, of course; the Fog Hounds would never have figured the northern Void Sea routes without her." He glanced at the ginger woman behind him as she scowled. "I could have gone straight to Vale, but she's on the ship entertaining private company right now and you're the one I want to talk to anyway. Now that you've unloaded your cargo from the Dagger Isles and you're looking to spend your spoils."

"Not bad," Zalrin grudgingly admitted, eyes wide. "How the hell did you find out my first name?"

"I know all five of your names, Zalrin," Sanction replied, eyes not leaving Bear. "The take-away here is that I've studied your crew and I know enough about who you are and what you can do that I am confident you can take on a little job for me."

"I don't like it, I don't like *you*," Bear growled, rising to his full impressive height. "Maybe I just kill you."

"You won't," Sanction replied, looking him in the eye. "Will this go on much longer? You're very frightening, yes, but I want to be done with this conversation before dark."

"He will probably tell *me* to kill you," Zalrin clarified with a conspiratorial shrug.

"I don't know, maybe not this time," Bear rumbled. "I really don't like this guy's face."

"What's the job," Goldie demanded, matter-of-fact as she crossed her arms.

Sanction turned to her. "You need to take the fight to the Hive before they consolidate their position enough to confidently take on your sponsor," Sanction replied. "I know their assets are well protected, and that's why you need to strike at their coordination. There are two main targets."

"Don't you want to talk pay first?" Bear muttered, sullen.

Sanction continued talking to Goldie. "For Silkshore, the first target is Barness. He handles the invisible money, the network of bribery and corruption. He's out of reach at the moment; Bluecoats hit his lair and disrupted his communications. He's in hiding."

"Oh, you can't find him?" Bear scoffed.

Sanction didn't even glance over at him. "The second target is Dalia. She handles the invisible property the Hive controls, working through proxies and organizations that can obfuscate ownership and tax issues."

"What, you need us to find *her*?" Bear interrupted.

"Excuse me for a moment," Sanction said to Goldie. He deliberately turned and looked Bear in the eye, unimpressed by his height and mass. "Barness was raided by the Bluecoats," he said quietly, "and I don't know if they got his coded ledger of bribes to law enforcement or not. Regardless, he's compromised and not the highest value target now—especially if the Bluecoats assault his network. I know where Dalia is, and where she'll be, and when she's vulnerable." He turned back to Goldie. "If you Fog Hounds do not take on Orris and get the Hive to take a more cautious approach, you'll likely be cashed out by the end of the festival."

"You know where Orris himself is?" Goldie retorted.

"I don't," Sanction replied, "but you don't need him yet. You just need him busy. Triggering a power struggle sounds like a good idea, but the way each of Orris's aspiring successors would prove themselves starts with shredding your crew. You want Orris focused on protecting properties you aren't supposed to know about. Hit them in succession, stealing and killing and burning, and he will be forced to pay attention to you or his report up the chain won't look good." He paused. "The Hive is pretty harsh with failures."

"And you get something out of this," Goldie prompted.

"I'm not going to mount any attacks," Sanction replied, arching an eyebrow. "I was never here, we never talked, you won't look into me or who I work for. No reason for the Hive to connect us. We both need the Hive to take a hit. I'm doing my part." He turned to look Bear in the eye. "If you want to fight back, I'm giving you a target that will cause real pain."

"That's already the plan, smart guy," Bear frowned. "Hit the rail station. Hit the toadies that signed on with the Hive, those backstabbing bastards. Dry up the market."

"You have five members of your crew, maybe two or three gangs you can pull in," Sanction replied. "With that, you want to take on the protected customs office, the Doskvol transit guard, and the Bluecoats. Afterwards, the Inspectors and the military will get involved. All that to knock out a few mules and one or two supply runs." He looked at Goldie. "Good luck with that plan."

"Of course you—" Bear started, but Goldie cut him off.

"Look, mister," she said to Sanction, "we know shipping and transport. We've got plans. But," she added, forestalling other comments from her crew with a raised finger as she studied Sanction, "lots of our plans are aimed to find out Hive safehouses. You say this Dalia, she could fill us in."

"She knows them all," Sanction replied. "You take her alive, get her to trade that information for her freedom, then make sure no one ever finds the body. Under no circumstances should she walk free, or you'll pay the price for it; the Hive will see to that. You will have to frame her reality so giving you information is the only way out that she can see, right up until the end."

"That's chilly," Zalrin observed, subdued. "Is that what you're doing now? Framing *our* reality?"

Sanction looked over at him for a moment, then indulged a small sigh. "I have deep pockets and esoteric needs," he said quietly. "I want to use your services for my smuggling needs, I think we could have a great partnership. But for that to work out you have to survive, and you're on the edge of not managing that."

Sanction squared off with Bear. "Dalia will attend the opera tonight, Clashendo, Charterhall. It's over at midnight and she tends to leave early. She will have four tough bodyguards, and she will be using the alias Cynthia Forthright. If you need more than that, you aren't worth what I've already given you." He took a step back, nodded to Goldie, then turned and left the bar. Sanction did not spare a backwards glance as he crossed the street, walked a block, and pulled himself up into the carriage.

"Think they'll go for it?" Crackstone asked.

"Oh yeah," Sanction replied, finally allowing himself a bleak smile.

The whip cracked, and the carriage rolled away.

SADSACK'S HAPPY TAVERN, FOGCREST, SILKSHORE.
25TH VOLVINET. TENTH HOUR PAST DAWN.
SAIL LIGHTING FESTIVAL, DAY THREE.

"I screwed up," Daava growled, slapping her leather satchel on the splintery table. "The only way I could get a look at the Skullface Killer files was to sub in for filing duty on special Inspector assignment. So I did, and I got a look at the files as they came and went. A whole army of Inspector support staff and Bluecoat administrators are brushing up on the history. So that part went fine."

"What part didn't," Cellar demanded.

"The problem is the files. They've been tampered with. Before I got them. Hell, before *any* of this happened. Pages are missing. There are new pages with different handwriting. Somebody got in and adjusted things without leaving a trail in the sign-in protocols. Now, since I subbed in, once somebody figures out that the files were adjusted I'll be a suspect." She dropped her head down on her crossed arms and groaned out her frustration.

"Blood and bone," Jayan said, forlorn. "That hagfish, she keeps on chewing."

"Tell me you found some kind of connection to the Spirit Wardens," Cellar said.

"Uh, just one," Daava replied. "Doctor Vanwhyle told us there were four people who saw, you know. From last time," she said with a meaningful look to Cellar.

"Right," he nodded.

"Wait, what is this secret?" Jayan demanded.

Cellar looked him in the eye. "Are you sure you want to know? Really sure? Think about this for a second."

"Yes I'm sure, dammit," Jayan retorted. "I break the law for you all the time and no one will believe you spared me the details. If I'm going to get tortured, I want some answers to give them. I can't even begin to make up something as weird as the truth for this."

Cellar looked over at Daava, then made up his mind. "There was a symbol carved into the flesh of Spur's chest," he said quietly. "Under where the cut-off face was nailed on."

"Golden brown pants litter," Jayan breathed. "That's—really great."

Daava opened her book to the page with her sketch, and slid it to where he could see it. "That symbol looks like a Spirit Warden glyph, now that you mention it," she murmured to Cellar. "So the one connection I found to the Spirit Wardens is the people who knew about the glyph in the chest. The records don't mention the symbol, of course, but there were two lead investigators who were sure to have seen it. The Spirit Wardens insisted on a joint operation to hunt the Skullface Killer. The Church backed them up, so the Inspectors allowed it. Spirit Wardens are anonymous, but they get mission-based callsigns. We had Sephimous on this one. Also, Chief Inspector Dartfire was on the job. Dartfire died three years ago, and Sephimous—we have no way of knowing."

"So," Cellar said slowly, "the only person that we know for sure saw this glyph thing... that's the doctor." He leaned back. "This file was *watched*. By the authorities. High profile, unsolved case." A frown contracted his face. "Whoever modified the file... that's bold. Bold and smart enough to get away with it. Comfortable enough to attempt tweaking our bureaucratic systems and risk exposure." He shook his head. "That's a different kind of brazen than public murder."

"The Skullface Killer is going to take a shot at Doctor Vanwhyle," Jayan said, eyes widening.

"She knows something that she may not even know she knows," Cellar agreed. "She could be a threat. I mean, why kill ten people?"

"Seems more ritual than thrill," Daava mused. "Probably needed all these sacrifices to make some demon happy."

"Maybe," Cellar said. "Maybe so. It is a nice round number." He looked to his specials. "What do you think? Is Doctor Vanwhyle a target?"

"If you think it's a lead, we should shadow her," Jayan said immediately. "Research is just going to get us in more trouble. Even if we find something that *wasn't* tampered with—it doesn't look good. It won't look good at our trials."

"And apparently you *can't* go home at this point," Daava said. "None of us can. We've disobeyed orders and made things much, much worse for you and for ourselves. The only way we get out of this now is by solving it, or facing execution. Banishment. Prison. Whatever."

"It's a couple hours until dusk." Cellar looked to Daava. "Any insights on timing?"

"Dusk, dawn, mid-day, midnight. The Skullface Killer struck when the clock was at its highest and lowest," Daava replied.

"If you're doing rituals and trying to shut people up," Jayan began.

"The Blind Hour," Cellar agreed. "When the dusk fog rises that's a prime opportunity. I don't know how long we can stake out the doctor as our sacrificial lamb, but we've got to at least make an attempt to lure this bastard in. That's what, two hours?"

"Less," Daava agreed.

"I'll get transport," Jayan said as he rose from the table and pushed through the jostling crowd.

Cellar bit his lip, not looking at Daava. "I can't think of anything to say that doesn't sound stupid," he said. "I know—the risk—"

"Even that sounded stupid," she agreed. "Forget it." Standing, she looked around the room, then hefted her pack. "Make it up to me by solving this thing."

"I promise I will," Cellar said as his heart sank. Then it was time to move.

REMEMBRANCE ARCHIVE, CLERK STREET, CHARTERHALL. 25TH VOLVINET. TWELFTH HOUR PAST DAWN. SAIL LIGHTING FESTIVAL, DAY THREE.

Lightning thrashed against the spikes of Bellweather Crematorium tower, flicking an alien white light over the streets below. A thud of thunder followed, rattling windows as the light evaporated. Rain sifted down over the rising mists. The Clerk Street bureaucracy was closing, so workers streamed out of the massive buildings.

"I thought this was a bad idea at first," Jayan confessed as he hunched deeper in his Bluecoat half-cape, gazing at the crematorium tower several blocks away. "I had no sense of scale for *how bad* an idea it really was. That's just a lack of imagination on my part."

"What the hell is wrong with you," Cellar said, his voice distant as he studied the crowd pouring out of the government archive buildings. "I mean, if you think it's a bad idea, why did you come?"

"I'm desperate for friendship," Jayan admitted. "I'll do anything. It's pathetic." He squinted up through the rapidly cooling rain as it intensified. "Are you kidding me right now?"

"Doctor Vanwhyle should be finishing her briefing with the Chief Inspectors, if you're right about her schedule," Cellar said.

"I don't know if she'll do what's on the schedule, but I'm sure I got a good look at it," Jayan said. "Can you believe her assistant didn't buy my cover story that I was a doctor from out of town who wanted to consult on radiant poisoning?"

"Somehow I can," Cellar sighed. "I think you're right. This, what are we doing? We don't have the resources for a stakeout. Nobody does.

This is festival," he muttered, glaring at the crowd of pale government workers streaming out of the massive blocky institutions lining the street. "This... is a terrible idea."

"There," Jayan said, pointing. "Green light. That's Daava. She's spotted—"

Cellar was already moving, pushing through the crowd. Jayan waded in after him, a stern expression hiding his glee as he shouldered bureaucrats aside and knocked satchels and cases out of hands in his rushing bustle.

A strange synchronicity settled around Cellar as he struggled against the flow. The faceless masses fueling the government machinery pressed around him, dragging him away from his path. The lowering sky writhed with lightning and rain as everything seemed to slide inexorably down towards the invisible throat of the hourglass his world had become.

Then he reached the spot where Daava had signaled. Climbing the capstone of a fence pillar, he looked around and spotted the light she left on the street. He dropped down and ran towards it, moving much faster since the side streets were largely unused by the end-of-day exodus. Stooping, he picked up the green-tinted glow orb, and he spotted Daava only a block or so ahead. He broke into a run to catch up, his foot-falls muted as he chose his steps and hunched into a stealthy sprint.

Mist rose from the warm pavement into the cooling air, the exhalation of the earth confusing the eye and baffling sounds. Cellar was only a few paces behind Daava, and he could see the unmistakable tall form of the doctor almost a block ahead. Before satisfaction was properly settled, his blood chilled.

A man's dark shape unfolded from a side alley, closing in on the doctor in a couple noiseless strides.

"Hey!" Cellar shouted. As the doctor pivoted towards the noise, the dark shape snatched her and clapped a hand over her face. She struggled, clutching at the arm that wrapped around her neck and hauled her around between himself and Cellar. Daava jumped to the side and knelt, pistol out, squinting through the fog at the overlapping shadows. Cellar kept walking towards the doctor and her assailant, empty hands up to the sides.

"You don't want to do this," Cellar said clearly. "Witnesses. Backup in place. You aren't getting away, and if you hurt her I'll verify you did it. That's execution for you."

The doctor sagged in her assailant's grip as the drugged face cloth did its work. The assailant lowered to a crouch as she swayed down, losing her balance and lucidity.

Drop your weapons, the shadow hissed. The glint of reflected light on a small, sharp blade stopped Cellar in his tracks as the knife touched the doctor's throat.

"Do as he says," Cellar said, not taking his eyes off the shadow for a moment. He heard the reluctant clack of Daava's pistol laid on the cobbles behind him.

"It's been a day for surprises," Cellar said to the shadow, his voice as neutral as he could make it. "You may be able to kill the doctor, but there's no way you escape if you do."

Mist drifted past, isolating the confrontation, like the rest of the world was a muffled party in another room. The shadow did not move. The doctor groaned, vaguely gesturing with one hand. Cellar gauged the distance between himself and the assailant. A rush, the results measured in fractions of a second.

Cautious, Cellar took a step towards the hostage standoff. Another. "Maybe we can work something out," he said. "Maybe you forget about this and go have a drink, and we let you." Cellar leaned forward, as though listening, as though his stance would draw the eye away from the small steps that brought him ever closer. "What's that? I can't hear you," he said.

Close enough? Close enough!

Cellar launched himself forward—snatched the doctor! The shadow shoved her at Cellar just as he lunged, and Cellar barreled into the hostage as the shadow raised a thin-barreled pistol and fired with a sharp crack. Cellar's heart stopped as his body flashed a reaction, anticipating the smack of the bullet, but the bullet didn't hit him.

Staggering to the side and dumping the doctor's limp form, Cellar dragged at the pistol in his coat—so *fast*, the shadow was on him as the lightning flashed, revealing a tangle of beard and a crazed eye as the shadow batted his gun hand aside and drove a blow under his collarbone.

Agony seared through Cellar as though he had been cut in half, and a scream burst from him. The shadow overbalanced him, and he only dimly felt himself crash down on his back as the stab wound in his chest blared an impossible wave of sensation through him. His attacker loomed over him, gripping his lapel, face dipping close yet deep in shadow. Cellar felt the puffs of air and the tickle of his assailant's beard as whispered words—Hadrathi maybe?—spattered at him. Then the shadow leaped to his feet and sprinted away, almost soundless, half real in the fog and the rain.

Cellar heard a sizzle and hoarse sobbing. He clutched at his chest. Pressure on the wound! Pressure on the wound! His fingers were numb, and running steps closed in. He tried to squint through the intensifying rain, and he saw a Bluecoat approach; Jayan.

"Boss, hey, I'm here," Jayan said as he knelt by Cellar. "Let me look. Let me look!" He pried Cellar's hands away from his shoulder, and Cellar became vaguely aware he was the one sobbing as he hovered on the edge of consciousness.

"What—what the hell is that?" Jayan said in a hushed tone, staring at the wound.

"Daava!" Cellar yelled. "After him! Daava!" His voice broke, and he clutched his burning collarbone.

"Oh, no," Jayan said, looking over at Daava. Where she lay sprawled on the cobbles. Motionless.

Close, too close, the Bellweather bell tolled once. Twice.

"Doctor?" Cellar gritted out, trying to blink the rain out of his eyes.

Jayan's heart tried to pound its way out of his chest as he took in the sight of the collapsed doctor, and the darkening pool around her huddled form.

"Yeah, boss, there's no explaining this away," he said. His voice trembled.

"Dammit! Dammit!" Cellar screamed from the blending streams of pain flowing through him. "Okay we go!"

Jayan hauled at the injured Inspector, dragging him most of the way to his feet. As whistles shrilled in the surrounding streets, they struggled away from the lights.

CHAPTER FOURTEEN

*It's no surprise you didn't hear about the Claycourt mummies.
Back in the summer of 840, I was on the work crew that took
down that façade on the Zellmaker Theater along the canal.
Filthy work, on scaffolding, over the water a couple stories
up. The façade was built, what, twenty years before. But the
Ministry was going to put a bridge across to access the theater
on the fourth floor and it would connect where the façade was.
We had to clear the connecting point, so we cracked the façade
open. This row of stone blocks was built into the wall, the
perches for statues. Turns out the blocks were hollow.*

*I was one of the guys opening the first box. Inside, a corpse,
preserved and long-dead. You could see how the poor bastard
clawed at the walls, it wasn't a quick death. There were air
holes in the box; it wasn't supposed to be quick. There was
some kind of writing carved inside, and looking at it made my
head hurt.*

*Right away the foreman got us away from the boxes, yelled at
us that we didn't see a damn thing, and got the Spirit Wardens
involved. I only opened the one box, but there were six, and I
would bet they all had somebody inside. Lucky for me, I didn't
give a damn.*

*There was nothing in the papers about the discovery, nothing
official released, as far as I know there was no investigation.
The foreman had my back, he didn't give my name to the authorities as someone who saw what was in that box. Dawson
was at my elbow when we breached that box, and he just had
to find out more. A week later he was knifed by a mugger. Me,
I got to live a full life, and it's about over anyway, so what the
hell. Enjoy the story.*

*— Interview transcript, Mendar 847,
discovered in the investigation of the disappearance of
Polonia Waylund, reporter for the Gnasher Street Report*

TATTLER'S TOWER, IRONHOOK PRISON, DUNSLOUGH.
25ᵀᴴ VOLVINET. TENTH HOUR PAST DAWN.
SAIL LIGHTING FESTIVAL, DAY THREE.

The approaching footsteps roused Piccolo to a drowse, and the clatter and jangle of keys woke him fully. He cleared his throat and rolled his shoulders, stretching as best he could while wrapped in an inmate jacket and caged in the gibbet hanging in the center of his cell. He settled into position to watch the door as it swung open.

"There you are," the Bluecoat officer said with a jovial tone as he stepped into the cell holding a lantern. A blank faced Bluecoat pulled the door closed behind him. "So glad you had time for a meeting." His smile widened, and the effect was unflattering.

"You know I wouldn't duck you," Piccolo said with an answering smile, "but I've got places to be and I'm late. Let's move this along." He was vaguely surprised by the rasp in his voice.

"I'm Chief Hamstead, I run Tattler's Tower along with several other neighborhoods in our little community," Hamstead said with an airy gesture. "You've brought me a thorny little problem."

"Really?" Piccolo said with genuine surprise. "I've been behaving myself in this little box since I got here. No biting, stabbing, none of that. Did the medic complain?"

"Heh, you aren't my problem, you just brought me one," Hamstead clarified. "No complaint from the medic. Report I got suggests you'll survive getting shot and all the rest. Trouble is, I can't have that," he shrugged.

Piccolo was instantly quiet and watchful, subtly flexing to make sure he was ready.

"You may have heard," Hamstead continued conspiratorially, "sometimes people in Ironhook have convenient accidents. There's a whole unfortunate economy around it, based on who is likely to give a damn and how the death must appear, and how much scrutiny it can withstand. Quite a process. The Silkworms have been good customers in the past."

"There's also an economy for keeping prisoners alive," Piccolo replied, terse. "The Silkworms will be good for that as well. Are we negotiating?"

"No no, the negotiations are over," Hamstead said. "You also know that life and death in Ironhook is a communication medium. A way to send messages, so to speak. And there are some people on the outside who really need to have a face to face conversation," he said as he mournfully shook his head. "All this proxy nonsense means the messenger gets shot, and the messenger who took a message to the messenger, and... it's really rather a lot of killing to clarify various points. The diplomatic equivalent of yelling," he mused.

"That sure does put you in a tough spot," Piccolo agreed. "When one group wants things to go a certain way and another one wants something else, how do you look after your own interests? These people are obviously willing to order someone's death," Piccolo nodded thoughtfully. "They don't leave you a lot of room, do they."

"Thank you, of course you're right, they don't. Where is their sense of fair play and consideration? Truly tragic," Hamstead sighed. "But before you embarrass yourself, let me get to my next point."

Piccolo said nothing, poised between a number of options, feeling his heartbeat in his wounds' stitches and his cracked rib.

"The gondoliers are pissed," Hamstead said frankly. "They've offered me a princely sum for overseeing your accident in prison. A number of them are in custody in Ironhook, and all I need to do is transfer you to an area where one of them can reach you. Or, for a little extra bonus, I can handle it here in solitary, in Tattler's Tower where snitches are supposed to be out of reach. More scrutiny, but this accident alone will secure my retirement. I guess the Silkworms are over, after you failed to stop that sniper. The gondoliers suggest that your screw-up and subsequent capture has left you desolate with no reason to live, and they suggested some of the points you could make in a suicide note." His smile returned.

"Let's not stop there," Piccolo replied, wary.

"Indeed, let's continue. You were brought here personally by a shiny new Bluecoat, Rutherford. He took me aside and had a very specific conversation with me. He told me that I would be instructed to get rid of you, and he paid me a handsome sum in advance to pretend I complied with those instructions but to instead squirrel you away in an even danker, even more secret hole than this," he said with an expansive gesture at the narrow cell. "He didn't want a cut of the gondolier payment, either, he told me to keep it—and keep you here off the books." Hamstead cocked his head to the side. "If that's a message, it's encoded. But I think you'll notice who is missing from the bargaining table."

"The Silkworms," Piccolo said through his teeth.

"Just so," Hamstead nodded. "Word is, the Silkworms are through. I don't think anyone is coming for you, at least not in a way you'd like. I don't need more enemies among the Bluecoats, and I do like getting paid, so we're going to fake your death and put you somewhere you'll never be found unless Rutherford comes looking for you again. Unless, of course, you want to try a daring move. This is the time," Hamstead said with mock sympathy.

Piccolo watched him for a long moment. "I'm bored with these walls," he said. "Let's look at another apartment."

"Yes," Hamstead said, brandishing the keys. "Let's. You make any sudden moves, you try something heroic, and I will ventilate you with my suicide shiv. Failing that, you know I have backup."

"I know," Piccolo agreed. "If I had a drink, I'd offer a toast. To the long game."

"To the long game," Hamstead echoed. He approached, and unlocked the gibbet. Grasping the chest of Piccolo's jacket, he pulled him out to land unsteadily on the stone floor. "Just think," he said with a crooked smile. "You've been here about a day and a half. Imagine how bored with the walls you'll be by this time next year."

"Cheery," Piccolo said grimly. "Let's go."

Hamstead chuckled, then let out a whistle. The guard opened the door, and they shuffled out, leaving the empty cell in darkness.

TIRIAL RESERVE CANALWAY, THE EASE, SILKSHORE. 25ᵀᴴ VOLVINET. TENTH HOUR PAST DAWN. SAIL LIGHTING FESTIVAL, DAY THREE.

Mistress of Tides sat erect on the cushioned seat in the gondola's tent, feeling the dim thud of her heart, the strain that spiced her blood. "Nevi," she called out. Only a moment passed before the tent flap shifted and the acolyte joined her. "We have changed course," Mistress of Tides observed.

"Festival traffic," Nevi replied apologetically. "The main channel would take hours. We have diverted to the Tirial Reserve Canalway. Unless you object," she added respectfully.

"No, proceed," the Mistress of Tides murmured. "I need to get back. Make preparations. It is time for decisive action." Her frown was audible.

Nevi bowed, then moved to raise the tent's flap, halting as the Mistress of Tides raised her hand.

"Nevi," the Mistress of Tides said, "how is Yelsir doing? Her back?"

"The salve has numbed and relaxed the area," Nevi replied. "She is moving alright, and has not complained."

"Thank you," the Mistress of Tides said. "I understand your studies are going well," she added.

Nevi had been poised to leave, but she responded to an unspoken signal, gracefully lowering herself to the bench opposite the Mistress of Tides. "Thank you."

"You have joined my retinue at a complicated time," the Mistress of Tides said. "A time of change." She gazed into an indeterminate middle space for a long moment. "I wonder... I wonder about many things that are not clear at this time." The Mistress of Tides shifted. "How strange."

"Strange, my lady?" Nevi asked politely.

"In this moment, between us, I am aware of a thing that is so second nature that I can only detect it in its absence, when it does not exist where expected," the Mistress of Tides mused. "I feel a reluctance to end the conversation, and yet I have not planned out my objective for it. In my role, I do not have the patience or need for... small talk. Hm."

"I sense isolation is usually not uncomfortable for you," Nevi replied. "I most often want someone nearby when I need proof I am not as alone as I feel." She blushed slightly as the Mistress of Tides considered her for a long moment.

"I did not expect such insight in a novice," the Mistress of Tides said. "I am not sure I agree with your idea, but I am pleased that it has some depth."

Nevi blinked. "Thank you, my lady," she said.

"When we return," the Mistress of Tides began, then she paused, cocking her head to the side as though listening. "Do you feel—"

A thud reverberated through the wood of the gondola, followed by a splash behind it. The Mistress of Tides and Nevi were on their feet as shadows loomed then shrank on the cloth walls of the tent, fore and aft. A tearing hiss resonated against the underside of the bridge over the canal as some unseen force tore the tent from its footing on the gondola, twirling it off to the side as armored figures leaped at the Whisper and her acolyte.

The Mistress of Tides had only a moment to glimpse the metal mask of her assailant before she ducked the sledge hammer that whipped over her. Tugging a blade from her boot, she slashed in a crescent as she rose, slitting a pale line on the metal breastplate of her attacker as her other hand came around in a defensive posture.

The gondola trembled and bucked with the force of the assailants moving on it, but the Mistress of Tides had a steady stance. Her attacker thrust with the hammer, firing it forward, but she slapped it aside and took a step back; behind her, Nevi cried out as she thudded against an armored attacker, and the Mistress of Tides heard the boarder crash down through the surface of the canal.

A moment of relaxing her senses told the Mistress of Tides there were six attackers—three on the gondola, one in the canal, and two on the bridge above. They were easy to detect now, as the dimming ritual that cloaked them lit them up to her senses now that she was inside the ritual's influence.

A smile twisted the Mistress of Tides' features, invisible behind the veil.

The Mistress of Tides cried out a single Hadrathi word, *retreat*, and she dove cleanly off the gondola.

After all, *she* wasn't wearing armor.

Trusting her acolytes, the Mistress of Tides pounded her fists together (one fist still gripping the knife) and clenched her eyes shut, ignoring the pressure on her torso as her body drained the nourishment from the air in her lungs. Instead she focused on the water, the inevitability of current seeking balance, and the things that did not belong in this corridor of liquid. Her energies interlaced with the tatters of death that saturated the canal.

The Mistress of Tides was dimly aware of Nevi driving a kick into the chest of the armored attacker who was already in the water, pushing him away from her as she concentrated. The Mistress of Tides pulled the threads of interconnected reality into her fist.

The canal depth. The current. The shallow draft of the gondola, deepened some by the weight upon it now. The drifting tent, now saturating rapidly on the canal surface. One living acolyte, one dead. No tolling of the bells, no Deathseekers for this fight—the swaddling boundaries of the ritual were designed to hide killing from the supernatural senses of the bells and the crows. The ritual wasn't a Whisper design, nor did it pull from the dead, so the gondola's defensive protections didn't interact with it.

Whispers would know better than to attack the Mistress of Tides on the canal. So too would the Spirit Wardens. So these attackers were something else. She would satisfy her curiosity, but first things first.

Shall We Drown, she whispered in Hadrathi, galvanizing the threads she collected to herself in her motionless casting of the lethal ritual. She did not sink, nor did she float. She could hold her breath for over three minutes. She would now see to it that her attackers could not.

She tightened her fist, feeling the flex of her foe's chest, tripling the pressure of the water and surprising a bloom of air out of him; bubbles spurted all around his metal mask as he wildly swung his hammer, too slow underwater. Nevi had twisted around already; she snatched the back of his collar and yanked back as she drove her knee between his shoulderblades, finishing his air.

Smiling, the Mistress of Tides felt the water pressing at the man's face, and she felt his starving and empty lungs trying to inflate. She flexed, and the water drove through all obstacles between the canal and those flattened lungs, filling them to the point of tearing flesh.

Now her ritual was simmering in the canal all around her, and she was ready. Her other hand clawed towards the gondola, and she felt a ripple in the enchantments layered into its hull. She felt the energies woven through it respond to their master, responsive to her influence. Sifting through the possible commands, she found the one she knew waited for her.

Capsize, she whispered, and the gondola violently lurched before upending in an unlikely flip. Her drowning ritual hissed through her mind's eye with the bubbles from the disrupted surface. She felt her dead acolyte, and two others. She could taste the blood filtering through the turbulence. There, one dying assailant. She felt three more, living and startled, passing through the surface into the canal.

The Mistress of Tides contemptuously flicked a finger, and the squirming animated water in her victim flexed hard to snap his neck. She released that grip and shifted; she felt her ritual connection to her acolytes, and she tugged at it. Both relaxed their defenses towards her, and she drew from their life energy to fuel a hard and sudden squeeze on the torsos of the other three armored assailants. Convulsing, the attackers released gouts of bubbles that glittered towards the surface.

Yelsir's face flickered in the Mistress of Tides' consciousness, jarringly abrupt, as though the two of them were alone together.

Mistress, the image breathed, *I am hurt—I will die.* The Mistress of Tides twitched as she felt Yelsir's shattered bone, a direct blow from a hammer in the center of her back, blood rioting beyond its channels and bounds inside her body. *These are Foundation assassins. Take all I have and let none escape.*

The Mistress of Tides was bombarded with the last breaths of her acolyte. She felt Yelsir's shock at her former master's death, felt her agony and surreal echoes of pain, felt her cold and desperate need to matter. To serve. Here at the end.

The Mistress of Tides accepted her gift. No bell would toll for Yelsir. Her spirit was not freed.

The human sacrifice flared through the Mistress of Tides' ritual, burning. It illuminated the Foundation assassin on the edge of escaping her ritual's range as he savagely flailed at the water to get distance before he drowned. The other two had not panicked; one caught hold of Nevi as the other pushed back at the Mistress of Tides' ritual using a potent spiritbane amulet and remarkable concentration.

No.

The Mistress of Tides screamed into the water. The spiritbane amulet shattered. A wild current swept Nevi's attacker into the wall of the canal with a bone-shattering smack. And the swimmer—the swimmer was gripped by the ankles and torn down through the water, its pressure forced up through the mask and into his sinuses. Her grip was inexorable. With a series of throaty crunches, the three assassins were broken in the water's shapeless grip.

Spent, the Mistress of Tides regained her buoyancy as she released the water from the force of her will. *Right yourself,* she breathed to the gondola with the last of her air. The gondola shivered, then flipped, and she reached up to ride its movement out of the canal and onto the deck. Then she opened to the air, breathing once more.

The Mistress of Tides tingled as she sensed the edge of the cloaking ritual passing over her; the two remaining Foundation Assassins were withdrawing.

"No!" the Mistress of Tides shouted. A number of truths folded together, blended in her instincts. The Foundation assassins were somehow marked or warded by a ritual to suppress the sensation of death in the city; also, their life force was not directly vulnerable to detection or manipulation by Whisper abilities. However, four of them were dead and broken, and her energies lingered in their corpsemeat. And she was still within their ritual. She tasted the cost, but was beyond caring as anger unfurled through her overtaxed blood.

You will answer to me, she believed with brutal force. Ruthless, she peeled the panicked echoes of the dead assassins out of their cooling flesh; the firm corral the Foundation ritual created behind the Mirror made them easier to access than they would be in the diluting weight of the city's background noise. Hissing out her air, she flexed hard, yanking the four spirits to herself, feeling their wails of agony breathe across her skin leaving patterns of ice. She lost feeling in her arm as it clenched harder than mere muscle could close. She was dimly aware that the two survivors bumped into the edge of the ritual; it was no longer moving with them, she pinned it in place. They only had moments to recognize what might be happening, to take steps to prepare—The Mistress of Tides drew the ghosts into herself, and she felt her blood writhe with chill.

Freeze their hearts solid. The Mistress of Tides fired a punch towards the unseen survivors on the bridge above. Bone cracked in her arm, she felt sinew rip, and cold blood burned her muscle as she hurled the exhalations at their former allies.

Screams tore loose on the bridge above. The Foundation assassins were warded against ghosts—until they were connected by the rituals of the Foundation, already within the defenses.

The screams abruptly stopped. The Mistress of Tides dropped to her knees on the gondola, her arm useless. As the Foundation ritual imploded, there was no bell to mark the passing of the assassins. Still, the Mistress of Tides needed no confirmation. She felt their glow extinguish. And she smiled.

Splashing awkwardly, Nevi dragged herself up onto the gondola, out of the canal. "My lady," she gasped. "Are you alright?"

The Mistress of Tides tugged her veil out of the way and spat blood. "Take me home," she croaked.

Nevi only paused for a moment. "The others?" she said, her voice small.

"All dead." The Mistress of Tides leaned to the side, laying her head on the bench cushion, half-conscious.

Nevi nodded, glanced around, then took hold of the sculling oar and leaned into her work.

DOSK RIVER
25TH VOLVINET. HOUR OF SONG, 2 HOURS PAST DUSK.
SAIL LIGHTING FESTIVAL, DAY THREE.

"I don't suppose you have any counsel on my meeting with the Hive," Rutherford said, breaking the silence. He leaned against the outer wall of the wheelhouse, appearing casual with his arms folded over his chest as he looked out over the flotilla of festival celebrators on the river.

"Be polite, aim for good news," Laraman said, not taking his eyes from the river as he gripped the helm with both hands. The tidy little steam launch chugged along at a modest speed, generating a low wake that didn't draw attention from the rest of the river traffic.

"I'm missing out on my nap for this, so if you aren't taking me to Orris I'm going to be very disappointed," Rutherford said mildly.

"That puts you on the short list of people who look forward to a face-to-face with the boss," Laraman retorted. "I like your confidence, but maybe think twice about what you're after. This guy is high up, and if you slip it's a long way down."

Rutherford didn't respond, but he did step away from the wheelhouse and lower himself to the back bench of the open stern, next to the thrash of the paddlewheel. Minutes slid past uncounted, and the moon emerged from behind a cloud. Refracted by a crack in the sky, its image splintered, casting two dimmer sisters into the sky.

The launch maneuvered past the buoy marking the shallows of the opposite shore, approaching the rear quay of the Waxmelt Theater in Brightstone. Rutherford nodded to himself, deliberately calming his breathing and heartrate. He caught himself cracking his knuckles, and crossed his arms to hug himself.

Laraman expertly maneuvered the launch parallel to the quay, tossing a rope to a dockhand, who secured the casting line to the cleats. Rutherford waited for Laraman to disembark, and he followed close behind as the dockhand boarded the launch to power it down properly. Laraman led the way up the back stairs, into the rear dock, past the massive stair exchange connecting the many levels of the theater, down a back hallway by the kitchen. An unobtrusive and narrow stairwell connected to a restricted access corridor, and Laraman stopped by an unmarked door with a hospitable gesture. Rutherford nodded to him and stepped through the door.

The room smelled of cedar and spice, and it was lit by an oil lamp with a glass chimney on the table. Ornate chairs surrounded the hand-carved wooden table. A solidly-built man with slicked-back hair and elaborate dinner dress leaned on the arm of his chair at the far end, ignoring a number of papers and books arrayed before him. He looked up as the door opened, but he did not rise.

"You must be Rutherford," he said, his tone warmer than his smile. "And you know who I am."

"Orris," Rutherford said with a nod. "Thank you for saving me the trouble of working out a meet." His smile was unusually guarded.

"About that," Orris said, leaning back. "This is your chance to set the tone for our conversation."

"Let's be frank," Rutherford replied. He reached into his coat, and tugged out a leather bound diary. "You want this back." He tossed it on the table. "I did not make a copy, and I did not make an attempt to crack the cipher. The Bluecoats don't know I found it, though it seems likely they suspect it exists."

"And what is that?" Orris asked calmly.

"Barness tracked your payments to Inspectors and Bluecoats in that book," Rutherford replied.

Orris frowned slightly. "I still do not understand. Why would you take the risk of pursuing something like this, something that a lot of people would kill you for touching, if you did not want to take advantage of it?"

"I'm taking advantage of it right now," Rutherford said. "I wanted to convince you that I'm serious, without wasting a lot of time. I put myself in a position to wreck Hive operations, so I could show you that I chose not to. This is my job application."

"Job application?" Orris echoed, eyebrows raised. "You want to get on the payroll?"

"Yes and no," Rutherford said. "I'm not interested in grunt work or petty graft. Far as I can tell, the Hive currently has a vacancy—the Unseen Hand. That's going to be me."

"Really," Orris said, sitting up straight. "The Unseen Hand. You think you can just stroll in and ask for that."

"I'm not asking," Rutherford said, still calm. "I'm offering. I'm applying. You'll consider me. And if you think I'm the best candidate for the job, then I'll do the work. My credentials are unique."

"Because you're a Bluecoat?"

Rutherford smiled. "Because there was a time you were pretty close to approaching my husband for the job, but he blew up his life and founded the Silkworms instead. And because his uncle is Lord Belderan. I know Belderan used to be the Unseen Hand. What I don't know is why you let him walk away, or what leverage he has now. Considering the Silkworms are targeting Hive infrastructure behind the scenes, that's got to rankle."

"Those seem more like cautions than qualifications," Orris said, unreadable.

"Maybe," Rutherford shrugged. "Maybe not. I know Trellis is dangerous. He is only still alive because you are wary of the contingency plans that might expose some critical facts, or put some plan in motion should he meet with foul play. Any time you try to infiltrate his circle, you pay a price for your failure. What you need is someone who can get close to him, figure out his secrets, and put him down safely. I'm your man."

"Really."

"The only one who can take the old man down is someone who can inspire enough affection that Trellis hesitates before defending himself. You may not know this, but the old man has a soft spot for me." Rutherford's smile was bleak.

"Surely you know that no one trusts a traitor," Orris said, cocking his head to the side. "You offer to betray Trellis, so I suspect you'll offer to betray me before long."

Rutherford watched him for a long moment. "Anyone with the necessary initiative, opportunism, and ruthlessness to function as the Unseen Hand is going to be a threat," he said, "but the Hive has the position anyway because it's about managing risk. Maybe you think that the risk of bringing me on is greater than the risk of letting Trellis continue to operate. Maybe you have a better idea. In case you don't, here I am."

Orris shifted in his seat, eyes narrow. "You had to know that coming in here and saying these things meant you would either persuade me or disappear," he said.

"If those odds were daunting then I wouldn't be the one for the position," Rutherford replied. He looked Orris in the eye, fearless.

Orris grinned, almost involuntarily. "Blood and bone, Rutherford, you've got spirit," he said as he rose to his feet. "Style. I like that. Dashing and arrogant to the point of insanity; and of course you're right, that's just what the Unseen Hand needs to survive. But, you? Surely you know you look like a ploy, like an obvious attempt for the Silkworms to get into the Hive, close to our operations."

"That did occur to me," Rutherford replied. "Make up your own mind. But consider these two things. Do you think Trellis would resort to something so straightforward?" he asked, raising one finger. "Second, Sanction was unfaithful to me with multiple partners. I left him, burned down his house, interfered with Silkworms business to get them crosswise of the gondoliers, shot and captured his lurk, and broke off his Hive contact point. Maybe you think I'm done expressing my feelings in a way Sanction can understand. Perhaps I'm done mourning the loss of the life I was trying to build with him." He paused. "I promise you I am not."

Orris looked him over, then nodded to himself. "Alright, consider this an initial interview. You have intrigued me. I put more thought than I care to admit into figuring out your angle, but this? Not what I expected. I'll honor that by giving you a test. You manage it, with style, without connecting it to the Hive, and we'll talk again."

"I'll do it," Rutherford said.

"The Fog Hounds are a problem. Remove the threat they pose to our smuggling consolidation."

Rutherford raised his eyebrows. "See you soon."

He let himself out.

CHAPTER FIFTEEN

Don't make this kid an Inspector. He doesn't know how to pick his fights.

You know his story? Cellar was maybe fourteen, washed out of the Bluecoat Academy, a tragic urchin trying to scrounge coin to support his hungry family. Inspector Daubry, who was in the twilight of his distinguished career, took an interest in the kid. So Cellar joined my cadets, running messages for Inspectors. That wasn't enough for Cellar, he figured he'd become an Inspector even though he lacked education and his only connections were through Daubry. Cellar was righteous; if he thought he was correct, he tried to force people to defend their opinions or admit they were wrong—even if they were instructors, officers, aristocrats. He figured truth should outrank authority.

He was in an evidentiary class with Master Sulwin, who often said when you find yourself in a hole you can climb out or keep digging. He asked Cellar which he should do; it was meant to be a teaching moment with the argumentative kid, a signal the cadet should stop challenging the instructor. Cellar's response? "Depends where the truth is." Sulwin ejected Cellar from his class. He was exasperated when Daubry intervened on Cellar's behalf. Unwilling to cross Daubry, Sulwin kept Cellar on—but he required the other cadets to call Cellar by a new name, "Digger." The other cadets gleefully complied and got a much-needed high score on that assignment.

— Sayers Canless, Headmaster
— Clearance interview notes, Suran 12, 846

Screaming woke Cellar from a dead sleep, and an open-handed blow cracked across his face. The screaming abruptly stopped, and he blinked at his confusion.

"Welcome back," Jayan said, grim as he loomed over Cellar.

"Who—screaming," Cellar slurred.

"You, asshole," Jayan growled.

Cellar clamped his teeth and convulsed with sudden agony, snatching at Jayan and the padded bench next to him. Spent and numb, he sagged back.

"What. Stabbed?" he winced at Jayan.

"I don't even know," Jayan replied.

Cellar registered the lapping wash of water, the unsteadiness of his position. He peered around, realizing he was on a small boat, on water, the air suffused with the chill of the River Dosk breathing up into the night.

"Leave it alone," Jayan said, swatting at Cellar's hand as he reflexively moved to touch at the bandaged wound. "This is like the fourth time you woke up, but you probably don't remember. I stole a boat and we're headed to Tangletown to get your injury looked at."

"That seems like a good plan," Cellar breathed, letting his eyes drift shut.

"Oh no, you stay awake now, you hear me?" Jayan demanded. "I gotta keep this boat moving, but you just can't start screaming again." He glanced around. "We are in no position to explain what's going on to a Bluecoat."

Cellar tried to chuckle at that, but the noise was more of a strangled half-sob. "Right."

"You aren't getting me deep into this nightmare then taking the easy way out and going insane," Jayan said with a stern tone. "I want you rational and suffering, dammit."

"Best—best I can hope for," Cellar slurred.

"We're almost to Tangletown, hang in there," Jayan insisted.

Cellar resumed blinking at the fog in his eyes. "Where?"

"You have like one friend in this haunted nest," Jayan replied. He nodded towards Tangletown, dead ahead. The shipwrecked Leviathan hunter formed its own tilting horizon, its flank clustered with a jumble of masts and sails, unevenly lit by lanterns shining up from its floating apron of watercraft. "We are going to see Stanchion."

Cellar coughed, arrested by the jolt of pain from the motion.

"I know," Jayan replied quietly, "but I don't have any better ideas."

A few minutes later Jayan sculled the craft past the outer picket to the flotilla neighborhood, and tied off the craft with a mooring line affixed to a cleat on a free-standing piling that anchored a number of other craft. Dragging Cellar to his feet, he hauled him up out of the boat and onto the rickety gangplank to a neighboring boat, where an old woman with one long horn regarded them through yellow slitted eyes as she slowly drew on her pipe; a pack of cats stared at them as they crossed her boat to the next, stumbling to a lower level and avoiding a stack of crates full of creatures that hissed at them.

"I can walk!" Cellar insisted, desperately hoping he was right. He pushed off of Jayan, took a staggering step, and resonated with the thrum of the current sliding under the boat's hull.

"You sure?" Jayan said skeptically.

"If I can't, just leave me," Cellar retorted. "Now... how much further?"

Jayan looked over at the child sitting on the hatch cover, watching them steadily. "Hey kid, you know where Stanchion is berthed?"

"Two lengths hullside," the kid replied.

"Yeah, I don't know what that means," Jayan said through his teeth, brows drawn.

"I'll guide you for a knife," the kid said with a shrug.

Jayan tugged a clasp knife from his boot, holding it up to the lamplight. "You get this when we arrive."

The kid nodded, then rose and pulled on a broad-brimmed hat. He scrambled up a rope net holding his family's craft to its neighbor, whistling a passcode. Jayan and Cellar followed, climbing through an interconnected maze of platforms, cables, and planks, with the hungry river winking and whispering below as they made their way.

"There you go," the kid said, pointing at the grungy barge that was berthed between a rotting riverboat and several repainted lifeboats that were obviously residences now. Jayan handed his clasp knife over, and offered his arm to Cellar, who reluctantly took it and leaned on the Bluecoat as they clambered aboard Stanchion's craft.

"And that's far enough," came the reedy voice from the shadow of the pilot house. They saw the barrel of a pistol illuminated by the dim light from the neighbor's barge.

"Inspector Cellar here," Jayan said with a gesture. "You remember him, you worked that apothecary theft ring together last year. He got hurt, and it's weird, and you are going to help us," he explained.

Stanchion stepped out into the light, lowering the pistol somewhat. "That's generous of me," he observed. His narrow features were crooked, his lank hair was indifferently braided, and he wore a shirt that was far too big for him restrained under layers of belts and vests. "Are you offering gratitude in the form of threats as usual, or do you have something valuable for me?"

"Bragging rights, you know?" Jayan said with half a pained grin. "I've been a Bluecoat for six years. I've seen stabbings, shootings, nasty falls, half eaten corpses, ghostburn, walking rot, six plagues, and a dozen ways to drown on dry land. But this? I never saw anything like this."

"Okay, that's fun," Stanchion agreed cautiously. "I'll take a look. I suppose I will trust you to offer some reward to counterbalance all the regret that's going to find me for not telling you to get off my home right now."

"Right, good," Jayan said, and he guided Cellar to an overstuffed chair under a tattered tarp stretched over the deck. Stanchion beat him to it and swept some clutter off the seat, and Cellar groaned as he lowered into the chair.

Stanchion snapped his fingers, and a light glowed to life in a globe that filled out a cage set on the deck. The light swelled to offer a yellowish clarity to the scene. Prodding Jayan out of the way, Stanchion squared off with the dirty rag bandaging Cellar's upper chest and collarbone area. Without warning, Stanchion tugged the cloth out of the way; Cellar clenched around a shout, not letting it past his teeth as tendons stood out in his neck like cables.

"Points for the Bluecoat," Stanchion murmured, eyebrows raising. "For creativity." He picked up a hand mirror, adjusting its angle in the sickly light so Cellar could see the wound.

Purple grit was worked into the seared flesh, which struggled to clot and scar around what looked like a chemical burn in a twisted shape. Several blisters had formed, and they glowed with an unhealthy dimness.

"What." Cellar stared at the wound's reflection.

"That means you pissed off a cult," Stanchion said. He glanced around. "Okay, Bruisecoat, keep your pistol out and your eyes sharp. Usually this kind of thing means the sacrifice got loose, and there is— you know, there's some kind of *investment* that goes with a branding like this. Cults tend to want to finish the job in the privacy of their gross ritual chambers or whatever. This is a step in a process you don't want to finish," he confided in Cellar.

"What?" Cellar squinted.

Stanchion heaved a sigh. "That's a first reaction, if you want more I want more too. This thing has to be cleaned, see how clear the symbol is. I get the general shape, and it is part of a family of signs, you know? This is technical stuff, closer to the limmer tradition than my divination studies. It's old. Like, closer to the demon bone Whispers than the drowning Whispers. It's part of that slow and quiet hiss that underlies the chatter of the dead. This here is part of the spectrum people like me tune out when we listen to the other side."

"So if we clean him up, look at some books or something, then you can tell us?" Jayan demanded, his back to them as he scanned their surroundings. His hands were under his half-cloak, resting on his weapons.

"I really can't," Stanchion shrugged. "But you came to the right area; there are some adepts who work with cults, or belong to them—hell, *lead* them. But you don't know what they'll do if they get somebody who is marked like this. Maybe they will try to finish the job."

"But you have a recommendation," Cellar said, looking Stanchion in the eye.

"Oh, sure," Stanchion replied quickly. "Suicide. Just knock yourself off, right now, before they get you. I don't know what will happen to your spirit, but at least then you've got some control. I mean, these sacrifices, some of them are downright nasty. Drawn out. Painful." He shook his head. "That's the trouble with cults. You can go back to your buddies in the Tower but you never know who might be under the influence, ready to betray you for their cult."

"What *else*?" Jayan demanded, turning to face Stanchion.

"Payment and next steps," Stanchion retorted. "All I want for this is for you to tell me who you pissed off so I can watch out for trouble, and then you can go find yourself some other expert."

"We are hunting the Skullface Killer," Jayan said. "And we're not done with you yet."

"Oh, the Skullface Killer, very nice," Stanchion said through his teeth. He raised the pistol, aiming it at Jayan's face. "Bye now."

"You already know too much," Cellar said softly, watching Stanchion. "Whoever we talk to next, we tell them we were here. You shoot us and dump the bodies, that doesn't mean *this* is over," he said with a gesture towards the brand on his chest. "You want us to go, we go, but you must connect us to the next step. Make this someone else's problem. Have answers, in case someone tries to extract them," he said, barely audible.

Stanchion stared at him. Seconds passed.

"We might have been followed," Jayan said, too loud. "We need to get moving—all three of us." He raised his eyebrows. "So where are we going, Stanchion?"

"I suppose there's no reason to play it safe," Stanchion mused aloud. "There is one expert... she keeps her circle of contacts small and elite. But there's nobody better versed in the ways of the limmer Whispers. Her demonic studies..." Stanchion shook his head. "She's tied to the water now, I don't think she can get far from it even if she wants to. I did a favor for one of her people once, and my payment was special knowledge of where she berths. I might even be able to arrange an audience," he said slowly, "if it is an emergency."

"Okay," Jayan said, controlling his impatience. "Let's do that."

"Guys, this is serious," Stanchion said in a solemn tone. "You don't waste her time. You don't want her attention. She is one of the top three mystics in Tangletown. She might be immortal. I really don't know how she'll react." He paused. "Maybe you better go back to your

Tower and consult the Spirit Wardens," he said. "I can't believe I'm saying this, but that might be safer."

"That is not an option," Cellar replied. "We will meet with your expert."

"I mean, I'll do it," Stanchion said, "but... you gotta be ready. This isn't going to be pleasant. That mark you've got? The mark of the sacrifice? It's not just about your body. These cults, they strip your identity. They change you into an energy vessel, then they empty it into their rituals. This is the old stuff, man, this is a magic of blood and bone that reshapes how you feel reality. It's the echoes of these rituals that got sanitized into the Church of Ecstasy. That mark on you... you'll never again be who you were before it hit you. And right now, you don't know who you are, who you are becoming." The mystic's dark eyes were unsettling, steady, almost pitying.

"Who are we going to see?" Jayan demanded.

Stanchion turned to face him. "I've got some paper, so you can send any notes you need to send, say anything you don't want to leave unsaid. Because tonight, we're going to pay a visit to the Empress of Gulls." He swallowed hard.

For a moment, the river itself seemed to shiver.

WRECKRIB MARINA, FOGCREST, SILKSHORE.
25TH VOLVINET. HOUR OF THREAD, 4 HOURS PAST DUSK.
SAIL LIGHTING FESTIVAL, DAY THREE.

Rutherford slowed, squinting at the berth numbers painted on the retaining wall opposite the boats. Then he nodded to himself, leaning his back against the wall as he breathed in the spicy stink of the night air. The cookfires aboard the various craft wove the scent of food into the breeze, mingling with the low-tide rot and the castoff corruption of civilization's trash in the fine mist that coated everything. Dozens of boats in various states of disrepair were moored in the still waters adjacent to the canal, and during festival many of the owners had guests taking a break between outings. Rutherford felt his impatience strain at its boundaries, but he took a deep breath and released it, waiting. He watched a low-waisted canal patrol boat, decommissioned for age, its official designators painted over.

The wait was not long. Clamp stepped out on the deck, fists planted on his hips, looking Rutherford over. Then he shook his head, and beckoned, turning back to re-enter the cabin. Rutherford strode over, mounted the plank, and joined him in the bright confines of the wheel-house.

Clamp was already seated at the narrow table, and he held up his hand as Rutherford entered. "Me and the boys are curious, that's all, we don't mean anything by it. You don't have to come here and chew me out; there's a generally understood exception to privacy for Bluecoats that you should already know about," he said.

Rutherford blinked, then shook his head. "I'm not here about that," he said. "Gear up, we've got a mission."

"It's all business with you, isn't it," Clamp said, struggling to regain his balance. "Except that none of it is."

Rutherford's bemused smile deepened. "We don't have a lot of time," he said gently.

"Sure we do," Clamp retorted, leaning back with his arms crossed over his chest. "Captain Smiles tracked me down this afternoon and specifically told me that you were off duty until after dawn. You are off the Barness ledger follow-up activity. You are going to support the festival. She wanted to make sure we had eye contact and the message got through. Because apparently I'm your keeper or something."

"She knows I rely on you," Rutherford said. "She suspects I'm not going to get a good night's sleep. Now, I'm not following up on decoded ledgers from the Barness strike, but I'm also not directly following up on festival duties. Maybe we don't get any tangible success from tonight's efforts, maybe we do. Either way, I don't know what tomorrow holds." He paused. "But I want you to come with me."

"And if I don't, you'll go alone. Won't you," Clamp said.

"I will." Rutherford waited. For a long moment, neither man moved.

"What do you want, anyway?" Clamp demanded with a peevish tone.

"I'm looking for some smugglers, the Fog Hounds," Rutherford replied. "They are breaking the law and upsetting people and I'm going to put a stop to it."

"You make it so hard to trust you," Clamp said. "I think you are doing it on purpose. You weren't always like this. I can feel it," he said. "I don't know you, but... I don't think this—I don't think *this* is you," he said with a general gesture.

Rutherford waited. Clamp heaved a sigh.

"Captain Smiles," Clamp repeated. "She tracked me down. I don't like that she knows my name. I don't like that it occurred to her that I mattered in her ongoing plans. I do not want to be noticed. When I stand next to you, the follow lights land on us both."

Rutherford continued to listen even though Clamp did not continue to speak.

"It is customary," Clamp said through his scowl, "to bring a Barrow-cleft vintage not less than a dozen years of age as a gesture of gratitude when inconveniencing a fellow Bluecoat outside the boundaries of official—"

Rutherford drew a dusty bottle from his sling bag and thudded it down on the table between them.

"Well okay then let's go," Clamp grumbled as he rose to his feet and reached for his overcoat.

EMPRESS OF GULLS' WORKSHOP SLOOP WRECK, TANGLETOWN, CROW'S FOOT.
25TH VOLVINET. HOUR OF PEARLS, 6 HOURS PAST DUSK.
SAIL LIGHTING FESTIVAL, DAY THREE.

"It's not too late to leave," Stanchion said through nerveless lips. He stared at the tar-painted exterior of the sloop, at the platform at the end of the walkway, at the door cut into the side of the ship. "We should sleep on it. Think this over."

"This isn't going to get easier," Cellar growled, "and I don't want you to have time to think up better excuses. We're here. Let's go."

Jayan loomed behind them, sensing the fragility of Stanchion's morale. He knew better than to risk saying the wrong thing, but he also knew just how to speak with his size. Stanchion glanced over his shoulder at the Bluecoat, then an expression like a sneer crawled over his face.

"What the hell," he muttered, striding forward, his hands clenched to fists to conceal their tremors.

The door creaked open as they approached, the light inside spilling on the platform. A half-naked man stepped out and rose to his full height, his youthful musculature impressive. He was shaved and shined like a living statue, a work of art.

"We come in humble supplication," Stanchion said in Hadrathi. "We bring a puzzle as a gift to the Empress of Gulls."

"Have you any other gifts?" the door guard replied with surprising politeness.

Stanchion shot the others a sideways glance. "Of course," he said with a pained wince, and he reluctantly untucked an amulet around his neck. "She will know its provenance, and its dearness to me."

The man accepted the gift, and stepped back inside, closing the door.

"I'm not going to get that back, you know," Stanchion murmured, almost to himself, grief flavoring the words. Cellar clapped him on the shoulder, and nodded curtly.

"Thank you," he said. "How long do you think—"

The door opened again, and the man stepped out and waved them in. Stanchion bowed from the waist, and led the way into the sloop.

Inside, the floor was slightly tilted with the resting angle of the wreck. The long room was close, the air choked with incense and less readily identifiable exotics. Bands of writing, glyphwork, and sigils covered the walls. The end of the room was dominated by a throne crafted from driftwood and bone, flanked by braziers. The woman on the throne was knobbled and thin with age, but her strength was apparent somehow; the bone and driftwood of the throne seemed to resonate with her tenacity. She was veiled, but her posture was regal. Two more of the shiny-fleshed guards stepped in behind the supplicants as the door was closed and barred behind them.

"My lady, Gracious One, I am deeply moved by your generosity in agreeing to see me," Stanchion said in Hadrathi as he swept into a deep and elegant bow, his legs trembling slightly. Cellar and Jayan exchanged a glance, then hurriedly dropped modest bows of their own.

"You have brought me a puzzle," murmured the woman on the throne, switching to Akorosian. "Show me."

Stanchion flexed his eyes at Cellar, dipping a nod at him and at the throne, anxiety flowing from him.

Cellar took a step forward and shifted his shirt aside, then winced as he peeled the bandage back.

The Empress of Gulls shot to her feet. She barked two words.

As Stanchion flinched back, one of the guards snatched him and cleanly slit his throat. A gun barrel jabbed into Jayan's back hard enough that he stumbled forward, half-turning to see the other two guards leveling pistols at him as the third dumped Stanchion's gurgling body. The dying man clawed at the air that surrounded him, forever out of reach.

"Who is the Dark Tooth?" the Empress of Gulls hissed at Cellar.

"The—what?" he blinked, mind racing.

"Your master," she pressed, one of her hands shifting into a deeply uncomfortable and physically improbable angle as the air tingled and their senses glittered with adjusting energy.

"I was attacked!" Cellar said, almost shouting. "This was done to me! I came here to try to understand what it means!"

"You are within my power," she hissed, "and I can end this whole thing, right now."

"Can you?" Cellar demanded, hardly knowing what he was saying. "Are you sure? I'm tied to something bigger. Maybe you break it through me. Or maybe it breaks you. Are you sure there is no other way? Are you sure of how all of this works?" He hesitated, desperate for more words. "I'm not sure at all! I came to you to understand; maybe if you already do you can at least explain it to me—why I have to die!"

She stared for a moment. "Submit to me," she said with lethal intensity, "and I may choose to spare you. Or do not, and I will slay you right where you stand."

"I submit," Cellar blurted, echoed by Jayan.

The Empress of Gulls relaxed back, and seated herself. Her guards did not waver, the guns pointed firmly at Jayan.

"No one really understands why they have to die," the Empress of Gulls mused. "Your whole life is an air bubble. Spun off from impact through the Mirror, twirling back towards its natural state, pushing through this mysterious realm in a package of life that is desperate to break. Drawn to the barrier that separates it from what it was before and after this side trip. Yet unable to resist the inexorable pressure as the living world squeezes your energy out of itself, back through death, through the Mirror, to where it belongs."

"This—this doesn't help me," Cellar said through his teeth, struggling to think.

"Why you, I wonder," the Empress of Gulls mused.

"What do you mean," Cellar asked, pushing his frustration back, aiming for a respectful tone.

"You bear the mark of the Herald of the Dark Tooth," the Empress of Gulls murmured. "Now the ritual is nearly complete, and the end of the world is nigh. My confidence that you are unwitting is growing. And yet." She cocked her head to the side. "I have both Heralds. Why should I not destroy you and prevent any chance of what is to come?"

"I really, really hope you can think of an answer," Cellar breathed.

Far away, a bell tolled to mark Stanchion's passing.

MAURO OVERVIEW, ZEPHYR STREET, MASTER MARKET, SILKSHORE. 25TH VOLVINET. HOUR OF FLAME, 5 HOURS PAST DUSK. SAIL LIGHTING FESTIVAL, DAY THREE.

Bone-weary, the Mistress of Tides pushed the door to her inner chambers open. She shuffled in, her customary grace drained from her. Gingerly lowering herself into the chair before her meditation mirror, she heaved a deep sigh. She paused to listen, and heard Nevi tidying up in the adjacent chamber.

Struggling with her good arm, she tugged off her headdress and veil, draping them on the mannequin head by her seat. She lightly touched her face, then covered her eyes, feeling the tendrils of death energy trying to creep through her shoulder from the devastation of her withered arm.

Rising, she crossed her chamber to the side board, pouring out a glass of wine. She downed it, enjoying the simmer of flavors on her tongue. The death echoes of her acolytes and her victims resonated in her flesh, thrumming in her sinew and veins, flexing in her muscle. Sleep would be impossible without meditation.

She shrugged out of her heavy vestments as best she could, leaving them in a heap. She pulled on a simple shift, then arranged herself on her meditation mat. Breathing flowed into her, then out, a rhythm as trustworthy and instinctive as the moon-pulled sea. She began to settle in among the day's events, touching them to drain the emotion and pain from them so they could be folded and stored instead of left in a jumble for her to trip over as she moved about her internal space.

This afternoon, she received her new gondola; it had already been connected to death by her hand, and quite possibly contributed to saving her life as well. Her acolytes, faithful in their service and uncomplaining in their deaths. Like any physical exercise, her pursuit of her own path would bring unavoidable pains and discomforts. She breathed deep, preparing space to manage those consequences, to get past them into the strength that took time to deepen in her.

Something was wrong.

Her eyes drifted open. She was alone. Rising, she crossed her room, standing in the doorway. Silence. She listened to life force, and detected several acolytes.

Wrong.

Frowning, she closed and barred her door, and took a step back. Uncertainty bloomed in her gut. She turned to approach her mirror, and stumbled. Shaking her head, she felt panic rise as an unsteadiness wobbled around the movement, her balance threatened, darkness soaking into her peripheral vision.

She meant to snap out "What is this?" but all she heard was "Whu ths," as she took another step, and dropped to one knee, palms slapping the floor.

Drugged. The wine.

Retreating deep into her mind, to her deepest discipline, she aimed for her most profound focus—from there she could reshape her body, elude this chemical imbalance. It was already too late. She concentrated like an experienced athlete dropped on a sheet of ice; her mind was frictionless, she crashed against the slickness that coated her racing thoughts.

In a single burst of effort, she reared up, her eyes shining with a terrible panic. To her horror, she saw a figure part the shadows in the corner as though they were a curtain, and step out of hiding. She confronted the man dressed in simple clothes, his expression somber, his eyes bottomless, his wild gray beard a backdrop as he raised one finger toward his lips. Sssh.

The Mistress of Tides fell into darkness.

CHAPTER SIXTEEN

According to common understanding, the gondoliers of Iruvian descent who settled the Ease chose to belong to Doskvol. The Sail Lighting Festival commemorates that choice. In 368 Imperial Era the gondoliers burned the sails from their masts in a symbolic act of commitment to their new home. Ever after, they navigated with shallow boats in canals, eschewing the open sea.

The boat families see more complexity in the celebration. In the year 368 IE the Onyx Hermitage had been in Doskvol for three generations. The Conclave of U'Duasha sent an emissary to them, insisting that all vessels under Iruvian sailcloth must answer to the Conclave. They required an arranged marriage to solidify ties with the homeland.

Myrsaka, the contemporary Onyxite, dramatically rejected their order. She demonstrated her command of the solidarity of her people by showing the emissaries every Iruvian sail in flames, the Ease burning a fortune for spite. That rebellion triggered a shadow war of assassinations in Doskvol and U'Duasha that lasted until Iruvia joined the empire as a tributary state over a century later. Myrsaka did not last a week after her symbolic act, but her many successors were steeled to resist because of her example.

They burn sails as a signal of their unity and their willingness to kill and die to keep the distance they earned from the tribal politics back home. They burn sails to signal that they are one tribe here, now, sacrificially if need be. This is not loyalty to Doskvol. They are loyal to the other emigrants from Iruvia, becoming family in a strange and cold land. This is how they remind each other that they choose resistance unto death rather than accepting an outsider's orders. The Sail Lighting Festival re-enacts costly rebellion.

— From "Stranger Inside: Immigrant Insights"
by Croftwood Simmersale

The grimy plaster walls flickered, the central firepit spraying shadows from the columns around it as the server stirred up the flame. Dozens of pale statues looked on from their pillars and niches all around the smoky common room. A discussion of artistic perspective rambled through a series of gesticulating interruptions in the corner as the shabby students mixed drink and art to somewhat slurred effect.

Trellis sat motionless in a shadowed corner, eyes lost in the flames of the pit, empty wineglass untouched on the chipped table before him alongside a sealed and dusty bottle of wine.

The door creaked loudly, admitting a lean Bluecoat. Conversation continued undimmed; the patrons here were too tame to grow wary in the presence of the city's enforcers. A bleak smile spread across Trellis's features, and he leaned back, life returning to him.

"I was hoping you'd make it," Rutherford said under his breath as he approached the corner.

"I got Celia's message, and I must say, I am relieved to see you alive. I take it Orris sends his best?" Trellis said sardonically.

Rutherford seated himself, glancing around. "I am to take on the Fog Hounds."

"If you want to pile on your momentum, you could hit them tonight," Trellis murmured. "I know where they'll be, just before midnight. There is even a crime involved that you could interrupt."

Rutherford blinked. "Midnight—that's less than three hours. I mean..." His mind was racing. "Of course I'll try it," he said.

Trellis's smile shifted, gaining a little warmth, almost wistful. "Wreckrib arena," he said. "Berth twelve." He settled back against the wall.

"I'll set something up," Rutherford nodded.

"Oh, no, that's not where the Fog Hounds will be. That's where Clamp's home is moored," Trellis said.

"Clamp?"

"I figured I'd save you the time of tracking down his location," Trellis said. "You plan to take him along, right?"

Rutherford paused. "I mean... he's a good man." His forehead creased. "What are you thinking?"

"I'm thinking you should take the wine," Trellis said with a nod to the dusty bottle between them. "May come in handy. Be sure to check in with the Tower, the Fog Hounds are brawlers. If they feel threatened they'll fight before they think," Trellis said. "The Glint Row Tower is closest to the Clashendo Operatic Auditorium, they'll be receptive because you'll be protecting a patron leaving the opera. Cynthia Forthright and her guards. 'Cynthia' is really Dalia."

"I see," Rutherford said, eyebrows raised. "Seems like a bold move for the Fog Hounds." He took the bottle, slipping it into his bag.

Trellis's smile was stitched together from loose secrets. "I'd love to chat," he said, "but the clock is ticking. My best to Celia."

"I'll be sure to pass that on," Rutherford said, rising as the server approached the table.

"Something for you to drink?" the server asked Rutherford, polite.

"Not here, not now," Rutherford replied, eyes still on Trellis. Then he glanced at the server, nodded, and left.

"And you, sir?" the server said to Trellis.

"No, thank you," Trellis replied, his eyes distant. "I'm already gone."

GLINT ROW TOWER, CHARTER WALL, CHARTERHALL. 25TH VOLVINET. HOUR OF PEARLS, (ALMOST) 6 HOURS PAST DUSK. SAIL LIGHTING FESTIVAL, DAY THREE.

The carriage didn't fully stop before the door flew open and Rutherford sprang out, surefooted on the landing and racing up the steps of the Glint Row Tower. The doors were open, mingling the stuffy interior's air with the cool night breeze.

As soon as Rutherford was through the door into the narrow but tall corridor, he let out a shout. "Pikes UP!" He looked almost regal in his crisp uniform.

Heads turned, and one of the Bluecoats was at his side in a few steps. "What's going on," she demanded, frowning at Rutherford's insignia for Silkshore.

"Reliable tip, we're dealing with some smugglers who have an imminent plan to kidnap somebody rich. What's going on in the area right now?" Rutherford demanded.

"Opera house, gets out at midnight, we've got six pikes already on-site," the woman replied in a sharp tone. "What the hell do you—"

"Fine," Rutherford interrupted. "Follow on. Which way?"

"Down the street, can't miss the auditorium," the pike replied. Rutherford pivoted, darting down the stairs past Clamp, who reversed course and gamely did his best to keep up.

As Rutherford pounded down the street, long legs propelling him at impressive speed, he sighted a lit clock in a storefront; ten till midnight. The assault was probably already in progress. He cut across the street and sprinted down a broad alleyway that was wider and better maintained than many of the thoroughfares in Silkshore. Rounding the corner, he heard the clatter of a squad behind him echoing from the other end of the alley, and a smile twisted the corner of his mouth. An aristocrat with a taste for privacy would exit early, maybe from the delivery gate; a vulnerable point for an interception if attackers could figure out which exit.

A pistol shot snapped its report off the massive slab wall of the auditorium, echoing between the stately facades of Charterhall. Rutherford redoubled his effort, closing in as several other shots cracked out in the thick night air.

Tucking up in a hurdle, he cleared the wrought iron planter lining the roadway, dropping into the lane for delivery carts supplying the auditorium's kitchen complex. He saw an elegant carriage under a plume of smoke, and he saw the woman in an evening gown jammed behind a pillar for cover as one of her guards was hit squarely in the chest by a couple shots and the other pressed between her and danger; another was sprawled on the steps, and the fourth was grappling with a massive bearded Bluecoat. Two other Bluecoats had taken cover between the woman in the gown and the carriage, cutting off easy retreat. Their backs were to Rutherford. He did not hesitate.

Tearing his pistol from its sheath on his baldric, he lined up and fired while running, his shot crashing into one Bluecoat's back and slamming him off the column he thought provided cover. Startled, the other Bluecoat looked over at him and pivoted, then ducked as a bodyguard fired at him and knocked a chip of stone from the column next to him.

With a roar, the big Bluecoat on the steps bodily shoved the guard trying to wrestle him, unbalancing his opponent. The guard recovered fast, plunging at him with a knife, but the big Bluecoat slapped the attack out of the way and headbutted the man, knocking him senseless to tumble backwards down the stairs.

Rutherford clattered behind a stone post for cover, lining up his pistol—some instinct blared, and he twisted to the side—bang into his arm, he sailed through the air to rebound off the wall. The pain from the gunshot wound hit the same time the rifle report caught up to the bullet, washing over the alley.

Dazed, Rutherford squirmed towards the best cover he could see through the haze of agony. Some distant part of his mind helpfully remembered that Vale, leader of the Fog Hounds, was a sniper.

One of the bodyguards jammed his shoulder into the door to the auditorium, but it had been barred behind them, trapping them in the ambush; another shot rang out, and he twirled as blood sprayed. One, two, three sepulchral tones reverberated from the Bellweather tower, marking the deaths.

The thin whistle of approaching Bluecoats sounding the alarm penetrated the echoes of gunfire and bells, and the remaining imposter Bluecoats had seconds to make a decision; the big one loomed over the woman in the gown, and she produced a hold-out pistol and snapped a couple shots into him. He teetered for a moment, and she dropped to one knee and snatched up a pistol dropped by one of her guards.

"Go!" yelled one of the Bluecoat impostors, and he ran away from the approaching reinforcements. Snarling through his beard, the big Bluecoat stumbled down the stairs. The woman with the pistol lined up on him and squeezed the trigger, blasting a shot into his back that hurled him forward. She withdrew behind the pillar again, darting a glance towards where the plume of smoke still lingered over the abandoned sniper nest on the rooftop across the street.

Half a dozen Bluecoats arrived on the scene, out of breath, guns drawn. Clamp immediately spotted Rutherford, sliding to a stop and kneeling to check on him.

"Arm," Rutherford slurred. "Shot."

"We'll get you out of here," Clamp said through his teeth.

The pike joined him, standing over Rutherford. "Looks like we were just in time," she observed. "Your tip was accurate. I suppose you'll want—"

"No," Rutherford gritted out. "All yours. Paperwork and glory." He bared his teeth with something like a grin.

"Done," the pike said coolly. "You can take your man to the tower, get him patched up. I'll have a coach sent around."

"Yeah," Clamp said as he tugged a compression wrap out of a belt pouch, busying himself with putting pressure on the wound. The pike moved on to take over the scene and order the Bluecoats.

"How many got away," Rutherford hissed to Clamp. "The sniper— one other?"

"Yeah, two, that's about right," Clamp muttered. "Don't you worry about that now."

A deep peal rolled through the world, barely audible, as the bell marked the passing of the big man who bled out on the stairs.

Clamp glanced up, surprised, to see that the woman dressed in an evening gown stood by his side. "Be with you in a moment," he said, gruff.

"Thank you," the woman said to Rutherford. "Impeccable timing. What's your name, officer?"

"This here is Rutherford," Clamp said, not looking up.

"Thank you, Rutherford. Any idea who my assailants were?" she asked, her tone light.

Rutherford blinked hard. "Fog Hounds," he said.

She displayed a tight, wintery smile, then turned away.

Water slithered past her ankles, bitterly cold in contrast to the humid night air. Trying to shift position, her body clanked against metal, rousing her consciousness; she opened her eyes and saw the unfiltered world. She was not wearing her veil. And she was in a cage.

The Mistress of Tides recoiled from the bars only to tremble around in the narrow cage. She coughed at the metallic slime in her throat, then peered out as she pushed back the disorientation that threatened to overwhelm her.

She wore her meditation shift, and nothing else, and the hump of an incoming wave again rushed through the bottom of her cage. The cage itself was fixed to a piling on the pier, out at the end, just above the waterline. The angle wasn't good, but the Mistress of Tides saw the supplies stacked at the entry to the pier, and the signage. The pier was closed for construction. No one was nearby. No one was going to be nearby.

The tide was coming in. Her eyes darted over her prison, heavy metal bolts holding the cage in place against the algae-slicked piling. It only took a moment. She had maybe two hours until the cage would be underwater.

A bang startled her. She craned her neck to see the steps leading down from the pier to lower platforms, for servicing docked ships at the waterline. The bearded man she saw in her quarters had closed his toolbox, and he worked the shoulder strap up over his back with the practiced ease of a professional laborer. His bottomless eyes took her in, and the cage, and the water swirling around her legs. He said nothing.

"Let me out of this now," the Mistress of Tides growled.

He watched, expressionless.

Another wave carried away her patience, and her expression twitched. She opened her senses, feeling the water, the ambient life force of the city... the energy was brownish, singed, and it crumbled as she reached for it.

"What did you do," she demanded, her voice flat.

He did not break eye contact as he nodded sideways at the neighboring warehouse. The Mistress of Tides saw the North Hook Annex branding painted on the wall in fairly fresh paint. It took a few seconds, but realization of where she was dawned in her eyes.

"That's the test warehouse," she said. "Rowan's ambient suppression field." Now she could feel the distinct resonant buzz of the machines in the warehouse, the machines that drained the background energy behind the Mirror so Whispers and ghosts were disarmed—starved of the plasmic residue they manipulated with their wills. Cutting edge security apparently extended somewhat beyond the walls of the warehouse itself. Another wave distracted her tumbling thoughts, and she looked down at the dark waters pushing past her knees, foam swirling around her.

Setting her teeth and releasing her panic, the Mistress of Tides focused past the first taste of the devastating headache that was hovering at the edge of her vision. She pulled hard on her surroundings, drawing energy into herself—she slipped. Instead of energy flowing into her she felt the emptiness enter her, squeezing out some of the glimmering energy she already had. The Mistress of Tides broke off the attunement as abruptly as she could, gasping for air, dehydration rupturing her sinuses and oozing blood into her breathing spaces. She struggled to calm herself as terror snatched handfuls of her guts, twisting and squeezing.

"Alright," she said, loud, her tone as neutral as she could make it. "You are still here. So let's negotiate. You wanted my attention, and you have it."

The stranger raised one eyebrow slightly, then glanced up over her head. She followed his eyes, looking up to see the metal plate bolted over the cage, out of reach. It was rimed with distillations, and over time evaporations had been focused on the surface to form runes that would wash off when submerged. The Mistress of Tides recognized elements of the ritual that protected the Foundation assassins from alerting Bellweather Tower with their kills.

She would die alone, her passage unmarked and her fate unknown. Her heart raced, but there was nowhere for her blood to go except through her veins again and again and again. Insistent, a higher wave dragged at her legs, but she could not follow it out of the cage. The water could not feel her commands. The Mistress of Tides focused on her breath, trying to press the tremors from it.

"You always knew how it would end. That you would drown," the stranger said in a voice rendered gravelly by disuse. His Hadrathi was marked with an odd accent. "Looking within and without, we shall *not* see. We shall *not* be seen. With the brush of Time, I erase you. The Void within you will join the Sea." The Mistress of Tides felt a twitch, a crumple in her chest. She felt the ritual seal in place, containing only her.

She tasted her death.

Furious, she screamed after the stranger as he turned away and mounted the stairs. He did not look back. No echo returned to her. Her voice was tinny and distant in her own ears. The Mistress of Tides pushed hard against the fear that swelled around her, the advance tide of the killing sea that rocked back and forth ever higher in the fixed cage.

Her withered arm burned as life slipped in and out of her chest and her mind raced.

For the first time in decades, she could not find her center.

Her scream became a wail.

EMPRESS OF GULLS' WORKSHOP SLOOP WRECK, TANGLETOWN, CROW'S FOOT. 26ᵀᴴ VOLVINET. HOUR OF WINE, 8 HOURS PAST DUSK. SAIL LIGHTING FESTIVAL, DAY FOUR.

"This is all very enlightening, but why don't you summarize the situation for me once more," the Empress of Gulls said, inscrutable behind her veil as she inspected the grease pencil fixed to the end of the pointer.

Cellar was panting, slightly dizzy. He was naked, his wrists and ankles secured to a circular metal frame hanging in the middle of the Empress's throne room. The grease pencil had sketched out the various blood-draining vulnerabilities and potential butcher cuts on his shrinking and clammy skin. To one side, Jayan scowled, hands tied to a ring bolted to the wall, stripped down to his undergarments. His damaged flesh had only just started coloring with bruises. Four large men stood at attention, hanging on the Empress of Gulls' every word. They flanked the iron ring, and the captive Bluecoat.

"My name is Inspector Kobb Cellar. Someone is framing me, giving the impression I'm the Skullface Killer even though a decade has passed since the last round and I was too young to be the killer at that time. I've been trying to figure out who the Skullface Killer is so I can shed the suspicion and stop the murders." Cellar paused for breath. "I think the last victim was killed because she was the doctor who was present for the last round, a decade ago. I tried to save her, but the Skullface Killer was there and I thought he stabbed me, but he must have had some chemical brand, he gave me that awful thing," he said with a head jerk towards the purple burn site. "Before that, this criminal, Spur, he was ritually murdered. Like a sacrifice maybe. I was checking through his room, and found a hidden chamber that looked like a workout room for a Spirit Warden. I think he was a Spirit Warden with a double identity." Cellar squinted at the Empress of Gulls. "I am not a cultist, I don't know any rituals, and I'm trying to protect people here. I only came to you to find out what this brand was. Please do not kill me."

"And you haven't told the Inspectors about this Spur fellow's secret identity?" the Empress of Gulls asked, her tone bland. She sketched a slash on Cellar's neck with the grease pencil on the pointer, wielding the marker with the skill of a calligrapher.

"No!" Cellar shouted. "No, I can't go to the Inspectors, I'm a suspect."

"Don't like your tone," the Empress of Gulls said absently, and one of her agents slung a heavy punch into Jayan's gut. The Bluecoat was caught by surprise, staggered back against the hull.

"Please! Please don't do that," Cellar wavered.

"Still don't like your tone," the Empress of Gulls shrugged, and as Jayan squinted at his attacker, the other one swiped a blow at the back of his head that drove him awkwardly to his knees, arms over his head where he was secured to the hull.

Cellar gritted his teeth, but said nothing.

"Better," the Empress of Gulls nodded. "Let me guess. Spur was killed after you said stupid and vengeful things about him, while you had no factuals established to prove your innocence. Every way you turn, you find things out, but they increase suspicions around you, driving you to be more and more alone."

"Y-yes."

"Classic," the Empress of Gulls sighed. "You are being isolated. As you are cut off, your identity becomes malleable, to the point where you get the brand," she said with an airy gesture. "You are being groomed to become the Herald, sounds like the Dark Tooth has a careful touch. You are harrowed, a Herald unwilling. Your identity is being stripped away; probably why the Dark Tooth chose someone so young. The Dark Tooth is preparing you. The role of the Herald is to open or obstruct, and beforehand, it is very difficult to know which." Leisurely, she carved a distressing line along Cellar's flank with the grease pencil.

Another of the Empress of Gulls' bodybuilding guards emerged from the shadows. "A guest," he said in Hadrathi. "Neap, for Mistress of Tides."

"Let him in," the Empress of Gulls replied, cocking her head to the side to regard her art on Cellar's body.

Moments later, the sweating adept was escorted in. He bowed deeply, and the Empress of Gulls gestured at him to rise. "What brings you to me in the heart of the night?" she asked, dry.

"The Mistress of Tides is missing," Neap said, breathless, ignoring the Empress of Gulls' captives. "There are small signs, but signs I may read. I do not believe she left of her own accord, leaving no word or message. I believe she has been taken."

"And you come here," the Empress of Gulls mused.

"My understanding is that the Mistress of Tides was agitated greatly by her conversation with you today. On the way home she was assaulted by assassins, we believe they were elites sent by the Foundation to slay her. When I returned from the work she assigned I went to see if she was still awake, and she was gone." Neap paused. "Your wisdom penetrates time and space, and I beg you to assure me she is safe and has chosen this mystery."

For a long moment, the Empress of Gulls studied Cellar. "A ritual longs to complete," she murmured to herself. "Most of them require a certain... symmetry." She turned to Neap. "We had best establish her whereabouts," she agreed.

One of Jayan's handlers and one of Cellars' handlers stepped away from the prisoners, setting up a makeshift ritual table, bringing sands and small jars and implements. They quickly set the table in a peculiar parody of table manners, arranging the elements for a seeking ritual. Neap stood respectfully to the side, heart hammering.

The last element was a rat the length of a forearm, furious and wary, a vicious survivor of the docks, secure in a well-gnawed cage. The Empress of Gulls called out an invocation, and hammered her knife through the bars, skewering the rat; blood spurted then drooled down, and as her assistant held the cage above the table, the Empress of Gulls studied the spatter pattern.

"I don't see her," she mused. "A spirit of her magnitude burns clean, and is only invisible to the ritual if she has chosen to conceal herself..." she paused. "Foundation assassins," she echoed, brow furrowed. "They could... hide her."

She turned to Cellar.

"You and I are both tied into a ritual that includes the Mistress of Tides," she thought aloud. "It is possible that I could coax her location from my blood. But that could take time, time we may not have. You have an opportunity here, boy. You could contribute of your essence, to penetrate the mystery. Are you game?" Her tone was just short of mockery.

"I have conditions," he said through his teeth. "You release me and Jayan, and give up any thoughts of capturing, injuring, or killing us. Do that, and I'll see if I can find this Mistress of Tides."

The Empress of Gulls watched him, unmoved.

"I've played enough games to know you don't want to start trading pieces," Cellar said softly, improvising, thinking as fast as he could. "Maybe you normally would, but this is different, right? Sounds to me like the board is poised, and if you don't want to find corpses, you shouldn't make them."

"Done," the Empress of Gulls said, her tone flat. "Cut him loose and give him a knife."

Her man swiftly did just that, and Cellar found himself standing in arm's reach of the Empress of Gulls, naked, knife in hand. He successfully resisted the temptation to try to fight his way to freedom.

"What do I do?" he asked gruffly.

The Empress of Gulls held her hand out, palm up, and cut her forearm. She tilted her hand enough for blood to roll down her palm and gather, heavy. The first drop fell. She nodded to Cellar, and he cut his own forearm, bleeding on the spattered table.

The Empress of Gulls spoke quietly, with the rhythmic intonation of a musician, and the table shimmered and blurred. Her next drop of blood hissed on something invisible above the table, and melted down through it somehow, as though it was a translucent dome. Then Cellar's blood fell into the "hole" eaten away by the Empress of Gull's blood, burning still further; there was an inaudible popping sensation they felt in their chests. The Empress of Gulls frowned, and ran the ritual once more; this time it wavered around the edges, but the tablecloth began to singe and crisp, and a single chip of flame danced over the vague outline of a map forming on the surface.

"Of course it is on the water," the Empress of Gulls breathed, a fresh fear kindled in her voice. "Neap, go quickly. She is somewhere on the North Hook Annex. I doubt you will find her without him." She gestured towards Cellar, oddly weary.

"Jayan," Cellar said, his voice level. "Let's go."

The Empress of Gulls nodded, almost imperceptibly. Jayan was cut loose, and by the time he was free, the Empress of Gulls' agents handed the two men their personal effects.

"You have my gratitude, and the gratitude of my lady," Neap said with sincerity as he backed towards the door. "Looking within and without, we shall see," he added in Hadrathi.

The Empress of Gulls said nothing, settling back on her throne.

Discomfited, Neap bowed once more, then led the other two out of the workshop.

"You got a way to go fast?" Cellar demanded as they stepped out into the night air. He was unsteady, he felt the whole world tilted fifteen degrees. His ankles, wrists, back, and neck ached. His chest burned with the horrific brand. But he was still alive.

"Yes," Neap replied. He ran to where the docked gondola waited, two other adepts aboard. Cellar stopped in his tracks, staring at the elegance of the Sight, the spellbound craft almost humming on the water as one of the adepts sat cross-legged and attuned with it.

"This will do," he said, and he climbed aboard with Jayan in his shadow. "So who the hell is the Mistress of Tides?"

"The Docks, North Hook Annex, all speed," Neap said to Spring, who nodded and leaned into the sculling oar as Ebb frowned in concentration and added slickness and stability to the gondola hull. Neap turned back to Cellar. "First, who are you?"

"I am Inspector Cellar, I'm on the trail of the Skullface Killer." Cellar watched Neap's reaction closely.

"Your honor binds you to report all things to your masters," Neap replied, expressionless, "so I think we had both hope that we find the Mistress of Tides in a condition where she can explain everything to your satisfaction." He paused. "Please put some clothes on."

As Cellar and Jayan dressed, the gondola nosed away from Tangletown, headed downriver but against the incoming tide. Cellar and Jayan gingerly seated themselves, wincing.

"Adventuring with you is no fun at all," Jayan muttered under his breath, squinting at Cellar.

"Well," Cellar said, short of breath as he touched at the stinging brand, "at least we're getting somewhere."

CHAPTER SEVENTEEN

Ghosts teach us that solidity is an illusion. You move back and forth between the front and the back of the Mirror and you see that distance, time, and consciousness are not wholly defined by human senses. This is not to say that they are not defined at all—instead, you must understand that there are other points of view, other senses that humans do not have. A demon can stare into reality and see interconnectedness that a human cannot.

Water teaches us that energy focused through a malleable medium can forcibly erode the strongest material. Everything flows. Rituals are, at their root, the mechanization of different anchor points, lines, and planes than the ones our physical senses report to our minds. The most powerful rituals create a dam that isolates a reserve of energy necessary to the work of changing the shape of reality itself. Provided with pressure and focus, the stuff of life and death can be rendered a precision sculpting tool.

— From "Water Rituals: Five Centuries on the Canals"
by the Master of Crickets

"I mean, whatever he's dealing with, he can tell me, right?" Sanction continued, his speech distinct as he masked the slight slur in his voice. "It's me we're talking about! I'm his right hand man, the only one who has any idea what that vulture is thinking! If he can't tell me his plans then he can't tell anybody, and you know I'll back him up however crazy his stupid idea is. Like, with the girl, remember her? That big secret girl thing he cares so much about that he turned over to the boat people? Blood and bone!"

"I know, yeah, you are so right," Spindle agreed carefully. "You know, you've had a bit to drink. Maybe you should rest in one of Trellis's apartments in the mansion and talk it through tomorrow."

"You may not know this," Sanction retorted, nose high, "but I hold my liquor *extremely well.*" He arched an eyebrow and pinned Spindle with a blood-shot stare. "To the untrained eye I appear completely sober."

The carriage jolted over another shallow hole in the road, and Spindle squinted out into the darkness. "Well, we're almost there," he muttered, as much to himself as to Sanction.

The goats drawing the carriage let out a bleat, and the carriage momentum faltered then slowed to a stop. Sanction frowned, banging on the roof of the carriage.

"I know, but there's fire," yelled Crackstone from the buckboard.

"What?" Sanction growled, throwing the carriage door open and stepping out into the cool night, Spindle right behind him. Sanction blinked, and stared at the glow that underlit the column of smoke twisting up from the flaming mansion ahead.

"That's... yeah, that's not an accident," Sanction said as a level of inebriation metabolized, seared out of his bloodstream by adrenaline. His eyes followed the long ridgeline of the third story, the even sheeting of flame from two wings of the house. Even if the entire radiant lab in the attic burst into flame, the pattern of flame would not spread so fast it would be even at this stage. "We need a closer look."

"Do we though?" Spindle muttered through his teeth, eyes straining towards the manor.

"We do. I'm asking you—did Trellis die?" Sanction demanded, looking at Spindle. "Report."

"I don't know," Spindle replied slowly.

"That answer is *not* good enough. Because if Trellis died, there are likely some wheels in motion. Get me?"

"I get it," Spindle nodded. "I just... we can't go up in there," he said. "So unless he's in the yard, or they left a note or something..."

"And if they did, we'll find it," Sanction grunted as he hauled himself back into the carriage, Spindle right behind him. Crackstone flexed the reins, and the goats brayed their irritation but reluctantly resumed dragging the carriage towards the flames.

The thick crackle of energy tearing out of overheated wood punctuated the roar of air into the starvation of the burning building. Thick billows of smoke and chemicals tumbled down from the cloud of drifting debris ejected from the digesting structures, stinging the eyes and stuffing the nose and throat with unbreathable stink. Waves of heat were only visible as a shimmer, but they pushed hard at those who tried to approach the house, stopping them at the edge of the driveway.

Spindle stared at the fire as Crackstone jumped down to manage the two spooked draft goats. Sanction stepped out of the carriage and slowly walked towards the five still figures laid out on the withered grass. The butler. Two maids. The stable hand. The gardener. Throats slit, eyes glassy, the bloodstains invisible in the darkness. A harsh caw snapped Sanction's attention upward. He saw pinpoints of reflected light from the eyes of the Deathseeker crows perched in the tree. His eyes traced around the branches with dizzying speed, counting.

Five corpses. And five crows.

Sanction blanched slightly, surprised by the nausea that swarmed in his throat. Some deeper part of his mind stumbled. He connected the sight of a corpse at his feet to the memory of the formal but kindly man that made him sandwiches when he was a child. Sanction dropped to one knee as he felt a reverberation in the part of himself that predated the toughening of his criminal perspective.

A divot of the lawn exploded upwards with a dull whack. Sanction stared at it stupidly for a moment before the report of the gunshot reached him. Panic galvanized him, and he threw himself to the side and scrambled towards the low wall that encircled the drive.

Spindle did not react so quickly. A bullet hurled him off his feet. He landed in a full-length sprawl as his head spattered across the lawn. Crackstone clapped his hand on his hat and raced for cover, sprinting towards a tree that stood opposite the direction Spindle fell. A solemn peal rippled through the Mirror, mingling with the crack of the second shot. Crackstone was thrown into the tree; he rebounded with the force of the powerful gun, flopping down. Excited, the crows already on the scene cawed and flapped, hopping from one branch to another, eagerly staring at the draining bodies.

Hardly daring to breathe, Sanction felt his heart try to blast its way out of his chest, flexing and clamping with panic. He squirmed along the wall, wriggling into the muddy drainage pipe by the drive. Some disconnected corner of his mind echoed with the butler's stern warnings to his child-self; stay out of the drains. You could get stuck and drown, or be nibbled by the scavengers of the field, and no one would find you. Dangerous! The drains were dangerous. His shoulders and ribs flexed as he straightened his arms and hoped the mud that ruined his expensive clothes would ease the friction enough for him to make it into the pipe.

The shooters would have to confirm their kills. Taking on the Silkworms, they didn't dare miss. They would need to be sure of who they put down. They would look around. The pipe trembled as the frightened goats dragged the carriage over the roadway overhead, trotting anxiously away from the burning houses, the loud noises, the stink of blood.

Sanction's face seemed frozen in a silent scream as his mouth was wide open, desperate for air, his chest trying to expand against the narrow pipe walls to draw in breath.

Stuck. Drowned. Nibbled by scavengers of the field. Maybe shot. Sanction kept pushing against the pipe and against his terror.

The exit glowed with the light of the burning house. Escape seemed to become more possible as he squirmed onward, his shoes disintegrating against the pipe wall, clothes peeling off.

Echoing oddly in the pipe, Crackstone's cries for help seemed ghostly. Sanction ignored them. Everyone who succeeded in Doskvol had to master the art of turning a blind eye to victims. Just because you can still hear a call for help doesn't mean the victim can be saved.

Impossibly, the worst moment was squeezing out the far end; wrists, then forearms, finally shoulders, unfolding to leverage his chest past the exit. Filthy rags clung to his bleeding body as he dragged himself clear and stumbled upright, wild-eyed and streaked with filth.

The glow of radiant fields flanking the road was subdued this close to dawn, and Sanction knew from experience that trying to spot shadows against their backdrop was useless. He did not look for snipers, nor did he expect them to see him. Breaking into a limping run, he closed in on the hesitant and confused goats harnessed to the empty carriage. Banging into the side, he pulled himself up onto the buckboard, gasping for air and ignoring the stitch in his side. Gripping the reins, he flexed hard, and the leather slapped on goat haunches. One bellowed surprise and dismay, but both obediently broke into a trot.

A grim expression twisted Sanction's features; surprised and stung, the goats were still willing to work as long as the uncertainty resolved into clear action. Hunched low, he did not look back as he urged the goats to greater speed.

NORTH HOOK ANNEX, THE DOCKS.
26TH VOLVINET. ALMOST THE HOUR OF ASH, 9 HOURS PAST DUSK.
SAIL LIGHTING FESTIVAL, DAY FOUR.

The Sight listed violently, unsuited to the heavy swells of the channel. Again the bitterly cold shoulder of the wave slid along the gondola's flank, spilling across the hull and dragging at the crew. Only the adept interface with the gondola's spellcraft kept the gondola buoyant and driving forward through the surf.

Ebb shouted, gripping the prow and pointing at the docks. Relieved, Neap hauled at the sculling oar as hard as he could. Cellar and Jayan clutched the handles by the benches, and Spring's resolve was unmoved as the salty water slapped at him, failing to break his stone-faced concentration.

Sliding out of the swells into the relative shelter of a pier, the Sight nosed up to a row of cleats along the side of a piling. Ebb secured a casting line with the long experience of a gondolier.

"Okay, this is the North Hook Annex," Neap said as he sagged against the oar, exhausted. "We don't have much time, and there are dozens of piers."

"Maybe ten minutes until high tide," Ebb said, subdued.

"So how do we find her?" Cellar demanded, every bone aching, his chest aflame with the salt stinging into his chemical brand.

Neap gestured vaguely, his mouth working as he searched for words. "We—we look," he managed.

"High tide, this isn't an accident," Jayan said. "Some sick bastard is trying to drown her. We check the waterline. All the waterlines," he said, trailing off as his eyes immediately got lost in the forest of pilings.

"Wait! No! Hang on!" Spring barked, leaping to his feet. "North Hook! North Hook Annex!"

The others stared at him, and he shoved at his ideas to get them in order, to fit out through his words. "Last year—Lord Rowan—test site—"

"You're brilliant!" Neap shouted. "Spring, take them by land, we'll go by wave!"

Ebb slid back to the bench and arranged himself, attuning to the Sight, and Cellar and Jayan exchanged a confused glance before scrambling up the ladder behind Spring. The Sight cast off, heeling around. Spring scrambled up onto the pier and ran. Cellar and Jayan followed, doggedly ignoring their aches and pains as they raced after the slim acolyte.

As they pounded down the uneven and dim street, only a few others were out and about; it was hours until dawn. Weather-beaten warehouses, docks, and ruins blurred by as the men raced the tide.

Spring stumbled to a halt, his hands on his knees as his torso flexed for air. He vaguely gestured at a warehouse. It was freshly painted, the North Hook Annex clearly lined on the flanking wall and a coat of arms on the door. Two guards stood by the door in a pool of light, bored senseless but watchful all the same.

"Okay—warehouse—" Cellar gasped, clattering to a halt beside him, a block away from the guards.

"Ambient—defenses—disarm—ghosts—Whispers," Spring spat between gulps of air.

"Right!" Jayan yelled, and he slapped at Cellar's arm unthinkingly, then ran along the road that passed in front of the warehouse. If you wanted to kill a Whisper, of course you'd want to get close to defenses that could render them powerless.

Cellar started after him, but Spring caught at him, and Cellar rounded on the acolyte.

"No time to look around," Spring managed. He planted his hand on Cellar's chest, looking him in the eye. "If you really are—connected—open up—feel her!"

"Can you help?" Cellar demanded. Spring nodded, and grasped Cellar's shoulders, bowing his head and focusing hard. Cellar wasn't sure what to do, so he grabbed Spring's shoulders and also bowed, squeezing his eyes shut, pushing his starving lungs and their demands out of his mind for the moment. He tried to listen past the banging of his heart and the squirt of blood through his overstressed body.

Then he felt Spring's presence, deflecting him back, and he looked into the racing of his blood. There was another flavor in the sensation, a flavor that Spring knew. Cellar was not the only one with a racing heart, desperation careening through his flesh.

"Mistress," Cellar heard Spring hiss.

Cellar focused on the close-but-alien sensation in his blood, and felt a surge; he felt the bubbles twirling up away from his face, then the dip of the wave that for just a moment allowed a breath, snatched from between the metal bars of the cage lid. Sobered, he pushed Spring away, his eyes wild as he saw two overlaid scenes for a split second.

"No time to be sure," Spring said. "Guess. Now. Go."

Cellar pivoted, scanning the piers, docks, and quays, half-focused. His heart skipped a beat. There. Or nowhere. He lowered his head and drove himself towards the pier, snatching at a pole to swing around and line up with the boardwalk. Racing down the pier, he felt his heart hammer with a terror that he did not wholly own. Battering into a railing as he spun around it, he clattered down the stairs to a lower level that was chained to the pilings and resting on buoyant tanks, almost at the top of high tide. He spun, eyes everywhere, and he saw a spray of water come out of a wave. Three steps took him close enough to the edge to stare down at the foam-laced black shoulder of the next wave—and the glint of bars just under the surface.

With a hoarse cry, he dropped to his knees and thrust his arm into the water, clanging into the cage lid. His hand fumbled across it, finding the padlock immediately. Oxygen burned out inside him, he felt his body starve and drown, muscle trapped under skin sucking the air out of his blood. His heart battered out orders to drain his lungs, and they heaved air away to make room for more.

Rearing up, he spun in a tight circle looking for something that could break a lock or a hasp. Frantic, he clawed at one of the cleats on the side of the piling, but it did not budge.

A hand thrust up through the cage lid, fingers barely clearing the surface.

"I know I know!" Cellar gritted out. For a crazed moment, he flashed on the idea of trying to pick the lock with his belt buckle, an idea that was doomed before it occurred to him.

Thudding steps and a mad scrabble down the stairs, and Spring closed in.

"Knife! Something!" Cellar barked out. Spring flicked a stiletto out of his sleeve, and Cellar snatched it, pivoting and dropping so he could jam the blade under the surface. He found the lock, slid the stiletto between the padlock and the hasp, and took a moment to focus. Then he yanked on the knife, applying a sharp shock to the hinge. The knife flexed, but nothing gave.

"Please," Cellar whispered, breathless. This time, he knew that either the knife would snap, or the hasp would break. He tugged hard.

The hasp broke.

Dragging at the cage lid, Cellar freed it with a spray as it tore through the water's surface. He thrust his arms into the swirling surf and snatched at a cold hand, pulling. Spring grabbed him and planted his feet, leaning back and hauling the Inspector up away from the water's surface. A woman sloshed up through the water, and together they dragged her up onto the platform.

"Not breathing," Spring said, short. He pushed Cellar aside and knelt by the pale woman, expertly pushing on her chest. After just a moment, she fountained water out of her nose and mouth, and rolled on her side, quickly clearing her airways enough to cough. Cellar lay back on the planks, struggling to breathe just as she did. Spring stripped off his shirt, twirling it around.

Cellar propped himself up on his elbows as Jayan clumped down the stairs. Spring looked over his shoulder at Cellar, and glanced at Jayan.

"Thank you," Spring said, his voice choked with emotion. "She will live."

The Mistress of Tides pulled at his arm, and he leaned down to help her to a sitting position. His thin shirt was fashioned into a veil, concealing her features; she chose the veil over covering the shift that was plastered to her narrow body. Straining close to Spring's ear, the Mistress of Tides forced out a faint rasp.

"We need Trellis."

PAN SALT MOORING ROW, THE EASE, SILKSHORE.
26TH VOLVINET. HOUR OF WINE, 8 HOURS PAST DUSK.
SAIL LIGHTING FESTIVAL, DAY FOUR.

Bent with weariness and pain, Rutherford limped along the pavement next to the mooring pylons, the houseboats dark and quiet as he passed them. Looking ahead, a bleak smile tried to warm his features. He saw the light Celia left on for him.

The expression evaporated as he heard footsteps approaching from behind. He stopped, cocking his head to the side, not quite bothering to turn.

"Rutherford," said a husky voice with an Iruvian accent. "Trajan wishes to speak with you specifically. Will you accompany me?"

Taking his time to reorient, Rutherford looked over the gondolier. "Of course," he said. "I'll meet you by the landing there. Come pick me up." Turning his back, Rutherford continued forward, then down the steps. By the time he was on the landing, a sleek gondola drifted into position, three hooded figures aboard. Rutherford stepped down, then arranged himself on the bench, and the gondola glided ahead as one of the Iruvians leaned into the sculling oar.

"I don't suppose you know what this is about," Rutherford observed mildly.

"I assume the Silkworms," the gondolier replied. "You will know soon enough."

After a short interval of maneuvering around festival boats at anchor, the gondola closed in on a sturdy barge, and secured casting lines. The crew of the barge lowered a gangplank, and Rutherford scowled as he climbed it, enduring the pains from his gunshot wound. Moments later he was in the hold of the barge, glancing over its exits as well as its burnished brass trim and luxurious appointments. Trajan stood to greet him, expressionless, his arms crossed over his chest.

Rutherford waited as his escorts left. The two men were alone in the houseboat's main hold.

"You have had a busy week," Trajan observed.

"Festival," Rutherford agreed. "My temporary quarters are supposed to be a secret, by the way. How did you find me?"

"Your friend's barge touches the waters of Silkshore, so we know about it," Trajan shrugged. "I keep many secrets, and my friendship is valuable. I brought you here so I could ask you for a favor."

"Well," Rutherford managed with a squint as he lowered himself to a chair. "You can ask, of course."

"I need to secure something where no one else can get it," Trajan said. "I have thousands of hiding places in Silkshore, but I am trying to hide something from Trellis. So."

"Indeed," Rutherford agreed coolly. "And?"

"I do not know what plans Trellis might have, who he may have compromised among my people. If I want something truly beyond his reach, I must hide it somewhere so secure no one can get to it. No one," he repeated, scowling. "I know who your father is. I think you can help me do this."

Rutherford pursed his lips, then frowned. "What you ask is costly, if it is even possible." He relaxed. "I don't want to do it. I have troubles of my own."

"Please do not be hasty," Trajan said, trying on a smile as he seated himself opposite Rutherford. "Do you want assistance combating crime in Silkshore? My people can be invaluable to that kind of effort." He raised his eyebrows.

"You insist I consider this," Rutherford clarified.

"Yes. Please," Trajan agreed.

"Very well." Rutherford looked him in the eye. "If I do what you ask, then I will control one seat on the Fairpole Council. I will identify someone who will be added, with full rights." He paused. "Also, you will reconsider terms for the current contracts with Barness and Dalia."

Trajan's smile grew pained. "Cutting the Hive out is not so simple—" he began.

"Not cutting them out," Rutherford interrupted, his voice hard. "Renegotiating, offering more favorable conditions."

Trajan stared. "You? The Hive got to *you*?"

"Us," Rutherford corrected, "if you want me to consider your favor."

Trajan struggled to regain his poise. "Very well. We are disposing of the Silkworms, and we will need new influential partners to smooth our operations with the Ministry. Trading Trellis in for the Hive is... traditional."

"Yes, Trellis is at the center of all that, isn't he. First he strengthened the Hive in the Council, then he cut most of it out. If you are through with him, it's all about rebalancing." Rutherford shifted in his seat. "Are you planning to kill the old man?"

"I've sent two teams. I expect it is done already. However, we cannot assume success. If he does survive, we need his attention to be elsewhere. I have to accept the likelihood he has made plans to observe his prize, so if I relocate it that should absorb his attention and keep him too busy to enact revenge."

"You want this done tonight," Rutherford sighed.

"What's left of the night, yes," Trajan replied, looking out the porthole. "Mere hours until dawn. You can get in position to work out the finer points with your father over breakfast. Besides. If you wanted more time, you should have gotten home earlier," Trajan said with a crooked smile.

"Busy night," Rutherford replied, deadpan. "What is it you think Trellis will watch so closely?"

Trajan hesitated. "We have a deal, yes? You hide this treasure out of Trellis's reach, and in exchange we renegotiate terms and add a seat on the Fairpole Council."

"We have a deal," Rutherford agreed. "The prize."

Trajan scowled. "It is an Iruvian girl. From what my people tell me, she may be a powerful mystic, but she has not spoken and she seems to ignore us for the most part. Looks to be about twelve, name is Cromlech." He shrugged. "I have no idea. Daughter? Granddaughter? He spent several fortunes, drained accounts we knew about and others we didn't in getting this girl into the city." Trajan regarded Rutherford. "I have never known Trellis to care about anything in particular with such fierceness," he admitted, "so I feel I must protect this bargaining chip. In case I need to force him or his plans out in the open so we can deal with them."

Rutherford considered. "I wonder what her value is. There are much cheaper ways to satisfy pretty much every perversion," he mused. "He's also not terribly fond of family members, I've seen that up close. Must be something else."

"Whatever it is, what matters is that he finds her precious and I control her whereabouts and health. If I order her death, I need to know it will happen," he said.

"Sure," Rutherford nodded.

Trajan smiled, cautious. "Very good. Go with my man, he will take you to her and see to it that all goes well."

Rutherford struggled up out of his seat, and stood straight. "Sounds like a plan." They shook hands.

FLASHBACK.
BELDERAN ESTATE, BARROWCLEFT.
21ST VOLNIVET. TWELFTH HOUR PAST DAWN.

"Your plan has merits," Trellis admitted. "However, it could... it could be bigger in scope."

"I find your reaction to be completely unsurprising," Rutherford observed.

Trellis smiled, a troubled and soft expression that was out of place on his craggy features. "I have told no one," he said, "but I have a terminal condition. I will not live much longer." He refocused in the middle distance. "Priorities shift, approaching the end," he said quietly.

"I am... I am so sorry," Rutherford said.

"Don't be," Trellis said with a dismissive wave. "I have plans. The point here is, I want to give the Hive a proper sendoff. I want to give them what they deserve. They hate me, you know. I was once their Unseen Hand, many years ago."

Rutherford had no words.

Sincerity rounded out Trellis's smile. "Indeed," he nodded. "And you know what... I think *you* should be the next Unseen Hand."

"Me?" Rutherford blinked, again startled.

"Yes, if you approach this right, you could be a very tempting option. Once you are in with the Bluecoats, the moment you get enough clout to pull a squad together, you go hit Barness. He's got the secret ledger, documenting the Bluecoats and Inspectors under Hive influence."

"What, apply pressure on them?" Rutherford prompted.

"Don't try to run ahead," Trellis said, mild, one eyebrow cocked. "No, you get that secret ledger from him. He won't want to go to prison, or die, so he's likely to give it up to someone who knows to ask him for it. Once you have that, you keep it to yourself until you're contacted."

Rutherford waited, and Trellis savored the moment.

"Then," Trellis continued, "you give that ledger to Orris and tell him that's how you wanted to get an audience. To expose a vulnerability and cover it again. You want to provoke attention, this is about a big flashy gesture to show you know secrets but you're cocky enough to waste the opportunity they represent."

"Right," Rutherford said, thinking it through.

"The other ledgers are fine for the Bluecoats to crack, that will be a nice win for you," Trellis continued. "If the Bluecoats get stuck, the ledgers probably still use a number substitution filtered through a book code, most likely 'Behind Public Curtains' by Sydoloron. Anyway, Orris is petty enough to be attracted to the novelty; you may not know this, but Sanction—your very own Kreeger—was almost contacted to be the Hive's Unseen Hand. In the final stages of the vetting process, he veered off to found the Silkworms."

Rutherford stared. Trellis sipped his tea.

"He doesn't know," Trellis added. "At least I think he doesn't. Just as well. Now *you* know, and you're not supposed to, so that will discomfit Orris further. Here you are, Sanction's husband, a man with access to me, pursuing an elite Hive position. Currently, Orris is under pressure to deliver on consolidating North Port for smuggling, so he'll likely ask for you to prove yourself taking on the Fog Hounds or some other victim of the hour. You can handle that on your own," he said with a fluttering gesture. "Before we get into the details, I have a gift for you, and... and a request."

"I don't know what to say," Rutherford managed.

"First things first," Trellis said. "Take this." He pulled a folder from a desk drawer, sliding it over to Rutherford, who accepted it. "Inside are credentials to access an investment I made some years back. There is a substantial value there. Use it to pursue these objectives we've talked about, or to retire in style, or whatever you like. You can look it over later. Don't thank me," he said before Rutherford could interrupt. "It warms an old man's heart to know some of my resources will be put to good use. I cannot take them with me, after all. I was always going to leave this particular fortune to you, but the timing works out," he said, and for a moment he was almost grandfatherly. "Second, you and I are going to see to it that the Fairpole Council is very, very angry with the Silkworms." His smile lost all warmth. "When they turn on the Silkworms, they will see you as the one who can assist them in hiding something from me."

Still off balance and struggling to sort out the cascade of emotional responses, Rutherford blinked and said nothing.

"Why you, of course, reasonable question," Trellis continued. "Because I told them who your father is, and I told them that I was cultivating a friendship with you so I could get to some things tucked away in his keeping. Things I tried to access for years, to no avail," he added with a mock dramatic flair. "I've built up your father as an obstacle I simply cannot circumvent. That will stay with Trajan. When he decides to kill the Silkworms, he will hedge his bets; he is the cautious sort, that's one of the things I like best about him."

"So he will pressure me to influence my father," Rutherford said, eyes wide. "Hide something you care about." He paused. "What is it? What do you need to hide with my father?"

"That part is not something you need to worry about," Trellis said. "I need this object to go to Whitecrown. Nowhere else. And I need to be sure no one else can get it, not even the Bluecoats."

"I—I can arrange that," Rutherford said.

"Good. Good!" Trellis said, rising to his feet, all smiles. He rubbed his hands together. "Oh, this is a load off my mind," he confessed. "Thank you, my friend. Thank you. I must say, I always did like you best. Now, let's move on to the rest of the details."

"Yes," Rutherford echoed, disoriented by revelations. "Sounds like a plan."

Chapter Eighteen

My master may now be aware of our arrangement. I promised you information on the Pyressant Order in exchange for safe passage out of the city and a new life elsewhere. This is what I have learned. You had best come through on your end of the bargain.

The only candidates considered for membership are those touched by a Leviathan's Mark—it may not be something you can see, but it changes them. Gives them power. Shows a Leviathan invested in them to further some demonic plan. Members of the Order can see the Leviathan's Mark on others, informing their recruiting efforts.

Members have a naming convention—the title, of something. Like the Master of Crickets. There are a fixed number of titles in the Order that form a hierarchy, but only those of Lord level and above know any of the Order's secrets. The 'of something' is always whatever gave them life—what saved them from destruction. Like all mystics, they try to map their inexplicable experience to some rationale the human mind can grasp.

Their leader in Doskvol, the Empress of Gulls, has taken an interest in an orphan that washed up on Doskvol's shore during the Sail Lighting Festival. The Empress of Gulls says she is the key to

— From unfinished correspondence
suppressed in the investigation of Inspector Fanwell's murder,
Volvinet 829 (twenty years ago)

Jayan squinted at the lock, then rocked his heavy frame against the door once again. This time the bolt tore loose and the door banged open. He stepped into the musty dimness, alert.

The Mistress of Tides followed him in, and Cellar was watchful as he backed through the door.

"You are sure we were not followed?" he said between his teeth. "I feel like I'm being watched."

"We must all endure our vulnerabilities," the Mistress of Tides replied wearily. She lowered herself to sit on a padded bench, her eyes sweeping the common room. Chairs were upside down on tables across the space, a bristling forest. Massive windows let in the ugly glow of the lightning tower outside, the writhing film of energy twisting in coils rather than the usual sheets of light. An erratic red glow, somewhere between the shades of molten metal and an infection, curled across the etheric defenses.

"Never seen a lightning tower do that before," Jayan frowned, planting his fists on his hips as he looked out the window. "Should we be worried?"

"That's our signal," the Mistress of Tides said. "I sent Ebb ahead to sabotage the tower. We keep a hidden reserve of tainted electroplasmic fuel near here. Should the Silkworms need an emergency meet, one of us arranges for the signal tank to be loaded in to the tower. Even if my crew cannot see the display, gossip will spread. When the Spark Grounds burn red, they will come to this observatory."

"It's spectacular," Jayan muttered. One of his eyes was swollen shut, the other bloodshot; he could feel the pain of the burning fuel stinging in his bruises.

Cellar closed the door, propping it shut with a chair. "You are brave," he said, "trusting us. Sending all your acolytes away."

"I am brave," she agreed.

"Shouldn't Ebb be here by now?" Cellar pressed. "If he sabotaged the tower, he's on site."

"His instructions were to then climb the tower and serve as a look-out," Mistress of Tides said. She shivered slightly in her thin shift, but did not remove the shirt concealing her face.

"Maybe you should tell us the rest of the plan," Cellar said, his tone as neutral as he could make it.

"Neap is acquiring a cache of supplies for me," she said, "and Spring is taking the Sight on a roundabout tour with some passengers, to draw attention elsewhere." She regarded Cellar. "So you are an Inspector, with a Bluecoat, dodging the law and locating me with some sense of urgency." She paused. "That's unusual."

Cellar barked a laugh. "That's my week. Unusual." He rubbed at his face. "I went to see your friend, the Empress. She damn near killed me. Said I was a herald, part of some ritual. She's part of it too, that's how the two of us managed to locate you through the cloaking spell. We're all connected somehow by this demonic plot, so she thought maybe if she killed me you were more likely to die somehow." He shook his head. "I found you because Spring helped me feel you in my blood. What the hell are we into here?"

"The Dark Tooth is conducting a ritual, something massive. It cannot be good. I am apparently positioned to stop the Dark Tooth," the Mistress of Tides murmured.

"I got involved through investigating the Skullface Killer," Cellar said. "I confronted him, got burned with this." He shrugged his shirt back to reveal the burn. "The gull lady—"

"Empress of Gulls," the Mistress of Tides interrupted, unamused.

"She said the Skullface Killer was the Dark Tooth, and he'd been breaking my identity down to make me susceptible or something."

"You saw the Dark Tooth?" the Mistress of Tides demanded, energy in her tone.

"Kind of," Cellar replied. "It was dark. He had a hat, coat. Big bushy beard," he gestured. "His eyes." Cellar abruptly stopped.

"He is the one who put me in that cage," the Mistress of Tides growled.

"What did he do to your arm?" Cellar asked, almost reluctant. His eyes shied away from the blackened withering along her skin, the gnarled twist of burned muscle.

"That wasn't him, it was a cadre of Foundation assassins. I destroyed them," the Mistress of Tides said, something distant in her voice. "I too have had an unusual week."

"I've heard of the Foundation," Cellar said. "I thought they were a secret society, with some mystics, really into ritual, architecture, geography." He blinked. "So yeah, that checks out. You think the Dark Tooth is connected to them?"

"They have a prophecy about the Dark Tooth, the Bellweather Locus, recorded in 512," the Mistress of Tides murmured.

"What does it say?" Cellar prompted.

"I don't know, I just learned about it yesterday," the Mistress of Tides said. "The Empress of Gulls said there was a Fourfold Circle, a massive ritual, involving human sacrifice. This Skullface Killer, the Dark Tooth, finishing work he started a decade ago." She paused. "Maybe longer."

"So are you more powerful than the Empress of Gulls?" Cellar asked. "If she's *your* herald?"

"Roles in demonic rituals do not reflect the ability of their actors, though they do impart some power," she replied. "Demons do not see what humans see, when they glance across a person. Political influence, wealth, and skill do not matter to them. They touch upon and reshape the inner character."

"Well that's flowery," Cellar muttered. "Help me understand. The Empress of Gulls said heralds might open the way or close it. Something like that. Do you understand the job description?" he asked.

"The greatest danger," the Mistress of Tides said, her tone level, "is that you think you understand. What we are tangled within is a demonic ritual. As an Inspector, you are accustomed to getting enough facts to understand the motives, means, and opportunities of other people. You cannot get enough facts to understand the context we now inhabit. The perspective of an undying god monster drifting through the foundation of the world involves needs, information, and perspectives we cannot grasp."

"How is this ignorance a danger then?" Cellar demanded. "I don't understand the lightning walls, but they keep the ghosts out."

"The danger is that you think you can thwart the demonic will by acting counter to its interest. It is human instinct to either align with a greater power, or defy it. You will not know which you are doing, not really. The demon simultaneously understands you better than you know yourself, and also does not know you at all—not in the sense that people come to know each other. I am answering your question," she said, something sharp in her tone as her patience wore thin. "You asked me whether the heralds would open the way or close it. And my answer is that we cannot focus on the motives of the Leviathan or the Dark Tooth, not really. Resistance may be what they count on."

"Well I don't see much alternative," Cellar shot back. "If these demons know us so well, and pick us for these roles, how can we trust our instinctive responses?"

"They know us, if they touch on our lives, but they do not choose us. I cannot be sure I understand it myself, but what I've heard is that their plans align with their opportunities. If you are touched by the Leviathan, then you become an anchor point for its complex designs. Not the other way around. They do not recruit." She paused. "This is the machinery of fate, not politics."

"I don't understand either one," Cellar groused, crossing his arms then immediately wincing and relaxing his posture as the flesh around his brand bunched up. "I am trying to sift all this nonsense to find a course of action. Something to do. I feel like we are wasting time, and the Dark Tooth is up to something. For all we know, someone else is getting butchered *right now*." He bit his lip.

"We need a plan," the Mistress of Tides agreed. Then she rose to her feet, her good hand closing in a fist. Alarmed, Cellar scrambled to his feet.

"I didn't mean—" he said quickly.

"Not you," the Mistress of Tides snapped, orienting on the door as it shifted, sliding the chair along the floor. Jayan stepped over out of sight, ready to rebalance the situation if needed.

"All is well in the crimson shadows," Neap said carefully in Hadrathi, out of sight on the other side of the door.

"Tides of blood wash the bones of centuries," the Mistress of Tides replied, relaxing.

"And I found Sanction!" Neap said, doing his best impression of cheerfulness as he pushed the door open the rest of the way. He entered the room carrying a bulky chest, shrugging to settle a backpack.

Sanction followed, lean and wary. His hair was wet, and he wore new clothes.

"Neap told me you survived an assassination attempt," Sanction said, grim. "I did as well. And they burned down Trellis's mansion. It's the Fairpole Council. Trellis was supposed to settle them down," he said, the anger in his voice fueled by nerves. "Have you heard from him?"

"No, not yet," the Mistress of Tides replied.

Sanction's eyes widened. "Your arm."

"I was attacked by the Foundation," the Mistress of Tides said. "I do not believe the Fairpole Council was behind the attempt on my life. They have offered me gifts and extended an invitation to join them, and I do not think they were spurned to the point of trying to kill me. The timing is strange, yes. I think I have been targeted by a demon-slave attempting to complete a ritual."

"Is everyone else absorbed in personal business when the Silkworms need them most?" Sanction growled.

"How is Rutherford?" the Mistress of Tides retorted.

Sanction blinked, and swallowed his response, turning to look out the window instead. "I don't want to fight," he said firmly. "We need each other now. We have problems to address."

"That's why we're here," she agreed coolly. "I'll be back in a moment." She went with Neap as he carried the chest, behind the bar and through a door to the back room.

"Well. Sanction," Cellar said. "I've heard of you. I guess I didn't realize you were also Kreeger. You run the High Six, right?"

Sanction fixed him with a cold stare. "Well. Inspector Cellar. Why are you here."

"I rescued the Mistress of Tides from drowning," Cellar said, his tone mild. "Where were you when some maniac stuck her in a cage?"

"What?" Sanction blinked. "When was this?"

"A couple hours ago. It's been a great night," Cellar said. "I've been burned by cultists, tortured by a Whisper, and stymied by snakeshit." He sank down on the bench, weariness unexpectedly sapping his strength. "Saw my best friend die," he murmured.

"Here's to hoping your day goes better," Sanction sighed. He dug a candle out of his pocket and set it on the bar, lighting it with a finger sparker. "There we go."

"Ambiance?" Cellar said, raising an eyebrow. "Really?"

"A signal," said a voice on the balcony. Cellar jerked around, startled, then winced as pain shot through his injuries. Sanction casually blew the candle out. Trellis came down the stairs, his long black leather coat whispering around him. "It's good to see you," he said to Sanction.

"Likewise," Sanction said, trying to conceal the depth of his relief. "Glad to see you are keeping the crows lonely."

"Inspector Cellar," Trellis nodded, approaching him. "You can tell your shadow it's alright. I believe we're all on the same side here." His grandfatherly smile was a little too disarming.

"I feel like we've met," Cellar said, vaguely troubled as he studied the aristocrat.

"We most likely have. I am also Lord Belderan, out of Barrowcleft. You're learning quite a bit about the backstage operations of Silkshore tonight." Trellis's smile revealed a glint of teeth.

"I don't suppose you know how Piccolo is faring," Sanction said.

"I hope he's alright," Trellis said. "I've been keeping my head down. The Fairpole Council is eager for confirmation of my death. They've staked a fortune on it. This isn't the moment for me to contact my usual sources for information on the doings in Ironhook."

Jayan returned to Cellar, glaring up the stairs. "Balcony," he muttered. "Hell of a blind spot."

"We've all had a rough day full of things we didn't anticipate," Cellar said, his hand on Jayan's shoulder.

"So Daava was your best friend?" Jayan said, squinting against the pain in his face.

"She was *our* best friend," Cellar replied, serious. "What, you jealous?"

"Yeah, of both of you," Jayan sighed. "My best friend is Crabcake, bartender at Snozzles. He's totally worthless."

"Not much of a looker, either," Cellar said with the ghost of a smile, relaxing into the joke. "Couldn't fill out those pants worth a damn. Not like our Daava."

"Not like our Daava," Jayan echoed.

The Mistress of Tides rejoined them, Neap at her heels. She wore her customary headdress and veil, along with a loose outfit sashed and secured for rigorous activity.

"Trellis, you're here," she said. "We need you, for the challenges we face have escalated and we have more difficulties than time."

"I will help however I can," he replied, serious, ignoring the flash of incredulity that washed over Sanction.

"My priority is the Dark Tooth," the Mistress of Tides said. She nodded at a table, and Neap stepped over to it, pulling chairs off and arranging them as the rogues drifted over to it and seated themselves. "Inspector Cellar has been looking into the Skullface Killer, who is apparently active again. In that pursuit Cellar confronted the killer briefly, and was branded. Cellar met with the Empress of Gulls to identify the mark. She reckoned he was a herald of the Dark Tooth; she connected the marking and events to the Bellweather Locus prophecy held by the Foundation, describing a Fourfold Ritual and some sinister outcome."

"Wait, hold on," Sanction frowned. "My priority is not some demon ritual. My priority is the survival of the Silkworms, and we need to deal with the Fairpole Council. Trellis, you went to talk them down. What happened? They torched your house! We lost Piccolo to Ironhook because of our Fairpole Council difficulties. I think we need to get him back and get ourselves squared away before we go chasing trouble with demons."

Trellis leaned back and fixed Sanction with a steady gaze. He let a moment of quiet gather. "The Fairpole Council," he said.

Sanction nodded. "The Fairpole Council. You told me to make arrangements with another faction regarding some future business opportunities instead of focusing on making amends with our allies," he said, regulating his details with a sideways glance at Cellar. "I did what you asked, I trusted you. Because you agreed to patch things up with the gondoliers."

"What can I say?" Trellis shrugged. "Apparently I offended Trajan. You know how touchy he can be. You said they burned my house down, so that's a high price for my failure. Did you at least turn Dalia in?" He did not look at Cellar, he focused his attention wholly on Sanction, who struggled against a feeling of intimidation.

"I did, I set that plan in motion," Sanction said. "The gondoliers killed Crackstone and Spindle. Shot them with snipers, I barely escaped. The price of your failure is not paid in full, we're handling this in installments, and accruing interest the longer you enjoy this complacency that seems to have—"

"Sanction," the Mistress of Tides said, firm. "Enough. We understand that the Fairpole Council is a problem, and we will deal with it. The timeline may be tighter with the Dark Tooth. If the ritual—"

"Timing matters," Trellis said sharply, eyes still on Sanction. "I don't have to justify my actions to you, young man. Frankly I'm weary to death of your nagging. We are going to deal with the Dark Tooth, and then when the festival is over, we'll deal with the Fairpole Council. The matter is settled. Don't bring it up again." His stare bored into Sanction, who felt a buoyant frustration and fury growing in him, threatening to shrug off his better judgment and alarm in the face of Trellis's scolding. Still, he found himself speechless.

After a moment, the Mistress of Tides gestured between Trellis and Sanction. "Is this over?" she asked coolly.

"Give it another minute," Trellis growled. "In case he can think of anything else that must be said." He waited, looking Sanction in the eye.

Sanction cleared his throat, trying to swallow his feelings. "You've been clear," he said, bitter. "Let's discuss the Dark Tooth."

"Good," Trellis nodded, and he leaned back, reorienting on the Mistress of Tides. "Proceed."

"We need to get a look at the Bellweather Locus," the Mistress of Tides said. "If the Foundation is supporting the Dark Tooth, we need to stop them, and him."

"I studied the Foundation, years ago," Trellis mused. "Fortunately they are very, very conservative. Much of what I learned then will still serve. I am an old man, and I don't need much sleep; you all look like you've been through it. Go ahead and get some rest, I'll work on a plan, check in with you individually as needed. I think we may need a few rituals; can you access the overview undetected?" he asked Neap.

Startled to be directly addressed, Neap swallowed, glancing around the table, and nodded. "We have secret ways," he said.

"Excellent. Get some ritual materials for the Mistress of Tides. Do you know the location of the infused gem I sent over last week?"

"I do," Neap replied with a sideways glance at the Mistress of Tides.

"We'll need that too. Now," he continued, addressing the table, "this restaurant had some recent fiscal difficulties, and isn't likely to have visitors for the next few days. Help yourself to the supplies behind the bar and in the kitchen. Some rooms are made up for you."

"Sound like you've been here awhile," Cellar said, reflexively probing.

"I anticipate," Trellis said. "You are with us until we get this issue resolved. We don't want to lose track of our game pieces. That's not a winning strategy." His smile was mostly sincere as he seemed to study the Inspector.

Sanction abruptly rose and stalked towards the stairs; no one watched him go.

"Why," the Mistress of Tides said under her breath, focused on Trellis.

"This isn't the time," he replied quietly. "I need to start my planning."

The Mistress of Tides rose. "Do not let us oversleep," she said.

"You can count on me."

DOSK RIVER, *ELDRITCH CHAIN* BARGE.
26ᵀᴴ VOLVINET. HOUR OF CHAINS, 11 HOURS PAST DUSK.
SAIL LIGHTING FESTIVAL, DAY FOUR.

"I'll take the boat the rest of the way in," Rutherford said, absently cradling his injured arm as he gazed at the shoreline across the dark waters. "If we have a deal, I'll flash the lantern red, and you'll come on in."

"Got it," the barge captain nodded. "Once you have a deal, we'll be ready to turn the package over to you."

Rutherford stepped over the stile into the boat where two sailors waited for him. Others released the lines, lowering the boat as the pulleys overhead squawked and wailed. Waves slapped the hull, the cables released, and the boat closed in on the pier as Rutherford ordered his thoughts.

A house sentry waited for them on the pier as they secured the craft. Rutherford stepped onto the pier with confidence.

"I'm here to see my father," he said, and the sentry squinted at him for a moment before nodding.

"Welcome," he said, indifferent. He turned and led the way down the pier, through the back gate, and across the broad lawn that glittered with dew. "You may freshen up in the guest cottage before coming up to the house if you'd like," he said. "Breakfast in half an hour. I will announce you. If Master Silvercrane is unavailable, I will see to it that you get breakfast before you go."

"Thank you," Rutherford replied. He let himself into the guest cottage, and rubbed his face as he struggled over the wave of exhaustion that rose through him. He glanced around the familiar but updated cottage, and frowned. Then he washed his face, combed his hair, and focused.

He was ready when the sentry returned, and he projected confidence as he mounted the shallow sweep of stairs to the back lanai, crossing the complex tile work to enter the gallery dining area lit by candles. He seated himself at the table, and the server brought him a pale slick of eggs and cheese. He ignored the server, watching the doorway. He heard his father approach, the light tap of a cane resonating through memory and reflexively raising defenses long relaxed.

"Rutherford my boy, don't get up," the lean man said in a brusque tone as he swept into the room. "I've a busy day, your timing is minimally inconvenient. Tell me what you need." His practiced smile had no sincerity.

"I have a person that I must hide out of reach of all interested parties on every side of the law," Rutherford said quietly. "I would like you to shelter this person for a little while."

"You ask me to break the law," Master Silvercrane said, the wrinkles in his face deflecting the eye from his features. "What is it you offer me, inducing me to take a risk on your behalf?"

"I expected you'd want to see me again," Rutherford said, calm. "Here I am. I am provoking some calculation in your mind. Maybe, if this interaction goes well, I might be opening the door to resuming our relations. That is something that would be quite a victory for you, both as a parent and as a stubborn man accustomed to having his way."

"Cheeky," Master Silvercrane observed. He lifted his teacup and sipped, watching Rutherford over the rim. "A bold move to insult the man you ask for favors, bringing nothing valuable in return."

"Favor, singular," Rutherford corrected. "If you're not interested, say the word and I go." He made no move to rise.

"What happened to your arm?"

"Shot in the line of duty, last night," Rutherford replied. "Saved a noblewoman from capture. I'm a hero," he explained.

"I heard you're in line for some kind of commendation from the Ministry," Master Silvercrane mused. "Yet here you are, in the throes of your heroics, bending the law and involving a despicable lawyer who toils in service to the rich and guilty. Doesn't seem heroic to me."

"Heroes lose," Rutherford agreed. "You tried to teach me that, and I'm a slow learner."

"Oho, that admission cost you something," Master Silvercrane said, leaning on his walking stick. "You must be desperate indeed."

"I've always been desperate," Rutherford shrugged. "I finally found a prize worth taking big risks to secure, and the obstacles in my way are at last ones that are within your power to address. Will you do this for me?"

"You know I will," Master Silvercrane scoffed, "if only out of curiosity. This is no random need. You've got a bigger plan in play." He cocked his head to the side. "You will tell me about it."

"Providing a service to the Fairpole Council of Gondoliers," Rutherford said, "as an off-the-books service. I'm recently reinstated to the Bluecoats, as you no doubt know."

"I actually allowed my surveillance contract to lapse on you some time back," Master Silvercrane said. "You were profoundly boring, I gave up on you. Perhaps too soon," he said, a glint in his eye. "You're different. I don't miss the righteous judgement. It never suited you."

"You take your lunches at the Regal Forge still, yes?" Rutherford said. "I can meet you there in a day or two. Fill you in. I may have work for you that registers on your pay scale."

"Where's the contempt in the tone?" Master Silvercrane demanded, eyes narrowing. "Are you even my son?"

"When I left," Rutherford said, maintaining his white-knuckle grip on his temper, "I had not yet truly had my heart broken by betrayal in love."

"Ah," Master Silvercrane said, nodding, finally in on the joke. "Excellent. I like the look of reality on you, it's a much better fit than your old outfit."

"I'm in line for a promotion," Rutherford observed. "Looks like I've got a successful career ahead of me."

"Don't let Kreeger gum it up," Master Silvercrane said, back straight as he looked down his nose at his son. "All that moral posturing, only to end up with a crook—one you couldn't keep. He dirtied you up, though, didn't he. Here you are."

"We all have our inadequacies," Rutherford said, his voice level as he looked the old man in the eye.

"I plan to enjoy yours to the fullest," Master Silvercrane said. "Now. I'm headed to the Ministry in a few minutes. Bring this mysterious guest around to the front carriage. I'll put some thought into how you can repay me. Hero Bluecoat that you are. Silkshore in the palm of your hand," he smiled, darkness in his eyes.

"I'll meet you out front," Rutherford said, rising. They parted ways, Rutherford returning to the dock.

Rutherford's hand trembled as he lit the red lantern.

The boat from the barge drifted up to the pier, and Rutherford lowered the gangplank. A burly sailor clambered up first, and extended his hand back to the slim cloaked figure on the boat. He helped her onto the pier, and she turned to face Rutherford.

His greeting was lost in the calm of her eyes. Just a child. Yet her center... Rutherford felt her stance, felt a stability that could balance a world. "You—your name?" he managed.

"She does that to everybody," the sailor said, a bit sour. "She's called Cromlech. Some Iruvian mystic." He shrugged. "You'll get over it."

Rutherford sensed the girl's regard shift slightly to curiosity. He wondered if that curiosity was perhaps the highest compliment he had ever been paid.

"Please come with me," he said. "Pay no mind to the man you are about to meet. He will take you to a safe place, that's all. We just need to move you beyond the reach of all others, for a few days. Do you understand?"

She nodded, and he did too. "Very well," he said, and he took a step back and managed a deep breath. "Let's get you out of the open." He glanced around, then escorted her up the broad sweep of shallow steps, away from the breathing mist of the riverside.

He was surprised when she pressed her chilly little hand into his hand. He gently squeezed, strangely aware that if he had the opportunity right now he would take a bullet to protect her.

"This better go right," he breathed to himself.

Then he put her into the carriage, and watched it go.

CHAPTER NINETEEN

We are the Foundation of the future. This means financial security, in the sense that stone provides the secure foundation for a Great House. Any sensible observer would agree that rocks do nothing to hold up the towers and chambers of a Great House; a pile of boulders provides no shelter. Stone is clutter and obstacle in the absence of design. Order shapes the paving stones. Discipline aligns the courses. Vision brings architectural majesty to the strength of the arch.

Mere Coin is naught but raw material. It is the vision for managing Coin that transforms currency into true wealth, which can only be described as power. To build a future upon our resources, we must shape our funds to provide influence, access, and obedience in pursuit of a future we have already drawn out in detailed plans. One does not improvise the majesty of a Great House, nor does one accomplish the impossible with a blind stumble through the years.

— Excerpt, Grandmaster Sakath Keynote Address, Annual Ministry of Preservation Philanthropy Convocation, 842

The carriage jolted, snapping Rutherford awake, stabbing agony through his arm. He leaned away from the wall, wincing as he gingerly pressed his bandage.

"Smoke Tower," the cabbie called out.

"Right," Rutherford growled, hauling himself forward, out the narrow door, into the light rain. He squinted up at the cabbie, who expectantly waited for a tip.

"Duty served," Rutherford said with a casual salute, his coat shifting to show the uniform beneath. The cabbie swore under his breath and lashed the goat, who bawled irritably and dragged the cab back into the street. Rutherford took a deep breath and tried to exhale his weariness, then he turned and headed into the bustle of the tower.

The crowds were a blur, but he could taste the energy of the final day of the festival. People were losing their long-anticipated freedom from the daily routine. Their celebration was shrill defiance of the rules that would lock in place tomorrow. The end loomed over everyone, intensifying the need to make the most of today.

Rutherford shuffled down the spiral staircase and followed the corridor to the boat house. He spotted a knot of Bluecoats chatting over steaming cups, and he smiled to himself as Clamp spotted him.

Rutherford leaned against the crate wall as Clamp excused himself and crossed to him, frowning. "You got shot last night," Clamp pointed out, "*and* you are late to work. I figured even you would take the day off for a gunshot wound. But if you are planning to put in a day, you are tardy, and that sets a *terrible* example." His humor was too half-hearted to get a grin from either man.

"Captain Smiles wanted me on festival duty," Rutherford replied, "and this is the last day of festival. I don't want to disobey orders, do I?"

"You got a big head start on getting yourself killed," Clamp muttered. "Coming in bloody, that's impatient of you. What is the rush, man? Why are you pushing so hard?"

"I won't tell you, Clamp," Rutherford said in an unexpected moment of honesty. "I need you to stop asking me. I need your help, now more than I did three days ago. The festival—it's—it's almost over," he said

"I've been patient," Clamp replied, serious. "Taken risks. Done some crazy stunts. I don't even know why. But I won't die for you." He understood his thoughts only when he heard them aloud, and the stakes left both of them sober.

"Neither of us wants you to," Rutherford agreed. "I won't slow down, though. I believe you understand. My friend told me how you lost your wife. I think he was trying to cheer me up, I recently suffered a—a similar loss. You think you'll do anything to get her back, but you only know for sure when you find out what it will take. When the choice is real. And you have to choose, and live with your choice." His eyes searched Clamp's face. "No matter what you choose, you aren't whole anymore. Every choice means part of you dies and part of you lives. You try to—to choose the parts you want to keep the most."

Clamp was dangerously still. "I don't know who told you about my wife, and I don't *want* to know, but that's the last time—" Clamp shifted, eyes moving to the hall behind Rutherford. "Help you sir?" he said, his tone erasing any respect in the 'sir.'

"Yes, I just need to chat with Rutherford for a moment," said the sleek and solidly-built man as he approached in easy earshot. Rutherford turned, unreadable.

"Well hello," he said to Orris. "What a pleasant surprise."

"Is it?" Orris asked, eyebrow raised.

"Pleasant, yes," Rutherford replied, squaring off with him. "Surprise, no. Let's step into my office."

Orris followed Rutherford around the corner. Clamp did not.

Passing the crowded and noisy holding pens, Rutherford mounted a narrow staircase awash in the stink of the canal and the crowd. He let himself out through a door to a modest courtyard converted to a target range, currently abandoned as the Bluecoats were fully absorbed in regulating the festival.

"You botched the hit on the Fog Hounds," Orris said.

"Did I?" Rutherford arched an eyebrow. "I prevented Dalia's abduction, and told her who attacked her. Surely she has stitched up the survivors by now, it's been eight hours."

Orris didn't try to repress a small grin. "Shrewd!" he said. "Spinning your failures to look like successes is a pretty critical job skill for the position you're after. Tell you what, I'm persuaded to give you a chance. I want your undivided attention and loyalty, so I've got a job for you. Demonstrate you are willing to provide both." He looked Rutherford in the eye. "Kill Sanction. I want it done today."

"Understood."

Orris nodded. "We'll talk," he said, and he left the courtyard. Orris passed Clamp, who glanced back at him as he approached Rutherford.

"Who the hell is that guy?" Clamp muttered.

"He's nobody," Rutherford sighed. "What's up?"

"Smiles is looking for you."

"I'll check in," Rutherford nodded.

"Oho," Clamp grunted, "she told me to escort you up to her office, immediately."

"Where's the trust," Rutherford mused, bleak.

Clamp waited a moment, then turned and headed out, Rutherford in tow.

Rutherford's normally crisp pace was sluggish, his shoulders bowed, and each step seemed a task. Clamp slowed to match his speed, and did not comment on it. All too soon they approached Captain Smiles' office, treading on the creaking boards.

"Enter," Smiles called out. Clamp pointed a meaningful look at Rutherford, then swept the door open and stood at attention before the captain's desk, Rutherford close behind.

"You've been busy," Captain Smiles said without looking up. "I thought I told you to go home."

"I understood you to say I was to go home, get some rest, and not return to the tower until today. I complied with those orders." Rutherford's eyes pointed straight ahead, unseeing.

"Is your idea of 'restful' tangling with kidnappers in Charterhall, outside the boundaries of our territory?" Captain Smiles asked, looking up from her papers.

"That encounter was after I rested at home," Rutherford replied, deadpan.

"You are injured and you look like hell," Captain Smiles said. "Take the week off. I don't want you to burn out, you have a lot of work to do."

Rutherford blinked, and looked her in the eye. "Yes Captain," he said. "Thank you Captain."

"You want the week off too, Clamp?" Captain Smiles said to the mustachioed Bluecoat.

"Do I gotta get shot first?" he retorted before his better judgment stopped him.

"No," Captain Smiles mused, "but Rutherford here apparently needs a keeper and I want you to look after him."

Any lingering possibility that Captain Smiles expected Rutherford to rest evaporated.

"Yes Captain," Clamp said stiffly. "Thank you Captain."

"Dismissed."

Outside the office, Rutherford looked to Clamp. "You can *actually* take the week off," he said, serious. "I know—"

"You know?" Clamp retorted. "Do you? What the hell do you think you know about me?" For the first time, Rutherford heard genuine anger in his tone.

"I know nobody owns you," Rutherford said quietly. "That's why I trust you." He paused. "More than I trust myself."

Clamp bristled, jammed between conflicting impulses.

"Plus," Rutherford said with half a shrug, favoring his injured arm. "The obvious."

"Obvious?" Clamp snapped.

"Yeah." Rutherford paused for a beat. "That magnificent moustache."

"You silly son of a bitch!" Clamp ground out, struggling not to yell, a laugh startled into his growl.

"Come on, I owe you a bunch of drinks," Rutherford said. He turned and walked away.

After only a moment, Clamp followed.

NINE AND NINE TAVERN, THE SPARK GROUNDS, SILKSHORE. 26TH VOLVINET. FIFTH HOUR PAST DAWN. SAIL LIGHTING FESTIVAL, DAY FOUR.

The world drifted, unmoored. He was motionless in the void before the gaze of the drowned child's face. Then harsh cawing roiled Cellar's dreamscape.

Cellar was propelled through the surface of consciousness by the buoyancy of his life force. Gasping, he flinched, and pushed himself up to a seated position as he stared wildly around the dim room.

"Fishmix?" Jayan said mildly, offering a tin of chopped fish and a two-tined fork.

"Jayan," Cellar breathed, feeling strangely relieved. He winced as a stinging burn threaded into his mind from the brand, followed by a tumble of aches and pains reported from all corners of his body. "Ugh, what the hell is going on."

"The old man came up with a plan, there's some ritual magic going on downstairs," Jayan said with a grimace. "They didn't offer details, and I didn't ask."

For an awful second, Cellar looked to Daava for her take; he caught himself and said nothing, feeling the ache of her absence. Unsteady, he climbed to his feet. Right. The restaurant, Spark Grounds, the sky burning red with tainted electroplasm. A criminal crew on the run from the gondoliers. A demon ritual. He took the tin of fishmix and the fork from Jayan, frowning at the pungent slurry.

"What's the time?" Cellar asked.

"Fifth Hour," Jayan replied. He squinted at Cellar through the eye that wasn't swollen closed. "After dawn," he clarified. "You got nearly six hours of sleep. I hope it helped."

"So do I," Cellar groused. A crackle of light caught his eye. He crossed to the window, looking out at the field between the restaurant and the lightning barrier.

A crowd of hundreds was gathered outside, their backs to the closed and darkened restaurant. They craned their necks, watching two spark flycro riding the updrafts overhead. The pilots guided kites flanked with metal, swooping alongside the lightning wall and drawing coils of coruscating energy to flash and twist between the kites and the barrier.

"Idiots," Jayan editorialized, joining Cellar at the window.

Cellar was lost for a moment, feeling a vertigo as he watched the two swooping fliers cross paths and nearly tie a bow with energy streamers. Adrift, jolting with energy, wheeling above the masses as though they could shrug off the bonds of the earth, swimming in an upside-down ocean.

"It's the last day of the festival," Cellar murmured. He paused, narrowing his eyes, wondering what he meant by that. Then he frowned. "We had better find out what's going on."

A few minutes later they were dressed and clumping down the stairs to the main room. An inhuman shriek tore through the air, followed by a horrible croaking rattle; Jayan and Cellar exchanged a glance, and raced towards the kitchen.

They burst in to see two acolytes holding a massive crow's wings down in a ritual circle as the Mistress of Tides slowly drew a long needle from its heart. The dying crow's blood pooled, almost contained by wax patterns on the floor.

"Unsettling, is it not," Trellis murmured, startling them. He stood by the door, watching the ritual, unmoving.

"That—that's a Deathseeker crow," Cellar said, pointing at the ritual. "An attempt to trap one is highly illegal, actually killing one—"

"Very upsetting to the Spirit Wardens," Trellis interrupted, nodding his agreement.

"How did you even capture—" Cellar started, then he paused. Trellis looked him in the eye.

After all, everyone knew there was one very reliable way to attract a Deathseeker crow.

"The Mistress of Tides cast a shadow," Sanction said, approaching from the other end of the kitchen. He held a plate with a half-eaten meal, hard cheese and spore crust with a mushroom spread. "An echo on the back of the Mirror. She knows how to lure a Deathseeker crow to confirm whether there was a death or not. We do not kill at random."

"Why are you killing a Deathseeker crow?" Jayan asked, unable to take his eyes from the ritual as the Mistress of Tides gently wrapped a paper-thin strip of meat around the crow's beak, whispering in Hadrathi.

"For its power," Trellis replied. "The Foundation has mastered ways of setting alarms and traps on the back of the Mirror, to detect intruders. They use ghost doors for secret travel. Many of these techniques manipulate the same kind of connection the Bellweather Seminary and Deathseeker crows have to life and death reflected through the Mirror. We aim to isolate and interrogate a master. We don't want chases, distress calls, or interruptions. The Mistress of Tides will take over the Deathseeker crow connection and then repurpose it to meet our needs."

"Conviction for attracting, killing, and ritualistically interfering with Deathseeker Crows... that's a hanging offense," Cellar said in a subdued tone.

"The law is the least of her worries," Trellis pointed out. "Something goes wrong here, she could be permanently marked as a crowslayer, visible to all Spirit Wardens, Whispers, and Deathseeker crows. She could also get pulled partially through the Mirror and fused with it, unable to move her body because her life-force is rooted in place. Or death energy could swarm through her body and spirit, tearing them, infecting them to make her undying and unliving." A bleak smile twisted his face. "The Mistress of Tides is profoundly capable. She will be fine."

A cleaver flashed down, whacking through the Deathseeker crow's neck.

"Still," Sanction said with a look pointed at Trellis, "the Spirit Wardens are red-flashed when a Deathseeker crow dies. So we had best be gone in ten minutes."

"I'm already packed," Jayan said through his teeth.

The plump and grandmotherly woman hefted her document case and shifted her grip on the embossed key ring so she was ready to open the door as she approached. The receptionist looked up and smiled.

"Minister Nalaya, your Eighth Hour meeting was rescheduled. Would you like me to evaluate the waiting list and see if any of the supplicants are available on short notice?"

"No thank you, sweetie," the minister said. "I've got plenty to do and I'll take the time as a gift. Any new supplicants come in while I was gone?"

"No, minister," the receptionist replied. "The festival is keeping everyone busy."

The minister slotted in her custom key and turned it carefully; quarter turn left, full turn right. The lock and its various defenses clicked out of the way, and she swept into the office, the door drifting shut behind her.

"Let's talk," the Mistress of Tides said, regal in the throne-like seat behind the massive desk. The minister drew up short, startled.

"You can't be here," she said as anger sparked.

"That's the disadvantage to back doors," the Mistress of Tides disagreed, inscrutable behind her veil. "Especially ghost doors. They can be breached. I did not come alone."

The minister glanced around at the shadows, uneasy. "There will be consequences for this, no matter what happens to me," she said.

"You ordered my death already," the Mistress of Tides observed.

Minister Nalaya paused, then shrugged. "Well there is that," she said. "You are here for revenge?"

"I do not care about revenge," the Mistress of Tides said. "You will tell me how to locate Paving."

"Paving," Nalaya echoed. "But this isn't about revenge."

"It is not. My view is wider." The Mistress of Tides rose. "You will give us what we need to stop the Dark Tooth."

"The Dark Tooth!" Nalaya retorted, slinging her document case to rest on a chair. "So you have not revealed to your crew that you are, yourself, the Dark Tooth?"

"This is no time for games," the Mistress of Tides replied.

"I agree completely," Nalaya said. "Demonic screens are never simple to penetrate, but we've been at it for years. Divinations, oracles, predictions from various sources. All signs point to you. The Dark Tooth is a Silkworm. I met with you in person to confirm."

"Your divinations did locate key ritual roles. I am involved, but I am not the Dark Tooth," the Mistress of Tides said coolly. "I have been identified as the one person positioned to stop the ritual. My Herald is the Empress of Gulls. We have located the Dark Tooth's Herald, a hapless Inspector. He was assaulted by the Dark Tooth, who branded him with his heraldic glyph. The Herald got a look at him, described him as wearing worker's clothes, big bushy beard, eerie eyes. That description matches the man who assaulted me. The assassin you sent to kill me," the Mistress of Tides added, her voice unwavering.

"No. Paving is an Instrument of the Will. He does conduct ritual sacrifices and he does serve the Powers, but he is not a demonslave and he is not the Dark Tooth. You think the forces we employ are compatible with others? You think one of our assassin priests could possibly be in the employ of a demon?" She scoffed at the idea. "If there's one person in the city I know is not the Dark Tooth, it is Paving. The Foundation safeguards the city against intrusion by Leviathans. Your ritual targets our defenses, aims to shatter them. That's why you're here, really." She thrust out her chin, defiant. "Kill me if you can. You will learn *nothing*."

The Mistress of Tides stood, silent and unmoving, watching the minister.

Nalaya narrowed her eyes. "You have doubts," she mused. "Or you wish to appear as though you had doubts."

"I sense we are running out of time," the Mistress of Tides said slowly. "I...do not want to fail because I aimed poorly."

"Why *did* you target me," Nalaya pressed. "Am I the highest ranking Foundation leader you know? Were you to have the broader perspective you claim, you would understand that I am in no position to reveal the depths of the Foundation's secrets."

"Perhaps not in the general sense, but you *are* the one who has been assigned the task of stopping the construction of the cathedral bordering the Spark Grounds. You are the Silkshore Architect. You know where we would need to focus our efforts to put a stop to the ritual."

"I do not like the extent of your assumptions about the Foundation's workings," Nalaya said. "However... it is to your credit that you led with discussion rather than assault."

"I have no desire to be bogged down in a costly conflict with the Foundation. If the Foundation is not sheltering and empowering the Dark Tooth, you could be well positioned to put a stop to the ritual."

"You don't get Paving," Nalaya stated flatly. "What else do you want?"

"I want to see the Bellweather Locus, recorded in 512."

Nalaya frowned. "Really." Her expression grew thoughtful. "Really..."

The Mistress of Tides waited.

"I dare not trust you," Nalaya sighed. "The secrets you require are not mine to give."

"But if you did trust me," the Mistress of Tides prompted.

Nalaya watched her, unreadable.

"I will tell you a secret," the Mistress of Tides murmured. "Only one other in this city knows my true name, and I only told her yesterday." She took a deep breath, and let it out. "I am given to understand my name is embedded in the prophecy. My name is Venisana."

Nalaya stared for a long moment. "You know more about the prophecy than you should, that's certain," she said under her breath. "But that is... a critical insight within. If you are the Dark Tooth, you play a very clever game... for Venisana is the key element that can stop the Dark Tooth. In the end it all comes to you."

"Help me," the Mistress of Tides said with quiet intensity.

Nalaya slowly nodded. "I... I will," she said. "I will help you."

"Swear it," echoed a voice from the shadows, startling Nalaya.

"Who else is here?" Nalaya demanded.

"Those who are working with me to end this threat," the Mistress of Tides said. "One of our number is an expert on the Foundation."

"Then your expert should know that if I swear upon the Anvil and the Spoke, it is an oath I will not break. And I swear I will aid those who aim to stop the Dark Tooth. By the Anvil and the Spoke I so swear." She squared her shoulders with determination.

"That's good enough for me," Trellis murmured, stepping out of the shadows. He nodded to the Mistress of Tides. "Well done." He rubbed his hands together, an unconsciously gleeful gesture. The cloaking ritual faded, revealing Cellar, Jayan, and Sanction.

"Now what?" the Mistress of Tides asked.

"Now we go to the Thricebar Archive," Nalaya said. "We will speak to the Archivist of Crenellation. He will know what to do." She adjusted her grip on the oversized keyring in her hand. "I will change the combination as soon as our business here is finished, so I suppose there is little harm in taking you through the back way." She rounded the desk, still wary of the Mistress of Tides, and put her key in the lock of the unobtrusive door at the rear of the office. She hummed a tonal sequence as she twisted the key four times, then she pushed the door open and stepped through. The Mistress of Tides was right behind her, the others falling in line.

The doorway was more than a doorway.

Disoriented, they stepped out into the flickering shadows of a high-ceilinged chamber, its walls lined with glass-columned lamps and bookshelves. The floor was laid out in an intricate mosaic depiction of Doskvol, lit with glittering sigils and gem studs. Three glowed like tiny red stars.

"Here we are," Nalaya said. "This is the Thricebar Archive. Misbehave here and you will be destroyed."

"This place is not for prisoners," intoned the man that stepped out of the shadows, his lean form draped in dark robes. "Unless they be prisoners of ignorance, seeking the keys to move to larger cells." He offered them a thin smile. His broad forehead and pinched features were deathly pale.

"I beg your assistance, as is my right," Nalaya said with a deep bow. "The Master of Stone, Architect of Silkshore, invokes research access."

"The Archivist of Crenellation stands ready to assist," he murmured as he studied the others. "My my, you've found people involved in the Fourfold Ritual. They *stink* of it."

"We stand against the Dark Tooth," the Mistress of Tides said.

"I see," the Archivist murmured, eyebrows raised. "You have persuaded the Master of Stone, clearly."

"We have trusted the Master of Stone," the Mistress of Tides said, "and we are willing to trust a vampire as well. The stakes are high."

The Archivist's smile was thin. "Indeed, Whisper. I am undying, and that is to your advantage, as my memory is profound. The secrets you engage are embedded in the very roots of this city. The power of prophecy has been curated for centuries, and I have sampled its flavors."

"Not to interrupt," Nalaya said in a measured tone, "but time is an issue."

"Of course," the Archivist nodded.

"We wish to see the Bellweather Locus, recorded in 512," Nalaya said.

"What—what are those red lights?" Cellar asked, distracted. The glowing chips burned in his eyes. He pointed at the map.

"Distressing, are they not?" the Archivist murmured. "The energies behind the Mirror are in danger of overflowing, and those three spirit wells are at risk of flooding."

"Something about them," Cellar said as he stepped over to the map that stretched across fifty feet on the floor. He glanced around, spotting the spiral staircase leading to a balcony overhead. "May I?" he asked, pointing. The Archivist nodded, and Cellar led the way, the others following.

On the balcony, he looked down. "Coalridge. Six Towers. Silkshore, you can see the light is in the Exchange. Where the rivers meet."

"Yes, there is a spirit well there," Nalaya agreed. "Those are all spirit wells."

"And they are also sites where the Skullface Killer hung a ritual sacrifice," Cellar said. "In 839, that's ten years ago, there were ten murders in the span of a week. Surgical mutilation, bodies displayed publically."

"And two of them were on those sites in Coalridge and Six Towers?" Sanction said, skeptical. "Why do those two matter?"

"We look for patterns," Cellar rushed on. "More killings obscured the pattern. What if those were the only two that mattered? The one in Silkshore, that was done *yesterday* at dawn!"

"East, south, and west," Nalaya added. "Your pattern is no good. To bound the city in, the final piece would be in Whitecrown. There are no spirit wells in Whitecrown."

"None?" Cellar echoed, eyebrows raised.

"Not one. Never was," Nalaya said.

"Maybe there is," Trellis said through his teeth. "Damn."

Everyone looked at him.

"I did not realize the Skullface Killer was active again. Ten years ago, I got close to catching that monster. In the interests of keeping the peace. Couldn't quite catch him or her," he sighed. "But I did my homework with various mystics and seers. Followed up on scraps of lore. Discovered that the Skullface Killer was driven by the stars."

"Yes," the Archivist intoned, "the Sail Lighting Festival is always staged on the opening and closing of the Fracture. The alignment of the stars is complimentary this year to the Fracture ten years ago."

"When does the constellation close?" Trellis asked.

"Tonight," the Archivist responded.

"We are out of time, then," Trellis scowled.

"Explain," Nalaya demanded.

"When you cannot search out your prey, you find bait to draw your prey to you. I was intensely interested in the Skullface Killer's motive. My research sifted through the sites where the victims were hung, and discovered two of them were spirit wells. In my further investigations, I found a rumor that there was a portable spirit well. Such things have occurred before, but this one was unique. I had to know more. I invested substantially in gaining access to this phenomenon, as it was also fascinating from the perspective of a radiant curator."

"Unique in what way?" the Archivist asked.

Trellis crossed his arms over his chest. "I sent independent researchers to verify, then I took action when the reports turned out to be credible. There is a young woman in Iruvia who has unique access to a spirit well. She is the only one who can reach it."

"Spirit wells that are only accessible under certain conditions are not uncommon," the Archivist said skeptically.

"Of course," Trellis agreed. "But you see here; Whitecrown. There are defended areas there, areas with the most top-of-the-line security technology. This includes Rowan's ambient dampening fields. There is no way to get a ghost door to work, no method of traversing the Mirror can be effective."

"Then we are safe," Nalaya suggested, thinking through possible rebuttals.

"Completely," Trellis nodded, "unless the access is unaffected by the ambient conditions. This young woman, the one that I contacted in Iruvia; she can only access this unique spirit well through her *dreams.* If someone was able to join her in a dream, then even Rowan's defensive measures would not be able to prevent access. A spirit well could become real... to a site in Whitecrown." He frowned at the map on the floor below. "I invited this mystic to come to Doskvol, so that I might safeguard her. But... I entrusted her to the gondoliers, and I have reason to believe they have betrayed me and shuffled her off to Whitecrown for safekeeping." Alarm filled his eyes as he looked at the others. "Right exactly where we don't want her, and can't reach her."

"You are suggesting the Dark Tooth could," the Mistress of Tides said.

"I think we have to get there first," he said, subdued. "Protect her if we can. Kill her if we must."

"Could someone get into her dreams from elsewhere in the city?" Cellar asked.

"Not if she is under the ambient field defenses," the Mistress of Tides said. "The only way would be through physical contact, with her consent."

"Travel through blood to behind the Mirror, flesh to flesh and soul in soul," the Archivist quoted. "So it is written in the Bellweather Locus." His demeanor was troubled.

Looking past the Archivist, Trellis looked into Sanction's eyes, and saw the horror there.

With mounting irritation, Sanction listened to Trellis's explanation. Civic engagement and amateur sleuthing was not Trellis's style; it seemed unlikely he cared about a serial killer a decade ago, especially since he stopped caring about the Silkworms at all—

Then he realized Trellis was lying; he didn't *just hear about* this mystic.

Trellis spent *fortunes* to find and transport her, without any explanation. There was no *invitation*.

Acquiring the Iruvian girl was the most expensive, secretive, and elaborate scheme Trellis ever concocted. No one else could have done it.

Only the Dark Tooth would know why this mystic was important.

The Dark Tooth *was* a member of the Silkworms.

But it *wasn't* the Mistress of Tides.

CHAPTER TWENTY

The Whitecrown District Evidentiary is the richest treasure vault in Doskvol. Rather than accumulating the interest on investments, this vault has accumulated evidence in investigations. All tributaries flow to this mighty river, after all; the city cannot invest in maximum security for all evidentiaries, so one was chosen to be profoundly defended. This evidentiary collects leverage on the most powerful citizens in our city, across centuries and generations.

Obviously the evidence is valuable to those who want influence over the accused, the victims, and those who are actually guilty—no matter how the trial turns out. The gems may as well be glass, the gold could be sand, and the security would still be necessary to protect the leverage. Beyond that, the Whitecrown Evidentiary also has a vault deep below its more mundane security, under the roots of the island. The Undervault is where cursed or magical treasure is stowed away out of reach.

It is easy to understand how treasure and lore enter the evidentiary. Spare a thought to what is required to extract material, permanently. It isn't easy. Not even when the trials are over. The Ministry can't sell or use the evidence, or they appear invested in the outcome of the trial. Returning it to owners or their families can be complicated.

Part of the security must be secrecy. The Ministry must control access to information about the evidence as well as the evidence itself, and their systems of transmitting knowledge and handling inventory are imperfect. Additional tunneling and expansion is secret and ongoing to add capacity as needed, but information is compartmentalized. As a result, not one person alive or dead knows all of what's there.

— Second entry in "Top Five Hard Targets of Doskvol"
by Ronicus Forscut

"Sanction, a word please," Trellis said directly.

"No!" Sanction blurted, but before the next words could tumble out, Trellis focused.

"I need your help," he said with a strange intensity.

Caught off guard, Sanction could only stare at him for a moment.

"We have reached a critical point," Trellis said as he looked Sanction in the eye. "You know me, you know what I am capable of accomplishing. Together we can do the impossible. I have plans, contingencies, backups; I want you to think about that for a moment."

Sanction saw the glint of light behind the darkness in the center of Trellis' eye. Coldness rippled down the inside of his ribcage. He was speechless.

Trellis nodded to himself, continuing. "I know things between us have been difficult these last few days, and I appreciate your patience with an old man too used to having his way. We get through this next patch and things will be different. I promise."

Sanction wondered if the others could hear the threats in what Trellis was saying to him.

"I offer you a choice," Trellis said. "We need to go to Whitecrown, to find the Cromlech. But you aren't wrong. The gondoliers will be looking for us. You could go to Mother Grine and be seen entering the protection of the church. The church has some locations that the gondoliers could not easily breach, and their network is one of the only ways you might be able to move in Silkshore with relative safety. This is the moment," Trellis said, closing the distance between them and putting his hands on Sanction's shoulders as his stare bored into Sanction's eyes. "Please. Draw attention away. Give me room to work."

Too fast. Sanction felt the moment of truth flashing upon him. No time for deliberation: he had to choose between outing the Dark Tooth by crossing a prepared Trellis, or saying nothing and letting it all unfold. Frozen, he struggled to understand the stakes, to think up a frame, to dance around the confrontation. He felt hypnotized, but some corner of his mind felt the cowardice of that conclusion as it deflected blame and allowed him to be the helpless victim. He tasted the words, *You are the Dark Tooth*, smoldering in his mouth. His finger itched to point at the threat standing among his friends. The weight of what he knew threatened to crush him.

Mute, he nodded slightly.

Trellis didn't unlock eye contact. "Archivist, the door we entered; can you shift it to connect to the Waystreet exit?"

The Archivist frowned. "You think there's an exit on Waystreet?"

"I think that's the best one," Trellis said, "because it is in the shadow of the Sanctorium in Brightstone."

After a momentary pause, the Archivist nodded. "Follow me." He glided over to the stairs and down. Trellis gestured for Sanction to go first, and followed him. As they approached the door, the Archivist was already manipulating sigils and signs on a panel concealed in the wall by the door.

"Waystreet," the Archivist said.

Trellis gripped Sanction's shoulder. "Goodbye."

Sanction tried to swallow around the corpse of his voice.

Then Trellis ushered him to the doorway, and through. Trellis stepped back, and the door closed behind Sanction.

"Some tension?" the Archivist inquired, bland.

"Difficult to feel safe," Trellis explained. "He survived an assassination attempt earlier tonight, and I've just sent him back into danger." He shook his head. "Sanction is brave, and committed. But it isn't easy, doing what we do."

"Hm." The Archivist turned, leading the way back to the others, Trellis at his heels.

"...does seem to be the best chance of success," Nalaya agreed, looking over the Mistress of Tides' shoulder at the Archivist and Trellis as they approached. "Do you have something belonging to the Cromlech that we could use for a location ritual?"

"I do," Trellis nodded, producing a hank of hair from his pocket. "Her location is sure to be warded, prepared specifically to defeat divination rituals."

"With a direct connection like this," Nalaya said, taking the hair, "we can find anything in the city."

Trellis smiled.

SIDEARM PUBLIC HOUSE. SILKSHORE. 26ᵀᴴ VOLVINET. EIGHTH HOUR PAST DAWN. SAIL LIGHTING FESTIVAL, DAY FOUR.

"So," Clamp said, breaking the silence. "We are pretty bad at this."

Rutherford looked over at him. "Bad at what?"

"Getting drunk," Clamp observed, gesturing at the warm beer sitting on the table next to a couple empty mugs. "Here we are in the dank alcove of this piss-soaked barn, supposedly celebrating, and we're just staring at the table." He shook his head. "It's when they *won't* drink, that's when you worry."

"Just ask, if you must know," Rutherford sighed. He took a pull from his beer, and made a face.

"You stopped off at a half a dozen information brokers before we settled here," Clamp said. "What are you looking for?"

"My husband," Rutherford replied, studying his knuckles. "I need to have a word with him."

"Yeah, spouses," Clamp said.

"Speaking of which. I apologize for bringing up your wife earlier," Rutherford said, sincere.

"Good," Clamp growled, looking away. "You don't get to talk about Letty ever again. Not to me. Not to anyone." He snapped his mouth shut.

"You did what you had to do," Rutherford said quietly.

"What did I just say?" Clamp retorted, reddening.

"You said not to talk about her, and I'm not. I'm talking about *you*," Rutherford said. "You could have taken the easy way out. You were supposed to." He paused. "When I listen to you, I hear what you *say* and I hear what you *do*. You say you don't want to make waves. But you surely do, when you must."

"*Doing* didn't work out well," Clamp growled, over-enunciating. "I learned my lesson."

"Yet here you are," Rutherford observed. Then he brightened, sitting up straight, as a Bluecoat jogged over to the shadowed table.

"Message," the Bluecoat grunted, handing over an envelope with a wax seal. Rutherford stood up, snapping the seal and tearing the message open. He nodded to himself in satisfaction.

"Sir," the Bluecoat said, "do you need that wagon and squad you had on standby?"

"No," Rutherford replied absently, thinking fast as he stared at the paper. He tucked the letter into his lapel pocket. "Clamp and I can take care of this on our own. Dismissed."

The Bluecoat hesitated a moment longer.

"I'll take care of you," Rutherford said. "But we do this right, not handing money around in public. Go."

The Bluecoat turned and left. Clamp shook his head.

"You have a reputation for generosity," Clamp observed. "Encourages them to get pushy."

Drawing his pistol, Rutherford checked the breech, and nodded to himself in satisfaction.

"I hope all is well with your soul," Rutherford said, holstering the gun. "We're going to church."

THRICEBAR ARCHIVE.
26TH VOLVINET. EIGHTH HOUR PAST DAWN.
SAIL LIGHTING FESTIVAL, DAY FOUR.

Cellar sat on the wing chair, head in his hands, elbows on his knees, silently enduring the throb of his blood. Jayan paced the floor behind him. The Mistress of Tides appeared lost in meditation, or patience. Trellis sat at the side table with Nalaya, poring over a musty book.

"Intriguing," Trellis murmured. "This is the only original Holstairs Codex I've seen in person, though I've reviewed several copies. He had a steady hand," he said, touching the page. "I didn't think any floor-plans of the Whitecrown District Evidentiary existed outside Ministry control."

"Well, I *am* the Ministry Director of Structures," Nalaya reminded him with a secretive smile.

"Thank you, also, for that look at the prophecy," Trellis said. "Maddeningly vague, aren't they. I appreciate that you have some more actionable research."

Cellar cleared his throat. "You're absolutely sure you don't have a copy of that prophecy in Akorosian, or in a more accessible version of Hadrathi?" he said. "If I'm supposed to be in the prophecy, I'd really like to read it myself."

"Understood, but we're short on time for hand-holding," Trellis said. "I reviewed it, and the narrative there, such as it is, reinforces what we already know."

"Don't push your luck," Nalaya said, looking Cellar in the eye.

Cellar subtly bristled, setting his jaw. "On to the mission at hand, I guess. I get that your peoples' first pass with the ritual identified the evidentiary as the location of that Iruvian mystic," he said. "Do you really think your rituals can identify where this mystic is, *inside* a place like that? That's... really ambitious."

"They can," Nalaya said.

"We have to have a level of precision to pull this off," Trellis added without looking up. "Some places, you can get past the outer security and have freedom to wander inside. Not the evidentiary. Each area has its own precautions and protections. There are more than three hundred workers employed in various capacities at the evidentiary and they all have rigorous tests they must pass before receiving enough trust to get past the front gate." He sighed. "This isn't going to be simple."

"I think it's impossible," Cellar retorted. "Even if you know where to go, you can't get in."

The side door opened, and a black-clad adept stepped into the room. "Master," he said to Nalaya. "The ritual is complete. The mystic you seek is in the Carriage House Factual Annex."

"Perfect," Trellis said, rising. "That's where advocates sometimes put those who can establish factuals for high-stakes trials involving the aristocracy. I've contemplated hitting the evidentiary for decades, since it's one of the richest targets in the city; I happen to have some background on one of the most expensive advocates who is credentialed to store evidence there. We have a chance."

Cellar examined the clock on the sideboard. "In ten hours?"

Trellis looked up at him. "What's the most important case your Chief Inspector is currently building?" he asked mildly.

"No no no," Cellar said rapidly. "You want me to involve Prichard in this? Ask to look at evidence from *his* cases? Are you *insane*? Security will never buy that excuse, and even if they did—"

"We can get you the necessary paperwork, fast," Trellis interrupted, "but we need to start *now*. This has to happen tonight, or not at all." He paused. "You don't have to help," he said, "if you are sure the Dark Tooth will fail. Or if you don't care whether or not the ritual succeeds."

"What about the Foundation?" Cellar protested. "You seem to have people everywhere," he said to Nalaya.

"True," she agreed. "We do have some passwords, codes, and arrangements that may help someone get in. But it's influence. Favors. Not ownership, not of anyone with sufficient clearance at the evidentiary." She paused. "More to the point, a Fourfold Ritual runs deep in the city. These things play out over decades. We are just now learning the rules to the game, but the Dark Tooth, yet unknown, may have contingencies in place that compromise our agents. I do not know who we can really trust. And we're out of time."

Trellis looked Cellar in the eye, direct and unnerving. "We need a real Inspector. We need you."

Cellar said nothing.

"Or," Trellis said, "you can go back to work." He watched Cellar. "Hope for the best."

"Of course I'll help however I can," Cellar said through his teeth.

"Excellent." Trellis turned to Nalaya. "We need a portal exit near the Bowmore Bridge in Brightstone. There's a cache of supplies for an expedition into Whitecrown that I set aside for a special occasion." He eyed Cellar. "I even have a uniform that will fit you," he said with the ghost of a smile.

"I can get some access passcodes, phrase keys, and sympathizer identities to you. Some material that will help you get in," Nalaya said. "Don't cross the Foundation. I am trusting you far more than I would if the danger was not so great."

"Thank you," Trellis said, sincere. "Because of you... we have a chance."

Nalaya left the waiting room, and Trellis rose to his feet. He crossed to the Mistress of Tides and squatted down before her.

"We will need a very specific ritual," he began. Her eyes drifted open. "You are an expert with Breathe Into Dreams." He tried on a smile.

"That only works with a consenting subject," the Mistress of Tides murmured, sounding half-awake.

"We should not need it at all," Trellis said. "But if the Dark Tooth gets there first, we'll need a way to follow."

"I'm not sure that makes sense," the Mistress of Tides said slowly, reflective.

"I like to be prepared," Trellis shrugged. "We will go in a few minutes. Sand is slipping through the hourglass faster now."

"The energy in this ritual... It is becoming intolerable," the Mistress of Tides breathed. "It is saturating me. I can hardly think."

"We are almost through. Just a little further," Trellis said. "One more push."

"One more push," the Mistress of Tides echoed. "One more."

FEMORAL COURT, FOGCREST, SILKSHORE.
26TH VOLVINET. NINTH HOUR PAST DAWN.
SAIL LIGHTING FESTIVAL, DAY FOUR.

A steady rain tumbled down through the wind, spraying the street and the buildings. The festival was irrepressible, with music punctuating the crowd noise under the uneasy grumble of thunder. The smell of frying meat and cheese mixed with the stink of rinsing gutters.

Rutherford stepped down out of a carriage, Clamp at his heels. They approached the massive iron gate closing off the courtyard from the street, ignoring the miserable beggars huddled against the outside of the barricade and hunched under the rain. Church Guardians stood watch at the cramped station by the entryway.

"Bluecoat business," Rutherford said, curt.

"You need an exception to pursue answers here," the Guardian replied, bored. "If you have questions, take it up with your captain."

"Looks like there are forty three windows in the courtyard," Rutherford said in a low voice. "How many do you count?"

The Guardian masked his surprise well. "I count forty two," he said, replying with the answering code. "Best you confirm for yourself." He hauled at the metal bar, unlocking the gate, and it swung open. Rutherford led the way into the courtyard, and the gate clanged shut behind them.

"What was that?" Clamp muttered, eyeing the Guardian.

"Silkworm passcode," Rutherford replied. "Gondoliers have spies outside, they saw Sanction hustled in here for his own protection. They paid off the Bluecoats to look the other way, and that's how I got word; we don't have much time before they try something. Here we go."

"Nobody has more fun than us," Clamp observed as they pushed through the heavy door into the entry hall of one of the apartment buildings facing the courtyard. Two Guardians stood in their way.

"It's Rutherford, I'm here to see Kreeger," Rutherford said. "Got a report there are forty three windows in the courtyard." He paused. "Does that seem right to you?"

"Not sure," a Guardian replied, scowling. "I thought there were forty two. You can count them from suite 210." He consulted his ring, and handed over a key. Rutherford nodded, mounting the stairs, Clamp at his heels. When he reached the third floor, a Guardian was patrolling the hallway.

"Stop!" the Guardian said. Rutherford held up his key, and pointed down. The Guardian looked down the center of the stairwell, and a Guardian in the entry hall was looking up and offered a hand sign. The Guardian at the top of the stairs nodded, and threw a hand sign to the Guardian in front of suite 210. Turning away, the Guardians handled other business for a few minutes.

"Wait here," Rutherford said to Clamp in a low voice. "Neither of us wants you to know too much about what's about to happen." He was pale. Flexing his fist into his palm, he freed a couple pops from his knuckles.

Clamp nodded, alert, and he leaned against the bannister with his thumbs hooked in his belt next to his various weapons.

For a few long seconds, Rutherford stood outside 210. Long enough to breathe. The surging twist of stress squirmed through his guts, and he let out as much of it as he could with a shaky exhalation. Then he nodded to himself, and unlocked the door. He pushed it open.

Sanction stood in the middle of the sparsely decorated room, pistol in hand and pointed at the floor, waiting. His eyes widened to see Rutherford, but he said nothing.

Rutherford stepped inside and shut the door behind himself, squaring off with his husband. For a long moment, the only sound was the drip of rainwater from his coat to the floor.

"So what's this," Sanction said, bitter. "You plan to arrest me now?"

"I could," Rutherford said. "Drag you from this place. You'd probably make it to the tower alive, but you wouldn't make it through the night." He sniffed. "I don't want you dead. That's not my plan."

"Well it's just the two of us now," Sanction spat, "and I have had a *hell* of a week, so why don't you let me in on the joke."

"The joke is on me," Rutherford replied softly. "I fell in love with a man who scorned me. Insults me, ongoing. Even now. The level of your disrespect towards me is staggering. I was humiliated a long time before you started screwing anyone who caught your eye."

Sanction sensed his danger, but did not know how to respond.

"I have rehearsed this conversation so many times in my mind," Rutherford continued. "Won all the arguments, as one does in that sort of imaginary confrontation. They were arguments I did not want to have, and did not care to win. I envisioned demanding an accounting of you, of what I did wrong. Where I made mistakes, how I lost your respect and your interest. But that fiction was never satisfying, because I know you too well. You did not calculate my actions and calibrate your response accordingly. You followed your instinct for what you could get away with, and as you discovered I was not dangerous, you completely lost interest in me. You really are that simple."

"So," Sanction said slowly, "you put on the Bluecoat again, to recapture the forbidden romance of when I courted you? Really?" He blinked, and frowned. "You think you can just start over?"

"No," Rutherford replied. "Not at all. You fouled our life together, so I burned it down. If I could, I would walk away from you."

"You can't?" Sanction retorted.

"I can't," Rutherford agreed. "Because I love you. I don't want to go on without you. That's the joke. And it is cruel."

Sanction watched him for a long moment. "I don't understand what's happening right now," he said carefully.

"I put a lot of thought into how to respond," Rutherford said. "There can be no love without respect. And for you, there can be no respect without danger. Clear, demonstrated, memorable danger. That's all you really understand. The only power you feel is the power to bring danger to others and deflect it from yourself. In the presence of that power, you feel respect, and that's a foundation for the best love in you. That's the love I want. So I worked my way backwards."

"You—you did all this—so I would think you were *dangerous*?" Sanction sputtered. "You got people *killed* with your stunts!"

"People die anyway," Rutherford said, shrugging that off. "Now you *know* I am dangerous. Now you *feel* it. I destroyed your life," Rutherford said with quiet intensity. "I turned Trellis against you. I burned down your house. I wrecked your alliance with the Fairpole Council. I cost you the High Six. Anything you possess, any source of power, I can take from you. I have proven this. Nothing you have, nothing you can build, is beyond my reach. You know this. I see it in your eyes." He swallowed hard. "You hurt me," he said, a tremor in his voice, "then you threatened me. That stops now."

"Are you serious? You destroyed my life and now you want to get back together?" Sanction managed, incredulous.

"Convince me I can get what I want from you," Rutherford said through his teeth, "and I can give you your life back. Everything." He snapped his fingers. "Mounted on a pivot. Consider it courtship."

"You put a lot of work into this," Sanction said, subdued, his mind racing. "You sure I'm worth it?"

"Love is not a meritocracy," Rutherford said. "I don't care if you're worth it or not. I need your love. My plans end with you giving it to me again. Starting over. Understanding the stakes this time."

"What if that doesn't happen?" Sanction asked, his voice small.

"I don't know," Rutherford replied, looking him in the eye. "It doesn't matter. If I'm right about who you are, we won't need to find out."

"What about—" Sanction licked his lips. "What about forgiveness?"

"I worked out my feelings and I forgave you as best I can," Rutherford ground out. "The past is behind us. I am looking at the future. I realize I was wrong to treat you like a reasonable adult. I won't make that mistake again. You are the man I love, you love me to the best of your ability, and... relationships take work. It's up to me to make certain you never take me for granted again."

"You are out of your mind," Sanction said, awed.

"Look at your future," Rutherford said quietly. "Go ahead. Think about it for a minute."

Sanction studied Rutherford's face for a long moment, breathless at the conviction he saw there. The future was indeed bleak. His mind shied away from Trellis, and Piccolo in Ironhook, the Mistress of Tides at the mercy of a massive world-shattering demonic ritual; the Silkworms were done. Survivors would be hunted by the Hive, the gondoliers, the Foundation, and rival crews. Sanction could leave the city, perhaps, but survival was long odds. He thought of Spindle and Crackstone, now dead. His lovers, gone. He shivered, feeling his profound isolation.

"I don't know what I feel," Sanction said in a small voice.

"You are a bureaucrat, a fixer, and a confidence artist," Rutherford said quietly. "Right now no one has given you orders, and you don't know what you want." He nodded. "I know you, Kreeger."

"But do you respect me?" Sanction said, brow furrowed. "You said there can be no love without respect."

"You are amazing in your element," Rutherford replied, "so we need to get you back into it. I will make sure you have a chance to live into your best self. Trellis won't be around long. Then you step up. We shape a future. Build it and defend it." He paused. "Together."

"It is uncanny," Sanction breathed, "how you understand me."

"One of us has to," Rutherford agreed, solemn.

"I really want to kiss you right now," Sanction said, unsteady, realizing for the first time in a long time it was true.

"Come here," Rutherford agreed, eyes burning.

They kissed, swift and deep and passionate. Sanction felt Rutherford's body heat, soaking it in, stark contrast to the frostbitten isolation that had set in deeper than he realized. Hope flickered to life in the ashes of his desolation. Betrayal, demon machination, and impending doom seemed somehow distant.

He leaned back, dizzy. "You—you said something about a pivot?"

Rutherford's grin was feral. "You're going to love this," he promised.

BASEMENT, BROADSHOULDER TENEMENT, TURNABOUT COURT, BRIGHTSTONE. 26TH VOLVINET. TWELFTH HOUR PAST DAWN. SAIL LIGHTING FESTIVAL, DAY FOUR.

"The Blind Hour coming up," Cellar said, squinting out between the cracked wooden slats of the cellar window, careful not to stand too close to the wall as the rain's runoff trickled down the cracks. He fiddled with the cufflinks of his dress uniform. "You were right," he said as he turned to look at Trellis. "Surprisingly good fit."

"Sometimes we get lucky," Trellis murmured, eyes bright as he adjusted his own uniform. He glanced over at Mistress of Tides, already dressed and deep in contemplation. "So, who wants to go pick up our forged documents?"

"Me," Jayan said, rising from the rickety chair in the corner. "I'll do it. Need to walk off some of this nervous energy," he said with a crooked grin, winking with his swollen eye.

"Excellent," Trellis nodded. "I'll get the payment." He crossed to the moldy workbench, knocking out a slat in the back of the cupboard and pulling out a dusty box. Opening it, he pulled out a bag of coins. "This should do it."

"Great," Jayan nodded, reaching for the bag. Trellis arched an eyebrow as he handed it over.

"Did you write a note too?" he asked. "You got some charcoal on your cuff."

"Oh, it will wipe right off," Jayan said. "No problem."

"A goodbye to loved ones perhaps?" Trellis pressed.

"Don't worry about it, old man," Jayan frowned. "I'll be right back." He turned, hauling open the metal door to the sewer entry. The door slammed behind him.

Trellis pointed a meaningful look at Cellar. He didn't say a word. He didn't need to.

Cellar caught up with Jayan moments later. "Hey, what was that?" he demanded.

"What was what?" Jayan retorted. "I don't like answering to criminals!"

"So answer to me," Cellar frowned.

"What, are you worried about my personal grooming?" Jayan demanded.

"No, I'm not, but that old man has scary-good instincts and I don't like what I heard in your voice when you answered him," Cellar said, steady. "Just tell me whatever embarrassing thing he was picking on, and I'll keep it to myself. Love note? Draft of a eulogy? Come on, tell me something I want to hear," he said as he struggled against the insight his intuition was offering him.

"Can you just let it go," Jayan demanded, his tone flat.

"It's like you've never met me," Cellar replied, unable to turn it into a joke. He reached for Jayan's pocket where he kept his investigator notepad. Jayan slapped his hand away, and for a shocked moment the men stood face to face in the dim tunnel, tense.

Cellar reached out again, slowly, taking his time. Jayan trembled, but did not resist. Cellar pulled the note pad out, and flicked the cover aside, able to read the scrawled text by the dim light filtering through the grate above.

"Tonight. Whitecrown District Evidentiary. Carriage House Factual Annex. Trellis, Cellar, Mistress of Tides." He looked up at Jayan, expressionless. "What is this."

"Before the festival started," Jayan said slowly. "Somebody was working through a proxy, offered me a stupid amount of money for a couple notes on your movements. Right after my landlord promised to evict me. I figured what the hell. Dropped notes a couple times a day. Doubled my income. I didn't think anybody would get hurt," he insisted, earnest.

"But somebody did," Cellar said as coldness filtered into his bones.

"Yeah, when Spur turned up dead and you couldn't establish factuals. How could the Skullface Killer know to strike when you were most vulnerable? I wanted to tell you," Jayan insisted.

Numbness spread through Cellar. "Daava."

"Yesterday. Second note I got from this guy. Told me to hang back a little when you went after the doctor. The note just showed up at my desk, but there was a bonus. A big bonus," he said, troubled. "I didn't know."

"That you were informing to the Skullface Killer? To the Dark Tooth? But now you *do*!" Cellar shouted, his voice brittle as he crumpled the note in his fist and brandished it. "Now you know about the ritual! There's some threat to the whole city, and you're thinking about the *payday*?"

"Yeah, well, I'm being blackmailed too, okay?" Jayan yelled. "You think this is fun for me? I got some choices that are pretty ugly!"

"Give me the money and go," Cellar said, his voice cold.

Jayan looked him in the eye, overflowing with shame and anger. He tugged the pouch of coin out of his vest and threw it on the ground.

"I am *so sorry*," he ground out. Then he turned and ran down the dark tunnel.

Cellar dropped to his knees, gathering up the bag.

He could not immediately rise.

An hour later, the door clacked shut behind Cellar. Pale, he stood in the basement, oddly alone. He threw the oilskin pouch on the workbench.

"The forged documents," he said. "Jayan was informing on us. We may not have the element of surprise. I don't see how that changes anything."

"Agreed," Trellis nodded. "We must take our chances regardless."

"That's it? No surprise? No anger?" Cellar struggled to relax, and failed. "Did you know?"

"It seemed reasonable," Trellis replied. "The killer probably wouldn't be able to stay close enough to you to see your movements, and also remain undetected. You are an Inspector, after all."

"You didn't say anything."

"How would that conversation have gone, do you think?" Trellis mused. "Put it from your mind. We need to go."

"It's time," the Mistress of Tides said, and she rose. "Now or never."

Moments later, the basement was empty.

THE LAST CHAPTER

It was not some criminal title, not at first. Like many before him, Lord Belderan carried his school-days nickname into a seedier environ. He was in an arts finishing school between programs of educational coursework as a child. After an incident where the theatrical production was sabotaged with larger-than-life pornographic images painted on the drapes flown in to close the act, an investigation immediately turned up the scoundrels responsible.

In the justification for expulsion document, Headmaster Trowly described Belderan as a pernicious and enabling influence. I kept a copy for old times' sake. Here: 'Where the instinct and inclination to mischief are lazy blooms in most of our students, Belderan provides a trellis that supports escalation of his classmates' idle urges, providing pathways so their misanthropic ambitions climb to inappropriate heights.' Belderan immediately leaked the document as part of his resume. He became sought after as a planner and fixer for a dozen of the most rambunctious societies in privileged academic circles, just in time for the hardest shocks of puberty and rebellion to inspire their first truly regrettable ambitions.

I was right there with him. He became Trellis, and I became Lazy Bloom. It was beautiful. He rendered his friends' unearned confidence plausible by sketching out these genius little plans with roles simplified so we could understand them, roles that played to our strengths. We did such damage, and built such fabulous networks. The Belderan name got him into the best schools and social circles at first. Scandal would have ejected him soon enough, but he earned his place by befriending the popular and earning a reputation as a peerless fixer for students, instructors, and administrators alike. We only parted ways when the choice was underscored; follow the arts, or follow the power. I chose the arts. I suspect my broken heart added a certain depth to my efforts, so even now I can thank him for amplifying my work.

—Unpublished interview transcript
for Lady Vashlay's biography

"How do you stay so calm," Cellar said under his breath, looking to Trellis. "What we are doing... this is insane."

"The stakes have never been higher," Trellis replied, eyes bright in the shifting shadows of the coach, "but there comes a point where we've done what we can do and we're in the grip of fate itself. Can you feel it?" he mused. "As the Herald of the Dark Tooth, you very nearly touch on an ocean of energy that's built up over a decade." He shivered slightly. "Soon we will be past it, one way or another."

"Can I see the floorplan again?" Cellar asked, struggling to deepen his breath and his voice.

"Don't worry about the floorplan," Trellis soothed. "I've got it memorized, *and* the personnel list, *and* the passcodes. You are a vital part of this mission, but you don't have all of it on your shoulders. I've been training for this most of my life, one way or another, and we've got good preparation in place." He offered Cellar a smile. "Between the three of us, I think we can get in there."

"Do you really think the Dark Tooth got here first?" Cellar asked. He squinted out the coach window at the massive electroplasmic lamps drifting by as they closed in on the overbuilt entry to the evidentiary. His heart pounded in his chest, his mouth was dry, his hands trembled.

"We cannot assume otherwise," Trellis sighed. "For all we know, the Dark Tooth is a Ministry official." He paused, looking to the Mistress of Tides. "Not long now. Can you walk?"

"I can walk," she murmured. She clutched at her bag with her good hand, and let out a shuddering breath.

"Excellent," Trellis murmured. "Now remember, we're here on orders of Chief Inspector Prichard, to interrogate a nameless Iruvian girl in the Carriage House Factual Annex, one of Master Silvercrane's discretionaries. We have negotiated access with him," Trellis said, pressing the oilskin bundle of documents into Cellar's hands. "We must get in tonight."

"Blood and bone," Cellar whispered.

The carriage rolled to a halt, and Cellar led the others to the gate.

"Inspector Cellar, Silkshore, Smoke Tower," he said to the guard. "I'm here with my specials, dispatched by Chief Inspector Prichard." His voice was even, calm.

"Credentials," the guard demanded. Cellar handed his Inspector packet over, and the guard took it to a side chamber for review. Cellar and his specials stood in the rain for a long minute before the guard returned to the barred window. "With me." The massive gate clanked, and the sally port swung open. The three entered, and followed the Ministry guard up the side steps to the after-hours entry.

The elevated duty officer desk was designed to be imposing, towering over visitors. The sleek woman looked down her nose at them, her uniform immaculate. "Can't wait until morning?" she said.

"Chief Inspector Prichard has a lead on the Skullface Killer case," Cellar replied. "He sent me to establish some factuals in support of the investigation."

The duty officer raised an eyebrow. "I see. Your specials can wait here."

"Levyra, the medium, under command for the investigation," Cellar said quickly with a gesture to the Mistress of Tides. "Also Quinn, a Bluecoat who served in the initial investigation of the Skullface Killer a decade ago. I need them both for veracity and follow-up questions."

The duty officer considered that for a moment, then nodded. "Very well. What is your course?"

"Master Silvercrane's discretionaries, he had a young Iruvian woman brought in. We have negotiated access with him." Cellar handed over the oilskin pouch with the documents.

For an impossibly long moment, the duty officer examined the documents. "You do not have the notice of curiosity from the Chief Inspector," she said absently, "and your consent from Master Silvercrane lacks the needed specificity regarding berthing arrangements." She looked Cellar in the eye. "This will have to wait until morning."

Trellis studied her badge. "Spare a thought," Trellis said quietly, "for the sons of the ships."

Something like alarm flashed through the duty officer's eyes. "Ships of the sea?"

"The narrow traverse, canals without tides," he replied.

"I see." The duty officer cleared her throat. "Stay with your escort. We will keep your credentials and weapons here, you can pick them up when you leave. Enjoy your stay." Her smile was mirthless.

The guards searched them thoroughly, taking their blades and pistols. Then the guards escorted them down endless marble corridors in the company of two veteran Ministry escorts in crisp black uniforms. They descended several staircases and passed through a number of checkpoints.

They heard wailing up ahead, and the murmur of worried conversation. The Ministry guards exchanged a glance, and picked up the pace. A checkpoint had several Ministry guards and officials in a loose crowd. There was a coppery stink in the air and fresh blood on the desk and floor.

"What's going on here," the Ministry escort asked one of the guards.

"It's Sevelian," the guard muttered, barely audible to Cellar and his specials. "He wasn't feeling well earlier, and he just—he just started screaming. Clawing at his eyes. I guess he caught fire."

"We have some guests, here to see one of Master Silvercrane's discretionaries," the escort said.

"I don't know what to tell you, we can't put people through. Our adept is unavailable for the security scan. It's after hours anyway," the guard frowned.

"Captain Schrieveren sent them through," the escort said, "and I get the feeling she doesn't want them back." He pointed an unfriendly look at Cellar and his specials.

"Probably a malfunction in the ambient field," the Mistress of Tides lied smoothly. "Adepts don't handle those well at the best of times. And if the field is up, it doesn't matter if we're Whispers packed with ghosts or not, the site is secure." She cocked her head to the side. "The field is up, right?"

"It is," the guard replied through his teeth. He exchanged a look with the escort. "You're with them all the way, right?"

"Yes, through the questioning too," the escort nodded.

The guard frowned. "Alright, go on," he said. "You have thirty minutes."

"Thank you," Cellar nodded, subdued, and he followed the escort.

The sign painted on the wall indicated the ambient suppression field was ahead. Trellis moved to the Mistress of Tides elbow as they crossed through the doorway into the field-protected zone.

"Oh," she breathed.

"Are you alright?" Trellis asked, concerned.

"Yes," she replied. "Yes, this is… it is a relief." She took a deep breath. "The pressure is receding," she continued in Hadrathi, quietly, difficult to overhear. "I can feel the drain into the ambient field. The connection to the ritual is less oppressive here."

"I suppose you are not often overflowing with energy," Trellis said. "Well, that's something."

"Hey," one of their escorts said, frowning. "Keep up."

They dutifully followed through the well-appointed foyer, down another corridor that looked like an expensive hotel with guards. Examining the numbers on the wall, the escort stopped by a heavy door, and unlocked it from a ring of keys. "Visitor," he said, banging on the door. He opened it, and the five of them entered.

An Iruvian girl sat cross-legged in the middle of the floor, lost in meditation.

"That's one way to deal with the boredom," one escort said.

Trellis pivoted and thrust his hands out, one towards each of them. The dust ejectors sewn into his sleeves cast puffs of trance powder, catching the escorts off guard. They stumbled back, dazed, the powder doing its work.

"This is dull," Trellis informed the receptive guards, adjusting his cuffs. The drugged escorts believed his suggestion over the evidence of their senses as the magical powder warped their perceptions. "A bunch of stupid questions in a bad Hadrathi accent. Nothing of interest is happening. Ignore us." The escorts slumped back against the wall, saying nothing and seeing nothing. Cellar leaned against the heavy door, closing it.

"She is dreaming, it appears," the Mistress of Tides said. "We have no way of knowing whether the Dark Tooth has already moved through her."

"Would a body be left behind? If someone joined her in dreams?" Cellar asked.

"I don't know," the Mistress of Tides replied. "This is an impossibly rare corner case, there are no precedents I've heard about."

"We must use Breathe Into Dreams," Trellis said.

"She cannot consent," the Mistress of Tides pointed out. "Unless we rouse her, and if we do, that may affect the connection to the spirit well. If the Dark Tooth is there, we may not be able to get in if the door closes."

"I suspect she will be able to consent when we find her, between this world and that one," Trellis said quietly. "Please try."

"Maybe I should stand guard," Cellar said, uncomfortable.

"No! No. We need you to be part of this," Trellis said quickly. "Now, here we go." He sat down cross-legged next to the girl. The Mistress of Tides sat on her other side, and Cellar reluctantly sat between them, opposite the dreamer. "We need to physically connect, blood to blood," Trellis said. "The Ghost Field is suppressed here, so we must have mind and body connected physically. This may pinch."

The ritual seemed straightforward. They each drank a bitter shot in unison. The Mistress of Tides inserted a copper wire through the Cromlech's skin on one side and into Trellis's leg on the other. Another wire connected Trellis to Cellar, another connected Cellar to the Mistress of Tides, another connected the Mistress of Tides back to the Cromlech. As their stomachs churned, trying to reject the foul potion, blood trickled from the punctures. They murmured the incantation together over and over, feeling the dizzying drop of vertigo as they struggled to attune

to the dream

on the deck of a ship. Clouds towered overhead, giving the blank and empty sky cathedrals of turbulence frozen in mid-billow. Lightning streaked, pulsed, all around. Constellations burned below, their points of light elongating to streaks under the polished obsidian of very slowly flexing waves.

Cromlech sat with her back to the broken helm, her feet hanging over the edge of the aft deck, regarding them coolly as they stood amidships.

"Looking within and without, we shall see," the Mistress of Tides said in Hadrathi, bowing low.

"I am no Whisper, nor an adept," the mystic replied quietly, also in Hadrathi. "I have no need of the traditional forms."

"I understand," the Mistress of Tides replied. "Yet I am a Whisper, and I do have need of the forms." She paused. "We seek to stave off the completion of a demon ritual. Do you feel its shadow?"

"Your city is dark," Cromlech said, "awash in a terrifying fate. I do not understand why I am here." She squinted out at the oozing slowness of a raging storm around them. "Yet I cannot escape."

"You did not respond to an invitation to come?" the Mistress of Tides clarified.

"This is my fault," Trellis said in accented Hadrathi. "I was working through proxy agents, and they may not have communicated as well as I would wish. I tried not to micromanage, as Iruvia has different customs than we do, and I did not want to interfere in my agents' methods unduly."

"My guardians were slain," Cromlech said, "and my home destroyed. I was stolen from my people, smuggled over borders, and dragged along a trail of blood. I do not wish to be here."

"You have my apologies," Trellis said, shaken. "I did not realize. I swear I will make it right."

"Why *am* I here?" Cromlech asked. "I assume it has to do with the Garden."

"The Garden, yes," the Mistress of Tides said. "A demonic ritual has given the city the aspect you sense, and it is about to complete. Tonight. We do not know what will happen if it does, and we are determined to stop it. Have you allowed anyone else access to the Garden since you arrived?" she asked, breathless.

"No, I have not," Cromlech replied.

"And yet," Trellis mused. "Is it possible someone entered the Garden previously? Possibly years ago, and hid, not returning?"

"Trellis," the Mistress of Tides interjected, "we know the Dark Tooth is active now in Doskvol. How would it work to be simultaneously here *and* in a spirit well behind the Mirror somewhere?" She gestured to Cellar. "We have the Dark Tooth's Herald."

"You are sure Cellar didn't enter a fugue state and finish the ritual sacrifice himself, unwitting?" Trellis murmured. "How sure? Also, the prophecy isn't terribly clear. There may be may be another player. Demonic rituals may hinge on a few key figures, but they are often supported by cult activity. I think we need to check. I dare not leave it to chance."

Cellar stepped in close enough to overhear, and Trellis regarded him carefully. "Cellar, I leave this to you. Do we trust, or do we assure ourselves we are safe?"

"I mean... we should check," Cellar said.

"Then you must be the one to convince her," Trellis said. "Please."

"Why?" Cellar said, baffled.

"Because you have a sincerity I don't, and she's not going to listen to our reasons and ambitions. She will only listen to heart, and of the three of us," he shrugged, "yours speaks the most eloquently."

Cellar stared at him.

"We haven't known each other long," Trellis said, almost a whisper, locking eyes with Cellar. "Still, I feel l know you. And one thing about you that I envy; you have not steeled yourself to do awful things because you feel you must. You have not accepted that price, and you have not received the tainted rewards." Trellis put his hand on Cellar's shoulder, his voice wavering slightly. "I pray you never do."

Reluctant, Cellar looked away from Trellis, over to the Mistress of Tides. She nodded slightly. He heaved a deep breath, then stepped back, orienting on Cromlech. He crossed the deck to easy conversational distance.

"Hello," he said experimentally in Akorosian.

She cocked her head to the side.

"My Hadrathi never got much past a few key phrases that aren't helpful here," he sighed. "The problem is this prophecy. That the Mistress of Tides here" he said with a gesture "can stop the Dark Tooth from completing the Fourfold Circle. That the ritual would complete, and the only chance to stop it is her." He paused. "So if the ritual is going to complete, we need to be there. The stars are moving, the window is closing, and if we leave now without doing everything we can do... I don't know how we go back to our lives if we turn back now. We threw everything away to get close enough to take a shot, so it better be necessary." He looked her in the eye. "Please."

Cromlech reached out to touch Cellar's face, and he let her. Her hand cupped his cheek, and there was sadness in her eyes.

A deep glow shone up through the deck, limning the edge of the cargo hatch. Trellis vigorously hauled at the hatch, and it slammed open, light and the scent of green things billowing up from below. He dropped through.

"Goodbye," Cromlech said to Cellar, releasing him.

"Thank you," Cellar replied, feeling a strange surge of emotion. "Thank you so much."

The Mistress of Tides took his arm, and together they stepped down through the hatch.

The jarring transition from the waking world to the dream had been unsettling. The drop into the spirit well was disorienting. Cellar dropped to his knees, gasping, feeling the sensation of the sand that supported him echoing through his body.

The Mistress of Tides stared. They stood together on the sere coastline where Doskvol was built, but the city's echo glimmered in the corner of her eye, not yet real. For now, there were rocks and black sand, wads of washed-up algae, dark grass and bushes swaying from the breathing of a world struggling to remember its present.

"Finally," Trellis said. "Finally, this is where I die."

He stood apart from the others, feet in the surf. Raising the iron rune-stitched flask, he drank it down, the cold plasmic essence flaring and burning as it flowed down into him.

"Trellis, no!" gasped the Mistress of Tides.

His laugh was unpleasant.

With a jolt, the energies of the whole spirit well galvanized, and snapped into alignment with him. He threw his arms out, and energy coiled through him then stabilized until he was a flaring core, rippling with distortion. He smoothed his lapels, and the energy seethed around him almost invisibly.

"What—what is this," the Mistress of Tides demanded.

"Did you know the Deathseeker crows sing?" Trellis asked, strangely centered in the wake of the energy burst. "They do. It is an unpleasant song. Oddly melodic, but... it changes you, when you hear it. For a long time, I couldn't tune it out." His smile was peculiar. "I heard it again when I first saw you. I knew you bore the Leviathan's Mark. That was the last confirmation I needed. I finally knew who you were to me. The one who could stop me." He paused. "The *only* one, if you believe in prophecy."

The Mistress of Tides stared at him, the tumblers clicking in place. The Foundation identified the Dark Tooth as a Silkworm. Trellis brought the Cromlech to Doskvol. He was always involved in plans, wheels within wheels, and he didn't talk about his past. He was ruthless, driven, dark, a schemer to the core.

"But—this cannot," she faltered.

"I know, it's a lot," he agreed.

"How did this happen?" she gritted out.

Cellar also realized the danger, and he charged Trellis with his fists raised. Trellis pointed a mild look at him, waiting. Cellar struck Trellis as hard as he could, punching his face; Cellar rebounded with a crackling shock, plowing through the sand, energy flickering across his form and leaving him dazed. Trellis didn't react in the slightest.

"You know better, right?" he said to the Mistress of Tides.

"Why is this not over yet?" she countered. "If you are immune to interference here, at the end."

"An excellent question," Trellis nodded. "There is a possibility you will choose to survive this, and if that's the case, I need you to have some context. There are questions you will never be able to answer otherwise, and I would not... I want better for you." There was a distant look in his eyes as sensation coursed through him.

"You are not concerned I will stop you?" the Mistress of Tides said.

"I think there is a very real possibility you will, more's the pity," he smiled. "I have planned on it, in fact. Wondered, through many a dark night, how this moment would unfold." He let his eyes wander the skyline both real and echoed. "It is more beautiful here than I expected," he confessed.

"Do you know?" the Mistress of Tides asked. "What the ritual does, if it completes?"

"I do," he said. With a shiver, he looked down at his hand; his fingers peeled back, flaring around the nimbus of energy pouring from his palm, disintegrating in the colorless light.

"What is happening," the Mistress of Tides said, breathless. "How do I stop it?"

Trellis relaxed, closing his eyes. Light began to wear through to visibility like glowing veins under his skin. "First one question, then the other. What is happening? The end of the world." He shrugged as though settling a weight. "Will you permit an old man to tell a story?"

"I see little choice in the matter," she replied.

"Your choice is coming up." He opened his eyes. "Fifteen years ago, I was reaching a crisis point. I was the Unseen Hand of the Hive. I had subdued the Fairpole Council for them. The Hive approached the peak of its power in Silkshore. Still, in order to suborn the gondoliers, I had to learn them. Considering the Hive planned to use up and discard the boat people, they were suspicious of the connections I cultivated among the Fairpole Council membership. My handlers were threatened by the idea that I could harbor sympathies with these disposable chattel. They did know I was dangerous, so they were reluctant to move against me directly or indirectly. Instead they gave me a dangerous mission. I was to scuttle a Leviathan hunter at sea, at an opportune time. There was a suggestion of an exfiltration plan, but at some level I understood what was happening." He paused. "I went through with it anyway. Maybe I was tired. Maybe I understood that there were far worse ways to die. Maybe I wanted a level of control over my own end." A smile creased his features, weary this time. "Now I have the fate I chose. As much as I've chosen anything over the last fifteen years." He shook his head.

"It was a hell of a storm," he remembered. "Stinging a Leviathan tends to provoke terrific weather hazards. Breaching the hull was trivial in that kind of dangerous situation, and I wasn't looking too hard for my way out when I hit the water. I thought I had found it." His eyes flicked over to the Mistress of Tides. "Indeed I did. I passed through a wake of Leviathan blood, undying and vicious. A baptism in battle, consecrated in the wilderness of a storm at sea, the demon itself in the waters with you... you cannot imagine," he said with deliberate enunciation. "The battle was past, and the Leviathan transported me somehow. Eventually I crawled out of the filth at the waterline of the docks, back to Doskvol, completely insane." He arched an eyebrow. "I later found that it was the exact spot where you were fished out five years previously."

"How did I not know this?" the Mistress of Tides blurted, her lips numb.

"I was never forthcoming about my past, and I did not encourage intrusion into my business," Trellis replied. "Anyway, I was on my deathbed in a filthy alley, burning up with fever, hollowed out by exposure. An agent of the Hive recognized me somehow. I still had friends, some regard in the eyes of the leadership. I was collected, and returned to my home to die with some modicum of dignity." He paused. "But I did not die. Not exactly. Nor did I return to life."

A dangerous shine slid out of his hips and shoulders, cracks spreading under his skin. He glanced down, his expression curious.

"I left the Hive alone, as I began the slow recovery," he mused. "They ignored me as well. I seemed neutralized, yet a misstep could provoke danger from some of the failsafes I had planted along my path. For the first year, they thought I had lost my mind for good. After I regained my senses, I didn't seem a threat, so they moved on. They could not see the threat I had become. The Dark Tooth."

He looked Cellar in the eye, catching him off guard. "The Leviathan swept my mind clean and implanted a compulsion I could not fully grasp. This dark purpose drove me to survive, drove me to explore its urges and begin to piece together my task in terms I could understand, not just feel. The seed of the Fourfold Ritual had been planted in me, and my life's work became nurturing it to overflow its housing and grow, breaking into the light. I've never experienced anything like it. A whole different way of seeing the world, of experiencing my own feelings. You use sign language; you think differently, yes? When you say something with your hands rather than with your mouth."

"Er—yes," Cellar said, deeply uncomfortable.

"Something in the motion, in the physicality of it, you communicate differently. You think differently. So it is with the Leviathan urge, with the knowledge I cannot explain that is more compelling and trustworthy than my conventional senses. I needed to map out the pattern, and it took me a year to get a basic understanding of the task. It was impossible," he said, shaking his head.

"The Fourfold Ritual?" the Mistress of Tides prompted.

"Yes. Like constellations or the steps of the spheres, all of reality in its many internal and external forms is in motion constantly in orbits with unknowable intersections. But there were four points that needed to align exactly, and if they did, then a barrier would fall away. You already know that there were four points to anchor the ritual, bounding in the city. You already know that there were to be two framing the Fracture constellation as it opened and closed, and another two framing the Fracture a decade later. Child's play," he said with a dismissive gesture. "However, due to the spread in time, to keep the ritual anchored I needed to use life forces that were profoundly embedded in the energies of the city. With a little experimentation, I knew that adepts and Whispers weren't right. I came to understand that I needed Spirit Wardens. But I had to preserve my secrets for a decadal gap. How could I manage this?"

Trellis winced slightly as his forearm began to sift into nothingness. "I researched into the Spirit Wardens, and came to understand that several of their powers are imparted by a glyph. This glyph is burned into their chests, then concealed with a ritual designed to hide the connection from any test, even (or especially) a Whisper's sight. I also discovered a secret network of undercover Spirit Wardens. I began my work with radiants and alchemical processes in an effort to develop ways to detect these invisible glyphs. Eventually I succeeded. When I sacrificed multiple Spirit Wardens, they could only assume one of their own had gone rogue. Who else would know enough?" He grinned, warmed by the idea. Then he continued.

"As if stalking and murdering Spirit Wardens in accordance to the ritual form was not difficult enough, each sacrifice had to align with a different state of being within me, the Dark Tooth. The first sacrifice was my acceptance of this purpose. The second aligned with my commitment to complete the ritual. The third, a decade later, was a response to the call to continue." He looked the Mistress of Tides in the eye. "Now, for the final sacrifice, a Spirit Warden won't do. I am brimming with the energy of the Leviathan that Marked me. My life force is the only one strong enough to complete this ritual. For the final sacrifice, I must be ready to die for it. I have already consumed the plasmic essence to bolster my tolerance and capacity, here at the end; my death is irreversible now."

"Then what."

"Then the lightning walls contain the city, fueled by processed Leviathan blood, part of the ritual. Try to picture it. A Leviathan breaching through reality itself, in the center of the city, the shock wave killing everyone bounded by this ritual in a matter of seconds." Trellis's eyes gleamed.

"Why? Why destroy Doskvol? Revenge for the Leviathan hunter predation?" the Mistress of Tides asked.

"Leviathans care less about revenge than you do; it is a petty thing, beneath them. No, this ritual is to focus the death. All those souls sluicing into the Leviathan, all that energy at once swelling it with a spike of power unseen since the Gates of Death broke. Leviathans cannot die." He paused. "And they are not sufficiently powerful to consume each other. At least, not yet. But if one could consume another, both undying, then the balance would be broken. Melded, they would continue to grow more powerful, able to consume another, then others. This ritual is the beginning of the end of this wretched, broken world. At last!" he cried. "At last we come down to it, we come down to your choice. Yours and mine, really."

"Your choice?" The Mistress of Tides felt power growing in her, seeping along her bones, glowing under her skin. Firm, she set aside the clamoring built-in need for survival, remaining alert to the moment with the iron discipline of a warrior.

"I had to choose how to respond to my purpose," Trellis explained as the piercing light erased his feet, curling up his shins. "My capacity for love, whatever it may have been before my baptism, was unrecognizable in my new passions. My hungers and joys were rewritten through my past and my future, alien in the present. The only satisfaction I could feel was in pursuit of this new and impossible mission. However, I could engage it on my terms. Wrestle what meaning, what purpose was within reach from the morass of insanity swamping me. I knew I would give my mind, my heart, and my soul to this new purpose, to crafting this ritual. But in the end?" His smile was thin. "In the end, once I had crafted the lock, I would give you the key."

"You want me to destroy the world," she clarified, expressionless.

"I want you to choose," he said gently. "My purpose is not the only one in play here." Wincing, he twitched as one of his shoulders crisped open, light twisting the rest of the arm apart. His torso and stumps hung in the flameless light, unmoved. "It is—such a relief," he ground out. "Finally to be in this moment. Finally to be past all the impossible challenges. Accessing a spirit well where there could be no spirit well. Finding life forces that could ground ritual energy for a decade, and researching the ritual forms to anchor and preserve their capacity undetected, year after year. All that, and more, went into preparing for this. One of the most daunting challenges... swollen with undying energy and power as I am now, I thought I would be very difficult to kill," he said with a pained smile. "Still, die I must. As it turns out, this energy, the reserve, will do an adequate job of erasing my consciousness. I count on you to finish the ritual, as I have counted on you for the last few years. In my work with seers and cults, I came to understand the fate of the Dark Tooth. I could only succeed if I brought to the last sacrifice a powerful Whisper—and one who loves me." He shook his head. "For years on end I thought it impossible. That I could find someone who would know what you now know, and be willing to release me. To let me go. To finish the ritual without dispassion or hatred or ambition."

"What if I don't?" the Mistress of Tides demanded, startled by the tremor in her voice.

"I have no idea," Trellis whispered. "I only know that if I am not erased by someone with a high level of expertise, the ritual doesn't complete and it doesn't disperse. So the energy builds up, keeps building, ruptures somehow. You have felt the reserve; what do you think will happen?"

"That doesn't explain why you think I have to love you," she said.

"It's the only way—the only way to know what's me, and what isn't, in what I'm becoming. To care," he said, his voice a breathy reverberation as he struggled like a man treading water. "It cannot be an intellectual puzzle. That's not how we're built. Ah. My time runs short. And you have much to consider. This is your purpose too, you know."

Trellis coughed. "You were spared from the storm that drowned your family because you received the Leviathan's Mark. The power of the limmers, the legacy of corruption from exposure to undying blood, did not move through your linage. It was given to you in those turbulent waters, instead of a drowning death. You became a figure in the prophecy in that moment, a part of the exception stitched into reality's rules. From the moment I became aware of you, I have aimed our shared experiences towards this encounter—this opportunity. It's not about you, just as it is not about me. This Fourfold Ritual goes further back. Further and further. Perhaps to the arrival of humanity on Akoros's shattered coast," he said as he gazed across the broken horizon. "Perhaps humanity was always the long game, the concentration of life to allow one Leviathan to ascend. And within that scheme, perhaps there was always going to be a tribe of humans dipped in undying gore, trafficking with the dead, reweaving reality itself to eventually untangle this knot of balance. Insofar as there is any purpose in this world, perhaps you and I are the ones lucky enough to fulfill it at the end of all things."

The Mistress of Tides felt her breathing shorten as she felt Trellis's life force in the energies that were saturating her. She felt his identity just as she felt the thoughts and pattern of a ghost, filled out with plasmic energy, and she knew how to twist and manipulate them. He was haunting the ritual, he was its animating force, and however she was going to react to the ritual it was going to be through him. She swallowed hard, already grieving.

"A gift," Trellis whispered, more felt than heard. "All our lives we have seen the suffering. The darkness. The—the corruption. Do you see a future without them?" he breathed. "A child born into this world—innocent. Twisted from the start. Marred and broken and hurt. Is this to be humanity's punishment forever?" A sensation like swallowing, and Trellis's thoughts moved within her instead of to her. She felt his closeness as pulses and strobes of light burned through knots of his physical remains.

The Mistress of Tides closed her eyes. The dream was wrapped around her, and she sensed it still. Within the dream, she was inside the spirit well. Across those levels, and the waking world, she felt the influence of the ritual reserve of life force. Now, within her own life energy as it stretched across those realms, she somehow faced Trellis, surrounded by her memory-sketched audience hall in the overview.

"Let's hear it for exquisite timing," Trellis said, his smile gentle. "I am at last ready to go. I have come to see this ritual as a gift, from the Leviathan. Everything ends," he said. "Why not now? No more pain. No more violence. Just... quiet. The only peace humanity will ever know."

"You believe we save the world by ending it," the Mistress of Tides said, quiet, steadying herself on the ballooning sensation of grief that saturated the last moments together. There was no romance, and never had been, but as she witnessed the end of Lord Belderan, the Trellis, she realized she did love him in her way. He was valuable to her, she had trusted him, and in some way she trusted him still even as her heart broke. She wore no veil in this place, in this last conversation. She needed no veil here.

"You know, better than anyone. The moment of death has a pain and disorientation that doesn't ultimately matter to what comes before or what comes after." Trellis's image shivered, losing resolution. "Just that shock of cold water when you first get in the pool." There was a kindness in his smile that reinforced the loss of the man she had come to know.

"The end of the world. It *is* a gift," the Mistress of Tides said. "A way out. A fitting conclusion." She took a deep breath, or imagined herself doing so. Finally, she felt the tipping point, and she felt her heart might twist in two as she passed it. Something hardened inside her. "But it is a gift from a demon. A massive god-demon of the deeps—but a demon all the same. This end is not one that humanity earned. Not one that humanity deserves. I imagine those who broke the Gates of Death thought they were reshaping a better world too. This gift is tainted, and I reject it." She studied his face.

Trellis's image suppressed a smile. "I don't care what you decide," he said. "I completed this ritual. I have murdered and studied and schemed my way to this point, I am past my own finish line. Whether the world lives or dies. The suffering that follows, either as a shock or as a continuing cycle—that is up to you now." He opened his arms. "You will live with your choice, you will carry that weight. It is time. Either sacrifice me, properly, completing the circuit and powering the ritual... or pull me out of the energy and scatter my death, plucking loose the seams of the ritual, and letting the reserve drift apart in the winds behind the Mirror." He paused. "Either way, it has been my honor to know you. I have loved you. Venisana. Mistress of Tides."

"You b-bastard," she whispered, a bleak smile cracking her face. "Looking within and without... we shall see."

"See... and be seen," Trellis's ghost echoed.

She had already forgiven him, without even trying.

The rushing power seemed to build from every direction at once. She felt the vastness of the hunger of the Leviathan closing in, the onrushing velocity flattening the ritual reserve to a disc that would breach, forming a gate from somewhere in the impossible depths to crash through reality itself into Doskvol. Dimly, she felt columns of flame tearing up into the blank night sky from the bursting spirit wells anchoring the ritual.

No.

The Mistress of Tides lived and died on the shifting pull of currents and swells behind the Mirror. As this tsunami crested, she faced it, and the end of all things; the towering wave of her dreams, the destruction that had always hovered over Doskvol, the resonant growl of life force from the Leviathan that haunted her memories. This moment, now, reverberating through her whole life, finally in context.

The twist of demonic undying blood bound the vast reserve, anchoring it in the Spirit Warden sacrificial points and weaving between the lightning towers. She tasted the bitter lessons about demonic energy with the Empress of Gulls, feeling the Leviathan strains. The life force of the demonslave, the Dark Tooth, was bound up in the ritual—but she also felt Lord Belderan, another mask. And beyond that, perhaps the truest, the dark figure of Trellis reflected in the demonslave of the same shape, formed from the original, the shadow both more and less than the identity that cast it.

The Mistress of Tides realized that she understood Trellis, in a way that he had perhaps never admitted to understanding himself. She understood the one constant that drove him across his early years, his time with the Hive, his time after, through the years with the Silkworms, up to the culmination of this vast ritual. He had always needed to feel himself in service, even if those he served were not worthy. Even before the Leviathan, he had been most himself when boosting the plans of others. Instinctively, here at the end, he had chosen to further her plans rather than those of the Leviathan—whatever her plans would be. Her bitter smile pushed tears from her eyes.

"I have found you," she whispered to the memory of Trellis, stretched through the ritual.

Like so many before her, she felt a bittersweet pressure to prove worthy of his support.

The principles were the same, even though she now toiled in a sea of energy rather than facing an angry spirit. She flashed back to the training exercises for her acolytes, hauling the sodden fabric along the water trench. Pulling at the threads of Trellis, she felt them slither free of connecting points. She dragged his life force away from the moment of his death, she twisted hard at the finale of the ritual. The life spark did not connect, did not seal the reserve into a portal, did not open the ground itself and eject a rampant Leviathan through the center of the city. The Leviathan loomed, inexorable, but the portal did not materialize. The moment came, and went; the Leviathan released a mournful bawl that shivered the roots of the world, then it glided on through the deeps alone.

As the ritual began unraveling, the energy sealing the Mistress of Tides to it separated. She slammed down on the spectral beach in the Garden, surrounded by a flaming coast, meteors drifting in the empty sky. Cellar shouted something, indistinct. Clutching at him, she clawed at her leg, twinging the wire still connecting her in the dream. With a jolt, she was back on the dream ship, its sails on fire. Cromlech regarded them, solemn.

"You are burning the Garden," she said quietly.

"You can stay in the evidentiary, or you can come with me," the Mistress of Tides said as she extended her withered hand to Cromlech.

With only a moment of hesitation, Cromlech took her hand.

The Mistress of Tides still felt the burning spirit wells, the last sensation of the ritual slipping away from her. Orienting on the strongest, she leaped off the dream ship, battering through the surface of the waves with her two passengers—

—and they tumbled out into the real world, collapsing on the barge in the middle of the Exchange. Behind them, a frenetically writhing column of flame burned, bright as the stars.

"Now what?!" Cellar shouted.

The Mistress of Tides vomited blood, then collapsed.

━━┑ THE FIRST CHAPTER ┍━━

You may productively envision unfolding history as an endless feast where the wait staff shuttle the food out and the dishes back, between the tables and the kitchen. Waiters are, in this conceit, the important people who are actually described in the stories we tell about our past. The guests are everyone else. And the kitchen? Let's call it fate.

Some waiters are methodical and organize the dishes both ways. Others are lucky to arrive with whatever confusion they can deliver. Some are careful in their stacking, others a bit drunk with a big mess on one or both ends of the trip. There are clumsy fools who drop trays all the time, and others who can deliver the new and carry away the old with grace that is a delight to witness.

They do not decide what the people order, nor do they prepare the food. How they comport themselves, the accuracy of the orders they take, and their ability to deliver can transform the dining room experience for those who pass through. In the end, they are paid through the meager rewards of the restaurant wage, and the tips that the people give them from obligation or gratitude. They are judged on their ability to serve.

Where we depart from the conceit is in noting that the waiters in our context are not trained and hired. They are the ones who get up from the tables, chosen by their fellow diners or by the kitchen itself, and act as the go-betweens. You are here because you want to be a public servant. So I will tell you one more truth: maybe a tenth of these waiters who shape the whole dining room are actually reported in our histories. Maybe you'll be one of those, with your name in history books, and maybe you will not. There are those whose names are recorded in occult lore, or in criminal legends, their heraldry inked on skin or painted in blood. If you become a waiter, you will connect the people with fate, and however the meal turns out, it's unlikely your payment will be fair.

> — *Minister Uradania's Last Graduation Keynote,*
> *Charterhall Diplomatic Academy, Class of 848*

Rutherford passed through the courtyard gate, back to the street. He paused, staring at the crowd gathering across the street. He recognized several gondolier agents disguised as beggars and dock workers. Some of them looked away, others stared right back, smoldering with hostility but restrained by his uniform. Rutherford nodded to them, clenched his jaw, and walked away, his mustached Bluecoat partner close behind.

Two blocks later they swung up into a coach, and Rutherford banged the ceiling and called out "Smoke Tower." The reins slapped, and the goat dragged onward down the street.

"Do you think I was spotted?" growled the Bluecoat.

"That's what you think Clamp sounds like?" Rutherford said with a genuine smile. "Spare me. And no, I don't think you were spotted," he said to Sanction. "You are about the same height and build. I've told him all week I picked him for his moustache, and that wasn't a lie; it's hard for people to see past it."

Sanction peeled the fake moustache off, flexing his face. "I don't know how people do it," he said, regarding the lip wig with a jaundiced eye. "Will your friend be alright?"

"He's already relocated in the building and he will leave through the service entrance. The gondoliers know him, he's Canal Watch. They would be foolish to take out their frustration on him. Anyway, he's no victim." Rutherford heaved a sigh. "Alright, so it's time to get on with the plan."

"I do love a clever plan," Sanction admitted, the glow of a smile under his schooled features. Rutherford was distracted in the moment, a bittersweet thrill shivering in him. It had been too long since Sanction had regarded him with anticipation, and he allowed himself a second to savor it.

"I'm dancing with the Hive," Rutherford said, "and I agreed to kill you today. So while I'm waltzing around that wrinkle, we also have to sort out the kill order from the Fairpole Council so we can get you back out in the open."

"While you're dealing with the Hive, we've got a complication with Dalia," Sanction said. "I sent the Fog Hounds to kill her last night. The High Six is going to be cracked open with an audit. She had everything she needs in place, so if she dies or is captured then information goes to the right people. The Silkworms get ground up in the system. The process may already be started."

"She survived," Rutherford said. "I took a bullet to assure it. Interrupted the Fog Hounds assault. She got away and I told her the Fog Hounds were behind it."

"You are a thorough and incorrigible vexation," Sanction said, half amused.

"Can the Fog Hounds tie the hit order back to the Silkworms?" Rutherford asked, serious.

"I don't think so. I didn't give them my name or any identifying clues. I gave them intel and appealed to their self-interest." Sanction shook his head. "Yesterday. How did you know to get in position to stop it?"

"Trellis," Rutherford said, looking Sanction in the eye.

"I see. He insisted that I set the Fog Hounds on Dalia, he was determined." Sanction paused. "I guess he was playing several games at once."

"Since before I knew him," Rutherford agreed. "I helped him with some of his plans, he helped me with some of mine."

Sanction flashed to the look in the old man's eyes, and cold rolled through his bones. The Dark Tooth. He opened his mouth to tell Rutherford, then closed it again. After all. The world could be tumbling through its last moments, right now. Why spoil it? He shied away from the idea of admitting his cowardice.

"Hey, it's all right," Rutherford said as he leaned forward, putting his hand on Sanction's knee, looking him in the eye with concern. "We'll get this worked out."

Sanction nodded, looking away. "You said it was all mounted on a pivot," he said.

"Yes. Still a few tricky bits," Rutherford replied, studying Sanction. "Our first stop is Ironhook."

Piccolo balanced, trembling, upside down. The balls of his feet were against the wall. He supported himself on his palms, his hair hanging down around his face, veins standing out in his forehead, eyes closed. Hissing air out, he lowered himself again, until his hair brushed the floor. Then with a sharp push, his arms straightened, sliding his feet back up the wall; his bandaged ribs twinged, and he flinched, toppling over.

He heard footsteps in the hall outside the heavy door, and he awkwardly scrambled to his feet and squared off with the door. A key rattled in the lock, and a Bluecoat opened the door to let in a couple more Bluecoats.

"Huh. Figured you forgot about me," Piccolo said to Rutherford.

"It's only been a few days," Rutherford pointed out. He looked over at the Bluecoat guard, who closed the door behind them. The three were alone.

"Came to see if you cracked," Sanction said, stepping into full view.

"What the hell," Piccolo said, his tone flat.

"I was drawing out enemies," Rutherford said, "and I needed you out of the way and safe."

"Safe? You *shot* me."

"True," Rutherford agreed. "I wasn't about to get in range of your knifework." He cocked his head to the side. "You are a hell of a lurk, but you aren't much of an actor. I needed my drama to be convincing. So I shot you. I'd do it again."

"Well please don't, because it hurts like hell," Piccolo frowned. "I mean, I was waiting for this; to find out it was some kind of big plan, and not the end of the Silkworms. It's not, is it? The end, I mean."

"It's not," Rutherford agreed. "The Silkworms are about to make a big play. It's very clever. The good news is, the run-up to this part was other people doing all the work while you were relaxing in a classic Ironhook vacation. I even paid extra to stash you in a luxury suite, away from the gum-chewers."

"Okay, you are just the worst at vacations," Piccolo pointed out, "and of course you had to do a bunch of work. Looks like you're the new provisionary member. You wanna be a Silkworm, huh, tough guy?" he said with his chin jutting out.

"On second thought, we *could* leave him here," Rutherford mused.

Sanction tossed Piccolo a bag. "Suit up, break's over."

"Bout damn time," Piccolo muttered, pulling a black bodysuit out of the bag. "Oh, I missed real clothes. I got rashes," he explained.

"We'll find you someone you can tell all about it," Sanction soothed.

"Don't you talk down to me, I blame you for all this," Piccolo said as he wiggled into his outfit. "Screwing around on Rutherford. He went crazy! Made a big mess," he said, muffled as he pulled his overshirt on.

"I know. And I'm sorry," Sanction said, looking Rutherford in the eye.

"What's that?" Piccolo said as he settled his overshirt. "Didn't hear you."

"I know you didn't, and I'm sorry," Sanction said with a grin.

"Better than I expected," Piccolo muttered as he pulled on his boots. "Let's go."

QUALITY DRYDOCK, FOGCREST, SILKSHORE.
26TH VOLVINET. HOUR OF SONG, 2 HOURS PAST DUSK.
SAIL LIGHTING FESTIVAL, DAY FOUR.

"Kind of a brash place to hide," Sanction observed in a low voice as they followed the alleyway flanking the drydock. "How do you know Barness isn't back?"

"Festival isn't over yet," Rutherford muttered, "and odds are good he will have some explaining to do. Besides, there's a Bluecoat guarding the front, there's no way they have the whole warehouse processed by now. Here we are." He triggered the catch for the secret door, and led them up the cramped stairs, out the concealed exit into the office.

"At least it's nicer than my cell," Piccolo said as he plucked a bottle of wine from the sideboard, twisting it open. "What's next?"

"I go tell Orris that I killed Sanction, and set up a meet. Then I find the Mistress of Tides. I don't suppose you can help with that," he said to Sanction.

"Her acolytes are distracting the gondoliers, last I checked," Sanction said. "She was with Trellis and an Inspector, they are trying to stop some demon ritual." He swallowed hard. "I was sent to the church to distract the gondoliers so they wouldn't see what Trellis was up to."

"Any idea where they might be?" Piccolo asked.

"No. They are looking for that Iruvian girl that Trellis smuggled in," Sanction sighed. "She is with the gondoliers, could be hidden anywhere."

"Iruvian girl?" Piccolo retorted, eyebrows raised. "What's that about?"

"I know where she is," Rutherford said, chilled. "Whitecrown District Evidentiary. We are not meeting up with them there."

"I was only gone for a couple days," Piccolo groused.

"Time for telling stories will come, if we make it through all this," Sanction said. "Are you going to pour that wine?"

"I'm letting it breathe," Piccolo said, patronizing. "What are you, a savage?"

Sanction just stared at him.

"You two keep your heads down," Rutherford said, "and if something comes up use the back water entry to the overview. If you aren't here, I'll look for you there."

"Who put you in charge, nucoat?" Piccolo demanded.

Rutherford flashed him a grin, then he was gone.

MAURO OVERVIEW, ZEPHYR STREET, MASTER MARKET, SILKSHORE. 27ᵀᴴ VOLVINET. HOUR OF SILK, 7 HOURS PAST DUSK.

The darkness resolved into a single candle, spilling light into her eye. The light tumbled through her, rebounding from her bruised and ruptured spirit, echoing through her physical pains, hissing out in her withered hand. She closed her eye again, and breathed deeply. She drew air and life into the wet darkness that languidly squirmed with what life she had left in her body. Again. Again.

Somehow, she was not dead.

The Mistress of Tides focused, applying her strength, and opened one eye. Iron door, stone chamber. Familiar smells. She was in one of the many secretive chambers below the overview. Relief welled into her, a bit.

"She's awake," Cellar said, hushed. "Okay, good." She felt a damp cloth touch the corner of her mouth, which was as unresponsive as a wax mask.

The Mistress of Tides relaxed back into the darkness.

Hours passed.

Foul smells soothed and reassured her. Opening her eyes with a lazy roll, she managed to focus on Ebb as he lifted a cloth from her chest. He smiled down at her.

"Still with us," he murmured. "Welcome back."

"Found me," she whispered.

"Yes, your exit from behind the Mirror gave us quite a beacon," Ebb said.

"Safe?" she managed. "My people?"

"The Fairpole Council's agents questioned us, but they do not want to anger you. They want the rest of the Silkworms dead. They still hope to recruit you." He wrung out the chemically treated cloth that was part of a ritual to restore her strength, and dipped it in a refresh of the solution. "Cellar did his best to tell us what you've been through," he said with a shrug. "If half of what he's trying to describe happened, then you've outdone yourself again. There are some parts he still cannot or will not explain."

"Silkworms," the Mistress of Tides breathed, struggling. "Bring them—here." Consciousness began to slip away, but she concentrated hard. "Take their—essences. Empress—of Gulls, locate them—ritual."

"I will do it," Ebb soothed. "Rest now."

MAURO OVERVIEW, ZEPHYR STREET, MASTER MARKET, SILKSHORE. 28TH VOLVINET. FOURTH HOUR PAST DAWN.

The heavy door swung open, admitting Ebb along with Sanction, Piccolo, and Rutherford. The Mistress of Tides sat up on a mound of supportively arranged cushions. Cellar sat on a cushion along one wall, opposite the Cromlech.

"You made it," Sanction breathed. "Rutherford, this is Inspector Cellar. And this is the Cromlech."

"Excellent," Rutherford said, more relieved than he expected to be. "Now, we need a plan. I have told the Hive that I killed Sanction, and it's only a matter of time until they find out otherwise. They will not take it well. Also the Fairpole Council is eager to kill the Silkworms, and they think Piccolo is already dead, so we need to smooth that over. Where is Trellis?"

"He didn't make it," Cellar said, blunt.

"You mean, he's not back yet?" Piccolo pressed.

"He died." Cellar snapped his mouth shut.

"Right, but are you sure?" Piccolo demanded. "It's easy to not be sure, I get it."

"Trellis is gone," the Mistress of Tides said, barely audible.

"So, we'll get back to that," Piccolo said. "For now we need a plan, like the nucoat said."

"Wait," the Mistress of Tides managed. She looked to Cellar. "Tell them. About Trellis." She leaned back, dangerously pale.

Cellar grimaced at the order, and looked dubiously at the others. "I'm just the messenger here, so don't blame me. You aren't going to like it."

Piccolo crossed his arms over his chest. "You better start talking."

"Trellis was the Skullface Killer. He did those ritual murders ten years ago, and also the one two days ago. He did the murders because he was the Dark Tooth, an agent of the Leviathans working the long game and pulling off an impossible ritual over ten years that would destroy the city. The Mistress of Tides stopped him at the last second, and he died." Cellar swallowed hard. "I know. It's a lot to take in."

As the others reverberated with the shock, Sanction trembled with a rush of relief.

"I thought he was sick," Rutherford said softly. "He told me he didn't have long to live."

"Sick can mean a lot of things," Piccolo said, blank. "Okay, we'll get back to that too. That's just too much right now."

"But it's just what we need," Rutherford said. "Trellis is the plan."

"Here we go," Piccolo muttered.

"Sanction, you'll be the face of the Silkworms to the Fairpole Council. I can work out a meet that's safe," Rutherford said. "We'll tell Trajan that Trellis was sicker than anyone knew, he went mad, and we didn't know until it was too late. Everything that went wrong was his fault."

"Hey now," Piccolo objected.

"No, it's good," Sanction retorted. "Trellis didn't care about his reputation, he cared about leverage. If this is what we need from him, I think he would have approved. Besides, he's the one that pushed them over the edge; we could have worked things out, but he provoked Trajan. I have no idea what he said, but it must have been something else. They had assassins on the job just hours after he talked to the man. If Trellis can get us out of a jam one last time, that's for the best."

"I have an idea for the Hive part," Piccolo said. "You could actually kill Sanction." He smiled brightly.

"Trellis is the plan there too," Rutherford said. "Now I have something real to offer the Hive, to make up for what I'm going to take away."

"This seems like a good time," Ebb said, subdued. "We received a package here at the overview, addressed to you." He turned to Rutherford. "It's from Lord Belderan."

Rutherford nodded. "I'll go with you, take a look. The rest of you stay here. I'll be back soon."

WAXMELT THEATER, BRIGHTSTONE.
28TH VOLVINET. SIXTH HOUR PAST DAWN.

"Fancy meeting you here," Orris said from behind Rutherford.

Rutherford slowly turned away from the balcony overlooking the vast foyer, and he smiled at Orris. "I thought it best we have a conversation," he said.

"I don't see how meeting here will help me confirm Sanction's death," Orris said without amusement.

"I put some thought into the situation and decided that the Silkworms were too valuable to waste," Rutherford replied.

"You don't do that," Orris said through his teeth. "You don't make up your own missions."

"The hell I don't," Rutherford responded coolly. "Is it possible I understand the Unseen Hand better than you do?"

"It's possible you're in the last thirty seconds of your life," Orris observed.

"The Silkworms are famous for standing up to the Hive," Rutherford said. "I want them to keep doing that. I want them to be the champions that offer an alternative to the Hive's overwhelming influence. So when people need to go up against the Hive they think of the Silkworms. With me as a member and leader in the crew." He raised his eyebrows.

Orris stared at him.

"Trellis is dead," Rutherford continued. "He was the real danger in the Silkworms, and you know it. Before he died, he sat back and let you have Gaddoc Station, and he didn't get involved. He waited because he knew that the gondoliers would only unite if they were faced with a monolithic threat. He wanted to organize them to take on the Hive in a more systematic way, to become a real competitor in Doskvol's smuggling market. You are walking into a trap. You keep the Silkworms active, and that reduces the incentive for the gondoliers to resist. They can believe your threat is diminished, that you've been handled. They will be less vigilant, more receptive."

"I told you to kill Sanction," Orris growled.

"I almost did," Rutherford retorted, "before I came to my senses. The gondoliers hold Sanction in contempt; they see him as a bureaucrat, a politician, a liar. If the Hive kills him, and takes over North Port, then Sanction is a martyr and a victim. He can serve as a better rallying point dead than he can alive. Consider. The Hive is a secret society, operating through proxies, when it is at its strongest. You do not want to be this close to the surface, this push in North Port exposes you. Use the Silkworms. Let the gondoliers organize and turn to the Silkworms for protection. Then run the Silkworms with your Unseen Hand while you control both of the biggest smuggling operations in Doskvol. If one gets smashed, the other survives. Both serve the Hive."

"Clever justification to get your way, I suppose," Orris said. "But that's not how it works. You do as I say or you have an accident, like Sanction will, whether you're involved or not."

"Trellis didn't have an accident, and I know why," Rutherford said quietly. "Before he died he passed a few things on to me, and I've made some arrangements to secure my personal safety. Because if I die, some things come to light."

Orris narrowed his eyes. "You didn't lead with that."

"I shouldn't have to," Rutherford shot back. "I will operate with a level of independence, looking after the Hive's interests in Silkshore. The question that remains is, will I report to you or will I work directly with your superior and adjust your assignment? If you want to stay in control of Silkshore, then you'll talk to Lady Maha and persuade her to align with my proposal. Or I go over you," he said with a finality built on utter confidence.

For a long moment, Orris studied Rutherford. "I would not have guessed the Trellis of Barrowcleft would pick you for his heir," he said.

"When you talk to Lady Maha—"

"Don't say that name again!" Orris snapped.

Rutherford looked him in the eye for a quiet moment. "When you talk to *Lady Maha*," he said, "tell her that the Unseen Hand finished off the Skullface Killer and settled things down in Silkshore. There will be no more ritual murders. Trellis is dealt with, and the Skullface Killer is too. You might want to keep it to yourself that they were one and the same." Rutherford nodded. "There is a reason that the Hive created the Unseen Hand, and gives latitude in its work. Let this be a reminder."

"She will want to meet you," Orris said, a new calculating look in his eye.

"I welcome the opportunity," Rutherford said. "Please invite her to my award ceremony. I suspect I'm going to get a medal for catching the assassin that killed Master Drassle during the festival. Now." He raised his eyebrows. "Are we going to be friends?"

"I very much doubt it," Orris said. "But for now, let's see how it goes. You are an arrogant bastard, it's true. But any Unseen Hand who is not a chronic pain is probably not doing the job. What about Sanction and the other Silkworms? Do they know you are the Unseen Hand?"

"No, and this works best if they don't," Rutherford replied. "I've taken steps to move into the inner circle of leadership, and I'll keep an eye on their operations. Influence where needed. They won't even know they're serving Hive interests."

"That's a bold move," Orris admitted, "and it's colder than assassination. Betrayal, profound and ongoing."

"You let me worry about my conscience." Rutherford's smile was bleak.

"I wanted you to prove your loyalty, and instead you proved your capacity," Orris said. "Let's see how that plays out."

"Yes, good reminder," Rutherford said. He produced a sealed pouch. "Codes and methods, how we'll communicate. Keep things quiet, move through the blind spots."

"Words to live by," Orris said. "I'll be in touch."

He watched Rutherford go, thoughtful.

MISTSHORE PARK, SIX TOWERS.
28TH VOLVINET. ELEVENTH HOUR PAST DAWN.

"I am alone," Trajan said cautiously as he looked at the massive stone pillars in the roofless courtyard, their shadows deep and straight. "You have news of the Cromlech?"

Rutherford stepped into view. "Yes. And Trellis."

"Go on then." Trajan crossed his arms over his chest.

"Trellis is dead," Rutherford said. "He had declining health and increasing episodes of delirium. Towards the end he was able to put up a good front, but his madness drove him to issue orders that were counter to the interests of the Silkworms and the Fairpole Council both. He was actively hindering the work of the Silkworms."

"You saw a corpse?" Trajan said, narrowing his eyes.

"Trellis chose me as his heir, I received some of his secrets. I want to do right by his memory," Rutherford said. "Part of that is repairing the damage that separates the Fairpole Council and the Silkworms."

Trajan's jaw tightened. "You belong to the Hive now, don't you?"

"Do I?" Rutherford asked, eyebrows raised. "What's important here is that I have friends with the Hive, and I have friends with the Silkworms. Friends with the Bluecoats, the Ministry, and the Inspectors." He paused. "Do I have friends with the Fairpole Council?"

"Of course," Trajan said reluctantly.

"I want to play the long game and continue Trellis's work of strengthening the Fairpole Council. Before his sickness confused him," Rutherford said. "You've got a foothold in the Ministry now, in Silkshore, with a chance to expand. I can persuade the Hive to invest in you also, and when we need to push back there's the Silkworms, who have their attention. I want to look out for your interests, not just do you favors." He paused. "Did you know the Cromlech escaped from the Whitecrown Evidentiary?"

"What?"

"Trellis is dead, so her role as leverage has ended. I wasn't involved, but I found out about it and I know her whereabouts. The point is, my friendship is valuable," Rutherford said, calm.

"Also, it has proven to be expensive so far," Trajan glowered.

"Perhaps, but I'm no mercenary," Rutherford said. "Can we work together?"

"Are you going to lower the rates with the Hive?" Trajan asked, arching an eyebrow.

"No need," Rutherford replied. "I come to peace talks with a gift. I'm going to see to it that you've got room to work in North Port." He watched Trajan, following the dawning light of the idea that spread through the gondolier's mind as it reflected on his face.

"You can limit Hive interference?"

"I can, and I will," Rutherford said. "You can set up an alternative to Gaddoc Station, for those who prefer not to work with the Hive. The profits will more than balance out the negotiations with the Hive for other services."

"I do accept your gift. However, you know they'll make a move on us as soon as we are successful," Trajan said, almost reproachful.

"Naturally. But we have some contingency plans. All part of the dance," Rutherford replied. "You paid to have Piccolo killed in Ironhook. I outbid you, and I've arranged for his release. You will allow this, and if anyone asks, you can explain you made your point and don't need to make it again. You will not retaliate against the Ironhook personnel involved, or I will interpret that as moving against the Silk-worms."

Trajan said nothing. Rutherford waited. Trajan shrugged at his discomfort, and nodded. "Fine," he snapped.

"When Trellis ran the Silkworms, you worked through Sanction. There are a number of reasons we need to return to that arrangement."

Trajan scowled. "I understand," he said slowly, "but I don't like it."

"You have a problem with him, you bring it to me," Rutherford said quietly. "We'll get it fixed. Because our alliance is important."

"I want the Mistress of Tides to serve on the Fairpole Council," Trajan said. "If I allow you your people, you must share one of yours with me."

"If she consents, we won't stand in the way," Rutherford nodded. "I will see you on the water. Eyes up."

"Eyes up, Rutherford," Trajan said. He shook his head slightly. "Give us twelve hours, to get the word out to the fringes. Then your people can move freely once more."

MAURO OVERVIEW, ZEPHYR STREET, MASTER MARKET, SILKSHORE. 29TH VOLVINET. ELEVENTH HOUR PAST DAWN.

The Mistress of Tides sat on her throne-like seat, veiled, a book stand in place before her. She looked up as her acolyte escorted Sanction in.

"Good afternoon," Sanction said. "You are looking much recovered."

"In some ways," the Mistress of Tides said. "But in other ways... I may never recover."

"I come with news," Sanction offered. "Well, news to share both ways. Hoping for some updates." He offered an approximation of a boyish grin.

"Yes?" There was weariness in her voice.

"Mother Grine asked if we, by which she meant you, would be willing to inspect the cornerstone for the new church going up on the edge of the Spark Grounds. They seem to have worked something out with the Foundation, and I didn't ask a lot of questions."

"Of course."

"Excellent, that will reassure them there's no hard feelings. Either way. They did offer me shelter when I needed it," he added. "Looks like Rutherford's work has paid off; enough of the ill will in various quarters has dried up that the open investigations into matters related to Silkworm activity will not find anything conclusive."

"It would be a shame," the Mistress of Tides said, "if we had to send Piccolo back to prison."

"Right," Sanction nodded, his smile strained. "Exactly." He paused. "Enough of all that. Have you decided what to do with the Cromlech?"

"I worked it out with the Empress of Gulls," the Mistress of Tides said. "We owe her for her assistance in the unpleasantness, and... the Empress of Gulls is a superb teacher. The Cromlech may no longer be able to access the Garden, but she is still a singular talent, and may develop into a Whisper with some encouragement." The Mistress of Tides paused. "At least the Cromlech will have a home, a future. Speaking of which. Have you found a place to settle in with Rutherford?"

"Ah," Sanction said. "Yes, we found a tidy little place bordering the High Six. Convenient location and all that."

"Nice. All... is well." She sat unmoving.

Neap moved up to Sanction's elbow. "She's asleep," he said quietly. "You held her attention for a long time today. She was... badly damaged. By the event."

"She'll get better though, right?" Sanction murmured, alarmed.

"We don't know, not for certain," Neap replied. "She paid one price after the other, just to survive. She was still injured and drained from the battle with the Foundation assassins, and a succession of rituals, then—whatever happened in the Garden. And after that, relocating physical bodies through the Mirror twice in a blind jump awash in ritual energy that was years in the collecting..." He shook his head. "I don't know how she's alive at all."

Sanction licked his lips. "Maybe tell her—when she wakes up, of course—maybe tell her that there will be no audit of the High Six, and it's still ours. Tell her we've got a feast scheduled with the Fairpole Council, and it's going to be a big expensive flashy show, but we're going to be alright. Tell her Rutherford is amazing as a crook, to no one's great surprise." He paused, and swallowed hard. "Has—has she mentioned Trellis?"

"We don't talk about it," Neap said.

"Oh, and remind her of the funeral at the High Six on the thirty second. I know she'll want to be there."

"We know, thank you." Neap watched Sanction, his gaze level, and Sanction got the message.

"Well then, I will see you soon." Sanction nodded to Neap.

"See, and be seen," Neap agreed.

Sanction smiled to himself, then headed for the door, the adept at his heels.

The hall was quiet for a while.

Cellar stepped in, uncertain, wringing his hands. He paused at the edge of the row of columns. Dressed in a simple shift and breeches instead of the Inspector uniform, he seemed young, more skinny than slender. He turned to go.

"You have questions," the Mistress of Tides murmured.

Cellar froze, then turned to face her. "I do," he admitted. "But who can I ask? The man with all the answers, he's gone."

"Ask me."

"Somebody out there paid Jayan to inform on me. Paid him really well. And the daft lump doesn't even know, he can't tell me who it was." Cellar hesitated. "Do—do you think this is over?"

"I think Trellis was the one hiring your man," the Mistress of Tides said. "It's just the sort of thing he'd do."

"What about the bushy beard? The guy who attacked me... I was sure it was the Dark Tooth. But he had a big beard."

"So did Trellis, sometimes," the Mistress of Tides said, a hint of amusement in her voice. "When he was undercover, he would... he would hide his features in this awful chin wig he kept hidden in a stash somewhere. For special occasions."

Cellar was not amused at all. "Will this thing ever heal?" Cellar winced, shifting his collar down to show the bandage over the Herald brand.

"You will scar, but when the ritual's energy has drained, the flesh will close over the weeping sores," the Mistress of Tides said in an almost dreamy tone, as though reciting.

"Will I? I mean, will I heal? The Dark Tooth destroyed my *life*, my... my identity," Cellar said.

"That's up to you."

Cellar frowned at that. "Why did he do it?" he said. "Why me?"

"All the spinning, twirling, parting and reforming configurations of energy in the universe... they hinge on physical locations, mental postures, lines of energy, whorls of time and space and stars. For this moment, for this role, the Dark Tooth needed someone who could be melted down, isolated, vulnerable. But still somehow sincere, even when stripped of all supports. Somehow, he found you. Somehow, you were already in hot pursuit of a disguised Spirit Warden." She paused. "Fate. It guarantees lucky breaks and increasing resistance. Spinning through the obstacles shapes a path, shapes the pursuer, shapes the context. How much was planned, and how much was accident? Difficult to know. He asked me to bring along an infused stone he crafted for me, as a gift." She turned her hand over, revealing the gleaming radiant stone. "Yet I did not need it. The omission troubled me, as your questions trouble you. But a stone of this kind... it could hold a ritual. Center it. Had I not been able to apply myself, had I been injured or distracted or weakened, I may have needed it to finish the job. It was a backup plan... and in the end, one he did not need. A reminder I now carry. A gift he gave me, a gift that his needs did not consume. Something from that space. Between planning, and fate. Still."

Cellar waited for a long, long moment. "Still?" he prompted.

"What difference does it make?" she whispered. Rallying, she cocked her head to the side. "You look to the future. What will you do now?"

"I don't—I don't know," he said, misery seeping into his tone. "My family. Without me, without my job, I don't know what they'll do. How they'll survive. But I can't go back. I mean, the least of my worries is my credentials, left in the evidentiary. I got no proof, nothing to show the Inspectors to clear me. The killer is gone, beyond justice."

"Tell Neap about your family," the Mistress of Tides breathed. "I will see to it. They will be cared for. They will want for nothing." She paused. "For your part in this... you may be Lost."

"Lost?"

The Mistress of Tides was still and unresponsive.

Cellar crossed the room, and looked over Silkshore. The view was breathtaking, jam-packed with activity, glittering and shadowed in the thick dimness of late afternoon except down among the busyness. Lights twitched and twinkled, carrying the life through the district as the canals carried the traffic.

"You have earned a stone," the Mistress of Tides said quietly.

Cellar startled, then pressed his chest. "I am sorry, I am intruding," he said. "You need your rest."

"Yet I do not get it," she said quietly. "Come closer."

Cellar approached her chair, and saw the glint of reflected light beneath her veil.

Tears.

"What I see... what I slip into... you cannot imagine it," she murmured.

"What do you see?"

"The suffering," she whispered. "The suffering that did not end. Because—I chose to allow it. To continue, ongoing."

He knelt before her. "What can I do?"

"Better," she breathed. "Do better." She was still once again.

Eventually, Cellar bowed to her, and left.

ARRIVALS AND DEPARTURES PUBLIC HOUSE, SORTING POINT, THE DOCKS 32ND VOLVINET. ELEVENTH HOUR PAST DAWN.

Cellar approached Jayan from the side, timing his movement for when Jayan scanned the other direction. Jayan was startled when Cellar slid down into the seat opposite him at the table.

"Did you get it?" Cellar demanded.

"Cellar!" Jayan said, eyes wide. "You—you made it."

"I sure did," Cellar nodded, eyes fixed on Jayan. "Did you run that errand for me last week?"

"Yeah, just like you said," Jayan said, intensely uncomfortable. He pulled an envelope from his vest. "Here's the sketch from Daava's book. Of the thing. They didn't give me any trouble, I told 'em I was all sad and needed to say goodbye, take her effects to her family." He paused. "I did. I took her effects to her family. Except that sketch. If anybody was watching me, they were a real light touch; I think the heat has died down around this one. I don't think anybody is looking for you now."

"Thank you," Cellar said, taking the envelope and pocketing it. "This doesn't make us even, but—thank you." His face was serious, to the point of pain.

"I would have gone with you," Jayan said under his breath, fierce. "Just so you know. Whatever else you think of me—don't—don't think I was a coward."

"I know," Cellar agreed. "You were a good friend to me. Best you could do." He stirred. "I hear you're still with the Bluecoats."

"Yeah, not a special anymore, too many questions. About you, but questions about you are also questions about your specials," he said. "Whatever. Not sure I'm cut out for it anyway. How about you, what's your plan? You looking for revenge?" Jayan forced a light tone.

"Revenge? Seriously? No." Cellar heaved a sigh. "We just got tangled up in some crazy plot that was way bigger than us. Everybody in the whole thing was just—just playing their part. Even you. I get it. I understand what you did. It's just who you are. I don't—I don't hold a grudge. You betrayed me, but it wasn't personal. You were loyal, even when you weren't." He shook his head. "Just—don't carry this around with you forever, alright? Let it go. Leave it behind. In the old world. The sun came up, and... that's not a guarantee. So now you've got a new world. Make the most of it."

The drinks Jayan ordered arrived. Cellar winced at him.

"Really?"

"It's suspicious to sit down in a tavern and not drink," Jayan retorted. He gripped his mug. "To Daava."

"Yeah, to Daava," Cellar said, almost twitching with the force of frustration in the moment. He took a long drink. "I promised her that I'd figure out who the Skullface Killer was. Solve it. Deal with it, you know? To pay her back somehow for going along with me. When it was bad. And, you know, I did figure out who it was, and I saw to it that the killings stopped." He paused. "But I didn't fix it. I couldn't. I can't find my way back." He swallowed hard. "I feel like—like I completely failed to rise to meet this challenge. I'm still alive, but my life is gone."

"So you're leaving town?" Jayan said, eyes drawn to the sailor's bag slung down by Cellar's seat.

"I am," Cellar said. "I have some things to figure out."

"You and me both," Jayan agreed. "I hear the Hive was behind putting the Skullface Killer down; I guess the Spirit Wardens owe them a solid or something. There's some chatter that they might be collaborating on something, for the first time ever as far as I know."

"I really don't care," Cellar said. "I've had it with this city, and it's time to go." He squinted over at the bar. "I get to carry the weight of what I've seen. What I've done. What I was a part of. That's... not something I can ever put down, you know?"

"I'll—I'll check in on your family," Jayan said, at a loss.

"Don't bother, I made other arrangements," Cellar sighed. "Anyway. I've got a ship to board. Just... be careful, okay? And don't get bitter. Put this thing in your wake."

"In my wake, yeah," Jayan said, rising. "I mean... good luck." He thrust out his hand for an awkward handshake.

"Eyes up, you idiot," Cellar said with a sardonic grin, rising. He shook Jayan's hand, then turned, and left him behind. His shadow was empty.

THE ROOTED DELTA, HIGH SIX, SILKSHORE. 32ND VOLVINET. TWELFTH HOUR PAST DAWN.

A small crowd was assembled beneath the massive spreading arms of the radiant oak that stood at the highest point of the High Six radiant garden. Luxuriant bushes and flowerbeds and vines glowed, their light reflected in the crushed crystal among the gravel of the path. A string quartet droned through one of Lord Belderan's favorite tunes.

In a modest tent set up in a courtyard behind the tree, the memorial servers checked their formal wear. Piccolo was sleek and trim, struggling with his dress glove buttons. Rutherford had already straightened out the glowing flowers in Sanction's lapels, and he was striking in his Bluecoat dress uniform. The Mistress of Tides was flanked by Neap and Ebb, and she was seated in a rolling chair, resplendent with crystals and shimmering fabric. She wore a thick veil, for mourning.

"I'm supposed to be the fixit guy," Piccolo scowled at his glove. "How come I can't fix this damn thing?"

"Here we go," Sanction said, stepping in and managing the button. "Don't get all dramatic."

"Screw you, this is a memorial service and I'll be dramatic if I want. I hate this," Piccolo said, passionate. "I hate being here. I should have been there with him, you know. He shouldn't be gone."

"Keep your voice down," Sanction murmured, studying the button, finishing it up. "What killed Trellis—he chose it. As much as he could choose anything. It was done to him when you were just a kid. There was no saving him." Sanction looked him in the eye. "Trellis was beyond saving. He didn't even want to be saved. We have to move on."

"At least he died playing those stupid games he loved so much," Piccolo said, his chin unsteady. "He was playing a shit game, but at least he won it. Dammit, now my mascara is going to run. What numbnut made white dress gloves?" he said with some savagery.

"You don't have to be here," Rutherford said, quiet. "I'm surprised you came. With Skelranna and her family, no less."

"Why *did* I come?" Piccolo snapped. "I don't understand it. But I know I'll miss it if I don't. And there's no second try." He snarled at his wince of pain. "Dammit."

"Later, we'll do this right," Sanction said around the lump in his throat. "We'll shake down a blackmailer at a fancy restaurant and stay for dinner, brassy and bold. For Trellis. But for now, this is what we do. For appearances."

"At least it's not in a church," Piccolo said, sullen. "Alright, let's do it." He sniffed heavily, then mopped at his face with a towel. "Screw it."

"We can't lose focus again," Sanction said, his tone serious. "We're the Silkworms, and the reason we're a crew instead of lone rogues is because we have to draw the best from each other. If we don't, if we get distracted, then we... we don't really understand each other. We don't see the warning signs. And it all... it all falls apart. Yeah?"

"Save it for the speech," Piccolo grumbled. But he pulled Sanction into a quick, fierce hug, rumpling his flowers. That put a crook of a grin at the corner of his snarl. He wiped his face again before throwing the towel on the ground and stalking out of the tent, taking his place in the lineup, his makeup more like warpaint. Rutherford quickly fixed Sanction's jacket and flowers as best he could, then they were all in the line and headed around the tree, facing the mourners.

A cleric spoke of breath and life and our print upon the earth, and there was more music, but the event drifted past the Silkworms. It was for a man they never knew, certainly not the one they mourned. The service was for Lord Belderan, not for the Trellis of Barrowcleft.

The glow of the massive tree suffused the scene, on the perfect autumnal day under a bleak and broken sky. Simmering leaves drifted out of the tree, a handful at a time, carried by the unsteady breeze. Skelranna sang a farewell, acapella.

Finally, time for Sanction to speak. He stepped forward, clearing his throat, and his prepared remarks evaporated from his mind. That was not the worst nightmare he carried, and he continued all the same.

"Here we are," he said, reflective. "We honor a man who was a philanthropist, a scholar, an artist, and an aristocrat. He was my uncle. He taught me so much about success and decency, what this city is and what it can be. He taught me the difference between control and connection. And, ultimately, which one is more important. You can lose control, but if you are still connected to the people and values you care about... there is a way back. And if you lose connection, then all that control just helps you do the wrong things more efficiently." Sanction found himself in eye contact with Nebs, and he looked away.

"He was a great man, and he did great things, and some of them were good," he said with as much of a smile as he could manage. No one laughed. He did not look at the gondoliers, stone faced, in a row at the back. "He found his way in and out of more challenges than I've ever even heard of, and he lived his life with purpose and grace. I will miss him, his steady influence and his inspiration to be more, dig deeper, and see an ever-bigger picture. We live in a short sighted age. This man... he lived always in the future. Now it is our turn to live in it, without him." Sanction bowed, then stepped back.

The music began. Rutherford clasped Sanction's hand. Leaning back, Sanction gazed up into the overlapping glow of light, layered endlessly above.

SMOKE TOWER, BOOKEND SQUARE, FOGCREST, SILKSHORE
34TH VOLNIVET. NINTH HOUR PAST DAWN.

"Didn't you come into money?" Clamp said, squinting at Rutherford as he approached in his crisp uniform, still unique in a tower full of Bluecoats. "I thought the whole point of coming into money was not having to show up at the job anymore."

"Got bored," Rutherford said, "and there's the greater good to uphold. Oaths, the Mandates and Provisions, and so on."

"Plus, you missed my moustache," Clamp prompted.

"And of course that glorious growth," Rutherford said with his wistful smile.

Clamp scowled. "Never call it that again," he said. "It isn't official yet, but they're working on a date for the award ceremony. Looks like you'll get a medal for nabbing Belltongue. They're working it out so it's a double ceremony, hanging him and honoring you. Figure they'll promote you to a pike, to go with the medal?"

"It's a start," Rutherford mused. "How about you? Looking to be promoted? And what I mean is, would you accept a promotion? Canal Watch is about to come into a *number* of unique opportunities. We might be sponsoring a new tower based in North Port, and if we do, we will need veteran leadership."

"Look at you, kingmaker of the cave already and just barely past provisional bands," Clamp said. "Are you planning to drag me around in case your husband needs a body double again? Or did you need one of my other qualities for your plans?"

"Well, after the moustache, it's the wit," Rutherford said. "An acquired taste, but now? Can't live without it." He poured himself some hot brew, glancing over at several other Bluecoats closing in with congratulations and welcome; it was possible his heroics attracted acclaim. It was far more likely his newfound wealth would make him popular.

"Any regrets?" he asked Clamp, sideways, before the others arrived.

"Of course," Clamp sighed. "But who has time to learn from mistakes."

THE ROOTED DELTA, HIGH SIX, SILKSHORE.
39ᵀᴴ VOLNIVET, 849. SIXTH HOUR PAST DAWN.

Rutherford closed in on the giant radiant oak, where Piccolo waited for him. "You wanted to meet here," Rutherford said as he strolled in easy speaking range. "Is everything alright?"

"I don't know," Piccolo said, watching the slow pulse of light through the leaves as the wind rustled them. "I'm trying to figure out what I think, and I don't think I'll know until I have to explain it. And there's not a lot of people I can talk to about this, not even Skelranna."

"Because it's about Trellis," Rutherford said. "And me."

"Yeah," Piccolo said. "Yeah, it is. Trellis would do this with me. Tell me what was bothering me, and why. Said it would just save everybody time and energy if I wasn't expected to work out my own knots. Condescending bastard," he smiled. "He was totally right, and I'm missing him now that I got knots."

"What has you knotted up?" Rutherford asked quietly, turning away from Piccolo and gazing out across the glorious garden. A haze was rising from the plants, tinted with their radiance.

"I'm trying to figure out why I miss him so much," Piccolo said. "He was selfish, and evil, and mean, and he barely helped at all in the day-to-day stuff. Plus it turns out he was a crazy demonslave."

"You miss him for the same reason I do," Rutherford replied. "I felt safe with Trellis in the background. I felt like nothing would sneak up on me. Like when I was a kid, and I had this rat-catcher dog, slept at the foot of my bed. Nothing moved in the house without that dog knowing it. I didn't have to pay attention, because if anything was coming, I'd hear a little growl first, then he'd start barking."

"Huh," Piccolo said. "I mean, you're right, now that you say it. I could relax with Trellis in charge. Focus on the task at hand. That's my job, you know? The task at hand."

"Yeah," Rutherford agreed. He waited, listening.

"I guess I always figured it would be Sanction," Piccolo said. "When the old man eventually moved on, one way or another. That Sanction would take over. And it looks like he did. But he'll never be Trellis." He looked Rutherford in the eye.

"I won't either," Rutherford said quietly.

"Maybe not," Piccolo said, "but—but you see further than Sanction does. You make opportunities for your people. Trellis made me a boss, can you believe that? Me! But yeah, he showed me how to do it without even showing me how to do it. He didn't have to threaten me. He was still scary. And I didn't want to impress him—I wanted to live up to the way he wanted to use me. It wasn't about his opinion. It was about—you know? About the plan. About being part of something, about being elite and bold."

Rutherford waited.

"I didn't see you coming," Piccolo confessed. "You were out past the edge of the circle, Sanction's personal life. I didn't think about you. But here you are. If we're going to be something, it's because of you. I had no idea you were selfish, and evil, and mean, and that you'd barely help at all in the day-to-day stuff—but here you are, the new Trellis. You're with Sanction so you're clearly crazy. You burned your own house down and blew up the crew to make a point. Who does that?" He paused. "I'm trying to figure out why you make me feel—safe. Like I can focus on the task at hand. Like you're the big picture guy. Even though nobody has said so, I think everybody knows you're in charge."

"That bothers you?" Rutherford asked.

"Knots," Piccolo repeated. "I just keep chasing these thoughts around in my head, I don't understand it. So if you're the new Trellis, you know, work out my knots. Tell me what I'm thinking."

Rutherford nodded to himself. "Knots," he echoed. "Yeah, it's a lot."

Piccolo frowned. "Doesn't usually take this long," he said.

Rutherford smiled. "You're so *needy*. Alright, I'll tell you what you think. You don't know me. And now you find out you didn't know Trellis. The one person you trusted to be consistent, more than anyone else, turned out to be human after all. Driven, haunted, compromised. So you feel like you want to relax again, but you don't like feeling stupid and you don't like betrayal. So you don't know how to be part of the team but not a chump who falls for another flawed leader."

"Less words," Piccolo said, gesturing. "Sum it up. I have places to be."

"I am never going to plot like Trellis," Rutherford said, serious. "But I know what I want. I'm willing to take a hit to get it. And if you stick with me, you'll become more than you are now." He crossed his arms. "Take it or leave it."

"And Sanction? What do I think about him?" Piccolo demanded.

"You wish he was more. You wanted him to see the bigger picture. But he doesn't. So you need to focus in on where he shines. Because he is gifted, in his way, and we need him. Just get out of your own way and let him be who he is, instead of who you wanted him to become."

"I think you're projecting," Piccolo sniffed.

"I fell in love with him," Rutherford said. "I know how disappointing he can be. I know who he is when he is at his best, chasing the high, maneuvering through the challenges, seducing the odds. That's who I see, even when he can't. Sometimes he's the fogged-up window, but I can see through who he is, to who he can be."

Piccolo rolled his eyes. "You are halfway to writing a mushy poem. It's gross. Besides. You're *in* the *Bluecoats* while you're also kind of in the Silkworms, you're handling Sanction instead of partnering with him, and I think you have other stuff going on. So... how does this line up for you?"

"Those are *my* knots," Rutherford replied, his smile shifting.

"There's that Trellis look," Piccolo said. "I guess you're haunted. He picked you."

"Is that why we're meeting under the Rooted Delta?" Rutherford asked. "Because you haven't let go of Trellis yet?"

"You don't let go of Trellis," Piccolo frowned. "He lets go of you. On his terms. When he's ready. Even if he's dead." He looked up into the glowing canopy. "He loved this tree more than any other living thing." Piccolo's eyes lingered on the saw-cut scars, mostly healed, marring one side of the trunk. "It wasn't easy being loved by Trellis. Put you in a lot of cross-hairs."

"You can't blame Trellis for that," Rutherford retorted. "I cannot imagine you living a life outside the cross-hairs one way or another. I remember the day you got kicked out of the River Stallions."

"Good times," Piccolo nodded to himself. Then he blinked, and actually blushed. "Yeah, sorry you got shot that day."

"Because of you," Rutherford prompted.

Piccolo grinned. "See, this here? How uncomfortable and guilty I feel right now? You *are* Trellis's heir."

"Well, if that's so," Rutherford said, crossing his arms, "you must have a problem you need help with, something that will likely involve all of us."

Piccolo thought for a moment. "The Sidearm's Golden Hook tournament—I think it might be fixed, and my fighting fish Nibbles is in danger of hagfish tampering."

Rutherford leveled a look at him.

"Make it epic," Piccolo prompted.

A slow smile spread across Rutherford's face. "All the competitors in the Sidearm's tournament could use secure facilities with coastal access for breeding and training their fighting hagfish," he said. "We could set up a competing tournament in North Port, focused on expanding the range of competitors to attract talent from all over Doskvol. Secure travel containers, dangerous animals inside, and a reason to move back and forth."

"That sounds like a smuggling thing," Piccolo said with a grin.

"It's a smuggling thing," Rutherford confirmed.

For the first time in a long while, Piccolo laughed.

DOSKVOL
ALSO KNOWN AS DUSKWALL, NORTH HOOK
Imperial Province Of Akoros
Circa 847 AC

N

Governor's
Stronghold

WHITECROW

THE LOST
DISTRICT

NORTH HOOK CHANNEL

NORTH HOOK CHANNEL

BRIGHTSTONE

THE DOCKS

SIX TOWERS

CHARTERHALL

CROW'S FOOT

NIGHTMARKET

SILKSHORE

CHARHOLLOW

COALRIDGE

Gaddoc Rail
Station

BARROWCLEFT

Ironhook
Prison

RADIANT
ENERGY FARMS
& EELERIES

DUNSLOUGH

DEATH LANDS

DUSK RIVER

OLD
NORTH
PORT

TIME	HOUR	
1 AM	SILK	
2	WINE	
3	ASH	
4	COAL	
5	CHAINS	
6	SMOKE	
7	1	DAWN
8	2	
9	3	
10	4	
11	5	
12	6	NOON
1 PM	7	
2	8	
3	9	
4	10	
5	11	
6	12	
7	HONOR	DUSK
8	SONG	
9	SILVER	
10	THREAD	
11	FLAME	
12	PEARLS	MIDNIGHT

THE IMPERIAL CALENDAR HAS SIX MONTHS, SIXTY DAYS EACH.

A MONTH IS TEN WEEKS WITH SIX DAYS EACH.

MENDAR	
KALIVET	WINTER
SURAN	
ULSIVET	SPRING
VOLNIVET	
ELISAR	FALL

PATREON SPONSORS

Thank you for your support while I was writing. You change what is possible.

Benjamin Hamdorf

Brett Casto

David Brock

edchuk

Elizabeth Parmeter

James Robertson

Jeremy Collins

John Harper

Jonathan Shields

Kelsa

Kevin

Logan Waterman

Mark Robison

Michael Liebhart

miller ramos

Per Falk

Petri Wessman

Phyllis Hurshman

R. A. Clark

RavenRavel

René Lößner

Thomas